A PATH OF STONES

A PATH OF STONES

by

Nathan Boutwell

NJB MEDIA
2017

Chapter One

AURA LOCKHAVEN KNELT on the grass in the center of the meadow behind her home. The moon long since set, the earth held its breath for the rising of the sun marking the spring Evenday. She always heard that the sky was blackest before dawn. This sky seemed blacker than any. Listening for the usual sounds of crickets and waking birds, she heard nothing but her own breath. Still tinged with winter's farewell kiss, the breeze across her naked body sent a shiver down her back. She tested the rope that bound her hands behind her. It was useless, but she tried to free herself anyway. She knew not to cast an untying spell. The charmed ropes would only come off at the will of the man who tied them. His will was even more firm than the steel of the sword pointed toward her.

The fire in the pit cast yellow light on the eastern standing stone opposite her, as well as the two on the north and south, and her own body. She did not need to turn around to know the fire cast her shadow on the stone behind her. Was that what she had reduced herself into, a mere shadow on a rock? The blade of the sword before her glowed with cold red light. That sword would soon end her life. Testing the rope again, she winced as the hemp stung her wrists.

Aura looked at the eastern standing stone. Illuminated by the fire, it loomed into the black sky, crushing her spirit with each inch of its granite face. The sun would rise behind it soon. This was supposed to be a moment of celebration, the day when ten years of hard work concluded. Instead, through her own carelessness, she faced her hour of execution. Aura wanted to vomit.

Aura's feet were still free. For a moment, she thought about leaping up and running away. The thick forest of oak, rowan, and laurel known as the Big Hedge stood like a forbidding wall to her right. If she could reach it, she might escape. No one knew the Big Hedge like she did, not even its owner.

No, she decided. She had never denied responsibility for her actions. She had done the deed, five seconds of mindless indiscretion that could plunge her whole country into a holy bloodbath. Whatever happened next, she would endure it.

Sagacius, the wizard of Hartshorn, the man she had called her friend and teacher for ten years, stepped between her and the fire. The tallest man in Lodwynnshire, in the predawn darkness, his body carved from shadow, he looked even taller. The firelight transformed his flowing silver hair into gold. For a moment, he no longer looked seventy, but a man in his prime. Aura could not see his face, much less read it. She was glad she could not. For the past month, the usual kindness had vanished from his deep blue eyes, replaced by alternating fury, concern, and despair. Over his heathered blue robes, he wore a black cloak. He reserved that for solemn occasions. Aura wondered what could be more solemn than executing his own apprentice.

He lifted the sword and held its point to her bared chest. The end of her life rested one inch away. The sword point never wavered. Despite his age, Sagacius' hand remained as steady as the standing stones around them. She strained at the rope. If she had to be executed, did she have to endure this humiliation? While Aura loved being skyclad, she did not like being bound. Besides, the bonds were supposed to be for another occasion, one she would never see now.

"Aura Lockhaven of Hartshorn," Sagacius said, his deep voice firm with authority. "You are naked and bound before me to receive judgment for the high crime of violating the Twelfth Command of the Order of Wizards. *For no reason shall a magical curse be used to cause physical harm against a nomagian except in the matters of self-defense or to defend another.* For this sentencing, I am no longer your master. As the only member of the order within riding distance, I am your judge and executioner. You have already admitted your guilt, but before I pass judgment, I shall hear your side of the story once again. Do not assume to rely on my kindness as your teacher in this moment."

"I had no choice, Master," Aura said.

"You always have a choice, Aura."

"I acted to defend another, Master. The crowd threw stones at that woman, just because she was a Geilltian." Aura gulped. "She looked like me. She had ... green eyes."

"Your claim is not valid, Aura. When you defended the Geilltian peddler, you merely stepped between her and the mob, giving Constable Lamrock time to arrive. That was highly commendable, especially given that you do look Geilltian to those who don't bother to learn the differences between the Tangoi peoples. You did not employ magic at that time. You violated the Twelfth Command immediately afterwards. On your own volition, with the Geilltian woman already protected by Constable Lamrock, you struck Cecil Fowler in the face. When you did, you imbued your fist with a throwback spell of enough strength to break his jaw. He heard you utter the incantation *tenthatora*."

Aura sighed. She lowered her gaze to the grass. "I am guilty, Master. I did that."

"Do you know the full consequences of your rash act? Not only did you violate the Twelfth Command, but you set in motion a potential landslide. Even as big and strong as you are, Fowler did not think you capable of inflicting such injury with your hand alone. He told Sire Thaddeus that you used a curse against him. The priest wrote the High Temple in Bellicia." He lowered his voice to a growl. "We do not need the Knights of the Holy Torch launching a purge of magicians in Ayrdland just because of you."

"I realize my mistake, Master. I realized it as soon as I did it. I have no excuses. I won't insult you by offering any. I do have my reasons, weak though they may be. I am still angry with Cecil, and I allowed that anger to overflow. He seduced me and bedded me last year. When he finished with me, he called me Snake Eyes and slapped me. Then, last month, as I defended that woman, he called me a Geilltian giantess and –" Aura paused, realizing that as she spoke, her voice rose and grew tighter. A sword waited for its signal to slice through her breast and end her life as she knew it because of that very anger toward that very man.

Why in the name of all the gods did she allow herself to erupt in anger. Why had she not performed a white candle ceremony a year ago and forgiven Cecil like she knew to do. Why had she held onto her anger, her contempt, her hatred. The point of the sword now looked inviting. All she had to do was thrust her body forward and Sagacius would not have to do the deed himself.

No, she thought. Perhaps there was a chance. Perhaps she could prick her master's pity. Aura continued her defense. "I admit my error, Master. I lost control of my temper. I wanted to hurt him. I'm sorry. I truly am. I wish I could promise that I wouldn't do it again, but I can't make a promise that I may not be able to keep. Master, I beg mercy! Give me a second chance."

She heard nothing. His face still shrouded in shadow, she could not tell if her plea even made him ponder, much less reconsider. Aura sighed. Sagacius was right. Her one rash act may lead to a disaster. She had not even thought about the consequences of just a little magic to push her hand into Cecil's face. All she thought about was her own hurt pride. One little moment of selfishness.

"No, Master," Aura said. "No. I don't deserve mercy. I accept full responsibility. That is what you taught me to do. I was wrong. If my crime were just the Twelfth Command, perhaps I may earn mercy. Considering what I may have set in motion, then ... I acted without wisdom, in pure anger, perhaps even malice. In my desire to hurt one, I may have hurt hundreds. I deserve no mercy." Aura lowered her head and said, "I condemn myself."

"You know what I must do," Sagacius said.

Aura closed her eyes. She knew this sword would not kill her, but she expected to feel excruciating pain anyway. The wound would heal immediately upon the sword's withdrawal from her body. Charmed with the order's sole executionary spell, once thrust into her heart, the spell would remain behind and become part of her. It would strip her of all ability to perform magic. She would not even be able to utter a simple wish for luck like the common people did. The sword would leave her defenseless and helpless. Her anger was about to return her to the life she left when she was twelve.

At the thought of being alone again, Aura squeezed her eyes tight. She fought to keep her lips from trembling, to hold back the tears gathering at the edge of her eyes. That was worse than losing her ability to perform magic. No, she thought. She closed her eyes and begged the universe to kill her then, and not force her to live alone again. No, no, no. Not living in barrels, begging for loose change and enduring the taunts of children who called her Snake Eyes. No, anything but that. In her mind, all she saw were spiders and the cold muddy cobblestones of Hartshorn's alleys. All she smelled was smoke, always the smell of smoke.

She tried to fight the fear, but the flood of memories drove her strength away. Her heart wanted to burst from her chest. She heaved, trying to catch her breath. This could not be happening, she thought. Old nightmares, memories, horrors lived and not imagined, took tangible form and forced their way from her eyes and down her cheeks. Perhaps the executionary spell wasn't quite as strong as Sagacius thought and the steel would kill her. That would be more merciful.

The sword an inch from Aura's heart faded into mere happenstance as the shadows of memories took form. Her body shook as she felt the scrambling of tiny feet across her shoulders and stomach. She choked her scream as the miniscule fangs penetrated her skin on yet another night. Her hands convulsed and strained at the ropes as the burning tunic ripped once again and the agony of fire from the flaming beam shot through her left hand. She jerked her head to her right to avoid the onslaught of smoke heavy with the stench of meat left in the fire far too long.

With a growl, Aura drove her will to push the memories back to the mental room where they lived. She was about to be executed, and if she had to face that, then she would with dignity. Aura shut out all memories

of Cecil's abuse, his insult, and her retaliation. She inhaled and exhaled
several times, not thinking about the wizard before her or the sword at her
heart. The staccato crackle of the fire created a rhythmic assonance. The
huff, pop, snuff, crack caused a sweet memory to float through Aura's
mind, of men and women dancing reels in her father's tavern, their
footsteps pounding on the floor, and echoing throughout the ale and wine
cellars beneath. The predawn song of sparrows and warblers drifted from
the rowans nearby. The notes of spring filled in the missing notes of fiddles
and pipes in her memory of the dance. That memory stepped before the
others. Issuing a silent prayer to her matron goddess Ystlena, she felt calm
enough to speak.

"Please act quickly, Master," Aura whispered. She clenched her teeth
and tightened her muscles, anticipating the strike. Her breath quickened.
Whether by steel or by spell, this thrust would end her life. Any second
now.

"I already have," Sagacius said.

Aura opened her eyes. She had felt nothing. The sword still pointed
toward her chest, its tip still an inch away. She saw no blood on her skin,
felt no fire. She expected searing agony as the blade sliced through her
breast, striking her heart. At least, she anticipated a tingle as the spell fused
with her body. Sagacius pulled a letter from the pocket of his robe. In the
light of the fire, she saw the broken seal.

"This is my judgment," he said. "I wrote to the Chieftain as soon as
you told me. His reply arrived three days ago. He is privy to information
that you and I are not, such as Sire Thaddeus' actual missive. As it was an
official charge, Sire Thaddeus had to report it to the Supreme Sire in
Bellicia, but he did so by saying that Cecil Fowler is, and I quote, a self-
serving crypuppy, and a notorious dispenser of fine whines. The good priest
said no evidence existed to, and again I quote, support the base accusations
of Hartshorn's champion of buffoonery. He also wrote, The younger
Fowler may as well be the town idiot because the fool has more gold in his
purse than brains in his skull." Sagacius looked up from the letter into

Aura's face. "Sire Thaddeus and I may not agree on faith, but we are friendly enough with each other for him to cover the tracks of a certain wizard's certain apprentice." He returned to the letter. "The Supreme Sire told Sire Thaddeus to completely forget the matter. Our Chieftain wrote that in light of the circumstances, and in light of the High Temple's response, he is willing to declare that you used magic in defense of a nomagian, instead of to harm one. He instructed me that I should forgive you, especially if you showed true remorse, which you have. So, Aura Lockhaven, apprentice of Sagacius, the wizard of Hartshorn, in the name of the Order of Wizards, it is my great pleasure and sincere relief to forgive you of your crime."

As Sagacius withdrew the sword from her chest, Aura sank forward and sighed. She said, "Thank you, Master. Thank you! But if you knew I was forgiven, then why –"

"To drive home the point that you need to learn to control your feelings, Aura," the wizard growled, shaking his finger in front of her nose. "I hate invoking fear in anyone, especially you of all people, but perhaps you will remember. You are far more powerful than a nomagian now, and could have killed Cecil. We're here to help people, not harm them. There are plenty of other spells you could have used if you felt the need to retaliate. We may frown on them, but we have no command against casting a tickling spell, making him speak backwards, or even causing him to run naked through the marketplace crowing like a rooster. You were blessed this time. The next time, the Chieftain won't be so forgiving. Believe me, I know! If I had expelled you from the order, I doubt if any of the others would have accepted you. An expelled member of any order is marked for life. If I had pierced you with the sword ... Well, you have no idea how happy I am that I did not have to do so."

"You're happy!"

"Now that that unpleasant business is finished, shall we proceed to our real reason for being out here before breakfast? We have some time." Sagacius looked at the eastern standing stone. He smiled. It was the first time in a month Aura had seen his usual happy visage. "It will be a beautiful morning."

"Yes, it will," Aura said. She wanted to vomit again, but from relief, not horror. A tear formed at the edge of her eyes, but from gratitude, not fear. She had survived. The Gweryn had smiled on her. "Yes, it will."

Now that she could relax, Aura noticed that the sky had turned blue with streaks of salmon. The stars retreated from the approach of their big brother. The sun was about to peek over the horizon. No moment before looked so glorious.

She tested the rope binding her hands again. This time, it was a reflex. Being bound naked was part of the order's highest ritual, but she wondered if it was also part of the formal sentencing of an accused. She doubted that, as she shivered again. Why couldn't she have been permitted to wear clothes during her judgment, or at least been closer to the fire. If Sagacius wanted to drive home his point, he succeeded.

Only the morning star remained now. The sky turned bright blue as the sun broke the horizon. Shafts of light shot by the standing stone and struck Aura in the face. The warmth felt good. The end of her ordeal and her survival felt even better. She vowed to the rising sun that she would remember, that she would exert all her strength to control her anger. She would perform a white candle ceremony. She would forgive her former suitor. She would! The next time, if Cecil provoked her, she would simply kick him in the groin.

Sagacius lay his staff down on the ground, with its gnarled head pointing north. He still held the sword in his hand, but with a muttered incantation, the blade ceased to glow. His black cloak popped in the breeze that blew through the stone circle. Again, Aura shivered, but this time, she did not mind.

"Day has broken. Shall we begin? Today is Bloomstead, the spring Evenday," Sagacius said. "In the old calendar, it is the midpoint of spring. In the new calendar, it is the first day of the season. In both, it is a day of fresh beginnings, a day for growth. So, it is fitting that we are here this morning.

It is my great honor to initiate you into the Order of Wizards as a full wizardess."

If Sagacius the wizard looked imposing during her judgment, he now transformed into the visage of a very god. He stretched out his arms and as he did, he seemed to grow to ten feet in height. His form blocked all light from the fire and the sun. His hair no longer looked the color of silver, but made of the metal itself. His heathered blue robes transformed into those of an emperor. The black cloak billowed behind him like wings.

In a voice that all of Hartshorn must have heard, he said, "Aura of the house of Lockhaven, the town of Hartshorn, the shire of Lodwynn, and the nation of Ayrdland, as your master, I declare that you meet all the requirements for full membership in the Order of Wizards as a wizardess. You seek to wear the mantle of wizardess. With this mantle comes tremendous respect, authority, and responsibility. This mantle is not light. You may be called upon to perform acts that others would deem foolhardy. You may be called upon to stand in battle and sacrifice yourself to save the lives of others. You may be called upon to carry the weight of the needs of an entire city. Are you prepared to wear this new mantle?"

"I am," answered Aura.

"You are bound to signify that you have been helpless in the face of the will of others. You are naked to signify that you have been powerless in the face of social custom. You kneel to signify your place as an apprentice."

Sagacius stepped behind Aura. Lowering the sword, he slit the rope around her wrists. Her muscles still taught, her wrists jerked apart as the bonds split. She felt the rush of air across her back and heard the whistle of the blade as it flew upwards. A few minutes ago, that sword could have destroyed her. Now, it ceremonially freed her. The rope fell to the ground. As she rubbed her wrists, he said, "In the name of the Order of Wizards, I free you from the tyranny of helplessness. Exercise your own will in all freedom and wisdom."

Sagacius removed his black cloak and draped it across Aura's shoulders, fastening the clasp over her collarbone. Her shivering ceased as the warm cloth settled over her body. He said, "In the name of the Order of Wizards, I free you from the tyranny of powerlessness. Be clothed in the power of magic, the wisdom of lore, and the blessings of nature."

Sagacius knelt in front of Aura. He took her hands in his. His smile widened into a grin. He said, "I've waited a long time to say what I'm about to say. In the name of the Order of Wizards, I free you from your duties as my apprentice. Rise now, as my equal."

Aura stood. With each inch, she felt she climbed a yard. As she reached her full height, his words settled into her mind. No longer the apprentice to the wizard of Hartshorn, she was his peer.

Sagacius motioned for her to remain where she stood. He stepped back, across his staff. As he did, Aura looked around. For the first time since they left their house for the stone circle, she noticed the plants in the meadow that surrounded the knoll. Lazy heather and bright violets greeted her like old friends. Although still chilly, the breeze carried the aroma of the wild roses growing in the Big Hedge. Aura smiled.

"Do you vow to use your power and office for the benefit of all humanity?" Sagacius asked.

"I do so vow," she answered.

"Do you vow to work in harmony with the forces and powers of nature?"

"I do so vow."

"Do you vow to use your power and office for the gain of others and not purely yourself?"

"I do so vow."

With just a little more firmness, Sagacius asked, "Do you vow to only use your power and office to harm another as an act of self defense or to defend someone else?"

With a sheepish smile, Aura replied, "I do so vow."

"Do you vow to let your actions reflect honor upon the deities that you worship?"

"I do so vow."

"Do you vow to maintain the dignity and honor of the Order of Wizards, even at the cost of your own life?"

"I do so vow."

"You have sworn these things to me, your master. Do you also swear them to your gods?"

Beginning at her left thigh, Aura drew an invisible line to her neck with her index finger. From there, she continued to draw the Sacred Star upon her body. One point for each of the seven elements; Spirit, Fire, Earth, Metal, Water, Light, and Air.

"I swear these vows by all the Gweryn. May they smite me if I do not uphold my vows," Aura said.

Sagacius placed his hands on top of Aura's head. She felt warmth flood her scalp and her mind. He said, "By the power invested in me by the Order of Wizards, in the name of my gods the Wealdenda, and your gods the Gweryn, I pronounce you a wizardess." Sagacius stepped back and said, "Please cross my staff."

Aura placed her right foot on the other side of Sagacius' staff. She saw no light, no shimmer in the air, but it felt as if she passed through a barrier, a wall of force that slowed her body. Her hair lifted from her scalp as she stepped across with her left foot.

Sagacius spread his arms wide and shouted, "I call to the East! I call to the South! I call to the West! I call to the North! I call to Above! I call to Below! I call to the Sun! I call to the Moon! I call to the nation of Ayrdland! I introduce to you Aura Lockhaven, the wizardess of Hartshorn!" Sagacius turned to Aura. His countenance returned to that of any other elderly wizard. He grinned and said, "Congratulations, Wizardess Lockhaven."

Aura clapped her hands to her face. It was real! She had succeeded. She was a wizardess. She was no longer the old wizard's assistant who followed him around and handed him herbs. She was now his peer. As her arms and legs trembled, Aura did not know whether to sink to her knees and cry, or throw back her head and laugh. Instead, she hurled herself into her master's arms and screamed for joy.

Sagacius said, "Uh, Aura, perhaps you shouldn't hold that body of yours so close to mine. Despite my cloak, you are still skyclad. I am an old man, although my heart could use the exercise. I also wish you wouldn't squeal in my ear. That rather hurt!"

"Oh, I'm sorry, Master." She released him and stepped back. He had seen her wandering naked around the farm plenty of times, and also at rituals for high holy days, but he always said he did not think anything about it. She had not considered the impropriety of hugging him. She thought about casting a healing spell on his ear, but he just turned to pick up his staff as if it were a mere annoyance than actual pain.

Sagacius said, "Well, my congratulations, again, Aura. This day has been a long time coming. I am so proud of you! Come. We have much to discuss. There are things I can tell you today that I couldn't yesterday. But first, we need breakfast and a few tankards of your ale." With a wave of his hand and an incantation, the fire diminished to smoke and embers. Picking up his sword in his other hand, he started down the knoll, back toward their house. Aura walked next to him. "You may return my cloak now."

"No!" Aura said, pulling Sagacius' cloak around her body.

"When did you decide to become modest?" Sagacius asked.

"I haven't," Aura said. "I'm cold."

Chapter Two

WHILE SAGACIUS FUMBLED in the kitchen, Aura dashed up the sagging stairs to to her bed chamber. On this day, after all she had just been through, her room smelled like the most beautiful spot in the world. Only large enough to allow her to walk between her bed, wardrobe, table, chair, and bookcase, today the room felt as large as the whole country of Ayrdland. She inhaled the aroma of the aged oak walls, the pine straw and goose feathers in her mattress, the lavender stuffed inside her pillow, the ink on the calfskin of her books, and the unfortunate stench of a blouse she needed to wash.

She tossed Sagacius' cloak on the bed. Since the man's clothes had more wrinkles than his face, she saw no need to fold it. Grabbing the linen towel draped over her chair, and her pot of soap from her table, she ran back down the wooden spiral stairs, as fast as she could without tripping over the loose treads. Through the door in the hallway, she saw Sagacius sitting at the kitchen table, staring at nothing with an expressionless face. Aura noticed the small black bottle in his hand, the cure for *his condition* as he called it. Every morning, he drank the potion. In the ten years she knew him, he never described *his condition*. As always, his hair had turned iron gray and his beard almost black. The sags in his face tightened and the wrinkles and folds almost vanished. For the next fifteen minutes, the old man may as well be a statue. That gave her plenty of time to take a bath before he began issuing the day's orders.

"The most dismal glamour spell ever," Aura muttered as she stepped through the door and walked around to the back of the house.

Aura stood naked behind the stone first story of their small house. She didn't care. If anyone happened upon her, he would stare open mouthed at her actions, not at her body. Placing the towel and soap on a table, she stepped underneath the cask resting on a frame of oak beams. Closing her eyes and tilting back her head, she gritted her teeth. Then, she grabbed the rope dangling from the cask, and tugged. As the stream of cold water droplets struck her face and ran down her chest, she squealed.

The cask collected rain water and run off from the cedar shingled roof, fed it down a pipe, and out a sheet of tin perforated with tiny holes. Sagacius called the contraption a shower. All she knew was the thing kept her clean and free of fleas. Along with the outhouse and the indoor cistern in the kitchen, the shower was just another marvel of her home. Shivering, she released the rope and reached for her pot of soap. Her hair still felt clean from the morning before, so she decided to concentrate on removing the crust of sweat and grass stains on her body.

As she lathered, Aura looked around her. She remembered being afraid of the insignificant farm when she was little. Names lived long in Lodwynnshire. Children knew the farm as the Wizard's House, because the town's wizard lived there. Old folks still called it the Hermit's Place. Like most her age, Aura referred to it as the Big Hedge, the unruly oak and rowan thicket separating Hartshorn from the tidy farms to the west. Her big brother Richard always said, *Stay away from the Big Hedge. It's full of banshees!* She lived on the place for ten years and never saw one banshee. Just behind her grew their modest kitchen garden and herb beds. She frowned. Apparently, initiated wizardesses still needed to weed. Beyond the garden, the Big Hedge crept into the uncultivated fields of heather and blackberries.

Finished with her soap, she replaced the pot on the table. Then, she reached for the rope again. This time, the brisk water felt invigorating. As it poured across her, washing away the physical remnants of her trial and initiation, she smiled. She released the rope and the water stopped its downpour. She tugged it again, and watched as it fell in thick droplets across her body. Somehow, this combination of wood, steel, hemp, and water bathed her. Sagacius always snickered whenever she called one of his inventions magic. To her, the shower was magic, a combination of will, personal vitality, and the powers of solid materials given by the earth. Like the shower, magic was tangible. Unless one called upon a deity or celestial being, magic lacked any supernatural power. It simply existed, just like the water in the cask over her head.

Aura grabbed the support beam closest to her as the reality of the day sank into her soul. Her knees trembled. Ten years of dreams and work came true. She now stood on the other side of those dreams and work. She had been initiated. Just as the wood in her hand was solid, so was her status as a wizardess. Sagacius made her a promise ten years ago. She made herself one as well. At the time of issuance, both seemed like mere hope. Over the years, they became solid, not unlike spells or the shower itself. Now, both manifested within the space of an hour, in the stone circle not far from where she stood.

"What is magic except to give a lost girl her life?" Aura muttered. She rubbed her hand across her chest, dragging her fingers through the film of water. Looking up at the lazy clouds drifting overhead, she said, "Dearest Ystlena, how can I repay Master for giving me my life, except to give someone else his or her life? Help me to do that."

The wind picked up. A dust devil danced in the grassless spot of clay where Sagacius always planned to build a barn. As the air blew across her still wet body, Aura reminded herself that it was just the first day of spring and she needed to dry herself. Otherwise, her first act as a wizardess would be to cast a healing spell upon herself for the ague. She stepped from under the dripping cask and onto the grass. Reaching for her towel, she looked up at wood and mud second story of the house. Above her, a whitelark sat on the sill of her lone window, chirping at the morning.

After drying herself, Aura tossed her towel over her shoulder, picked up her pot of soap, and walked toward the door. She paused at the stone threshold, her hand on the iron latch. The thick oak planks of the arched door reflected the sunlight back into her face. The whitelark continued to sing overhead. The wind whistled through the needles of the pine next to the house. In the grassless patch of soil, the dust devil continued its dance. Everything felt more alive than it had earlier. Earth quivered beneath her feet. The Fire of the sun warmed her back. Brisk Air delighted her skin, and moisture clinging to her reminded her that Water was never far away. Light struck Metal, reflecting back from the door latch. All six elements greeted her at once, echoing the serenade of the whitelark.

"What are you telling me, Ystlena?" Aura whispered.

Back in her room, Aura sat on her bed, brushing her long hair. When it felt smooth enough, she pulled the tangled mass from the brush and left it on the sill for birds to use in their nests. Choosing a red ribbon, she tied her hair in a tail in a futile effort to keep it out of her face.

Most women hung mirrors over their tables. In place of the usual polished bronze, a smoke stained portrait covered that spot on the wall. She blew a kiss to the faded images of Henry Lockhaven and Aurora Nightshade. The anonymous artist who drifted through Hartshorn that day the year before Aura's birth had been fairly accurate. At least, as far as her father's visage was concerned. If she closed her eyes, she still saw his smile. Her only memory of her mother came from the portrait. For a moment she stared at her left palm, as she did every morning, her eyes tracing the edges of the scar left there by fire. Closing her fist, she looked back at the picture.

She recognized her own long humped nose as that of Henry. According to the portrait, she inherited her round chin, high cheekbones, full mouth, and dark auburn hair from Aurora. Neither parent bequeathed their daughter their blue eyes. With a sigh, Aura whispered, "I wish I had your eyes, Mom. Ester's were the color of the sky in spring. Mine look like duck weed."

Aura smacked herself on her cheeks and snarled, "What is the matter with me? I've just been initiated. Today is the happiest day of my life. I don't have time to drown in self pity. If the people of Hartshorn want a wizardess, they're going to get one with green eyes."

Casting a glance at her bookcase, she visually counted the precious thimble of her mother, the glass goblet of her sister, her father's pewter tankard, her brother's still sharp sword, and especially the notebook of her father's tales. Aura whispered, "Did you see? I am a wizardess. I finally made it." Then, she walked to the wardrobe.

"Decisions, decisions," she muttered looking at her clothes hanging from pegs in the self-standing closet. Except for the rather obvious feminine bustier, anyone looking at her wardrobe would swear Sagacius' apprentice was a man. Aura's trousers scraped the floor of the wooden chest. At five feet eight inches tall, she towered over all the women in the village of Hartshorn, and looked most of the men in the eyes. That, too, she inherited from her father, down the lineage of the giant warrior still toasted in tavern songs.

The blue blouse was filthy. Initiated wizardesses still needed to do laundry. Last week, she popped the seam in the back of the red blouse, so that left the white one. Pulling it over her body, she loosely laced the ties across her chest and on her wrists, then pulled the blouse down to bare her shoulders. Now, which of her two black trousers to wear. She chose the pair that looked newer and did not have holes in the knees. After lacing them over her full hips, she donned her only bodice, adjusting it so her deep cleavage showed. Sitting on her bed, she pulled on her left boot. Through the hole in the tip, she saw her big toenail. If the eyelets wore any larger, she would no longer need laces. That was good, as the lace snapped when she tied it. The right boot was in worse shape, but it held together.

"I suppose I should pay more attention to my appearance now," Aura said.

Sagacius still sat at the kitchen table, his gaze unfocused and lost. Aura turned from the kitchen door and walked to the window in the sitting room. It always amazed her how fast fear fled in the face of joy. The horror of her trial and her terror attack seemed an eternity behind her. The heather outside shouted its color, blending with the deep, lush green of the grass to form a tapestry of glory. The wind in the spring leaves of the rowan outside the window sang a hymn of exuberance to the whole farm. Out on the road that led to the village, One-Eyed Rupert and his sons Lodd and Ed drove a herd of just-purchased sheep toward their farm next door. She smiled, knowing that Rupert would call on them later in the day to perform a blessing on his new livestock. The bleating of the sheep reminded her of life, of the lusty march of the season across the calendar from Esgor to Parin, of warming days and shorter nights. Aura closed her eyes and breathed deeply, letting the smell of spring fill her nose.

One wish came true today. Perhaps, another could as well. Granted, the first just involved ten years of hard work, and a few almost fatal mistakes. The second involved other people, and a pair of disgusting green things. Still, it was spring, and spring was the season for love. Perhaps, the next man would be color blind.

"Composing a song to celebrate your promotion?" Sagacius asked, walking into the sitting room behind her.

"Not exactly," Aura said, turning around. Sagacius looked like his usual elder, but still vital, self again. She didn't feel like explaining her thoughts to her teacher. Some things belonged only to her. A little fib would not hurt. Besides, it was more an exaggeration of time than an outright lie. "I was just thinking about my clothes. I look rather like the urchin you found ten years ago. What do wizardesses wear?"

"Whatever they wish. I have yet to meet the man insane enough to tell a woman who can levitate a cow what she can and cannot wear."

"I can only levitate seventy-five pounds," Aura said.

Sagacius ignored her comment. "You've met my wizardess friends. Some wear loose robes like I do. Others wear form-fitting and revealing dresses. Still others dress like any other woman. You may continue to wear trousers and a bodice if you want. Our order has no dress code. I do recommend that you wear a cloak and carry a staff so the people will recognize who you are. Speaking of staves, I need to show you how to carve one. After your last little misadventure –"

"Oh, please!" Aura groaned, thinking of her failed attempt to carve a staff. The ruined oak branch now served as the curtain rod in her room.

Sagacius clapped his hands and said, "I also think a journey to Welcaster is in order. You need your own magical tools, and I know just the person to equip you."

"Desiree? I finally get to meet Desiree?" Aura asked.

"I think it's time," Sagacius answered. "She will set you up with everything you need. That witch is the best purveyor of magical items I've ever met." He frowned, and continued. "I'm not sure how she finds what she sells, and I'm not sure I want to know. I have a feeling her methods are quite larcenous." He clapped his hands again and said, "But before we do any of that, we must have ale, and not a little of it, either! Ale for breakfast. That is the order of the morning."

Sagacius walked into the kitchen and grabbed the keg sitting on the table. Picking it up, he shook it. He frowned, removed the cork from the keg, and upended it over a pitcher. After the last drop fell from the now empty keg, he sat it down. Selecting two tankards from the cupboard, he filled them from the the pitcher.

"I'll get another keg from the cellar," he said, walking into the sitting room. He handed a tankard to Aura. He lifted his tankard, and added, "To Aura Lockhaven, the wizardess of Hartshorn and the finest apprentice I have ever had the pleasure to teach. And, the best brewer of fine ales, thanks to your father's wisdom in teaching you." A wistful look crossed his face. "I'm really going to miss you, Aura."

"What do you mean? I'm not going anywhere."

"Perhaps not, but I am. No one thinks twice about an apprentice living with her master, but a man and woman who are not married to each other? That does present a problem. Sire Thaddeus would say we are living in sin, not that I pay Iricanists any mind. Villagers can be quite the blabtales and breedbates, too. The last thing the emerging wizardess of Hartshorn needs is gossip and scandal. Hartshorn is your home, but it isn't mine. I only remained here because Mayor Hunter begged me to stay. Besides, I felt you needed to be in a familiar place, after all you had experienced. Now that you're initiated, I intend to turn the farm over to you and return to my old travels."

"I don't want you to leave!"

"Aura, Hartshorn may be the largest town in three shires, but it hardly needs two wizards. Now that you're a wizardess, you can handle all the local problems." Sagacius said.

"I need you! I'm not ready to be alone," Aura said.

Aura turned from Sagacius and walked to the window. Staring out at the road, she drained half her tankard in several deep gulps. She felt the familiar tightening of her stomach and the shortness of breath. She smelled the whispers of smoke in her nostrils. Her hands began to tremble. No, she told herself. Not a second terror attack. She had not had two terror attacks in one week, much less the same day, since she was fifteen. Not on a day like this, the greatest day of her life, the day she accomplished her dream. This was a day to celebrate, not to mourn. Aura closed her eyes and inhaled. She counted to ten, and then exhaled, willing calmness and joy into her mind and heart. She heard Sagacius take a step toward her, and held up her hand, her signal that she was grounding herself and he needed to keep his distance. Aura stood at the window, inhaling and exhaling until the trembling stopped, her stomach loosened, and the odor of smoke vanished.

"You promised me that you'd never leave me, and I'm holding you to that promise, Master," Aura said over her shoulder, speaking and breathing in a measured tempo, while willing herself to be calm. "I feel like I live up to my name, a light that's there, but isn't seen, a presence that's felt, but not comprehended. I've been your little shadow for ten years."

"You haven't exactly been my *little* shadow for some time, Aura. You're only four inches shorter than I am."

"You know what I mean!" Aura snapped, turning around. The brief flare of anger drove the last of the terror from her. "You trust me not to make stupid mistakes, but I'm afraid I'm going to and who will be there to correct them? Look at the mess I almost caused from one flash of fury. Besides, I still have nightmares about Daddy, Ester, and Richard. I'm not just a shadow, Master. I live in shadow. I know, it's shadow in my own mind, and I need to free myself from it, but I can't do that overnight. You may have taught me how to duel, but I still feel like a frightened little girl. I can't just step out into the light in one day."

Aura crossed her arms over her chest. She smiled as memories drifted through her mind. "I remember when I first came to live with you," she said. "I had terror attacks every day. I woke up screaming every night. You comforted me telling me stories from your life. The funny people you met. The duels you fought. The terror and nightmares aren't nearly as bad now, Master, but until I have my own stories to support me, I need you and yours. Please. Give me six months to adjust. Then, I will release you from your promise to me."

The wizard walked up to Aura. He put his hand on the young woman's shoulder and smiled. He said, "You will never have to release me from that promise, Aura. I don't want to be released. You were never just my apprentice. You are my friend!"

"And you're mine. You were never my father figure. I want you to know that. I had a great father. You were more the uncle I never had."

"Your uncle is a damned fool," Sagacius snarled. "I saw him the other day. He looks miserable."

"Good!" Aura snapped. "I may have forgiven him, but that doesn't mean I want to see him again. If my anger toward Cecil almost started a purge, then what will happen if I run into Uncle Cedric? Until I find out, I don't want you very far away."

"Then I won't leave," Sagacius said. "I'm sure that between our minds, and a few tankards of your ale, that we can figure something out. I could sell you the farm for a mere farthing and take a room in town." Sagacius snapped his fingers. "Bart the wheelwright! His last son moved out and Bart lives all alone in that big house. I'm sure he would enjoy having some company, hearing my tall tales, and receiving a few extra quid per month. That would give you the room to grow and gain your own reputation without being a shadow. If you need me, I'll be a mere horseback ride away."

"We don't own a horse," Aura said. When Sagacius frowned, Aura added, "That was a joke, Master. I like the idea. As long as you're nearby, I don't mind being alone in the house. I just don't want to be alone in the world. I need someone to turn to that I trust if I do something stupid."

"Don't worry, you will."

"Thank you! I appreciate your confidence in me!"

The old man winked at her. Realizing he teased her, Aura chuckled. Then, she giggled. Then, she laughed. The last of the fear's embers crumbled to mental soot. Her happiness returned in a flood of thoughts. Oh, merciful heavens, so much to do. Clothes! Oh, joy! And ale! More joy! And making a staff, no a trip to Welcaster first, then a staff. Oh, they'd have to walk. But first, ale. Aura looked at her empty tankard. Well, when was the old man going down into the cellar for that next keg?

"Now that we've settled that crisis, and you're happy again, there's something I need to discuss with you while we're both still sober," Sagacius said.

He refilled Aura's tankard from the pitcher, then his own. She leaned against the windowsill, waiting for the wizard to continue. Sagacius sat in his chair, staring into his tankard. He seemed to ponder something. She wanted to ask, well, what was it? He looked at her with an intense gaze. Aura gulped. The last time she saw that look was when she misfired a Divine Thunderbolt and almost killed him.

Sagacius said, "This is not my idea, Aura, but I have been overridden by the authorities in my order. They know about you, and they want to meet you. They are rather insistent."

Aura sighed. "Is this because of what I did to Cecil?"

"Oh, no. I don't mean the Order of Wizards." He paused again, before saying, "I mean the Order of Enchanters."

"Why do they want to meet me? I mean –" Aura stopped. Sagacius had said *my order*. "You're not an enchanter."

Sagacius sighed. With a slow nod, he said, "Yes, I am very much an enchanter."

"How is that possible? You're old. I mean, oh, I'm sorry Master. All the stories I've ever heard, enchanters were young. They also didn't wear nearly as much as you. Besides, that order is extinct now. They died out long before I was born."

"It would seem that way, wouldn't it," Sagacius said, rubbing his chin. "The Order of Enchanters is quite extant, despite their folly. Most live in a place called the Valley of the Mystic Moon. As far as I know, there are only five of us out in greater Ayrdland. You actually met an enchantress when we visited Barthwick two years ago. Her name is Leynda."

Aura remembered the woman, but thought at the time she belonged to an elite branch of the Order of Witches. Leynda had long flowing golden hair and eyes so brown they looked black. She wore silver bands that wrapped around her arms and legs. Her purple blouse barely covered her breasts, and her matching skirt only hid her hips. When Aura heard her speak, the deepest peace she ever felt filled her. Confidence and magnetism radiated from her. She watched, amazed, as Leynda healed a dying child with just a touch and a whisper. Then, the woman refused payment for her services, accepting only a hug in exchange. As she departed, the enchantress looked at Aura with a loving, yet ferocious gaze. It was if someone befriended a lioness.

"So, she was an enchantress," Aura mumbled. "I've always wanted to be a woman like her."

"Don't say that in haste, Aura," Sagacius said, frowning. "The Order of Enchanters wishes to extend you an invitation to join them."

"Why? I'm not an enchantress."

"In a manner of speaking, you are. I trained you as a wizardess, yes, but also as an enchantress, save for how one empowers her magic."

Aura frowned. In a firm voice, full of the most steel she could muster, she said, "The Order of Enchanters wants to meet me. You're an enchanter. You trained me as an enchantress." She held her growing irritation in check. "Why didn't you tell me any of this before today, Master?"

"You won't like my answer, Aura," Sagacius said.

"I already don't like this conversation, Master," Aura snapped, irritation giving way to anger, and overflowing. For two years, she lived without any sovereignty, in the glowering shadow of her uncle and the whim of weather. This morning, Sagacius himself severed her bonds of helplessness and covered her nakedness with power. Now, he implied that the past ten years had been duplicitous, or perhaps outright fraud. Through clenched teeth, she snarled, "Give me your answer and let me determine if I like it or not."

"I didn't mean to rile your Lockhaven temper, Aura. Please forgive me. My reasons are complicated, and many are personal. You said the order was extinct? Well, we may as well be. Fifty years ago, we divided along philosophical lines. The two sides took up arms and fought a very bloody war, leaving half the order dead on the battlefield. When the smoke blew away, those who remained fell into listlessness. The Order of Enchanters is a bunch of lascivious drunkards now. What I saw broke my heart, so I chose to leave the Valley of the Mystic Moon and walk among my fellow men, where I could do some good. Here, I am just Sagacius the wizard. In the Valley of the Mystic Moon, I am the final pupil of the greatest enchantress of all time. Any apprentice of mine is going to attract the attention of the council of the Order of Enchanters, despite my efforts to keep her shielded. The council has known about you for quite some time and has insisted that they meet you. I did not tell you about them because I did not want their problems to become your problems."

"The problems of an entire shire are going to be my problems," Aura said.

"Yes, but the people of Hartshorn do not hump on the public green," Sagacius said. "I would like to keep my other reasons to myself, if you do not mind."

Keep your little mysteries, Master, Aura thought. Just another line to add to the list of mental questions she kept about the man. How old was he anyway? He looked seventy, but talked about ancient history as if it happened just yesterday. Where was he from? He spoke Ayrdish with a distinct southern accent, yet he never claimed any village or city as his home. He spoke perfect Nebelish, Flumantine, all four Tangoi tongues, and Bellician, teaching all but the too-logical Bellician to her. Yet, she often heard him through the wall separating their bed chambers, talking in his sleep, and he spoke Nebelish. Out of the nearly one thousand inhabitants of Hartshorn, he alone had only one name. Surely, somewhere in those robes of his, he kept a surname.

"As for your training," he continued. "I joined the Order of Wizards to give myself some organizational foundation. So, I am a wizard. The training of a wizardess and an enchantress are not dissimilar. Both rely heavily on the elements and the forces of nature. But where a wizardess stops there, an enchantress goes farther. I decided to take you further, believing that the training of an enchantress would make you more flexible, and therefore, more employable. Dueling, for instance. No other wizard's apprentice knows how to duel like you. You are an initiated wizardess, Aura, but you know far more than most. I taught you everything an enchantress knows, save the most important. Perhaps, I should have taught you that, too."

"What didn't you teach me?" Aura asked.

"Tell me, Aura. What is it that you want to do for the people of Hartshorn?"

"We've had this conversation before, Master," Aura said. He knew her answer as well as she. For some reason, he needed to hear it again. Perhaps, he thought she needed to hear it again. "I want to defend the defenseless, help the helpless, and give hope to the hopeless. I want to help my town overcome its problems and I want my people to lead happy lives. If I can help them, I will."

"You want to do that for them, after what they did to you? They let you rot in that alley for two years. They let you sit under the hot sun and the freezing snow and the driving rain. They let you wear rags that became too small for you. They let you become a beggar for that rodent. They let you be covered in spiders. They let you be tormented by their own children. They let you be called ... *Snake Eyes*. After all that, you still want to help them?"

With each sentence, Sagacius' voice grew lower and deeper. By the last, he almost growled like a cornered dog. Aura felt his anger at the townspeople rise. As it rose, so did her own. Each word drove another iron spike into her heart. She felt the cold cobblestones and the prick of the feet of spiders. She tasted stale crusts of bread. She saw people pass her by as if she were just a stone in the alley wall. She smelled her own stale body. She heard those words, *Snake Eyes*. For a second, her anger flashed into fury and she wanted to hurl a fistful of curses into the town and splinter Piper's Knob into gravel. No, she told herself. That would not only violate the rules of her new order and her own solemn oath, it would violate every single day she sat in that alley and forgave the people of Hartshorn. It would violate her own dream. How could she help the helpless if she hurt them? Her fury turned from the townspeople onto herself, for that one second of hatred, for that one moment of forgetting she forgave them. It turned on her master for taunting her over the brink of her self-control.

Aura slammed her tankard on the window sill. She shouted, "That's exactly why I want to do it for them! They were not responsible. They were terrified of Uncle Cedric. Let me tell you something, Master. Many of them were kind to me. When they could, they snuck behind my uncle's back and brought me food, and a blanket, and their daughters' dresses. They sat with me and told me stories while I ate with them. I didn't understand why my world had been crushed and I had to live in that alley, but I knew my way out was to love people. Love, and that little book of the tales Daddy told me, were all I had. Is that good enough for you?"

"The question is, Aura, is that good enough for you?" Sagacius asked.

"Yes, it's good enough for me," Aura said. "I don't blame them for holding me at arm's length. Even when I was Hartshorn's little princess, I was different. Look at me, Master! Jack, Roderick, and Cecil were right. I'm a freak. I'm the tallest woman in the shire. My eyes are the color of grass, while everyone else has either blue or brown eyes. They're simply afraid of me. Perhaps, if I can love them, I can help them overcome their fear."

"Oh, Aura. I do look at you. I wish you would look at yourself! After all you've accomplished, even after your initiation, you still can't see yourself as anything but an urchin, can you? The woman I see and the woman you see may as well be two completely different people." He stared at the floor. Aura heard him mumble, "Gods forgive me, but she reminds me of ... Nightshade."

"That was my mother's surname," Aura said.

"Hmm?" Sagacius muttered. He looked at her. For a brief moment, she saw horror in his face, as if he just revealed a terrible secret. It vanished with a blink, and he smiled. "Of course it was. I do know your family story, Aura. Well, it's fitting. A nightshade is a very beautiful and helpful plant, but most people are terrified of it because they don't know what to do with it."

"I see," Aura said with a nod. She didn't believe the reason for the wizard's answer for one second, but she also knew he was not about to reveal the truth. "Let's return to my earlier question. What did you not teach me?"

"Ah, well." The wizard seemed relieved at her change of subject. He clapped his hands together. "I didn't teach you the secret of an enchantress' power. The different orders each have a special way to empower their magic. The wizards use the forces of nature. Witches and druids have their faith. Sorcerers use their wills, while alchemists use their minds. The mages use the forces of the netherworld, and shamans channel spirits. Well, an enchantress uses her feelings. She empowers her magic with her emotions. You have withstood enough in your life to drive any woman to madness, or at least drunkenness. Yet, you still love with all your heart. I may have made a mistake in not teaching you. Now, if I had taught you how to harness your emotions –"

Three loud raps on the door interrupted him. As Aura walked to the door, she said, "I bet I know who this is."

Chapter Three

ONE-EYED RUPERT stood just outside the door. Shorter than Aura by two inches, a life spent in the sun turned his once brown hair and beard, and his once fair skin, the color of old planks. She could not remember how Rupert lost his left eye. He wore a black linen kerchief tied over it as far back as she could remember. He glanced at Aura with his one good eye, a blue eye. Rupert pulled back his hood in deference to her as a woman, but glanced down at the ground. Aura sighed. She knew what that meant.

"Mornin' miss," Rupert said. "Is Mr. Sagacius home?"

"Yes, please come in," she answered, fighting to keep the chill from her voice.

Aura held the door open to allow Rupert to step into the foyer. Closing it, she noticed that Rupert looked Sagacius in the face as the two men shook hands. She sighed again, and walked into the kitchen to give them their privacy. As she passed the tags of sage, she swatted them with a little more force than she wished. Sage dust flew around her face, forcing a sneeze.

"Mr. Sagacius," Rupert said. "I was wondering if I could hire ya to come bless my new sheep."

"Of course," Sagacius replied. "In fact, Aura should perform the blessing."

Upon hearing her name, Aura perked up. This could be her first assignment as a full wizardess. She fumbled around in the kitchen, making busy movement with the dishes and jars, just to look occupied. She did not want the men to know that she listened to every word.

"Your apprentice? I need a professional," Rupert said.

"Aura is a professional. I initiated her today. She is Hartshorn's new wizardess."

"But she's –" Rupert lowered his voice, but not low enough. Aura still heard him. "She's got them snake eyes, all green like. Probably from her mother. Geilltian, ya know."

The muscles in Aura's back tightened. She was sure the two men heard her loud snort, and thought she saw smoke rise from her nostrils. Calling someone a Geilltian was the worst insult she knew.

"Aura's mother was Coadic," Sagacius said. Aura heard the sharp edge in his voice. She silently thanked him for defending her. "I believe you knew the woman. If you bothered to try, you could tell the difference between a Coadic and a Geilltian. Coadics have red hair. Geilltians do not. Aura's hair is a shade of red, if you didn't notice."

"Them Coads are piskies, ya know," Rupert said.

Aura cringed. She had never heard that one before. Now her mother was a piskie! Usually, the whispered insults were limited to "that girl would be beautiful if she had blue eyes," and "is she part cat?" Ayrdish women had all shades of hair color, so that browned red known as auburn was fairly common. If only she had blue eyes, Aura thought, or even brown, then maybe people would just judge her on the way she acted. They would see her as strange, not as a threat. Maybe she would not be such a shadow.

"She won't suck out my sheeps' brains, will she?" Rupert asked.

Suck out sheeps' brains? What next? Stealing the souls of babies?

"I assure you that Aura loves animals," Sagacius answered. "Besides, I'll be right there with both of you to make sure nothing happens."

"Well, all right, but I don't like it none."

Aura ignored Sagacius the first time he said her name. She considered refusing the assignment. After all, Rupert just insulted her, in her own home yet. That was a first. Then, he insulted her mother, twice. Piskie, indeed! Feeling her anger rise, Aura ignored Sagacius the second time he called her name. Why should she help Rupert? Oh, she certainly wanted to help the one-eyed shepherd understand the difference between a Geilltian and a Coadic, not that he would like the lesson. She knew Tangoi history, and when the Coadics were finally angered, the most efficient and terrifying empire the world had known stumbled. Why didn't she just turn around and tell him what he – . She lowered her head and sighed, remembering her tirade to Sagacius just minutes earlier. Even if she did not use magic, yelling at Rupert would hurt him. Dammit, but the shepherd just insulted her and her mother at the same time! She told herself not to think about Rupert. Think about his sheep. The sheep deserved her best. That she could give.

"Are ya sure she's up for this?" Rupert asked. "I mean, she ain't hearing ya and she's only fifteen feet away."

Sagacius chuckled. "She's just excited about being initiated. If anything, she will be too exuberant with the blessing, and you'll end up with one hundred sheep next spring."

"That won't be too bad," Rupert mumbled.

"Aura," Sagacius said. This time, she turned around. She stepped through the hallway into the sitting room. "Rupert would like for you to bless his new sheep."

"I'd be delighted, sir," Aura said to Rupert. She meant it. "I'll be right with you." Aura ducked back into the kitchen and grabbed a small jar on top of the cupboard by the window.

Rupert's farm lay next door to the Big Hedge, a quarter mile down the road, on the other side of the creek and forest that separated their two parcels. Using hand gestures, Sagacius insisted that Aura walk ahead of him, and beside Rupert. They covered the distance in silence. Aura felt Rupert's disquiet in his occasional glances at her with his one blue eye. She walked with her head up, her shoulders back, and her chest out. Let Rupert see her pride in her office and her determination to bless his sheep with the best of her ability. Blast it all, but the man took short steps, she thought, trying her best to rein in her long stride.

The shepherd's house was the same type of building as theirs, without the tower but twice as big, suitable for a married man with two sons and three unmarried daughters. Behind it lay his barn, an old stone affair with a thin thatch roof. On one side of the barn sat Rupert's sheepfold. On the other, Lodd and Ed carried hay to the large, black bull in the cattle pen. Rupert and Sagacius leaned against the stone wall of the sheepfold as Aura entered. Counting fourteen ewes and one ram, she decided to start with the ram. The sheep circled around her, as if they knew her and what she planned to do for them.

Aura uncorked her jar and poured some clear liquid into her hand. Then, she placed her hand on top of the ram's head. Anticipating Rupert's question, Aura looked at him and said, "Moonwater. It's water that I sat in the light of the last full moon. It's full of all that wonderful cold heat of a warm spring evening. It absorbed all the wool dust left behind by the giants who lived in this area long before the dragons came, which was long before we came. Some say it contains the urine of the goddess Cygfran, but I'm not so sure about that. It's the finest wine in all the Forested Islands and it helps animals grow thick coats. It's like holy water, except without the priest."

When Rupert looked confounded enough to suit her, Aura turned back to the ram. As she did, she noticed that Sagacius held his hand over his mouth. Well, it *was* moonwater, she thought. She just did not feel like explaining to Rupert what it really did, and the sheep would not care. Holding her wet hand to the ram's head, Aura hummed. She raised and lowered her voice until she found the note she wanted.

"I call upon Dyoedda of the Gweryn bright," Aura sang, letting her voice float up and down like the breeze around her. "I bless this ram with your divine light. May his life be long and his wool be his wealth. May he be only strong and know only health. May his lambs be many and bring Rupert much worth. Lady Dyoedda of the fields, let this blessing go forth."

"Baniar's nightgown!" Rupert said. "Is she singing to the sheep?"

"Aura's chanting. She always chants her incantations," Sagacius answered.

"Piskies."

Aura moved on to the ewes, changing her words a little to fit them as females. The sheep looked at her, as if they understood and appreciated what she did. When she finished chanting over the final ewe, she corked her jar.

"There," she said, turning to Rupert and Sagacius. "According to plan —"

A young man screamed. The scream came from the other side of the barn. Rupert, Sagacius, and Aura bolted from the sheepfold and ran around the barn. Ed dragged Lodd through the gate of the cattle pen. The black bull tossed his head behind them. As they approached, Aura saw the spreading red stain on Lodd's shirt, and the dark trail in the dirt leading back through the gate.

"Brawny gored Lodd," Ed shouted. "He gored him!"

"No!" Rupert screamed as they reached the two boys.

Sagacius dove to his knees and ripped Lodd's shirt open. Aura turned her head when she saw the wound, a crater of crimson below the boy's chest. Blood spurted from the deep puncture. Lodd's eyelids fluttered, but remained closed in leaden stupor. He breathed in jagged, quick pants. Already, his skin had turned pale gray.

"Ed, ride for the apothecary!" Rupert snapped.

"It's too late," Sagacius said, standing up. "I'm sorry, Rupert. That wound is fatal. It's through his liver."

"Do something," the farmer begged. "Ya're a wizard."

"I can't! Magic will not heal that wound in time. It would take too long and he does not have time. The best I can do is comfort him and make his passing peaceful and painless."

Aura looked at Rupert. She saw the fear, the anguish, and the hopelessness in his face. She had seen that before, twelve years earlier on her father's face when four men laid her sister's limp body on the kitchen table. Tightening her jaw, she threw aside Rupert's earlier insults of her mother and herself. Life was more important than her pride.

Aura fell to her knees, slapping her hands over the wound. Closing her eyes, she said a silent prayer to Tanawynne and Adphyr. Then, she opened her eyes and stared at her hands as if she saw the wound through them. Now, Aura, she thought. She became a wizard's apprentice to help people. Time to prove it. Time to earn her new office. Someone had to act. Someone had to stop the bleeding. Someone had to keep Rupert's heart from breaking.

She had no idea what to do. Healing spells required their own natural time to manifest. Lodd needed immediate healing. That meant an explosive force of will. The only spells she knew of that power were dueling spells. This was a duel, a battle between her and the wound. The victor claimed the boy. Dueling spells required the incantations be spoken in old Karanthek. Instant healing spells were no doubt the same, at least she hoped. Deciding her course of action, Aura channeled her will into one image, that of Lodd standing up and walking away with a smile on his face.

"Ekos entola plagos epolotha natara!" Aura sang in the tongue of the east's first empire, belting the words as if challenging a storm for vocal supremacy.

"What is she doing?" Rupert shouted. "Get away from him, ya cat bitch!"

Behind her, Aura heard scuffling, followed by Sagacius saying, "Leave her alone, Rupert! That's a healing spell. She's ordering the wound to close. It may help a little. It may slow the bleeding. It may buy some time for Ed to ride into town. Aura, try −"

"Be quiet, Master!" Aura snapped. "I'm trying to concentrate." She continued chanting, "Ekos entola plagos epolotha natara!"

She felt the blood gush underneath her hands and saw it ooze through her fingers. Dammit, Aura! Forget singing, forget chanting, she told herself. Only a fool chanted dueling spells, and this was a duel. Lodd was dying. She shouted, "Ekos entola plagos epolotha natara!"

Focus, Aura told herself. Focus! She was a wizardess now. It was time to put all that training to work. Ten years of lessons, and reading, and potions, and practicing came together in Aura's mind. She drew on them all, channeling them into her hands. No, that was not enough. The blood still oozed through her fingers. More. She needed more.

"Ekos entola plagos epolotha natara!"

She could not bear to hear Rupert wail and keen like her father had. That face! The agony! That was it, Aura thought as her hands warmed. Think about Daddy! Think about Rupert! Give the farmer his son back!

"I won't let you die," Aura said, looking at Lodd's white face.

She turned back to her hands. Blank everything out but the wound. See the wound close. See the bleeding stop. See Lodd stand up and walk. "Plagos epolotha natara!" Her hands grew hot. Her arms began to ache. "Plagos epolotha natara!"

"Aura, you're driving yourself too hard!" Sagacius shouted.

"Silence, Master!"

The heat in her hands now began to hurt. Too hot! No! Don't think about the pain! That meant something was happening. Vitality released! Intent worked! Push harder! "Plagos epolotha natara!" An energy of the clarity of blue fire exploded inside Aura, beginning in her chest. It roared down her arms, tightening her muscles with cramps, and erupted in her hands.

Aura threw her head back and screamed. Pure vitality, an energy of such force it dimmed the sun, roared through her body and exploded out her palms. Her hands felt as if she thrust them into a fiery forge. Heat poured from them into Lodd's body, heat that she knew incinerated her own flesh. She no longer cared about herself, only about this boy. "Plagos epolotha natara!" she roared. She gasped for breath. She could not breathe! Her chest pounded. Her heart. Something was wrong with her heart. No! Don't think about that. "Plagos epolotha natara," she yelled. Closing her eyes tight, and biting her lip to keep from screaming again, she ignored the pounding in her chest, the pain in her arms, and the flames in her hands. She held it back, allowing the heat to pour from her into Lodd. She held it. "Plagos epolotha natara," she whispered with all her remaining voice. Her whole body trembled. Her strength fled fast. Just a little longer. Just a little ... no ...

Her hands cooled. The heat vanished. Had she stopped the bleeding, or had she merely exhausted herself? Was Lodd still alive? Did she still have hands? She peeked. Her hands looked fine. Moving them aside, she looked at Lodd. She gasped. Her arm felt made of stone as she fumbled for her jar of moonwater. Almost dropping it, she managed to remove the cork. Then, she poured most of the water on Lodd's stomach.

"Ya healed him!" Rupert shouted.

"By all the gods and goddesses," Sagacius muttered.

Lodd opened his eyes. His skin looked pale but pink. He said, "What happened?"

Aura looked at the healthy boy. Not even a scar remained on his stomach. Lodd breathed as any normal, but tired, boy of fifteen should. A tear trickled down Aura's face as she smiled at the bewildered Lodd. She raised the jar and washed the blood from her hands. Then, she collapsed onto her right side, exhausted. Her chest ached. She panted, trying to catch her breath.

Sagacius knelt by Aura. He touched her on the head. She looked up into his smiling face. Unable to speak, she cast him a look that said, *I did it, Master.* He closed his eyes, and nodded.

Rupert knelt by his son. He stared at the clean flesh of his son's stomach. He jerked his face toward Aura. His lip trembled. A tear formed at the edge of his one eye. He reached his hand toward her.

"I was wrong about ya," Rupert said. "Miss Aura, ya ... ya saved my boy. No Geilltian bitch or piskie would ... I'm a stupid old boar, weaned on barley squeezin's and ... I ain't got no ... Please!"

Aura pushed herself up with her right arm. With her trembling left hand, she took Rupert's. She smiled and whispered, "Of course, I forgive you, sir." Then, with what remained of her strength, she bent forward, and kissed Rupert across his knuckles. Her right arm buckled. Sagacius caught her as she fell backwards.

"How can I repay ya?" Rupert asked, grinning with tears flowing down his face. "I'll give ya up to half my farm! I'll give ya my new sheep!"

Still panting to catch her breath, Aura said, "You've already repaid me, sir. Now, Lodd needs to rest. He's lost a lot of blood. I don't know a spell to replace that. Feed him well. Give him some of those barley squeezin's if you have any. Just a few days. And I need to rest, too."

Aura looked at Sagacius. She expected him to help her to her feet. Instead, without a word, Sagacius slipped one arm behind Aura's back, and another under her knees. He lifted her to his chest as he stood up. Aura felt the bulges in his arms through his sleeves. They felt like iron. She felt the solid chest under his robe. How could this old man lift her, she thought. She weighed almost 150 pounds. She was too tired to think about it further. Just one more mystery about her master to add to her overflowing list. As Sagacius carried Aura to the road, she looked back to see Rupert and Ed helping Lodd walk to their house.

"How did I do that?" Aura mumbled.

"Aura, that wasn't just a healing spell," Sagacius said, carrying her down the road. "That was a miracle! Not even I could have healed that wound. I've only known a dozen who could do that."

"Who were they?" she asked.

"They were all enchantresses," he answered. "They are our order's finest healers. You used love, didn't you? You poured your compassion into that spell, even after what Rupert said about you."

"I don't care about what Rupert said," Aura replied. "All right, it hurt. It hurt quite a bit, Master. But it didn't matter how I felt. It mattered how Rupert felt. I can recover from my injured pride. He can't recover from the loss of his son. I remember the look on Daddy's face when Ester died. I never want to see that look on anyone else's face, not if there's something I can do about it. I don't know what I put behind that spell. Perhaps it was compassion. I don't know. It was something I've never felt before, a power I didn't know I had. Really, Master. I can walk."

"I've seen experienced wizards try that sort of healing spell, and their hearts burst. Rest, now, Aura. I'm going to carry you home. It's the least I can do for you."

When they reached their house, Sagacius asked Aura to unlatch the door, then he carried her inside and sat her down in her favorite chair. She ran her fingers along the hide upholstery on the arms, worn hairless by her hands years ago. Sinking back into the chair, she let the comfort of an old friend envelop her. Despite her exhaustion, she felt happy, happier than she had even when Sagacius initiated her. Initiation ... stepping across a staff ...

Aura wore a red dress of something like silk, but more shimmering in the moonlight. It flowed from her neck to her ankles, and revealed almost her whole body, as if inviting men to gaze, but warning them to turn away their eyes before she stole their hearts. Her eyes were no longer green, but black, all black, the color of purity and completion and mystery. Blue mist drifted from her fingertips. The six elements danced around her. Fire, Earth, Metal, Water, Light, and Air, waiting to grant her slightest wish. She glanced around at all of Ayrdland and healed with a mere flick of her finger, and drove away all nightmares with a laugh. Yes, she could banish nightmares! Yes, even spiders! Yes, even smoke! Aura laughed as she never laughed before, and the more raucous her laugh became, the more people stepped outside their shuttered doors. She aimed her palm at a pile of dry wood. With a lowering of her eyelids, it burst into flame, a bonfire of victory and joy. Then, she sang a song and all the people danced and laughed and ...

Aura opened her eyes. Her lips felt dry. She tried to say something, but Sagacius held up his hand. He told her she had been asleep for an hour. She smiled. Her body felt like stone. Her soul felt like a bird flying across the field. The old wizard stared at her with a strange look on his face. She understood the look. It was one she often carried on her face, that of a memory not wanted, but also invited.

"What?" Aura croaked.

"Old words spoken by an old friend long ago. Old words believed by another," he whispered.

"Huh?"

The wizard blinked. The strange look vanished from his face. He smiled and said, "Nothing. Just the prattling of an old man. Let me get that ale." Then, he turned and walked down the cellar stairs.

Aura laid her head back and stared at the ceiling. She recalled an old dream, one formed twelve years ago on cold cobblestones. It had been set in motion by the kindness of an old man, an old man who no doubt lifted a keg in the cellar beneath her. Until today, she had not known how strong that dream had been, nor that she could see it turn into such vibrant reality. Today, she gave hope to the hopeless. She wanted to do it again, but she knew Sagacius was right. She had almost killed herself. If the wound had been any worse, she may have died alongside Lodd.

Sagacius returned to the kitchen. He walked to the table and pulled the bung from the keg. He poured the pitcher full of ale, then filled the two tankards. Carrying them into the sitting room, he handed one to Aura. She took several long gulps.

"Master," she said, when she felt refreshed enough to speak. "I have a serious question to ask. Can an enchantress do what I just did without exhausting herself?"

"The answer is rather complicated," Sagacius said. "It's both yes and no. There are very few instantaneous spells, but we enchanters have two. Dueling and healing. Because we harness the power of our emotions, we can do both with instant results and that is because we base both on love. Love is an inexhaustible force. The enchantresses that I know who heal like that have healed even worse injuries without tiring. That's how I fight such lengthy duels. It isn't the thrill of victory. It's that I defend someone I love. Remember the day I defeated the ogre? It wasn't that he was an ogre. It was that Hartshorn was in danger, and so were you. That emotion kept me fighting."

"You could have healed Lodd, then," Aura said.

"No, I couldn't. Enchanters gravitate toward the dueling spells. They appeal to our chest hair. Enchantresses, who are more nurturing, prefer healing spells. It would have taken me a week to heal Lodd like you did. I trained you in dueling spells, because they are what I know. I never expected you to be able to heal with the same vigor with which you move stone. I have never seen anyone who could cast both dueling and healing spells with equal power. Until now." He lowered his head. Aura saw that strange look cross his face again. He mumbled, "Nightshade ... the most powerful ... no, don't. It was spoken to her, not you."

Aura ignored his expression but not his comment. That was the second time Sagacius mentioned her mother's maiden name. Not uncommon, she thought. Anyone whose surname was that of the most potent magical plant attracted the attention of wizards. She thought about the word power. It was such a strong word, and an even stronger possession. Many people sought it. Others fled it. Aura thought about the power she possessed. She had enjoyed blessing Rupert's sheep. As the village wizardess, that would be her job. Her day's work would include blessing livestock and crops, finding lost items, locating missing children, assisting the constable and the midwives, making luck and joy charms, healing people ill beyond the skill of the apothecary, and brewing lust potions for newlyweds, as well as divination and consulting lore at the request of Hartshorn's elders. It sounded like an enjoyable life and a wonderful occupation, one she spent ten years training to fulfill.

The prospects no longer satisfied her. She just tasted something better. Her dream refocused, refined, and reignited all at the same time. She realized her potential to help others. Not only had she given Rupert back his son, but Rupert gave her something in return, something she craved for years. He gave her acceptance. Her act of saving his son melted his prejudiced heart. She bested his ignorance and fear. Perhaps now, Rupert could step into a larger world, one she just offered him. In return, he offered her his hand. His hand! She felt like she just took her first step out of the shadows. She felt like she just became a little more tangible. Perhaps in giving hope to the hopeless, she found a little for herself, too.

Chapter Four

TONIGHT, THE GOOSE feather and pine straw stuffing of her mattress poked Aura in the back, if it was possible to poke stone. She stared up at the beams overhead. They mocked her with more movement than she could muster. Every joint in her body ached. Every muscle screamed as if she had been running for five miles, or swimming for five miles, or doing something that required a distance of five miles.

"There must be a better way," she mumbled.

She had dreamed about Lodd thrice. First, she healed him, but died in the process. Second, she failed to heal him, and they both died. In the final dream, she healed Lodd with a mere touch of her finger, just as Leynda had the child in Barthwick. With the third dream, Aura abandoned all hope of sleep. She sat up and swung her legs off the bed, staring at the darkened room. Placing her hand on her chest, she felt her heart beat. Despite a day of rest, and probably too much ale, it still raced.

"I asked for a chance to give someone his life, but I didn't ask to almost lose mine in the process."

Even though she knew she walked up to the threshold of the afterlife, Aura wanted more. She had tasted the joy that follows saving someone's life. Not only had she given Lodd his life, but she gave One-Eyed Rupert a new eye, as it were. His acceptance of her fueled her own acceptance of herself. For a brief second, she saw Aura Lockhaven as Sagacius saw her, and she liked the image. She wanted to do it again. She did not, however, want to die. How did she accomplish that? How could she summon that level of compassion at will? How could she perform instant healing without endangering herself? How could she become a magician like Leynda? Aura needed answers, from someone wiser and more powerful than even Sagacius.

She often prayed naked, feeling a little more sacred in her natural state. Besides, the gods saw through her clothes anyway, so why bother with the effort to cover herself. As fast as her stiff legs allowed, she stood up. No need to strike an alchemist's firestick and light a candle. She knew her tiny room and exactly where to find what she wanted. The air drifting through the closed shutters brought the evening chill with it. Grabbing the old tunic of Sagacius' that hung in her wardrobe, she pulled it on, leaving the laces loose. As tall as she was, it still draped her body like a sack. With a mere belt around the waist, it would have passed for a threadbare dress reaching to her mid-thigh. Usually, she wore it to work in the garden, or when she needed to dress faster than her usual clothes allowed. Tonight, it was more for warmth than modesty.

"Vey ist der beer, Mutter?" she heard drift from Sagacius' closed bed chamber door. She smiled, and whispered, "Et ist war et du geleffen." Well, it was true. The beer, or ale in their case, was right where he left it, on the kitchen table. That was a good thing, too. Aura wanted a pint. She felt her way down the stairs, hoping the squeaks and moans of the loose treads did not wake the old wizard. At the bottom of the stairs she paused and listened. His snorts and growls in Nebelish told her that he still slept.

Moonlight drifting through the slats of the shutters gave enough light for her to spot the keg on the table, as well as the pitcher and her tankard. After filling the pitcher, she reached for her pint mug. No, she thought. Tonight required more than a pint. Taking the pitcher, she walked out the door, closing it behind her.

Aura and Sagacius often wandered to the stone circle atop the knoll behind the house to pray, think, or just look at the stars. They kept the path to the circle free of the prickly blackberries encroaching from the Big Hedge. As Aura walked out to the sarsens, she wished she had thought to put on her boots. The grass felt a little too cold underneath her bare feet. Ignoring the discomfort, she continued her journey. Besides, the beauty of the night drove away the chill in her toes. Once she reached the center of the circle, she looked up. Overhead, the half moon drove back the stars, until they retreated to a safe distance from the silver pearl's light. There, they stuck out their tongues and consumed the blackness with their own glow.

In Aura's mind, the moon represented Cygfran, even though she knew the actual sphere in the sky was the grandmother of all the Gweryn. She nodded and gave a silent tribute to the supreme mother goddess. She poured a cup full from the pitcher onto the ground in tribute, then drank a good five swallows to honor the queen. Tonight, she wanted someone else. On the horizon, she spotted her target, the evening star. Most people knew the star by the name Allathara, the goddess of love for the Towering Ones. Aura believed the star represented Allathara's counterpart in the Gweryn, the goddess Ystlena of the dark Tywelch. In honor of the laughing goddess, Aura drained half the pitcher.

"Dearest Ystlena," Aura said to the star. "I was born on your day. Even before I knew you, you were my matron." She sighed. Keeping her eyes on the star, she began walking back and forth, from the northern sarsen to the southern one. "I need you, tonight. You embody everything I wish to be, everything I hope to be. You are love. You are beauty. You are sensuality. I try to act like you, but I fail. Despite how much I love, I still feel hatred and I can't control my anger. I'm about as ugly as a pile of dry bones. As for sensuality, I've never experienced the surrender of breath in bed. I think it's a fable. Today, however, I experienced something. I gave someone his life! The joy overwhelmed me. I'd give up love, beauty, and sensuality to have that again."

She held her hand up. In the light of the moon, it seemed to glow before her eyes. Holding the pitcher in her other hand, she drank deep swallows of her best ale. "How can someone so hideous do something so beautiful?" She sighed. "I know what you would say, if you actually spoke to me. You'd say that type of beauty comes from within. It doesn't matter what the vessel looks like, only how she acts."

She sat the pitcher on the ground, and leaned against the northern sarsen. The star glowed brighter, as if in answer. The evening breeze kicked up, shooting through the stone circle. Aura shivered. From the Big Hedge, a nightingale sang. Goddesses were so dramatic, Aura thought.

"Perhaps, if I learned to love on such a powerful level, I would also find pleasure in my bed, find a man who loved me despite my eyes, see myself as Master does, and eventually love myself," she said.

She heard a small whisper. It was her own voice, inside her head, so she knew her hope spoke. Still, she attributed the voice to Ystlena. It said, "You have that backwards."

Perhaps, she heard Ystlena after all. Aura knew she had her priorities backwards, but felt powerless to reverse them. No glamour spell turned green eyes blue. She sighed. Looking back at the evening star, she said, "Ystlena, I adore you. Please. Help me learn to use compassion to empower my magic. Master mentioned the enchanters. He implied that an enchantress does that very thing. Yet, he speaks of them in fear. I don't know what to do. Why does this order want to see me? Can they help me? Can they teach me to be who I want to be? I want to be like Leynda. Please, Ystlena. Help me. Help me to –"

Aura paused as a movement caught her eye. From the Big Hedge, a light emerged. Oh, merciful heavens, she thought. Who in his right mind would wander in that thicket at night? She answered herself. Someone up to no good. Her stomach tightened as she gulped. She stood one hundred yards from the house, alone at night, with only an old shirt between herself and a man's hands. From the neck down, she had everything a lust filled man wanted. The memory of Ester's dead body flashed through her mind. What if a rapist held that lantern? No, she could defend herself. Even if her order and vows allowed her to use magic, she preferred to use her fists and knees against a man with more than conversation on his mind. They hurt more.

As the light grew closer, Aura ducked behind the sarsen. She stood straight, blending her shadow with that of the stone. By now, she made out the figure. It wasn't a man. It was a woman. A naked woman at that. She also didn't hold a lantern. The light shown from the woman's open palm.

She looked to stand five feet tall, with silver hair and skin carved from alabaster. A Fae. She ran her thoughts through everything she knew about the Fae. This one was tall, for a Fae, glowed, wore no clothes, and had no wings. She was a nymph. Now, what was a nymph doing in Hartshorn?

The nymph walked to the edge of the stone circle. For a moment, she looked right at Aura. Then, she shrugged her shoulders, and walked toward the house. As she did, she held up her other hand to her mouth.

"Yoo hoo," the nymph sang out. "Where are you?" Aura heard something that sounded like bacon frying on a griddle. "It's Nocturna, you silly thing. Who else would it be? Oh, I'm here, all right. The thing is, she's asleep. Well, the window is dark, silly!"

She? The only *she* Aura knew in the vicinity was herself. Nocturna meant her, Aura Lockhaven. Who was she talking to, Aura wondered. Aura glanced around, but saw no one but herself and Nocturna. Nymphs were not known to switch people for changelings. Besides, at almost twenty-two, Aura was a little old to be switched. Nymphs usually danced around in the forests, seducing men, satyrs, and gods into trysts. Perhaps this one preferred to share a bed with a woman. Aura cocked her head and watched the nymph walk toward the house.

As a nymph, Nocturna no doubt had preternatural hearing. At her height and weight, Aura knew her very body would shake the air enough for the nymph to hear her. Despite her best efforts, as a human, she was the noisiest creature in the forest. Still, she did not want to lose sight of the being approaching her home. As silently as she knew, Aura stepped from behind the sarsen and followed, praying to every god and goddess she knew that a twig of oak did not lie across her path.

Aura paused in her steps. Nocturna strode towards the house, singing to herself. "Tralala, bom boop de loop. Nocturna is going skylarking. Oh, yes, she is. Little Nocturna in the world of big mortals. Isn't this fun!" This nymph was as daft as a barn full of loonies, Aura thought.

When Aura reached the outhouse, she ducked behind it to watch. Nocturna spun around four times, her arms outstretched, still singing. "Oh, what glorious fun! What big houses these mortals have! Must be for their big heads. Could be for their big beds. Oh, I do love big beds and bigger things in big beds." She watched as the nymph looked about the shower. Nocturna grabbed the rope and tugged. A plume of water poured down on her. The nymph released the rope and smacked her lips. "Well, that was rather wet!"

Shaking the water from herself, Nocturna walked around the side of the house, toward the front door. Aura dashed to the shower, and peeked around the corner. The nymph stood at the door. Closer now, Aura saw that she held a crystal ball in her left hand, and the light shown from her right. The wizardess frowned. A nymph trying to enter her home only meant trouble. With Nocturna's back to her, Aura decided to turn the tables on the hunter. She stepped from behind the house and approached. The nymph seemed too preoccupied with the door to hear her footsteps.

"Yes, she healed a boy this morning. Yes, it was instant. I saw it, didn't I? Of course I can't go inside, silly," Nocturna said to the ball in her hand. Aura heard the sound of bacon frying. "She has an iron door latch!"

"Would you like me to open the door for you?" Aura asked.

Nocturna screamed, jumping almost three feet into the air. She whirled and looked up at Aura, terror on her face. Up close, she looked as slender and as aged as a fifteen year old girl. No doubt, she was well passed her two hundredth birthday. The nymph gulped a few times before stammering, "Hello."

"Hello, yourself," Aura said. "You're Nocturna and you're a nymph. I'm Aura Lockhaven, and I'm a rather irritated woman."

"Aura Lockhaven. Why do you have five syllables to your name, but I only have three? That isn't fair!" the nymph said.

"I didn't give myself my name," Aura said.

"That's silly, you silly. Letting someone else name you. How utterly ridiculous. I named myself. But if I had known you had more syllables to your name, I would have picked something much longer. Something like

Nocturna Goldenrod. There. My name is longer, so nyahh!" The nymph stuck out her tongue. "My, but you're a tall one, aren't you?"

"That's what they tell me. Now, what are you doing here?"

"That's for me to know, and you to never find out," Nocturna said. She touched Aura on the nose and said, "Boop!"

Aura's father called it *getting his Lockhaven up*. It was the moment when the scales of feelings tilted a little too much in the direction of anger, and the master of mirth transformed into the ruler of rage. Aura got her Lockhaven up. She slammed her palms against the door frame on either side of Nocturna. An involuntary growl escaped her mouth. The nymph cowered and stepped back against the door as close as she dared. She yelped as her hand touched the iron latch.

Cats made themselves look larger in dangerous situations. Always fond of cats, Aura bent over Nocturna, putting her full height and weight to good use. She broadened her shoulders, bunched her arms, and spread her legs. This creature was not about to elude her. She remembered two things about Fae. First, never irritate them. Second, never look away from them. She didn't care about irritating Nocturna. That was just paying the piper. As for looking away, Aura locked her eyes on Nocturna's.

"Answer my damn question," Aura said through clenched teeth.

"Oh, and you have such lovely red hair," Nocturna said.

"I have a temper to match and you're about to see it. Would you like me to press you into the door? It has iron hinges and studs."

"No!" Nocturna screamed. She rubbed her burned hand. "Anything but iron!"

"Then answer my damn question! What in the name of the hells of five faiths are you doing here?"

"I'm doing what I was asked to do," Nocturna said, grinning a grin of fear. "I'm watching you."

Aura's hands slowly slid from the door frame. She stood upright, but kept Nocturna close to the door. "Watching me? Why?"

Nocturna shrugged. "I don't know, silly. Nocturna doesn't ask questions. Nope. Questions are dangerous. They aren't fun. Watching you sleep and sweat and yell at the tall old man and stand under that thing that pees on you. That's fun!"

Aura felt violated. Nocturna had watched her bathe. She had watched her scold Sagacius, probably that very morning. She watched her work and practice. Apparently, she also saw her heal Lodd. The very idea of a pair of eyes upon her as she slept made her want to take another bath. What else had this nosy Fae seen? She shuddered as she thought about her trips to the outhouse.

"For whom are you watching me?" Aura snarled.

"Not even iron can force that name from my lips!" Nocturna snapped.

"I understand that silver works well, too," Aura said, grinning. "Would you like to step inside? My home is full of silver."

Nocturna gulped. If possible, her alabaster face blanched. Then, the nymph grinned and said, "Oh, you are quite beautiful, you know. I'd love to have eyes like yours, and hair with color in it, and breasts that stuck out like those."

Aura made a mistake. She knew she made a mistake as she did it. A nymph, a creature of elegance and beauty, thought she was beautiful. A nymph, a legendary seductress, envied her eyes, hair, and body. Nocturna's words surprised her so much that she took a step backwards. That was all the room the nymph needed.

Nocturna touched Aura on the nose again, and said, "Toodles!"

With a whirlwind of silver, Nocturna vanished. Aura stood looking at the door, where only a moment before stood a nymph, a Fae spying upon her for some unnamed party. Now, she saw only oak and iron. She sighed and said, "Oh, merciful heavens!"

Chapter Five

THE SPRING SUN sat in the sky at precisely the wrong angle. Shining down on Hartshorn's Temple of Irican, it cast a dark shadow of the spire onto the cemetery. The silver circle atop the spire, marking the structure as the center of the town's faith, blocked the light, forming a black ring directly in front of the eight graves inside the low wall of stone. The ring stood exactly where Aura needed to stand. There was nothing for it, she thought, and stepped inside the ominous darkness.

As she did, she shuddered, feeling the baleful glare of Baniar, the Iricanist god of good. Worse, she felt the baleful glare of his priest, Sire Thaddeus, staring at her from the window of his study in the temple. He knew who she was, and tolerated her presence on the temple's property. Despite her status as one of Hartshorn's two pagans, this was her family's grave plot, and, despite her status as the practitioner of a craft specifically banned by the High Temple, she was still a daughter of Baniar. At least, to Thaddeus, if not to Aura herself any longer.

Once, Aura had been a faithful attendee of Eanstead ritual in that very temple. Faithful, as in, she walked through the doors just as the spire bells ceased tolling, following her father, sister, and brother. To call the Lockhavens' faith nominal would have been generous. Henry put his faith in his skills, not some stone god whose priests spoke a dead language. To the elder Lockhaven, Iricanism still represented the religion that drove the Ayrds from their original home in Nebeland 650 years earlier. He had little patience with it. However, attendance opened doors for him, as did his heavy contributions to the temple funds. God business is good business, he always said.

Twelve years later, Aura had even less patience with the Temple of Irican than her father. While she never learned the all-too-logical Bellician language, Sagacius insisted she learn the Book of Irican, reading it to her and translating it into Ayrdish. The lofty code of love and kindness appealed to her. The rigid rules of morality, however, seemed so dehumanizing. As she stood in the circle, she especially thought about Irican's lengthy diatribe against lust. How could bedpleasure be so evil, she wondered. While her three suitors barely pleasured her, she thought there must be some glory in bed, in the arms of a man who adored her. She wanted to find out, and the prophet Irican be damned. How could it be evil to enjoy the caress of her clothing, the kiss of the wind, the love song of birds, or the passion of food and drink? Irican believed it so, and that made her frown.

The High Temple had the Brothers of Curtian, monks who ritually gelded themselves so they could enforce the Supreme Sire's decrees about morality. Rumor reached her ears that the Curtians had successfully, and somewhat violently, banned most forms of bedpleasure, except for that of sheer procreation, on half the continent. The High Temple also had a brotherhood of zealots called the Knights of the Holy Torch. Holy indeed. They were witch hunters, butchers dedicated to eliminating all who practiced magic. The smoke of numerous burning bodies on the continent had reached Sagacius' nose, and the death screams of the innocent his ears. Aura snorted. Iricanism had only two gods. She worshipped the Gweryn; the eight children of Day known as the Dyddau and the eight children of Night known as the Tywelch. Sixteen gods against a mere two? She had the Iricanists outnumbered.

Today had been somewhat different than expected. The waters of the River Gourdvine flowed fast by the docks of Hartshorn, sped south by the cataracts known as the Cats Whiskers that roared just north of town. News flowed even faster, and Sire Thaddeus had heard of Aura's initiation as wizardess and her healing of Lodd. He met her at the door of the temple, where he offered her the same agreement he once struck with Sagacius. While he disapproved of her line of work, and more so her faith, he always approved of acts of kindness and mercy, even if done in the name of an idol. If Aura Lockhaven remained out of the town's spiritual life, then Sire

Thaddeus te Solambyr, priest of Irican, would permit her to take care of the townsfolk's physical needs. In fact, he even blessed her hands to heal. Believing she needed all the help she could get, she accepted the blessing, and agreed to the arrangement. That did not keep Thaddeus from watching Aura at the grave, and she felt his eyes like small needles pricking her back. Perhaps he longed for her to renounce her faith in her *false gods* and run back inside, rededicating her life to Baniar.

Aura shrugged off the eyes, and returned to her business. Two neat rows of stones lay inside the border of the grave. The oldest belonged to Grimstan Lockhaven, the progenitor of the family, at least in Hartshorn. Moving to the then insignificant river village from Vine Haven after the death of his wife, he built a tiny tavern that had grown with the town over the generations. His stone, a simple affair of rounded pink granite, grayed and half consumed by moss, lay in the far back corner. Next to him sat a square pink granite stone, that of Grimstan's youngest son, Garwulf. Rowdy, often absent on another foray for women and wine, and rumored to have had a wife and children in another shire, Aura remembered Garwulf's name spoken in either hushed tones or garrulous shouts, depending on which story her father told. Next to Garwulf lay a man whose name still circulated like fine gold throughout Hartshorn. Grimchester, Grimstan's oldest son and Aura's grandfather, warranted a small obelisk of blue granite. His wife Ester lay next to him, beneath a matching obelisk. Closest to Aura lay four more recent stones, matching cylinders that panged her heart. She recalled too clearly the sound of chisel against blue granite, as each stroke of the mallet chipped away another sliver of her life. Henry, Richard, her sister Ester, and the one she would give anything to have known, Aurora Nightshade, her mother.

In any given part of town, the sounds of Hartshorn created a cacophony of life. The steady rushing of the river, the shouts of sailors on boats, the squeals of pulleys on wharves. The clopping of hooves and the grinding of iron tires against cobblestones. The hoots of children vying with the bellowing of shopkeepers they just pranked. The calls of the men and women in the stalls of the market on the green mixing with the arguments over the prices of cheeses and cabbages. The drifting strains of fiddler and lutenist practicing for the evening's revelry in taverns. The thuds of many oaken and ashen shop doors slamming. Even on the top of Piper's Knob, one heard the song of wind through leaves, and the squeaking of leather gloves against spears of the patrol watching south for raiders. Here, in the Lockhaven plot of the Hartshorn temple cemetery, Aura heard only her own breath.

With a heavy sigh, Aura stepped from the dark circle into the plot. Kneeling before each stone, she reached into the basket that hung in the crook of her arm. She laid a nosegay of three asters and a sprig of fresh heather tied with red ribbon before each stone, offering a small prayer of gratitude for each of her family members.

Two empty spots stood out in the silent grass. One lay next to the younger Ester. She could already see the engraving on the non-existent stone; *Aura Lockhaven, born Haemmont 1, 1029*. With any fortune, that stone would remain non-existent for at least another fifty years. The other empty spot lay behind Aurora, next to the elder Ester. That would be for Cedric, should whatever sire reigned in the temple permit such a miser the honor of burial within the cemetery. For a brief moment, a moment that stretched for a century, Aura wished the space were already filled. That would not bring justice or satisfaction, but she could at least walk through town without scanning the faces of people fifty feet ahead. No, she paused in her thoughts. Such a wish came close to violating her recent oaths.

Aura sighed again, but this time with a wistful smile on her lips. As Iricanists, her family believed in an afterlife of pure bliss, a life with Baniar, devoid of any of Mallarian's wicked temptations. She, however, worshiped an entirely different set of gods, with an entirely different concept of an afterlife. In Aura's faith, all people went to the halls of the Gweryn upon death. There, everyone was judged by each of the sixteen gods in turn. How well had one loved his wife in Ystlena's name? How well had one tended his flock for Dyoedda? How generous had one been with her money as Arian watched? Did he remember Dalen, or did he cut down trees willy nilly? The good received new bodies. As at the dawn of man, Golau, the king god, and Cygfran, the queen goddess, carved a man or woman from oak, except in the afterlife, it was an eternal oak. That became the person's new body. From there, the person went on to whatever life he or she wished. Not even the druids, the remnants of the ancient Gweryn priesthood, knew what that was. Evil people were sent back to the mortal realm, to live as victims of their own evil. Aura hoped she had committed enough good, or would do so, to warrant an oaken body, and could visit her family, wherever they lived.

Eternity could wait, Aura thought. There was plenty of time yet remaining to die. There was not, however, plenty of time to run her errands. Aura turned from the graves and walked through the cemetery, by the reminders of generations of Hartshornians, some ornate, some simple, some unmarked. She passed from sunlight into the shadow of the temple, itself as glowering as that of the spire.

As she stepped from the temple grounds into the vacant lots once occupied by three shops fallen down decades ago, Aura frowned. "She looks a frightful mess" would have been an understatement. Some new town wizardess. *A poor magician is a poor magician*, the common proverb read, and Aura looked like a poor magician. Four days ago, she snagged the cuff of her red blouse on a bramble and ripped off the left sleeve. Finding the only thread in the house, she stitched it back on. Yellow looked horrid against red. It was her last blouse. The blue one fell apart in the wash and too much of Lodd's blood had soaked into the white one for it to ever look good again. Her trousers now sported a new patch, courtesy of an ember that popped out of the fireplace. Baling twine held the remnants of her right boot together. Her frown melted into a smile. At least, she would not leave town the way she had entered. Crossing the street, she she headed for the shop of Tammer the cobbler.

At a leisurely stroll, stopping to admire each dandelion, the long-legged Aura usually required only five minutes to cross the town green. Today, it took an hour. As soon as her ragged boot touched the grass, Mrs. Adwine grabbed her arm.

"Miss Aura! I am so happy to find you," Mrs. Adwine stammered in a breathless voice. "Listen, dear. I have a favor to ask, and I am more than happy to pay you. I mean, that is your work, and a woman ought to be paid for her work. Would you be so kind as to come by and bless my new loom?"

"Why, yes," Aura said, surprised. "When? I can come by on my way home, if you'd like."

"Oh, no rush, dear. Any time this week would be nice." The older woman's ice blue eyes darted all over Aura's blouse. "Er, would you like me to pay you in advance?"

Aura chuckled, understanding the unspoken offer to buy her some new clothes. "That won't be necessary, Mrs. Adwine." She paused, and thought to reassure the woman. "I must be going. Brythony has my new dress ready."

Mrs. Adwine brightened and almost sang, "Oh, that's wonderful dear! She is my best customer, so I know how well the fabric is woven. Well, I will see you when I see you. Please let me know when you'll be by, so I will have tea ready."

Before Aura could say goodbye, Bart the wheelwright grabbed her hand and pumped it, threatening to rip the other sleeve off her blouse. If possible, the man's wrinkled face looked even more lined from the grin he bore.

"Miss Aura, thank you for loaning me your old man," Bart said.

"Well, Sagacius is hardly *my* old man, now is he?" Aura asked, faintly blushing. Old man had three meanings, and she hoped Bart simply meant a man of advanced age, and not the other two.

"Tell me, what do you recommend for rheumatism?" Bart asked, releasing her hand and rubbing his own. "It's getting hard to work with this."

"Potato soup," Aura said. "Bowls of potato soup. Add chives, garlic, and sage. Stir it with the sun, not against it. I'll make you a copper charm to draw the rheumatism from you."

"Splendid," Bart almost shouted. "What do I owe you?"

Aura's eyes narrowed. A mischievous smile crept across her lips. "If you promise to laugh at Sagacius' jokes, I won't charge you a farthing."

"When did that old wizard become funny?"

"He hasn't."

"I understand. Splendid." With a wave of a stiff hand, and a bright smile, Bart walked away.

Aura turned around, to see five people lined up to talk with her, each bearing a hopeful smile on her or his lips, and an unspoken request in their blue eyes. More ran up behind them. Bewildered, she rubbed the hump in her nose. She wanted to help to the helpless, but this crowd implied that Hartshorn was a town full of the helpless. For ten years, these people doted on her, because of her father's status. Then, for the next two, they ignored her. Some even spat upon her. Then, for the past ten, they looked at her as if her eyes were red and her hair green. Now, those same people surrounded her with beaming faces, and tales of need and hope. Some even touched her, as if she were a saint from the continent. At this rate, she should take a booth in the market and hang up a sign. *Wizardess for Hire. Read Your Fortune. Heal Your Cat.*

Bless the new baby? That is Sire Thaddeus' territory and he might not like it, but I could stop by the day after his visit. Thyme heals, rosemary sparks lust. Yes, thyme. Oh, then you definitely want rosemary. Why of course I can make a love charm for your wedding. When is it? Tomorrow! Oh, merciful heavens. No, I will have it ready. I was born under the sign of Erasto myself, so we are both prone to overeating. That requires candle magic. Can you give me a week? Thank you. Why, what? No, I don't know any tallness spells. Blame my father for my height, not a spell. I bless houses after they are built, but I'm hardly qualified to offer ideas during construction. No, I'm a wizardess, not a witch, but I can still build warding charms into your new fence. You hung the horseshoe upside down? Go home and turn it right side up immediately. I have an oil that removes warts, but I don't have it with me. Can I bring it to you tomorrow? Oh, I have a wedding to work on for tomorrow. How about Fifstead at nine of the sun? Perfect. Yes, I did heal him. It was the right thing to do, ma'am.

An exhausted Aura staggered through the door of Tammer's shop. The new boots looked good. Dark brown, they came up to just below her knees ending in a nice cuff. Overlapping straps that buckled at the top held them against her legs. She loved the way they squeaked and the way the light bounced off them. Having no desire to muddy these in her garden, she decided to keep her tattered old boots for that purpose.

Alternately, she sat in one of Tammer's chairs by his window, and paced his floor, inhaling the delightful aroma of leather, and listening to his apprentice hammer while he stitched. She told Tammer she needed time to accustom her feet to the new leather. Really, she wanted to catch her breath before dashing the four doors to Brythony's seamstress shop. When she felt rested, or courageous, enough, she decided to leave. After paying Tammer, she stuck her head out his door. Doubting that the children kicking a sheep's bladder ball in the street had any magical requests, she stepped out and headed toward Brythony's.

Aura stretched out her arms. As much as she hated mirrors, she still admired herself in the gleaming bronze before her. She barely recognized herself. The hair looked familiar, but who was that beneath it? The tightly woven brown linen dress looked beautiful, with its bell sleeves, snug bodice, open lacings revealing her cleavage, and the flowing hem that almost reached her ankles. The simple golden chain embroidery on the edges of the sleeves and bodice shimmered in the light drifting through the seamstress' windows. It fit perfectly, accentuating every curve and every nuance of her figure.

"Miss Aura," Brythony said. "You look like a princess."

Princess, Aura thought, admiring herself in the mirror, at least, from the neck down. During a visit to Welcaster, she saw the king's daughter from a comfortable distance. Princess Miranda was welcome to her white silk gown, golden tiara, and whatever continental noble King Edgar chose for her. She preferred the sky for her crown, the trees for her palace, and the birds for her guard. She also preferred this dress. Her eyes darted all over the bronze, except to her face. Those damned green things still shone, even in the reddish-gold of the mirror.

Princess. Aura Lockhaven had once been the princess of Hartshorn, that green eyed little mystic girl who drifted through town on clouds of her own dreams, pestering the blacksmith and candlemaker with her stories. Perhaps they only tolerated her because she was Henry Lockhaven's youngest daughter, but that had been enough when she was six, eight, and ten. That was when Henry still lived and ruled the village from his barstool. That had been before Cedric ripped it all from her and turned her into the village outcast.

Fibers of wool, flax, hemp, and that new imported stuff called cotton drifted in the air. They tickled Aura's nose. She sneezed. Prior to that very moment, Aura would just have wiped her nose on her blouse. These billowing bell sleeves demanded more respect. She glanced around the seamstress' shop for something, anything, to remove the puddle of mucus from underneath her nose. Brythony smiled and handed Aura a scrap of undyed linen.

"You just keep that and shove it inside one of them pockets for a kerchief," Brythony said.

As Aura wiped her nose, she looked about the bodice and hips for pockets. She saw no sign of any opening. A slow smile crossed her lips as she reached inside the sleeves. Sure enough, she felt the flaps of two pockets just far enough in the bells for her fingers to reach without discomfort, as well as a long one in the left sleeve. So, Brythony expected her to carry a wand. She cast the woman a wry look. Apparently, a certain seamstress sewed garments for witches and wizardesses in the past. Folding the kerchief, Aura slipped it into one of the pockets.

Brythony wiped a lock of silver hair from her face. Putting her hands on her hips, the seamstress said, "Gardurn, girl. Doncha think another color would be best? Green would look so much better on you. It would match your eyes." Aura winced. Brythony just had to mention those. "So would red, especially with your hair."

"I like brown," Aura said. Her father always wore brown. It didn't show beer stains. It also hid the person inside. While she loved parading around the Big Hedge bold and skyclad, she preferred hiding in the shadows of Hartshorn. This color blended her into the dark areas between the shops and houses. No one would notice her, unless he needed her. So much for that idea. Apparently, everyone needed her, and everyone noticed her now. A faint smile crossed her lips. As news spread of healing Lodd, the people had grabbed her hands and pulled her from the shadows. The sunlight felt good. Aura cleared her throat and said, "Brown doesn't show potion stains."

The voluminous skirt felt cumbersome around her legs. Aura had not worn a dress in ten years. She thought trousers and a blouse much more practical. However, as the new wizardess for her village, she believed some formality was in order. For the first time in her recent memory, she enjoyed seeing herself in a mirror. A new promotion, healing the neighbor's son, some new cloth, and she thought she looked halfway pretty. Besides, a nymph said she was pretty, even if that nymph spied on her.

Aura spent the past week looking around every corner for Nocturna. She sat in her open window at night, peering out toward the Big Hedge for some sign of that mysterious light from her hand. She had seen nothing. Yet, she felt the eyes upon her at all times. Well, let the nymph see her in this new dress. Let her report back to her sponsor that Aura Lockhaven knew how to be half-way pretty, at least from the neck down.

"You plannin' on spilling your potions all over yourself, are you?" Brythony asked, giving Aura a crooked grin. After Aura chuckled,

Brythony continued. "Now that there dress was a real challenge, yes, ma'am. Those legs of yours. Whoowee, girl. I ain't made a dress that tall ever. You're your mamma stretched out on your pappa's bones. That old wizard must feed you good. It's a fine thing you can cast them spells, honey. You step out onto that road in that dress, and every boy in town will be throwing flowers at your feet and trying to take you out of it."

With one last look at the way the sleeves flowed from her arms to her hands, Aura turned from the mirror. She gave Brythony a wistful smile and said, "That hasn't worked out too well in the past."

Brythony snorted and gave Aura a look of disdain. "Don't you be minding that Fowler boy, Miss Aura. He carries his brains in his purse, and he's worth about as much as a farthing, if you ask old Brythony. Not that you did ask, but if you had, that's what I would say. There will be plenty of young men with brains in their noggins callin' on you, now that you're our wizardess. Listen to old Brythony now. Don't you go and give them your cheese, if you know what I mean. You let them bring you the ham, first. Then, you can make a nice sandwich with the bread of your choosin'."

Aura giggled. That was one way to phrase it. She returned to the mirror. Today, she spent more time before a mirror than the past twelve years combined. She never felt this pretty. She never felt this powerful. Performing two complete circles, she admired the gracefulness of the back and skirt. The hem and sleeves billowed like poetry written in fabric. "How did you sew this so fast?" she asked.

"Huh," Brythony snorted. "You were an apprentice, weren't you?"

Aura glanced around the small shop. Well lit from tall windows, and skylights set in the roof, she remembered her father saying that it once belonged to her mother. She watched an apprentice cut red wool cloth for a shirt at one bench, while a second stitched the sides of a skirt at another. A third worked a spinning wheel, turning raw flax into linen thread. The girls hummed as they went about their work, transforming woven plants and hair into competent, and sometimes magnificent, garments. Sagacius brewed complicated potions in an hour, as long as Aura performed the running, fetching, cutting, grinding, and stirring. Cloth shouldn't be any more difficult than herbs and oils, especially with three apprentices taking care of the routine work.

"Your mamma taught me how to do this, child," Brythony said. "She was Coadic, as you well know, and Coadics are the finest garment makers in all the Forested Islands. If Aurora sewed that there dress, it would have been done in a day. But I swear, that woman used magic. I ain't never seen hands fly so fast."

Aura turned from the mirror. Smiling in gratitude, she said, "Thank you, Brythony. I never knew that about my mother. Well, I should probably get home. I'm sure Master has something up his sleeve." She raised her arms. "Now, I have my own to match. How much do I owe you?"

"Nothing," Brythony said. "You don't owe me nothing for that there dress."

"No, please, Brythony! Let me pay you."

Brythony shook her head. The cold look in her blue eyes told Aura not to argue with Hartshorn's leading seamstress and supreme docent of iron will. "Your mamma was my best friend, child. Makes me feel like I'm doin' Aurora a good turn. Besides, I owe you for blessin' my shop last year. Business has tripled. You take that there dress as my blessin' on you. Now, if you –" Brythony froze, half way to her counter, as the sounds of a bell clanging pierced the air in the shop. "We're being attacked!"

"No," Aura said. "That's the Temple bell, not Piper's Knob."

"How do you know?"

"I can tell location from sound. Besides, the bell on Piper's Knob sounds like a woman screaming. The Temple bell sounds like a man singing. Peculiar. Today is Midweek. It isn't a holy day. Why is Sire Thaddeus ringing the bell?" Aura stiffened. She took a step toward the door. "Something has happened up at the Temple."

Chapter Six

FROM THE DOOR of the seamstress' shop, Aura saw townspeople running toward the temple. She took a step through the door, pausing long enough to glance at the building across the street. One of the older structures in Hartshorn, it had a stone first story and half-timbered wattle and daub second floor. The broad oak door lay open. Above it swung the sign, splendid in fresh paint. A lock with a key in it. Lockhaven Tavern. *It should be mine!* Aura tensed and clenched her fists. The scar on her left palm felt stiff. Memory caused it to ache. She gained the scar five nights before she last saw the inside of her father's tavern.

A man stepped through the tavern door, out onto the street. Aura gasped and ducked back inside the seamstress' shop. Twenty feet away was too close. He glanced in her direction. She moved further back into the shop, pressing into the shadows far enough to be hidden, yet still see him. Cedric Lockhaven no longer looked like a younger version of Aura's father. His shirt hung about him like a tent. What remained of his hair had turned almost white. His scraggly beard did little to hide his sagging jowls.

Aura whispered, "The result of greed."

Cedric took a step into the street. Several townsfolk, running toward the ringing bell, swerved in the road to give him wide berth. *Don't come any closer,* Aura thought. She did not know what would happen if they met. Sagacius often told her that the town dreaded the moment when the richest man in Hartshorn stood eye to eye with its tallest woman. The dread only grew with each passing year as Aura grew more skilled. It cringed at the thought of the moment when uncle and niece settled ownership of Lockhaven Tavern, and his betrayal of her twelve years earlier. The last time they spoke, he threatened to sell her as a bedslave. For years, she daydreamed of turning him into a smoldering pile of ash. From the shadows inside the shop, Aura saw Cedric lick his lips. She had not been this close to the man in five years. She made sure of that. Whenever she spotted him, she ducked behind stalls, threw herself into alleys and shops, and hid behind Sagacius.

Cedric took another step into the street, another step toward Brythony's. Aura felt her right hand rise, her palm extended toward the man in the street. At this short distance, her throwback spell always hit its mark. *Do you vow to only use your power and office to harm another as an act of self defense or to defend someone else? I do.* She had lit many white candles in rituals to forgive him. Saying it was easy. Acting on it proved her maturity. She closed her hand and lowered it to her side. With a shrug, Aura's uncle returned to the tavern. Aura bent over and rested her hands against her knees. She sighed so deep she thought Cedric would hear her. A warm hand rubbed her back.

"I should have stood up to his lordship," Brythony said. "I should have taken you in. You're Aurora's girl, after all. The bastard threatened to shut me down if I did."

"It's all right. I forgive you," Aura said. She stood up, and smiled at Brythony. "By the way, Cedric isn't a bastard. His parents were my grandparents, remember?"

"Oh. Sorry. Bad term of endearment."

"I'll return for my old clothes. Something tells me I need to be at the Temple."

This time, no one stopped her as she walked down the street, crossed the green, and entered the vacant lots. People ran by her, most toward the temple, but a few ran from it. Those who ran toward her sobbed. Aura frowned. While she was no Iricanist, most of the people of Hartshorn were. If something shook the town's faith, then she and Sagacius may have more work than they could handle. If the Temple Laws changed, then she and Sagacius may need to leave town that night. When she reached the cobblestone path to the temple, she broke into a run. For a moment, she wondered why she moved so slowly. Then, she remembered to hitch up her skirt to her knees.

From its perch on Morgan's Hill, the Temple of Irican loomed over the town. The first temple, built of wood, burned down. Its replacement, now nearing one hundred years old, had been built of granite. Many older folk recalled hiding inside its flameproof walls and tiled roof as Skols raided Hartshorn. Today, the spire jutted toward the sky, not as a symbol of faith, but as a waving hand in distress. The bell clanged in an uncertain way, as if the ringer was not sure if he wanted to call for worship, sound alarm, or create general panic.

Aura approached as close as she dared, remaining at the back of the crowd gathered in front of the temple doors. Even from this distance, she knew what happened. Sire Thaddeus had collapsed. Not able to move the priest, and unsure of what to do, the boy who served as Thaddeus' valet climbed the bell rope. The bell still tolled its madness, ringing an erratic peel from one hundred pounds of fearful boy swinging on it.

Thomas the apothecary stepped from the shadows of the temple door. Sweat beaded on his face and clung to his beard. He wiped his hands on his shirt. Looking around, he shook his head. Several women burst into tears, and some men dragged their feet on the cobblestones. Spotting Aura, Thomas dashed up to her.

"Aura, where is Sagacius?"

"He's at home," Aura replied.

Thomas sighed. "The Big Hedge is too far away. I need help. Sire Thaddeus' heart is beating like a drunken drummer. He can't move. I don't know what to do. I thought Sagacius might know."

The priest's heart was failing. He did not have the time for Aura to brew a potion, or even to collect the herbs. He certainly did not have time for her to walk home and fetch Sagacius. Thaddeus needed a healing spell. She frowned. Aura turned her face to the temple doors. Beyond, shafts of cold light shot through the dark like swords into ice.

She knew Iricanist law. The religion divided, often violently, over the issues of magic, magicians, and those of other faiths. One half saw people like her as heretics worthy of death. The other half saw them as odd relics of the past, but useful members of the community. Their compromise allowed magicians room to maneuver, at least on the Forested Islands where the High Temple's reach was weak. She was welcome on the temple grounds, but not inside.

To give hope to the hopeless. A town without its priest was also without hope. What is magic but to give a town its priest? Her ways be damned. The priest needed her. Aura grabbed Thomas' hand. "I'm here. Sagacius taught me everything I know. Let me see Sire Thaddeus."

"I can't, Aura," Thomas said. "You know that. You aren't allowed inside the temple."

Aura rolled her eyes. "Yes, I'm a pagan! So? Just this morning, Sire Thaddeus himself blessed my hands to heal. Let me heal him."

"I ..." Thomas glanced to the temple. "He's more important to Hartshorn than our temple laws." He looked at Aura with grim determination. "If he blessed your hands, then it must be all right." Jerking his head toward the temple door, he said, "Do your best."

Thomas took Aura by the arm and led her toward the door. The crowd exhaled a collective gasp as she approached the temple. The apothecary tightened his hand and gave her a reassuring smile. Aura did her best to hide the quivering she felt in her stomach. Setting her face as stern kindness, she looked forward, into the darkness beyond the door.

Maxwell, one of the sergeants of Hartshorn's townsfyrd, stepped in front of Aura, barring her way. He placed his left hand on his scabbard, just below the hilt of his sword, the sign that he would draw if she took another step. The silver horn of the hart on his short black tabbard, the sigil of the town, never looked so threatening to her before. She had known this man since she was eight. He often ate in her childhood home when he spent the day sparring with Richard.

"Maxwell, please let me enter," Aura said.

"You can't enter," Maxwell said. "You worship other gods."

"This is not the time or place for arguing over who worships whom," she said.

"For Baniar's sake, let her in," Thomas begged. "I trust her. Would you stop Sagacius?"

"Sagacius is also forbidden to enter."

Thomas threw his arms up and screamed, "For the love of ... Sire Thaddeus doesn't have time for this!"

"I'm sorry. Richard was my best friend, but I can't let you in. Go home, Aura," Maxwell said.

"She's Lady Aura, now!" The voice cut through the throng like a knife through lard. Its deep rumble echoed on the stones of the temple. Aura jumped at hearing her name spoken with so much force and with a title usually reserved for wives of thegns and eorls.

The owner of the voice shoved several people aside, moving through the crowd until he stood on the cobblestones in front of Maxwell. Galen Hunter was shorter than most men, but the width of his shoulders made up for his height. By trade, he was a carpenter. After repairing or rebuilding most of the town, the people decided to put him in charge of it, and elected him mayor. In fifteen years, he transformed a skittish target of Skol and pirate harrying into the most important river port in the center of Ayrdland. He ordered the watchtowers of Raven's Bluff and Crow's Bluff built atop Piper's Knob, and constructed the stone walls at the southern end of town along Rath Creek. He reorganized the townsfyrd from an inept band of cowardly farmers and trembling merchants into a fighting force capable of repelling two hordes of Skols and catching the attention of King Edgar. In ten years of watching Sagacius offer counsel to the man, Aura had never seen him angry. He looked as if he wanted to level the temple with his bare hands. She took a step back from Galen, bumping into Thomas.

Galen twisted the end of his once blonde mustache and glared at the sergeant as if the man just allowed a throng of raiders to have their way with Hartshorn. "I hired Mister Sagacius, and I'm hiring Lady Aura, right now this moment. Maxwell, step aside and let Lady Aura pass," he said.

With a brief nod of his head, the sergeant did as he was told. As soon as he stepped aside, Clyff the cheesemaker took his place, barring the door.

"Clyff, get out of her way," Galen snapped.

"Temple laws forbid a pagan to enter," Clyff replied.

"You heard what Lady Aura did for Lodd. Let her try it on Sire Thaddeus."

"Temple laws forbid a pagan to enter," Clyff said, again.

"Sire Thaddeus is Frankenist. He isn't that strict," Galen replied.

"Temple laws are temple laws, regardless of the priest's order," Bart the wheelwright yelled from the crowd.

"That's right. Thaddeus is Frankenist. While you people are bickering, he could be dying. Do you want Bellicia to send a High Temple priest to replace him? How about a Curtian? Do you want one of them? Hmm?" He glanced around the crowd. Several glances lowered to the ground. Some darted their eyes away from those of the glowering mayor. "Do you know what a High Temple or Curtian priest would do? Your wives would be forced to sell their shops and stay home. You could only bed each other on forty nights a year. Is that what you want?" Heads shook. "Your taverns would be closed on Eanstead. No more dancing or swimming naked in the Gourdvine. Is that what you want?" The crowd grumbled. "You'd have to drive the harlots out of Eastbank. Know what the boatmen would do without them? Rape your daughters. Is that what you want? Hmm?" Murmurs flowed through the crowd. "How about burning Mister Sagacius at the stake, after all he's done for us. Is that what you want?" Several people shouted no. "If that's what you want, then just keep standing there." Galen put his hands on his hips and roared, "If not, then get the bloody hell out of Lady Aura's godsdamn way!"

"I'm sorry," Clyff muttered to Aura, as he returned to the crowd.

Of all the buildings in Hartshorn, Aura avoided only two in the past ten years. Lockhaven Tavern was the first. The Temple of Irican was the second. With a gulp, Aura stepped forward, and approached the wide double oaken doors with their bronze hinges. Galen and Thomas followed close behind. She wasn't sure if the mayor and apothecary were curious, took interest in her actions because of their status in town, or protected her back from stones. Only an hour earlier, the people of Hartshorn adored her. Now, she violated their faith, an act that often turned love into hatred.

"Would someone stop that bell?" she asked, pointing overhead.

"Maxwell!" Galen shouted.

The sergeant bolted from the crowd and dashed inside the temple. The pealing stopped moments later. As the echoes of the bell faded, Aura heard a whitelark singing on top of the spire. She took a deep breath, and passed through the granite arch into the temple itself.

Aura stopped just inside to let her eyes accustom to the darkness. She inhaled, and smiled. As the aroma of the frankincense, sage, and dragonsblood wafted underneath her nose, she felt eight or ten again. Great shafts of light cut through the dark, almost quivering as they passed through the heavy leaded windows. It was not as dark inside as she expected. Massive iron chandeliers cast their glow down onto the benches, while burners illuminated statues of saints along the walls. At the far end, underneath the largest of the windows, sat the ornate stone altar, with a statue of Baniar on top, brilliant in the light of two burners and twenty candles. Aura breathed deeply, and stepped forward. The crowd gathered inside fell hushed as she approached the altar. The only sound she heard were the slaps of her new soles on the stone floor, and the raspy breath of the man slumped against the altar.

Aura paused for a moment at the fifth bench from the front on the left hand side. For ten years, little auburn-haired, green-eyed Aura Lockhaven sat at the end of that bench. She understood little, if any, of the weekly rituals. Performed in Bellician, they all had something to do with the eternal struggle of Baniar with his evil counterpart, Mallarian. While everyone else paid rapt attention, or at least pretended to do so, Aura's eyes always wandered, turning the temple into an ancient Ayrdic warship. That was easy, given the dragon heads carved into the ends of the beams that supported the ceiling. In her mind, Aura shouted commands to her warriors as they sailed the Sea of Anfern looking for Frysting ships to plunder, or faraway islands to explore. Sometimes, Aura's imagination got the best of her, and she began speaking her fancies out loud, resulting in twitters of laughter from the bench behind, and a sharp poke in the ribs from the stately blonde haired Ester, seated to her right. On Ester's right sat handsome princely Richard, with the patriarch, Henry, beyond him. To Henry's right, sat Cedric, attending even more out of duty than the rest of his nominally devout family. Aura had dim memory of a dignified woman with white hair seated at the end next to the center aisle, a woman for whom Ester had been named, and the only grandparent Aura ever knew.

Sire Thaddeus te Solambyr lay on the floor, propped up against the altar. Aura last saw that altar twelve years ago, on the first day of winter. She stood where Thaddeus lay, begging Sire Porthold to give her food, shelter, and hope. His heart calloused by Cedric's gold, he denied her all three, casting her out to become Hartshorn's newest street urchin. She never prayed to Baniar again after that.

Porthold had been a Palasian, a priestly order notorious for avarice, gluttony, and seducing the girls of the towns it served. Thaddeus was Frankenist, a branch that returned to the original words of Irican. Unlike the other orders, Frankenists did not shave their heads. Thaddeus wore his graying dark blonde hair neatly cut, with no trace of a mustache or beard on his face. Porthold adorned himself with enough gold to make King Edgar blush. Thaddeus wore only a silver circle by a chain that rested against his laboring chest, and the simple ring showing his marriage to the Temple. While Porthold had worn robes that looked like tapestries, Thaddeus wore a black robe with silver piping, open over a shirt and trousers that would be at home on any farmer. He breathed like a man who just ran five miles. He turned a red face to Aura. With what little remained of good humor, he whispered in the soft lilt of a Saporian, "I am happy that I blessed your hands."

Aura frowned. The man was only fifty. Despite the lavish manor left him by Porthold, Thaddeus took his vows seriously. No one ever saw him eat rich foods or drink ale. His morning walks about town were the stuff of legend. He often entered contests of strength at various holidays, and defeated much younger men. She saw no reason for a man of such health to look as if he were ninety years old, and had lived a life of sloth.

"May I touch you?" Aura asked.

"I am not as important as a son of a shepherd, but I would like to live," Thaddeus said, wheezing. "That means yes."

"His heart is as split as an overripe peach, Aura," Thomas said. "It's a wonder he's still alive."

Aura placed her hand on Thaddeus' chest. Thomas was right. She felt it. Two quick beats, followed by nothing, then three, followed by nothing. Sometimes a man's heart just failed, but not in one so fit and in his prime. She felt a pang, deep inside herself. She felt anguish, guilt, and turmoil. They weren't hers. They belonged to Thaddeus. She felt not just his torn, physical heart, but his torn soul. This was not just a physical ailment. It had emotional roots. She did not know how she knew. She just knew.

As she removed her hand, Thomas said, "There's nothing we can do. I can give him elixir of nightshade to ease his pain and passing, but –"

"You heard Mayor Hunter," Aura snapped. "Sire Thaddeus is important to Hartshorn." She looked at the priest and smiled. "He's important to himself. I won't let you die, sir."

"You cannot prevent that, my child. But you may postpone it," Thaddeus whispered.

"You're talking too much, sir."

"Aura, I know of no herb that will heal a ripped heart. Not even time can do that," Thomas said. "I don't know your craft all that well, but there can't be a spell that powerful."

"There is," Aura said. "How do you think I healed Lodd?"

A murmur flowed through the crowd gathered around. The air in the temple felt suddenly cold. What she needed to do posed no problems on a farm. Inside the Temple of Irican, it could be seen as blasphemy. Aura cast frightened glances around the temple. Baniar, towering over her head on

70

the altar, glared down on her. Across the temple, Irican himself dared her to even try inside his house. All around her, the men and women of Hartshorn looked at her with a mixture of confusion, hope, and fear. What would any of them do once she began chanting in old Karanthek? Just last month, a mob in Flumance burned a man alive for less.

She whispered, "Mayor Hunter, please protect me."

Thaddeus placed a weak hand on hers. He managed a faint smile. "We do not agree on faith, but we agree on love. You are safe in this place, my daughter."

"You heard the man," Galen said, a little louder than necessary. The murmur fell silent.

Aura nodded to herself. She looked Thaddeus in the eyes. They were so blue, but clouded by mists of pain. Time to focus herself. She imagined herself as the frightful town of Hartshorn, worried about losing its priest. She imagined herself as a man of faith with so much more to offer his town. She imagined herself as having many more years of life left, but facing a lethal obstacle. She poured all those thoughts into one, to see Sire Thaddeus stand up, smile, and walk away from the altar. Then, she placed her hands on his chest, and began chanting.

Aura awoke in her chair, the new dress clinging to her body in dried sweat. Sagacius sat in his, staring at her in bewilderment. When she opened her mouth, he raised his hand. She succeeded, he told her. Sire Thaddeus was well. In fact, the priest of Hartshorn personally brought her unconscious body home in his simple carriage, four hours earlier.

"Aura, we need to have a little discussion," Sagacius said. "If you insist on healing like that, then you need the proper training. This time, you fainted. Poor Thomas thought you died."

She did not remember a thing. One minute, she knelt by Thaddeus. The next, she sat in her chair.

"Sire Thaddeus told me what happened. For years, he's walked in the narrow gap between the High Temple in Bellicia and his own conscience.

The High Temple pressures him to enforce Temple Law. His conscience pressures him to help the people of Hartshorn find the light on their own with his guidance. Remember, he's Saporian. He doesn't have the defiant Ayrdish spirit that you and I take for granted. He is a very torn man. The pressure became too much. His soul broke. Then, his heart broke. When you healed his heart, you also healed his soul. Somehow, you revitalized him. When you healed his heart, he felt the confusion and torment sucked from his soul. He's ready, as Thaddeus te Solambyr said himself, *to tell the Supreme Sire to fill his pious belly with a library full of dusty scrolls.* Aura, that's beyond magic."

Through parched lips, she asked, "How did I do that?"

"The question is, why did you do it?"

"Sire Thaddeus needed me."

"Our vows preclude us from harming nomagians. They do not force us to help them, especially those who could kill us with a mere wave of their hands. Not that Thaddeus would have done that. He's a good man."

"He was helpless, and I had to help him. I knew the risk, but I was willing to take it." She tried to stand. Her legs told her to sit back down. She obeyed. "I'm still alive, so it was worth it."

"You're still alive today."

She knew what he meant. Her body felt made of lead. "Master, could an enchantress do what I did without harming herself? Could she heal Lodd and Sire Thaddeus without almost dying herself?"

"Yes," Sagacius said. "Aura, your emotions are like a gale in a cauldron. They are extremely powerful, but without form. An enchantress keeps hers harnessed, but frees them at will. As a result, her emotions are unstoppable, and she can heal without injury. With your great love, and your great anger, you could be a force of nature. You could be the most powerful ..." He paused. The wizard looked at the floor and sighed. He whispered, "Egads. I hate to say she might be right. Nightshade."

"That's the third time you've said nightshade, Master. Somehow, I don't think you refer to the plant or to my mother. What do you mean?"

Sagacius smiled. It was a cold smile. "Well, Nightshade is an old legend in my order, the Order of Enchanters. Nightshade was one of our most powerful members. He was known for his huge heart and tremendous kindness. Nightshade died long before I was born. It's just a coincidence that he and your mother share a similar name."

Coincidence my endowed arse, Aura thought. One thing the wizard pounded into her with all the subtlety of a millstone pulverizing wheat was that no such thing as a coincidence existed. Something about her mother's name, and her own actions, reminded Sagacius of this legendary enchanter. Let the old man keep his secrets. She now had her own. Twice, she healed men who lay dying. Sagacius had not taught her how to do that. She just did it. That power was hers, not that she understood it. Whatever it was, it belonged to Aura Lockhaven, the Wizardess of Hartshorn.

Yet, it almost killed her. Leynda faced no such peril. That boy had been run over by a carriage, his body nearly cut in two. Yet, with just a touch of her finger, Leynda healed him and sent him running off as if he had been bowled over by nothing more savage than a butterfly. If she only had that power and training. Apparently, someone gave it to Leynda. Despite their reputation in the eyes of her master, members of the Order of Enchanters knew how to heal drastic injuries without sustaining injury themselves. Aura wanted Leynda's abilities. No matter the cost, she wanted them. Defend the defenseless. Help the helpless. Give hope to the hopeless. Heal the unhealable.

Looking up at her teacher, Aura said, "Master, please inform the Order of Enchanters that I want to meet them."

Chapter Seven

THE EARLY MORNING light drifted in around the shutters, casting shafts of white in the otherwise darkened room. Aura blinked and wiped the sleep from her eyes. Something awoke her from her favorite dream, of the day Sagacius found her. Someone called her name.

"I never thought you'd stoop so low. Isn't that hard on your back, oh tall one?" a man asked. She did not recognize the voice. It came from downstairs. Whoever it was, he spoke in the clipped accent of the south. Aura heard a snort of derision. "Accusing me, of all people, of watching Miss Lockhaven. I may be guilty of many things, but spying is not one of them."

"Someone is watching her," Sagacius rumbled. He did not sound happy. "Someone has been lurking about, and I suspect in the employ of someone within the order. Aura saw her last week. She said it was a nymph, and I trust Aura's eyes and judgment."

Of course she was a nymph. She knew nearly everyone in Hartshorn and never saw that woman before. Besides, even if she came from another village, and if she were a woman, that meant she covered herself with phosphorus. Only an alchemist did that without suffering burns. That did not explain the sourceless light she held in one hand, and only a lunatic talked to rocks. Wait, Aura thought. She talked to rocks herself.

Aura settled back on her pillow. This would be an interesting conversation. Apparently, Sagacius spoke to someone about their eavesdropper. She knew the constable. This was someone else. Two wizards could handle a spy, if they caught her that is. Had her teacher called upon another wizard, someone more knowledgeable about the Fae? Why in the name of all the gods had he arrived just after daybreak, instead of a more civilized hour?

"That is impossible," the other man said. "Well, let me rephrase that. Perhaps a nymph is watching you, but if it is a nymph, it isn't one of ours. You know as well as I that ours never leave the Valley. She could have been sent by someone, of course, but I assure you that it was not the council."

Order. Valley. Council. Aura put the words together and arrived at the conclusion of the Order of Enchanters. Last week, she told Sagacius that she wanted to meet them. The man just wandered upstairs to his library, emerging a few minutes later to tell her the meeting was arranged. Afterwards, he answered all her questions with silence. He refused to tell her how he arranged the meeting, much less where it was to occur. Apparently, they came to her. She propped up on her elbows to listen. Yes, this would definitely be an interesting conversation.

The other man said, "If you're going to suspect anyone of doing such a thing, I suggest you suspect *her*."

"I suspect *her* of a great many things, but not of spying on me!"

"I thought you two grew up together. Was I wrong in that assumption? Did you spend your childhoods on opposite ends of the Valley? You don't know your own sister very well, do you," the other voice said.

Aura sat upright. Sagacius did not have a sister! Now that Aura thought about it, she was not sure. Unless Golau and Cygfran decided to carve people out of oak trees again, then the man had a mother and father like everyone else. In ten years, he never once mentioned them. Perhaps, he did have siblings somewhere. She threw back her blanket and stepped onto the cool wooden floor. Creeping from her room to the top of the stairs, she listened. The conversation no longer qualified as interesting. It crossed into the realm of irresistible.

"I am certain Miss Lockhaven saw someone, but I assure you that we did not dispatch a spy," the other voice said. She saw shadows of movement through the archway into the sitting room. They did not sit around the kitchen table. This was a more formal visit.

"If not you, then whom?" Sagacius asked, his voice taking the quality of a landslide. "I was merely annoyed before. Now, I'm concerned."

Sagacius believed Aura's tale of encountering Nocturna. For two weeks, they took turns sitting in the stone circle all night, hoping to catch another glimpse of the nymph and perhaps learn the name of her employer. They saw nothing. Then, three nights ago, about the time they both thought the spy had abandoned her mission, Aura awoke with the memory of smoke in her nostrils. She walked to her window for some fresh air. There, in the shadow of the outhouse, she spotted the nymph, or at least, a nymph. While still a woman, she looked shorter and thicker. The nymph spotted her, too, and vanished in a whirlwind of silver air.

"Shall I take a look around the grounds, sir?" a woman asked. Aura recognized the accent as that of Colebury, the city on the western shore. Only they trilled the letter R in the back of their throats.

"That won't be necessary, Captain," the other man said. "We won't be here long enough for you to find anything, or for anything to find you. Well, old friend, when do I get to meet this apprentice of yours?"

"As soon as she wakes up," Sagacius said. "She's had a challenging two weeks. I'm letting her rest. Besides, she doesn't work for me anymore. Now, listen to me carefully. Aura is no longer my apprentice. She is Ayrdish. She is twenty-one. As if she needed them, those are three reasons that she is free to choose her own destiny. I will tolerate no duplicity from you, do you understand?"

"Duplicity! You wound me, old friend. When have I ever been duplicitous?" Aura heard a long pause. "No, that time doesn't count. I was backed into a corner. And ... that other time was your idea. Duplicitous indeed. Such an accusation coming from the master of disguise."

Aura shifted her weight, leaning forward to hear better. As she moved, the landing creaked beneath her foot. She winced and held her breath. She began counting. One ... two ... three ...

"Aura, you may as well join us," Sagacius shouted. Dammit, betrayed by the aging house. She took a step down the stairs, then stopped. There was no need to greet the visitors while naked. She yelled, "Give me a minute," then dashed back to her room. A quick wash of her face, a fast brush through her hair, her new dress and boots, and she felt presentable.

Although she wanted to run down the stairs and dash into the sitting room, Aura took her time leaving her room and descending the stairs. She fought to control the breathless excitement filling her. The Order of Enchanters wanted to meet her so much that they travelled all the way from the Valley of the Mystic Moon, wherever that was. Dignitaries from another magical order required her own dignity to be in place. Besides, although she had her reasons for wanting to meet them, she did not know why they wanted to meet her. Whenever she asked Sagacius, his reply felt more like he said everything but the true answer. Pausing in the hallway, Aura checked her dress to make sure it lay properly on her body. Then, with the precise heel to toe steps her sister taught her, she entered the sitting room as if she were the hostess entering a party.

At first, Aura only saw shapes in the growing dawn light pouring through the open windows. As her eyes accustomed to the brightness, she recognized Sagacius sitting in his chair. Her own remained empty. In the third chair sat a man with blonde hair that fell in waves past his shoulders, and a short neatly trimmed blonde goatee. He stood as Aura entered the room. Thick chested and broad shouldered, if he stretched, he could look her in the eyes. They were such kind eyes, too, and green! The age and wisdom in them betrayed the youth of his face. He wore a Tangoi keld, also green, draped around his waist and thrown over his shoulder like that of a thane. He wore no shirt, allowing his blonde chest hair to stand out against his golden skin.

"Aura, allow me to introduce Lord Deofoyl Ashthorne, the Vice-Chancellor of the Order of Enchanters," Sagacius said. "Lord Ashthorne, Miss Aura Lockhaven of Hartshorn, our new wizardess."

Deofoyl took a step toward Aura. He grinned, a broad expanse of white teeth and deep mirth. He lifted her outstretched hand and kissed her across the knuckles. Taken aback, Aura blushed. She was accustomed to the firm grip of farmers and craftsmen, the quick squeeze of merchants, and the limp offering of those wanting to move away from her as fast as possible. No one ever greeted her as if he were gentry and she a lady.

Releasing her hand, Deofoyl said, "It is a delight to finally meet you, Miss Lockhaven."

"And this is Elisabeth Lovejoy," Sagacius said, waving to his left.

The woman leaned against the window sill. Elisabeth stood a good four inches inches shorter than Aura, with a figure every bit as full, accentuated by tight muscles in her arms and legs. The sunlight streaming through the window caught her golden brown hair. Her sapphire eyes watched the whole room in total observation, glancing at Aura as if she knew everything about her in one moment. Elisabeth wore a corset and short skirt of leather dyed purple with bronze edges. Plates of the same metal fastened to purple leather knee boots and to gauntlets that reached her elbows. From her left hip swung a thick broadsword, with a gold guard and a dragon carved into the pommel. The woman nodded to Aura. She returned the nod.

"Miss Lovejoy is the Captain of the Watchers, the second in command of the Order's standing army. She is also Lord Ashthorne's personal guard," Sagacius said.

Deofoyl Ashthorne looked every bit like Aura imagined Prince Owynn to have when he led his rebellion against his father. Elisabeth Lovejoy reminded her of Iryndelle, the princess turned free lance who lived in the pages of the smoke stained notebook in her room. Such people only existed in tales. They romped through songs in taverns and pursued adventure in stories told around fires. Yet, here they stood in her own house, no legend, but flesh, cloth, and steel. If they represented the Order of Enchanters, then Aura was definitely interested.

As he sat down, Deofoyl waved to the middle chair in the room. "At the risk of assuming control of your own home, please have a seat, Miss Lockhaven. We have much to discuss."

Aura settled on the edge of her chair. She looked from Deofoyl to Sagacius and back. Both regarded her with intense gazes. She felt the Captain's watchful eyes on her shoulder. Clearing her throat, Aura said, "Well, I seem to be the center of attention."

"Let me get to my purpose for being here," Deofoyl said. "I trust Sagacius informed you that I would be visiting?" When Aura shook her head, he shot the wizard a disapproving look, graced with a grin. Sagacius looked at the ceiling. "He has the sheer gall to call *me* duplicitous? Anyway, I am here. I represent the council of the Order of Enchanters. The council has known about you for some time. Any student of Sagacius is a natural enchantress. Otherwise, he would not have chosen you. We haven't had a new member from the outside in twenty years, not that you are a member, of course. Naturally, we have been eager to meet you." Deofoyl shifted his gaze to Sagacius, and scowled. "I don't know why your master refused to introduce us."

"I suspect that you suspect my reasons," Sagacius said. He smiled, a smile without any humor.

"Be that as it may, old friend," Deofoyl mumbled. He returned his attention to Aura. "We understand that the nature of your training as a wizardess is similar to our own. So, I am here to offer you an invitation to join us and take your place as an enchantress. Naturally, you cannot just say yes without seeing the order for yourself, and experiencing the life of an enchantress. I would like to escort you back to our capital, the Valley of the Mystic Moon."

"You want me to go with you?" Aura asked.

"Absolutely. You will spend several weeks with us to see whether or not we are a good fit for someone like yourself. In the process, we will introduce you to members of our order who will teach you new skills. If you accept our invitation, we will initiate you with no further ado." He smiled and chuckled. "I promise, you won't have to undergo any formal apprenticeship. If you decline, then you will have had a nice holiday in one of the most exotic parts of all Ayrdland, and learned something valuable. Does that sound agreeable to you?"

"Yes, it does," Aura said. "I would like to see if being an enchantress will help me further my dream."

"What dream is that, if I may ask?"

Aura smiled as memories flooded her mind. It had been her battle cry as she played behind her father's bar, leading her army of straw dolls against the troll of the tavern cat. It sustained her as she slept in the barrel behind the bakery. She told it to Sagacius the day the new village wizard saved her from the filthy vermin who forced her to beg for him. Every day, as she practiced spells and potions, she repeated it to herself. Sitting higher in her chair, Aura said, "I want to defend the defenseless, help the helpless, and give hope to the hopeless."

Deofoyl shot Aura an astonished look. His mouth flew open. He looked to Sagacius, and muttered, "Those are the same words ..."

"The exact same words," Sagacius said. "I didn't teach them to her, either."

"What words are those?" Aura asked.

Sagacius cleared his throat, a little too loudly to be the mere action of removing mucus. Deofoyl looked at him with an intense glare, then he smiled. He fumbled with his hands for a moment before saying, "Oh, our old motto. We were known as the Order of Love, once upon a time. We couldn't pass even a child with a sniffle without stopping to help. We, uh, were also known as the Order of Busybodies for that reason, too."

Aura smiled, pushing as much happiness into her face as she could. She fought to control her irritation, holding her jaws apart to keep her teeth from grinding. Her hands betrayed her, drawing up into fists. The man's answer seemed to be as evasive as those of Sagacius.

"From what I've heard about your recent adventures, I think you would make an exceptional enchantress, and –."

"I won't tolerate any undue pressure on Aura," Sagacius said.

"I am simply explaining our position to –."

"A little too forcefully for my tastes."

"If you interrupt me one more time, Sagacius, I swear –"

Sagacius didn't smile, but his eyes twinkled. "What do you plan to do about it?"

"That's it, old friend." Deofoyl stood and stretched out his hands. "Titilla costena!"

Sagacius' eyes flew wide and he shrieked, "You lout!" Then, he grabbed his sides and fell out of his chair, howling in laughter and screaming "Egads! Stop! A pox on you! Stop it!"

"I don't think I will," Deofoyl said. He turned to Aura and asked, "What has this monster done to you? One minute for every tribulation."

Aura cast a crooked smile. She said, "He made me cut wood and haul water and light the fire and cook. He's a terrible cook, too. I tried to teach him all my father's kitchen tips, but he refused to learn."

"Oh, that's a full hour!" Deofoyl said, grinning. Sagacius continued to roll on the floor, holding his sides, and alternating between screams and laughs. "Did you know your master was ticklish? I sure did. His mother used to correct him this way."

"Master had a mother?" Aura asked, watching her master writhe on the floor. The wizard of Hartshorn was trapped. She crossed her arms over her chest. A grin spread across her face. This man did what she always wanted to do, get the old wizard back for all those mundane chores.

"Of course, I had a mother," Sagacius stammered between laughter. "What do you expect?"

"I hate to interrupt this frivolity, but my hair is standing on end," Elisabeth Lovejoy said. The gravity of her tone erased the absurdity of the trilled R. With the tone of someone accustomed to issuing orders, and having them obeyed, she brought the levity to an abrupt end. Deofoyl waved his hands, and Sagacius sagged into a puddle of gasps and wheezes. "While you two gentlemen enjoy yourselves, someone is watching us. I dislike having eyes down my cleavage, unless they belong to a suitor. The sooner we leave, the better off we will all be."

"Nocturna," Aura said.

Deofoyl dropped his hands and whirled on Aura. A look of fury consumed his face. "Who did you say?"

"Nocturna," Aura answered. "She's the nymph who has been watching me."

"That's it, then," Deofoyl said. He glanced at the recovering Sagacius. "This is more serious than I anticipated, old friend. I know Nocturna very well. You were right. You are being watched, and by someone from inside the order."

"Nocturna must owe someone a favor, someone who could order her to leave the Valley," Sagacius said, standing up. "That someone could indeed be my sister."

"I think it's time that all of you told me what is going on," Aura said. "Why am I so important that a nymph is watching me?" To Sagacius, she said, "Master, no more secrets." To Deofoyl she added, "Sir, I don't know you, but please, tell me the truth."

Both men looked at each other. Sagacius wore the expression of the helpless. Deofoyl slowly nodded, and set his jaw in defiance. With almost imperceptible movement, he turned to look at Aura. In a slow voice, he asked, "Has Sagacius told you about Nightshade?"

Aura sighed. She closed her eyes. How did she know someone would say that name? Putting all her will into her face, she fought to control her irritation and not let it show. She opened her eyes to see Sagacius' frown. Without looking at Deofoyl, she nodded.

The Vice-Chancellor said, "Some of our more powerful members believe that you may well be the heiress of Nightshade. They are alone in their beliefs, but in their solitude, they have found strength of conviction. Even if you are descended from a man who vanished without a trace, that does not mean you inherited his mantle. Such mantles are chosen, not bequeathed."

"I've told my sister for ten years that it is a mere coincidence of names," Sagacius said.

Aura shot Sagacius a withering look, one he did not see. If it was all a mere coincidence, then why did he mention the name Nightshade three times in as many weeks? Surely, the word was not an uncommon surname, especially in Coadia where everything had magical connotations. If he made some leap of logic between a plant, her mother, and some legendary enchanter, then who else had done the same? Her stomach tightened. She felt as if she sprouted strings, strings that led to the fingers of someone she never met, and who pulled them just to watch her dance. She glanced at the Captain, who returned her scowl.

"As for myself, I agree with Lady Etheria," Deofoyl continued. "She is the Lady of the Valley of the Mystic Moon, the Chancellor of the Order of Enchanters. Our beliefs are simple. You are the first apprentice from the outside that any of our order has had in two decades. You represent fresh ideas and a new perspective, which we so desperately need. Our order has become somewhat stagnant. Someone from the outside, who is not tainted by our history, would be welcomed. We would be delighted if you joined us. If not, that is your choice. We believe firmly in the right of self determination."

"I know I want what you could teach me," Aura said. "I want to be able to control my emotions and use them to empower my magic. I want to be able to heal without endangering myself."

"We cannot teach you that," Deofoyl said. "We can, however, teach you to teach that to yourself. Does that make sense?"

"No. But I am willing to find out what that means."

"That is a refreshing new attitude, Miss Lockhaven," Deofoyl said, smiling. "Well, the Captain is correct. The sooner we are on our way, the safer we will be. Whoever is watching us no doubt already knows of my presence here today. Not everyone will view it with such high and lofty eyes as those within the order."

"Not him," Sagacius said, slowly. "Not Brightstar!"

"He's dead, as far as I know," Deofoyl said. He cast a cold glance at Sagacius, one full of suspicion. Slowly, with a hint of accusation, he said, "But he does have a grandson."

Sagacius leapt from his chair. He covered the distance across the sitting room in two steps. He grabbed Deofoyl by his keld and pulled him to his chest. Fire shot from his blue eyes. He roared in a voice Aura heard only once before, "This is exactly why I hid Aura from you people! I will not have her threatened by Brightstar!"

"I told you that he is dead!" Deofoyl snapped.

"Evil does not die that easily! I blasted off his right arm and he still walked away from that duel. You of all people know what he's like. He was your master's master. And no one, not even you, best ever compare that monster with his grandson. Do you hear me, Deofoyl?"

"You best release me," Deofoyl growled. "Even if we are friends, attacking a member of the council is a capital offense."

"Will you two please stop!" Aura shouted. She had no idea what or whom they meant. Nightshade. Brightstar. Those were just words. What had she done to warrant such attention, and to provoke a confrontation between her teacher and the Vice-Chancellor of a magical order. She was just Aura Lockhaven, a wizardess who performed magic she did not understand.

"You should listen to the woman, and stop fighting each other," Elisabeth snapped. Sagacius released Deofoyl and backed away. Deofoyl shook himself and nodded. The captain stepped away from the window and stood between the two men, her gaze on Aura. "You gentlemen have a greater enemy than each other. The eyes on my back belong to someone who is working for someone else. I for one do not want to meet the mastermind, not here, where I don't have a full squad, and you, sir, aren't free to unleash your full power."

"Leave it to a warrior to put a councilman in his place," Deofoyl said. He looked at Sagacius and said, "I apologize, old friend."

"There is no need," Sagacius said. "I'm the one who should apologize. Especially, to you, Aura. I was wrong to withhold things from you."

As he returned to his chair, Aura said, "Then, please tell me the truth. Am I in danger?" That was a silly question. Of course, she was in danger. Every day, life presented a platter full of danger to her, just as it did everyone else. Last week, Rupert spotted a pack of wolves on the other side of his farm, and Morgana's husband shot the largest bear seen in Lodwynnshire for thirty years. Her own calling presented its share of danger. The Knights of the Holy Torch itched to cleanse the islands of all magicians just as it had most of the continent. If they arrived in Ayrdland, then she would spend the rest of her life looking over her shoulder for witch hunters. "Let me rephrase that. What haven't you told me?"

Sagacius sat quiet for a minute before saying, "When I met you, I realized that you had a gift for magic. I saw it in your eyes, a knowledge that there was more to the world than just what could be seen. In other words, you have natural talent, not just learned skills. In the past ten years, you've proven that to me. Now, after you healed Lodd and Sire Thaddeus, I've seen your true potential. I suspect that you will only grow stronger with each passing year. Aura, someone like you is going to draw quite a bit of interest. Some of the interested parties are ... disagreeable."

"Are," Aura said. "Not were or could be. Are. You sound like you know them."

"We did. Deofoyl, Etheria, and I," Sagacius responded, saying the words with deliberation. "We knew them in our little disagreement. We three tried to be the voices of reason, and remained neutral. That earned us the wrath of powerful members on both sides. Some of those could decide to take their anger out on you, solely because you were my apprentice."

"It was a very bloody war, Miss Lockhaven," Deofoyl said. "I literally saw brothers kill each other. You will see the scars for yourself, in ruins and smoke stains on walls. Also in the memories of the people. You shouldn't concern yourself with them, although they may concern themselves with you. Don't let the possibility of someone with, shall I say, nefarious purposes dissuade you from taking this journey. I will be there, as will Lady Etheria. I have assigned close friends to guide you, so you will be safe."

"The Watchers will be at your service," Elisabeth said. She gripped her sword hilt in her left hand, a sign of promise. "Marshall Gemengna ordered me personally to see to your well being. At the risk of sounding boastful, my squad is the toughest, and it is at your call."

Sagacius sighed. He looked at his hands, and said, "Deofoyl is right. You should go with him. You have the possibility of gaining greater strength on this path. Perhaps, you will even come to see yourself as others see you." He looked at her and smiled. "The people in the taverns already have a new name for you. Aura Lockhaven, the Healer of Hartshorn. Your name will eventually reach the ears of King Edgar. You are important, and not just to Hartshorn, the Order of Enchanters, and whomever is watching you. You are important to the entire country of Ayrdland. You have the potential to write history."

The only history Aura cared about was her own. First, her brother died. Then, her sister. Then, her father died before her eyes while she, too, young and weak to save him, could only scream and burn her hand in a vain attempt to move the fiery beam from his body. Finally, her uncle banished her to the street. Hartshorn did not even have an old witch at the time. Sagacius appeared two years later. If only a magician lived in Hartshorn in 1039, her history may tell a different tale. Perhaps a wizard could not have prevented Richard's death in the war. He could have, however, prevented Ester's rape and murder, and levitated that beam from Henry before fire consumed him. No terror attacks. No devouring fear of being alone. No nightmares. If only a magician lived in Hartshorn that year. Perhaps if a wizard or witch lived in the village ten years before that, Aurora would not have had to choose between her own life and that of her unborn child.

One lived in Hartshorn now. While Aura's history lay inked in the annals of the gods, others faced blank pages today. Rupert lived a whole life, all because of her accidental blending of pure will and sheer compassion. Lodd could grow older and have his own life. Sire Thaddeus faced the possibility of a life with more faith for the same reason. Three people lived whole lives today because she existed. Aura Lockhaven mattered. If King Edgar sought her, fine. For now, all she wanted was the power to help the next Rupert, Lodd, and Thaddeus.

"I don't care about writing history, Master. I care about righting wrongs," she said. She clenched her left hand, feeling the vague stiffness of the scar. "That's all I want. Is that too much to ask?"

Sagacius smiled again. "I would be alarmed if you wanted anything else. Well, what is your answer?"

She looked at Sagacius. He stared at her with a mixture of concern and excitement. Despite his misgivings, he seemed to want her to go. She looked at Deofoyl. He stared at her with a mixture of encouragement and anticipation. She glanced at Elisabeth. The Captain returned her glance with firm resolve. What did she want to do?

So much about this gnawed at her, as if someone offered her a ripe peach she knew had been laced with arsenic. Sagacius' secrecy. A nymph shadowing her, a nymph dispatched by someone within the order. A worried warrior who grew more restless with each passing minute. The names of apparently ancient, but extremely powerful, people who may not have her best interests in mind. The order wanted her membership so much that its council dispatched the Vice-Chancellor to fetch her personally, when a written note sent via courier or pigeon would have sufficed.

Aura thought about the next little girl who was about to have her life ripped apart. No one was there for Aura. Well, she wanted to be there for Suzanne, whoever she was. What if Old Man Ryll fell out of one of Master Donal's pear trees and broke his neck? What if she died trying to heal him? Then, Aura Lockhaven would not be there for Suzanne. Based on what little Sagacius said, this new path offered her the ability to heal a potential Ryll without endangering herself.

"I am going with you," Aura said to Deofoyl. "Let me gather my things." She stood up, and turned to Sagacius. "Master, I have to go.

There's a chance that I can learn to heal like Leynda." Sagacius nodded. He smiled at her in sincere contentment with her answer.

"Leynda," Deofoyl said, as Aura walked toward the stairs. "Now, that is an enchantress I have not seen in years. Leynda is a good example for you to follow, Miss Lockhaven. She was smart enough to stay out of our war."

Aura stopped, halfway to the stairs. She turned to Deofoyl, astonished. "I thought your war happened fifty years ago. Leynda couldn't be more than thirty now."

"You'd be surprised," Deofoyl said, with a smile.

Aura grabbed a leather bag from the wardrobe. With a quick glance out the window for Nocturna, or anyone else, she returned to her table. Into the bag she thrust her brush, knife, pots of clay and berry juice makeup, red hair ribbon, and a purse containing a few pieces of silver and copper. Preferring to bathe every day, she added her soap and towel. Finally, she folded the old tunic and pressed it on top of everything else. Just in case a terror attack struck, she stuffed her kerchief into a pocket of her sleeve.

She paused at her bookcase. For a moment, she thought about taking Richard's sword and the notebook of her father's tales. No, the notebook was safer here, and she knew only enough about swordplay to get in the Captain's way if they faced attack. That seemed to be all she needed. Surely, the capital of a magical order had plenty of herbs, crystals, and other items should she need to perform a ritual. Pausing at the door, she looked back at her room, wondering how it would appear to her when she returned.

Sagacius waited for her in the hallway. He took her by the arm and drew her to the far wall. Windowless, its oak panels covered in the patina of age, it held only two iron sconces. She was accustomed to this, but his next action astonished her. Usually, he faced the wall with his back turned toward her, obscuring his motions. Today, he stood to the side allowing her to see his every move.

Grabbing the right sconce with his left hand, he said, "Pay close attention, Aura. Pull down." He did so, and the sconce slid on a hidden hinge. "Then, twist. Push it back, then, push it up."

As he followed his own actions, the wall slid backwards, revealing a hidden room. She followed him through the low door, and up the wooden spiral staircase to his library at the top of the tower adjacent to the house. Aura inhaled. She loved this paneled room, with its tall but narrow windows, the aroma of pipe smoke and ink, and all the books, boxes, magical tools, and jars of weird stuff. Opposite the door stood another door, one that opened out onto a balcony where wizard and apprentice spent many nights studying the heavens and watching for comets. He put his hand on her shoulder and smiled at her with a loving look.

"When you return, this will be your sanctuary. I'm leaving it all for you, except for a few personal items." When she opened her mouth, he silenced her with a wave of his hand. "You're my heir, and I'm bequeathing it to you anyway. I'd like the opportunity to watch you enjoy it."

"Thank you, Master," Aura said. She looked around. It was all hers. All those books, some older than Ayrdland. Spells of Bellician alchemists, potions of Nebelish wizards, rituals of Glasenyan sorcerers, lore of Tangoi druids, and the charms of witches from countries that no longer existed. Several shelves held scrolls of parchment, some believed to be written by Karanthek magicians well over fifteen hundred years earlier, in a language forgotten to the tongues of men. One book beckoned to her, a book that in ten years, Sagacius never once let her touch, much less open. According to the wizard, it contained magic darker than the black leather that covered it. Would he leave that book? Whether he did or not, she felt he left a treasure greater than if he filled the house with gold.

"Aura," Sagacius said, looking at her with love and awe. "All that you've experienced so far. All the horror. The death of your brother, your sister, your father. The two years you endured that alley without me. All the lessons I gave you. The ogre and the woman in the fire. Your trial. Rupert, Lodd, and Sire Thaddeus. All that was mere happenstance to prepare you for this moment. Are you ready? Are you ready to become who you are?"

She thought for a moment. "Who I am," she said. Aura looked at her hands. The left hand, her receiving hand, with the C shaped scar a dull pink against the flesh of the palm. The right hand, her power hand, with its calluses of apprenticeship slowly fading from view. "I'm not sure I know who I am anymore. Until a few weeks ago, I thought I did. So much has changed since then. The woman you initiated is not the woman standing before you. It's as if I were but a child then, and that was just two weeks ago." She clenched both her hands into tight fists. Staring at the knuckles of both hands, she said, "I have an ability I can't comprehend, one that threatens to kill me if I don't learn to work with it. Yet, if I ignore it, to preserve myself, I will die the death of the bear in a cage." She looked up at her teacher. "I have to become whoever I am, Master. Whatever it takes."

Sagacius pondered her statement with indecipherable eyes. He spent an entire minute studying her face, and contemplating a response. Finally, he said, "Then go, Aura Lockhaven, with the blessings of your gods, your goddesses, and your teacher and friend."

"You speak as if you aren't coming with me."

He said, "That is because I am not."

"What?"

"Not this time. You've been under my influence for ten years. For this decision, you need to be free of my opinions."

"Now, I'm scared," she said.

"There is plenty to fear, but not of being without me. You will always have my voice and mind, Aura. Now, listen. You will no doubt learn things about yourself, things that you do not want to know, and you will not like. But they will only make you more powerful. Do you understand?"

"Yes, sir."

"Even though I won't be with you, I am sending a friend with you. Although you were born under the sign of Erasto, an Earth sign, I have always associated you with the color red. I believe it's your favorite color anyway. Your birthstone is an emerald, but you look like a ruby to me. Perhaps, it is your hair." He turned to the simple table he used for a desk. He lifted a small black box, no bigger than those that contained alchemists' firesticks. With the love of a man cradling his child, he opened the lid. He removed a small object, and said, "Therefore, this is yours."

Sagacius placed in Aura's hand a ruby an inch across and as thick as her thumb. Cut round, the light from the windows struck it, sending shimmering fire shooting across the library. As she held it, the fire intensified. The stone grew warm in her palm. It called to her. It was as if she knew the stone.

"It belonged to my teacher," Sagacius said. "She left it to me. Now, it is yours. Let it guide you. The ruby is the stone of passion, not that you need any more of that emotion. Perhaps it will help you refine yours. When you feel lost, or unsure, look deep into it. You will find the wisdom of ages and counsel of many souls within its facets. It guided me for decades, but now, it wishes to belong to you."

"Master, I don't know what to say," Aura said, gazing deep into the crystal.

"Keep it close, Aura. It's powerful, and not even I know all its secrets. It belonged to a woman, and I believe it prefers speaking to a woman." As he returned the box to his desk, he continued. "I'll have moved in with Bart by the time you return, but I'll make sure to visit for a few days. You will no doubt have much to discuss and many questions." He turned to look at her, and grew silent. With a smile, he said, "I am so proud of you, Aura. No matter your decision, I will be proud of you."

"Thank you, Master."

"Don't you think it's time to stop calling me Master?" Sagacius asked.

Aura smiled. She threw her arms around the old wizard and held him tight. She said, "After all that's happened to me since the Evenday, please allow me some more time to break that habit, Mr. Sagacius, sir."

Chapter Eight

Ten Years Ago

WINTER'S FIRST KISS made the waif shiver. The chill in the air nipped her through the shattered shell of a once nice blue dress. Absentmindedly, she scratched the spider bite on the back of her right hand. She wanted to scratch the other bites, itching in the growing cold, but scratching one's buttocks and girlhood was best left for the shadows, not a street. Perhaps, if she made a decent take today, Fulbert would leave her enough to buy an old sack down at the docks. She could cut that up into a cloak, enough of one to cover her bare right arm. Her dress once had a sleeve there, hadn't it?

Her left hand ached. It always ached in cold weather. It also always ached in wet weather. It always ached. More from the memory buried beneath the thick layer of scar tissue than from actual pain. The waif flexed her hand, opening and closing her fist, trying to get some movement into it. She held it out to passers-by, letting them see the scar as they heard the quail in her voice.

"Please, sir, can you spare a copper so that I may buy a muffin?" the waif called to the man who hurried by. Not so much as a glance in her direction. Tom Harper, the cooper, she remembered. He used to tell her the funniest stories, but that was two years ago.

She had not been quite so tall then, a mere forty-four inches, short for a ten year old girl. Mr. Harper said she looked cute sitting on his workbench, pawing at the wood shavings, kicking the air. Now, she worried about her dress. Two years ago, it ended just below the knee. She knew she now topped sixty inches, based on how much of her legs stuck out of her barrel. Already, she had lost one button to the strain of the dress across her growing chest. If she grew any taller, the dress would be immodest, ending just below her swelling hips. That is, if she didn't lose any more of the hem, catching it on stones trying to elude drunken boatmen. While she did not understand the terms, she all too well comprehended their intentions.

Mr. Harper used to muss her red hair as he told her tales. He needn't bother today. The wind did that for him, turning it into a snarl fit only for a razor. That is, if the razor could cut through the almost brick like mud that caked it.

The waif wanted to slip back into the alley and hide inside her barrel home. Overhead, the sky grew darker. Too early and too warm for snow. A torrent no doubt, one that would fill her alley with mud, and soak her to her bones. She sighed.

"They used to love me," the waif whispered. "Once, when the moon was younger. Once, when Iryndelle lived as I lay in bed listening." The girl sank to her knees. She shut her eyes. At one time, she prayed to Baniar, but the god of Irican turned deaf ears to her pleas. Now, she prayed to someone else. "Please, Lunambyra. I don't know if you were real, but Daddy always said you were. He said your name means Moon Shadow. I love the shadow of the moon. He said he visited your home long before I was born. I don't know where Saporia is, but it sounds beautiful. Please, Lunambyra. Send me someone. I need to see something beautiful again."

"Crying, Snake Eyes?" a voice said.

The waif opened her eyes, to see two pairs of boots about three feet from her. That was not the beauty she had in mind. The waif stood up, pulling herself to her full height and throwing back her shoulders. From her vantage, she could see that Reggie failed to part his hair straight. She allowed her fury to boil over into her emerald eyes. The boys wanted Snake Eyes? Those came with teeth, and the teeth with venom.

"What do you want!" she snapped.

"Hey, I didn't call you that," the other boy, Erik, said. "I'm here to remind you that it's Midweek, and you always come to supper on Midweek. Mom's cooking a roast pork. She's trying it the way you told her last time. It sure smells good."

"Heavy on the sage, light on the garlic," the waif said.

"And for Baniar's sake, will you take a dress from Mom? Gloria has outgrown all her stuff, and I know they'd fit you."

"She's too proud," Reggie said, grinning.

No, the waif was not too proud. She had accepted many clothes from many kind folk. Fulbert always took them from her, selling them to the women on ships at the docks. Why bother receiving a gift from Erik's mother if she could not keep it for one hour? The master beggar said he liked her better in the old dress she wore when her uncle threw her out. It made her more presentable to her clients. In other words, it made her look more like a beggar. Although, the look Fulbert gave her lately when he mentioned that dress made the waif shiver and want to hide.

"I can't believe you let this urchin in your home, Erik," Reggie said. He chuckled. "She might give you lice."

"Silence!" the waif yelled.

Reggie ignored her. He chuckled again. "What does she do, cry about dear old daddy all night?"

The waif clenched her right hand. Twice, she put boatmen on their backs, boatmen whose hands became too friendly with her budding breasts. She had no doubt she could do the same to Reggie. She didn't have the chance. Erik grabbed his friend by the throat and shoved him against the wall.

"That's enough out of you!" Erik shouted. The boy cut his eyes toward the waif and said, "See you at sundown?"

"I'll be there." Erik let go of Reggie's throat, but grabbed his lapels and dragged him away. As they moved toward the town green, the waif called out, "Thank you, Erik!"

The waif watched the boys disappear into the crowded market on the green. Erik was so kind. He might make a good priest. Reggie would probably end up like his father, swinging by the end of a rope.

She heard the distinct sound of leather against cobblestone. The waif knew most of the people of Hartshorn and their gaits. Bart the

94

wheelwright limped a bit on the left. Old Man Simpson must have had corns to make him pad like a sore dog. Mrs. Finch walked on her toes, making her footfall sound like rain on a roof. Jim the tailor walked as if his trousers were made of haircloth. This gait was peculiar, a firm heel to stone, then a roll onto the toes. The space of time between heelfall implied a long stride. It was one of purpose and self-knowledge. A stranger come to town.

The waif stuck out her left hand, stretching the fingers to emphasize the scar. Waiting until the footfall reached her, she said, "Please, sir, can you spare a copper so that I may buy a muffin?"

A form stopped before her. She looked up, expecting to meet a pair of eyes. Instead, she met a chest. At least, it looked like a chest behind flowing heathered blue robes and a golden medallion featuring the image of a raven. She continued to look up. And up. No mortal man could possibly be that tall! At first, all she saw was the short silver beard and the mane of silver hair that plunged down his back. Then, she noticed his face, a series of wrinkles caused by laughter that framed a pair of blue eyes that twinkled in kindness and curiosity.

"A muffin costs a copper in this town? That's robbery, young lady," the man said in a voice like that of a crackling fireplace on a winter's night.

"Huh?" the waif said, still staring up with wide eyes. "Oh. I apologize. Well, sir, if I earn a decent take today, perhaps Fulbert will leave me enough coin to buy a penny loaf and a cup of tea. Sir."

The man bent down until his nose almost touched hers. "Who is this Fulbert?" he asked, spreading the question out until it sounded like four one word sentences. The waif had once watched as the town guard tested a new defense, rolling logs and boulders down the side of Piper's Knob. The rumble in the man's voice made the din of that landslide seem like a mere hiccup.

"He's my master," the waif stammered.

"You're his apprentice?"

"Not exactly," the waif answered. She glanced up and down the street to make sure Fulbert was nowhere in sight. She whispered, "He says I must beg for him. Otherwise, he will sell me to the Frystings, who will sell me as a concubine in Faria. I know what a concubine does, and I do not wish to do that."

The man straightened so fast, the waif jumped. His face seemed to split in half. He roared, "Frystings do not steal, buy, or sell people, young lady! Those are the Skols, and there are no Skols in Ayrdland at the moment. If there were, I would have heard of the raid or battle, and all is silent."

The waif slammed her right fist into her left palm. She ignored the pain shooting underneath the scar. Of all the nerve. For nearly two years, she stood in the heat, in the rain, in the cold, in the snow, wearing a rag that grew smaller and thinner, out of fear of being sold as a foreign prince's bedslave. Fulbert could tie her up, toss her aboard a river cog, sail her to Vine Haven, ship out with her on a straitrunner, and hope to pass within sight of a Skol raiding ship, but not even Fulbert was dense enough to try something that foolhardy. With a tight grimace, she snarled, "That poxweasel! That dungrat! He lied to me!"

"He has been doing more than lying to you, miss," the man said, his voice returning to that of a warm fire. "He is using you, manipulating you, to serve his own laziness." The man rubbed his chin, letting the beard hair flow through his fingers. "I've seldom encountered an urchin with your vocabulary. You speak more like the daughter of a merchant. You also remind me of someone. I just can't place the name. Tell me, where is your family?"

The waif sighed. "They're all dead, sir."

The man's face softened even more. The pity that flowed from his eyes made the waif tear up in gratitude. "Oh, I am so sorry, miss. Please, tell me, what is your name?"

"They call me Snake Eyes," she said.

The tall man stared at her, as if trying to pierce her soul. He asked, "What do you call yourself?"

The waif sighed. "Even grownups call me Snake Eyes."

"Egads! That's horrible."

"I'm used to it, Mr. Old Man."

The man whirled around and doubled over. The waif saw him shake. He made a peculiar sound, as if choking on dry bones. She reached out her hand. For a second, she wanted to touch him, to see if he was all right. Before she could, he straightened. He gestured, as if wiping tears from his eyes, then he turned around. With a loud clearing of his throat, he said, "I have been called many things, miss, but that is the first time anyone called me Mr. Old Man. Do you not know who I am?"

"An old man?" she asked. "Well, not as in too terribly old, sir. Oh, dear. I think I insulted you. Well, you're certainly older than me, and I'm twelve." Her countenance fell. "I'm making this worse, aren't I?"

"The robes don't tell you anything about me?" he asked, gesturing toward his clothing.

"You're a priest?"

"Close enough," the man said with a sigh. "I am not going to call you Miss Eyes, so just miss will have to suffice. Well, miss. May I buy you something to eat?" The waif's mouth flew open. She wiped the saliva from her lips with the back of her hand and nodded. "Come with me, then." The old man stepped away and began walking up the street, toward the southern end of town. The waif fell in beside him. She tried to shorten her steps, but couldn't. It felt too awkward, but not as awkward as the sway that had recently invaded her hips when she walked. "I hope you don't mind eating at Antler and Drum."

"Mr. Hadrian is a friend of mine, even if he does have a Bellician sounding name. He always lets me eat behind his tavern. His pork is good, but his ale tastes like donkey piss."

"Aren't you a little young to know about ales?" the man asked.

"Listen, Mr. Old Man! My father was the best brewer in Hartshorn, and he taught me. I was weaned on beer, sir. Anyway, Mr. Hadrian sits with me while I eat, and tells me good stories. Not as good as mine, which are very good, if I may say so, sir. Have you ever heard the tales of the Sarethian Seven? Daddy told me all of them. Blood raising," she paused, rubbing the growing hump in her nose, "or is that hair raising? Hair curdling? Oh, merciful heavens!" She shrugged. "Anyway, stories of princesses turned free lance warriors in some place called Phrathia, although they came from Saporia. Do you know where either of those countries are? You do? You must tell me. Anyway, Iryndelle is my favorite, but I think I like the one called Lunambyra more now. She's their sorceress. I wrote the stories down just as Daddy told them to me." She paused. A note of anger entered her voice as she snarled, "But my uncle stole my book, just like he stole ..." She growled in her throat to clear away the rising anger. "Anyway, I have the tales all memorized, and tell them to Mr. Hadrian when he gets tired of telling his." With a swallow, she looked up at the tall man and asked, "Am I talking too much, sir?"

The old man laughed. It was a warm laugh that filled the waif with the first touches of joy she had felt in weeks. "No, miss. I'm rather enjoying not having to talk myself. In fact –"

"Hey! Where are you going with that bitchling?" a voice thick with phlegm and beer said from in front of the waif and man.

The waif stopped in her tracks. She ducked behind the tall man. Before them stood a man about as tall as he was round, his hairy belly jutting out over his belt and through his unbuttoned waistcoat. From the grime on his body, he had not seen a bath in at least three months. The waif smelled him from a distance of ten feet. Glancing at his mouth, she noticed he lost another tooth just that day. Greasy hair of an indescribable color clung to his oily scalp. The waif clenched the tall man's robes in her hand. A whimper escaped her lips.

"A friend of yours?" the tall man asked the waif.

"That's Fulbert," she stammered.

"Really," the man said. His voice changed again, into that of the rumble of a landslide. "You sir," he said, "are an abomination to all that is holy. How dare you use this child as a tool of your avarice!"

"What?" Fulbert asked. He blinked and wiped his mouth with his hand. "Oh, you mean her big words? Heh. Rich folk can't resist. She's my best beggar. When her body fills out, I'm going to make her one of my whores over'n Eastbank." He glanced at the girl clinging to the heathered robes. The waif gulped. She knew that look. Fulbert grinned with what few teeth he still possessed. "May just fuck her myself."

The tall man stiffened by the waif. He ripped his robes from her hands. If possible, he grew even taller. With the motion of a cat pouncing upon a mouse, he raised his right hand. The waif had never heard a lion roar, but she imagined that one sounded just like the tall man at that moment. He shouted one word in a language she did not recognize. The air crackled. Something formed in the man's palm, something there, then gone.

Fulbert flew backwards, flipped in mid air, rolled onto his stomach, and slid down the street. He stopped with his face in a puddle of water.

"Is he ... is he dead?" the waif asked.

"No. That was a throwback spell. I'm sure I shattered a few ribs." With a sigh, the man walked up to the limp body, and rolled him over onto his back with his foot. He looked down at Fulbert and said, "I should leave you to drown, but my Chieftain is going to scream at me as it is. Perhaps, you will have some decency when you awaken. I assure you, sir, that you will never pester this girl again, and that before sunrise, you shall depart this shire. That, I promise you."

"You just saved me," the waif said. She looked the old man up and down. She had never seen anyone like him, much less seen anyone do what he just did. Frowning, she asked, "Who are you?"

The old man smiled. He said, "My name is Sagacius. It seems at the insistence of your rather persuasive mayor that I am your new town wizard. That's why I can guarantee that you will never see Fulbert again. I have the authority to run him out of the shire."

The waif looked at Sagacius, then down at Fulbert, then back to Sagacius. "A wizard? Could someone like me become someone like you? I mean, I'm a girl, so I guess that makes me a witch, but can I learn to do what you do?"

"You're a little old. Most people start around age six. However, you don't have anything else to do at the moment, so why couldn't you? With the proper training, and a lot of determination, I'm sure you could, except you'd be called a wizardess."

The girl grinned. "That's what I want to do, then. You just saved me. I want to save others like you saved me. I want to defend the defenseless, help the helpless, and give hope to the hopeless. That is my dream."

The old man's eyes grew wide. His mouth opened. He took two steps back. Shaking his head in disbelief, he stared at the girl. "That is remarkable. The same words," he whispered. The waif swallowed. What had she said? Before she could ask, the man smiled.

"Well, young lady," he said. "I don't have a pupil at the moment. I would be honored to teach you."

Everything changed. In the span of half an hour, her life changed. It had taken less time than that for it to change two years earlier, except in the opposite direction. She looked up at the dark clouds. A single drop of rain splattered against her cheek, melding into the tears flowing from her eyes. Lunambyra had heard and had answered. If not the legendary free lance sorceress, then someone. Someone sent Mr. Old Man. Perhaps, tonight, she would eat a full meal. Perhaps, tonight, she would sleep in a bed. Perhaps, tonight, she would not feel spiders crawling on her body.

A new life faced her, one of mystery, but also one of promise. A life without begging from her father's old friends, a life without boatmen pursuing her, and a life without a master who lied to her and craved her body. Whatever that life held, it would be better than any day of the past two years.

The waif flexed her left hand. The ache seemed a little less intense now. She wiped her hand, and the other, on her dress. With a little fuss, she straightened her hair as best she could. She cast Fulbert a cold stare of triumph, one she hoped he felt inside his unconscious soul. She looked down the street, toward a sign of a lock with a key in it. She cast another cold stare of triumph in that direction. Then, she looked up into the face of the man who stood before her.

"I would be honored to be your student, Mr. Sage See Us, uh, Mr. Old Man, uh, Mr. Sir, sir," the waif said.

The wizard chuckled. "You will need a new name. Snake Eyes belongs to a victim of chance. You will learn to be mistress over chance through will and knowledge. Are you sure you don't have another name?"

She did, but no one spoke her name in so long that she almost forgot it. Once, it had been a name of pride, a name of stature. A pretty name for someone who ought to be pretty, not someone covered in grime underneath a mass of dirty hair and inside a wreck of a farrier's rag. A lyrical name for someone with eyes the color of springtime, not someone with eyes like pond scum. A dignified name for someone who ought to sit at a bar in a warm tavern and tell stories to happy customers, not extend a stiff hand while crying for a pittance. A name ripped from her grasp by a man with the same surname. Yet, it was there, just underneath the skin. It waited the chance to bloom again, and this wizard just offered it a beam of sunshine and a cup of water.

The girl inhaled. She stood taller. With a defiant set in her jaw, she looked the wizard in the eyes. In a dry voice, the waif whispered a name she thought she would never speak again.

"My name is Aura Lockhaven."

Chapter Nine

ORDERED FARMS OF wheat and barley surrounded by neat stone walls gave way to marsh as the party neared Rath Creek. Aura stuck her head out the carriage window to watch as they crossed the wooden bridge. The clear water rushing around boulders flowed east into the wide, brown River Gourdvine at the southern edge of Hartshorn. Ayrdish river cogs, Frysting longships, and Coadic straitrunners docked at Hartshorn to trade wares. Here, several boys netted fish in the waist deep water. Looking up, they waved at her.

Seeing the carriage in front of her house had surprised her. She thought Deofoyl and Elisabeth traveled by horseback. Unlike the ornate coach of the shire's eorl, this was a simple, but highly polished, wooden box with its windows and doors covered by leather flaps. Deofoyl explained that whenever a member of the council traveled in the outside world, he or she liked to appear as a middling merchant, not a powerful magician. Suspended from the frame on thick leather straps, Aura barely felt the rumble and bounce of the bridge. Deofoyl and Elisabeth sat side by side with their backs to the driver, allowing Aura to face forward. Looking down the length of the carriage, Aura saw the twin white drafters who trotted over the bridge as if the conveyance were air.

Bog formed by the confluence of Rath Creek with the Little Rath greeted her on the other side of the bridge. Wispy mist still rose from the wet in the mid-morning sunlight. Clumps of stubbly grass erupted from the muck, and stunted trees struggled to grow in patches. Men and women trudged through the mire, examining young stalks of rice. They looked up from their work to watch the carriage roll by. Even from that distance, Aura saw the contempt on their faces. The carriage slowed as the road changed from packed clay and gravel into rutted sop, throwing mud into the air from the turning wheels.

She jerked her head back inside the carriage and said, "We're nearing Kelton. Please tell your driver not to stop for anything, not even a broken axle."

"We passed through here in the night," Deofoyl said. "Surely the village can't be all that terrible."

"See for yourself," Aura said, nodding toward the window.

Slowed now to a walk, the carriage entered the village. On both sides of the mud road stood round stone huts without doors or windows in the holes, and smoke pouring from stumps of chimneys. That form of house vanished two hundred years ago, replaced by the square painted forms found throughout most of Ayrdland. All sat at crooked angles and one or two had already collapsed. The huts gave way to larger ones, some with signs over the doorways, some without. In between stood a few buildings constructed of interwoven twigs. One building loomed above the hovels. Square and built of cut stones painted a shade of brown, its proud walls reached toward the sky, with a bell tower standing higher than any tree within a mile. A circle of silver capped the tower. Aura frowned. The High Temple ought not parade itself in the face of wretchedness.

"This is the most dismal spot in Lodwynnshire. We Hartshornians call this village Balesville," Aura said. "Some fool thought it was a good idea to farm Arantian rice here, so he founded the village in a bog. Kelton is sinking, and so are the people. The only things that grow here are poverty and misery. Kelton's priest is pure High Temple. Two years ago, they hanged their village witch. They have a wise man, but he's a scholar, not a magician."

The carriage attracted the attention of the villagers. Listless people mingled next to the shops, watching it roll passed. They looked the same, faces blanked by drudgery, tattered clothes dyed the same colors of mud. To the people of Kelton, even a middling merchant was a wealthy prince. If the people saw more than the carriage and the faces of the occupants, there would be trouble. Deofoyl looked Cailliac or Garranian, while Aura could pass herself off as a comfortable woman from Hartshorn. No amount of talk would explain Elisabeth Lovejoy. The High Temple forbade the exposure of that much skin.

"So, the High Temple has reached this far inland," Deofoyl said. "That is not good. I much prefer the Frankenist branch of Iricanism. Their priests make more sense."

"The High Temple attempted to take over Colebury a few years ago, but we had none of it," Elisabeth said. "The priest wanted to hang our city wizard, so my father hanged the priest."

"Your father?" Aura asked. Elisabeth answered by looking out the window. Aura decided not to press the question.

Kelton ended as it began, with bog, rice fields, and people in mud colored clothing who glared at the carriage. Over the tops of the stunted trees, Aura saw the rounded shape of Dreadhenge Hill, supposedly the cairn of a tribe of giants. She sighed in relief. The road would soon become clay and gravel again, and Kelton would fade behind them. Sure enough, the carriage gained speed, the struggling trees changed into the usual groves of towering oaks, and the air dried to that of spring. Durtson would be the next village. Not as large as Hartshorn, it still boasted its prosperity with inns and taverns. Aura's stomach growled. In the excitement and consternation of that morning, and their haste to depart, she forgot to eat breakfast.

A thud echoed through the carriage, as if someone struck it with a rock. The driver brought it to a halt so fast that Aura lurched from her seat to the floor. She looked up to see alarm on Deofoyl's face. Elisabeth gripped her sword with her right hand, prepared to draw it.

"Highwaymen!" Deofoyl snapped.

"Everybody out!" a voice yelled.

"Let's see what they want," the Vice-Chancellor said, placing his hand over Elisabeth's to block her draw.

Deofoyl threw back the flap, and they descended to the road. The driver sat with his hands in the air, an arrow stuck in the wood beside him. Four men stood in a semi-circle in front of the door, swords drawn. Their greasy hair belied their mismatched fine clothing. Aura surmised that these men hailed from Kelton, but preferred robbing passersby to trudging through muck after ill-conceived crops.

"Well, well, well. What we got here?" said one with a long beard.

"Looks like a Tang, a lady, and ..." said the second, a short man with a missing ear. He looked at Elisabeth. "Whatever the hell you are."

"I expected a fat merchant. Looks like we got something better. We got girls," the first one said. When Deofoyl took a step forward, the man jerked his thumb toward the trees and snapped, "Don't. I got two archers up there. They'll kill you before you do anything."

"I can't fight this many, especially archers I can't see," Deofoyl muttered, peering into the trees. He raised his hands. With a nod to the first thief, he asked, "What do you want?"

"Smart man. Here's what you do. You give us your gold and silver. Then, you, naked boy, get back in that wagon and get out of here." He looked at Aura and Elisabeth, and licked his lips. "You girls stay with us." The other highwaymen grinned. The first man's eyes looked over Aura from her neck to her feet and back up, until she shivered. "We know how to treat ladies." They laughed.

Aura's stomach tightened. Her emotions began swirling. Sweat beaded on her forehead. She shut her eyes and grimaced. No, not a terror attack, not here, not over that. She drove the memory of finding Ester's dead body from her mind. Feel the air. Feel the ground. Think. she was a wizardess now. Time to act like one. Defend the defenseless.

As Aura struggled to regain control of herself, and before she thought of a course of action, Elisabeth said, "I challenge you men to a duel."

"What?" the first thief asked.

"I will fight all four of you at once. If I win, then the three of us go free and unharmed. If you win, then these two go free and I remain with you. You may have your way with me."

"This is a trick," the second thief said. "She's got a sword."

"Yeah, but she's a girl," the first thief said. He nodded to Elisabeth. "Four against one?"

"That does seem unfair," Elisabeth said. She smiled. "Perhaps I should fight you while wearing a blindfold. That would make us equal."

"Hey!" the second thief snapped.

"Personally, I don't think you know what to do with your swords, so I'm not concerned about you sheathing them inside my body. Oh, did you think I meant the ones in your hands?" The first thief snarled and shook his sword. The Captain grinned. "I've fought women who know how to hold a weapon better than you."

"Bite your tongue, bitch," the man said. "I have twelve kills to my name."

"Is that all? I'm not impressed," Elisabeth said. She sneered at the first thief. "Why don't you run home and let your mother give you a nice spanking before I do."

"Stuff your mouth!" the man yelled.

Elisabeth cocked her head and looked at the man's crotch. She examined him until he turned red. She chuckled. "Now I know why you carry a sword. You need something long. You've been gelded. You don't have anything with which to pierce a woman. No wonder you won't accept my challenge. You're afraid you'll win and have to unlace your trousers." Then, she laughed.

"That's it," the first thief snapped. "I accept!"

"Hey, now," the second thief said.

"I'm the leader," the first thief shouted. "If I say we fight her, we fight her. I want to seed her at least three times."

"Prove to me you have something formidable in your trousers, other than arrogance," Elisabeth said. The insult almost sounded ridiculous, given the number of times she trilled the letter R. The highwaymen did not look amused. She raised her right hand, then lowered it to the hilt of her sword. With deliberate movement, she drew it. Steel rang as it cleared the scabbard. She bowed to the four men, then stepped forward. The thieves circled her like wild dogs around a wounded rabbit. Gripping her weapon in both hands, she raised it until it nearly touched her right shoulder. Spreading her feet, she balanced and prepared.

"What is she doing?" Aura whispered to Deofoyl.

"The Captain is doing what she does best," he answered in a low voice. "She is correct. This is an unequal duel. I've personally seen her fight four ogres at once. Obviously, she was the victor."

The four thieves attacked as one. With a whirl of purple, the Captain turned, knocking aside each sword. She ducked the first and parried the second in one motion. The two behind her lunged forward, and struck at empty air. The fourth thief flew backwards as a boot landed in his stomach, while the second staggered under a countered slash. Elisabeth threw herself to the ground and rolled into a ball as the first and third collided with each other over where she once stood. Jumping up, Elisabeth grinned. The four thieves stood as a wall. They looked at each other, then back at the Captain.

"She's playing with them," Deofoyl whispered to Aura. "If she wanted to kill them, they'd already be dead."

"I thought this was going to be easy," the second thief said to the first.

"That's what happens when boys think," Elisabeth said. "Oh, you can't think. Your stones have been removed."

"Bitch!" the first thief roared. He charged her. She blocked his slash with her sword in one hand, adding insult by covering a yawn with her other. The others dashed in, each taking a different side. With the grace of a dancer, Elisabeth whirled, knocking aside each thrust. The air rang with the sound of steel on steel and shouted oaths. The Captain twirled, ducked, parried, and twirled again, dashing between each of the highwaymen as if she wove a tapestry.

Then, she stood still, facing the men. Her expression turned serious. Again, she wove her way through the highwaymen, but where before she assumed a defensive posture, now she pushed them into the defense. Steel rang louder as the thieves scrambled to block her thrusts and slashes. They failed. With each pass of purple, another lost a piece of his clothing. Gashes appeared across their chests. The third thief's left sleeve dangled around his wrist. The second tripped as his trouser leg fell to his ankle. With an oath, the fourth thief staggered backwards, holding his cheek. Blood flowed between his fingers. The Captain's seriousness just turned deadly.

"I am giving you gentlemen a chance to yield. I suggest you accept it," the Captain said from the whirlwind of purple and steel.

"How can anyone move so fast?" Aura asked.

"Her sword is blessed with a speed charm, not that she needs it. Lady Lovejoy earned her rank with her mind," Deofoyl said.

"Lady," Aura muttered. No noblewoman fought like this, not even the ones who still stood at their husband's side, axe in hand. In one fluid movement, Elisabeth knocked the sword from the second thief's grip, tripped the third with her leg, and punched the fourth in the face, sending him to the ground on his back. That left only the first. He stepped back, giving the impression that he wanted to drop his sword and run.

"That is enough play. I'm hungry and there is no tavern in sight," she said.

The Captain advanced on the retreating man, firm determination in her face. If he did not surrender now, Aura thought the woman would kill him. The second thief stooped to the road. He picked up a rock the size of his fist. Aura opened her mouth to warn the Captain, but before she formed the words, the man hurled the stone toward Elisabeth. It struck her on the back of the head. With a moan, she dropped her sword and fell to her knees.

Aura took a step forward. Deofoyl threw his arm in front of her. He looked at her and said, "This is the Captain's fight. For us to interfere would be dishonorable."

Elisabeth shook her head. Her sword lay three feet away. As she reached for it, the first thief stuck the point of his against her throat.

"I am going to pierce you, bitch!" he snarled. "It's your choice. Steel or flesh."

The Captain looked up the length of his sword to his hand. She slammed her fist into the ground. Fury poured from her eyes, more at herself than at the highwayman pinning her. Through clenched teeth, Elisabeth snarled, "Dammit! I yield."

"A deal is a deal. You two get out of here," the thief said, shaking his head toward Aura and Deofoyl.

"Captain," Deofoyl said.

"Go!" she yelled. Deofoyl threw his hand over his mouth. A tear formed at the edge of his eye. She screamed, "I said, go!"

With sagging shoulders, and a lowered head, Deofoyl turned toward the carriage door. Aura watched his back. Then, she looked at the defeated Captain. All hope fled from the warrior's face, replaced with rage. Aura's stomach tightened again. Three men raped and killed Ester. Six were about to inflict their lust on the fallen woman kneeling on the road. As valiantly as she fought, as tough as she appeared, no woman could survive that. Aura clenched her left hand, feeling the scar. Defend the defenseless. No one was there for Ester. Well, someone was here for Elisabeth Lovejoy.

"Not so fast," Aura said, stepping toward the thieves.

"What?" Deofoyl, Elisabeth, and the first thief said together.

"I want to make my own offer," she said. Aura cocked her hip to the right. She ran her finger from her throat down her cleavage. "Watching this duel aroused me. I am such a lustful woman, and I'm filled to overflowing."

"What are you doing?" Elisabeth yelled.

"Miss Lockhaven, this isn't wise," Deofoyl said.

"I can't help myself," Aura said. She took another step toward the thieves. "My loins are moist. I want you men!"

"I know this is a trick," the second thief said.

"Really, now," Aura said. "There's nothing under this dress except my body. I will stay with you and this woman. The gentleman here can go about his business. Think about it. Six men and one woman? The first two will enjoy themselves. The third will find things a bit messy. I pity the sixth man. Wouldn't you rather have two women?"

"Idiot!" Elisabeth shouted.

"She has a point," the first thief said to the second. "This one's mine. You can have the redhead. Her eyes look like snakes."

"It ain't her eyes I'm going to fuck," the second thief said, grinning.

"I like her tits better," the third highwayman said.

"It's been so long since I've been with a real man, and I can tell you are real men," Aura said, putting as much seductive purr into her voice as she could. "Why don't you take me out of this dress and see the goods for yourselves?"

The second and third thief grinned. They walked toward Aura. Her head spun and her mouth dried up. This was stupid! The spell required her to touch the victim on the face. What if they grabbed her hands? Ester's limp body appeared before her eyes. Remember the incantation. Just remember the words. The men approached side by side. She could tell they wanted to rip the dress from her and throw her to the ground. Her knees quaked. She wanted to vomit. Just another foot. She swallowed the whimper rising in her throat. They stood in front of her, their eyes locked on her breasts.

Reaching up, Aura caressed the men's cheeks. In a voice too dry and full of stammer, she said, "Oh, aren't you two handsome?" Then, with her fingers lingering on their chins, she said, "Batis upnota."

The men's eyes rolled up. They crumpled to the ground. Aura dropped to her knee and reached forward, her palms extended. She shouted, "Agis aspidar!" Blue light erupted from her hands. Putting her entire will behind the shield spell, she pushed it beyond anything she had ever cast. It extended into a plane, covering the carriage, Deofoyl, and the Captain. Just as it reached its full width, two arrows flew from the trees. They struck the shield and fell to the ground.

"Tenthatora!" Deofoyl yelled, aiming his own palm toward the fourth thief. A bubble of air shot from his hand. The throwback spell struck the thief on the chest, sending him flying. The first highwayman looked at Aura, Elisabeth, Deofoyl, and his fallen comrades in total disbelief.

Deofoyl dashed to Aura's side. "Excellent shield, Miss Lockhaven. Thank you. I know where the archers are now. Because of your actions, this is now our fight, and all is fair." He aimed his palms toward the treetops and said, "Lower the shield!" Aura closed her fists. The shield vanished. As it did, Deofoyl fired two throwback spells into the branches, and the archers plummeted to the road.

He stormed toward the remaining highwayman, his hands stretched out. "Drop your sword," he commanded.

The thief obeyed. "You coulda told me you was wizards," he said.

Deofoyl snorted. He said, "When your friends awaken, I suggest you find a new line of work, such as milking cows. Do you understand?" The thief nodded.

Elisabeth reached for her sword. Holding it, she began to stand. Aura held out her hand. The Captain looked up, her face full of awe and gratitude. She grabbed Aura by the wrist. They walked in silence to the carriage.

Once Aura settled into her seat, Deofoyl shouted to the driver. The carriage lurched forward and within moments gained full speed. Then, Aura collapsed against the wall, shaking. All the fear she bottled inside herself poured out. Tears streamed down her face. What if those men had grabbed her hands? They could have torn the dress from her. They could have ... they would have ... Closing her eyes, she saw Ester laying on the kitchen table as the village women prepared her for burial. That long swallowed whimper crept from her lips.

"Oh, merciful heavens! I've never been so terrified in my life," she muttered.

"That was outstanding, Miss Lockhaven," Deofoyl said. "Appealing to the lust of foolish men to remove two from the fight, then using a defensive dueling spell. You knew the archers would shoot at you, didn't you. Sagacius would be proud of you."

"That was a courageous act," Elisabeth said.

"Courageous! Look at me." She held up her trembling hands. "I'm treacle."

"Courage is doing what you must, even when you are emptying your bladder and bowels all over yourself. I saw courage worthy of the Watchers," the Captain said, smiling.

Aura managed her own smile. She pulled the kerchief from her sleeve and wiped her face. "Thank you."

"No," Elisabeth said. "Thank you." Her expression of gratitude slowly changed to one of curiosity. She cocked her head and stared at Aura. "Aura Lockhaven. Aura Lockhaven. That name is familiar. You are so tall." Her eyes flew open. "Lockhaven! Are you descended from *him*?"

Aura could not help but grin. Whenever anyone mentioned her ancestor, he or she always added a note of reverence to the word him. "Yes. The Locchaefen was my great-grandfather's great-grandfather's grandfather."

Elisabeth lost all expression except that of sheer worship. "That explains your courage. We have a statue to him on the green of Colebury. He saved the city from sack by Skols. They say he was eight feet tall."

Aura laughed. She had heard those songs, and he grew taller with every new one. "Not quite. From what Daddy told me, he was six feet eight inches tall. I guess that does qualify him as a giant."

"They say the Locchaefen's axe was the size of a tree."

"It hangs in my uncle's tavern," Aura said. She paused. She actually said that with no rancor. "Daddy measured it once. It's four feet long and two feet across the blades. It's big enough."

"They say his mother was a goddess and his father was a dragon."

"That's a new one. Where do those tales begin?" Aura asked. "Really now, do I look like I'm part dragon? My skin is oily, not scaly. I'm sorry to disappoint you, Captain."

"Please," she said. "Call me Elisabeth."

"Ah," Deofoyl said. "It looks like you've made a friend, Miss Lockhaven. Not even I address the Captain by her given name."

Through the open window of the carriage, Aura heard a whitelark sing.

Chapter Ten

THE RIVER PHANT cut Owynn's Vale in half. One hundred yards of pools and thick grass extended from the banks of the clear, rushing river, to the steep slopes of stony hills on either side. The Fingers, tall columns of grayed pink granite, jutted from the hills to the south, while the Giant's Testicles, a pair of boulders the size of tithe barns, dominated the northern side. Everywhere, especially in the expanse of the vale between the river and the northern hills, lay granite stones between the size of a pumpkin and that of a cow. The river flowed almost perfectly straight down the vale, tumbling over steps carved from rock and worn smooth by centuries of water, until it entered a wide arch set low in the castle walls. It did not reappear in the plain on the other side.

Aura could not believe she stood on the parapets of Ralthangarle, looking out on the legendary vale. She heard about this aging fortress all her life, the site of Prince Owynn's twenty year rebellion against his father, Trahern the Traitor, and his brother-in-law, the Emperor of Bellicia. Ralthangarle never fell to an enemy. It did, however, succumb to age. Most of the walls stood ragged, their uppermost parts toppled onto the stone floor or out onto the vale. The collapsed southern tower showed signs of quarrying, probably to build houses in nearby Castlebury. The gates and portcullis vanished long ago. If the old Geilltian form of Tangoi was anything similar to modern Coadic or Garranic, then 1,000 years ago, Ralthangarle may have been pronounced Ralta Tangar, which Aura roughly translated as the Fist of the People. Leave it to 650 years of Ayrdish occupation and the peculiarities of their tongue to ram the two words together and drawl the last syllable.

Aura and Elisabeth stood side by side at the edge of the round eastern wall, overlooking the river. The sun setting behind them cast the shadow of the castle down the vale, and the clouds overhead erupted in red, salmon, and yellow. Deofoyl sat on a square stone fallen from the mostly still intact northern tower, reading a chart and checking the sky. Pedyr the castellan, and Mark the carriage driver, rested against the western parapet, chatting about the fight with the highwaymen. With not a tree in sight, and the hills forming a funnel, the wind blasted down the vale straight at the castle. All five fought to keep their hair out of their faces. A flock of cranes, taking advantage of the wind, passed just overhead.

"The Bellician Empire threw four full legions away attacking Ralthangarle," Elisabeth said. "It's a wonder the Empire lived as long as it did, considering it did not learn from one, much less three, attempts to take this castle. The lay of the land forced the Imperials to march down the vale, in a full frontal assault. They always divided their troops to each side of the Phant. Crown Prince Owynn simply waited behind these walls, letting the wet terrain turn the enemy's march into a slogging crawl." She pointed to her left, to the high bluffs and the Giant's Testicles. "Battle Prince Marwynn stood up there, with his catapults. The back of the hills is made inaccessible by the Cliffs of Wrey. Marwynn destroyed the northern flanks. Many of the boulders on that side of the river were launched by his artillery." She pointed to her right, toward the Fingers. "Night Prince Alynn stood there, with Dark Princess Fayella and their apprentices. They rained incendiary spells down on the southern flanks. If the Bellicians didn't burn to death, they roasted in their armor. The survivors marched straight into the awaiting arrows of Owynn's archers." She nodded toward the river. "This is sacred ground. For twenty years, the Sons of Trahern flew the flag of freedom over these walls and died for that flag. Their blood is in that soil and in these stones." Stooping, Elisabeth grabbed a handful of loose pebbles and dirt. She held it up, letting it drift from her fingers into the wind. It flew out onto the old battlefield. "May your gods have mercy on your souls, and may you find laughter in the halls of honor," she said.

"You like battle, don't you?" Aura asked.

"I appreciate valor," Elisabeth said. "What is more valorous than fighting to free your people from the grip of tyranny? In Owynn's case, the tyrant was his brother-in-law."

"In your case?"

Elisabeth smiled. "I don't know you well enough to tell you." She put her hand on Aura's shoulder. "Perhaps, when I've repaid my debt to you, I'll tell you."

"I hope you never have to repay that debt!" Aura gulped at the thought of lying on the ground as a man knelt between her legs, ripping her dress apart. If anyone had to save her from such a fate, she preferred that someone be as fast and deadly as the Captain.

Deofoyl rolled up his chart and stuffed it into the bag at his feet. Standing, he said, "Well, Miss Lockhaven. The moon rises in three hours. We have some time, so how about some supper?"

"Where do we go after moonrise?" Aura asked, stepping away from the wall.

Deofoyl walked to the western wall of the castle. He spread his arms wide and said, "Into the Valley of the Mystic Moon!"

Aura looked toward the sun, halfway behind the curve of the horizon. A vast field of heather and lupines stretched before her, extending to the sun and beyond. The hills of the vale continued some distance, growing shorter and shorter until they appeared as no more than rocks vanishing into the heather. She cleared her throat, and said, "I hate to tell you this, Lord Ashthorne. That isn't a valley. It's a grassy plain."

Deofoyl chuckled. "You expected a magical valley to be visible to the naked eye? That grassy plain as you called it is a barrier spell so thick that people walk across it all the time, never knowing that one thousand feet below lies the most beautiful place in all of Ayrdland. In fact, over the years, the barrier has gained some topsoil and grown real grass. Shepherds graze their flocks on it. As residents of the Valley and members of the order, the Captain and I may enter at any time. You, however, are a guest, and may only enter by moonlight and in the company of a member."

"That barrier is about as solid as stale lard," Elisabeth growled. "It seems that anything with a will gets through it. Gwendolyn and I both found a way through it, without anyone accompanying us, and Akabara literally fell through it. I don't need to remind you of all the ogres, wyverns, vampires, shape shifters, and trolls."

Aura snickered. "Trolls only exist in tales told by big brothers to frighten little sisters," she said.

Elisabeth cast her a cold look and said, "I hope your naiveté is never shattered."

"We've done what we can, Captain," Deofoyl said. "The only things permitted through the barrier spells beneath the castle are water and fish. If an ogre can transform into a trout, I'm not sure what to suggest to the council."

Pedyr brought a basket from the north tower. On one of the square cut stones, he sat five crusty baker's rolls, eight boar and thyme sausages, a chunk of Ayrdish cheddar, five early peaches, and two flagons of wine that he swore was at least five years old. It wasn't, as their puckers attested. They drank it anyway. As the five ate, Deofoyl explained some of the history of Ralthangarle and the Valley of the Mystic Moon.

No one remembered when the castle was first built, but it was the seat of the crown prince by the time of Owynn's birth. When Trahern sold the island of Geilltia to the Bellician Empire, Owynn used the castle as his capital, rallying the south to him against the imperial minded north. He borrowed Bellicia's own designs and rebuilt Ralthangarle as a fortress. At the time Prince Owynn lived, the Valley was visible from the castle walls. Then, the castle backed up to a one thousand foot cliff that dropped into a canyon of barren rock three miles wide and ten miles long. No one knew why the original builders constructed the castle over a point where the River Phant flowed underground, but it made the fortress impregnable. The only way to reach the castle was from the east, down the vale, through a gauntlet of horror.

Vancinus the Younger wrote about the area after Owynn died, describing the western terrain as an inhospitable gorge that grew only stones, with a waterfall erupting from the canyon walls, flowing the length of the canyon, then disappearing underground again. The order's barrier spell presented a problem for anyone looking for Vancinus' canyon. Fortunately, Vancinus was notorious for exaggeration, and many Ayrdishmen couldn't read.

While the castle fell into disrepair, it grew in the estimation of newcomers. Taking advantage of the vacuum formed by the collapse of the Bellician Empire, the Ayrds invaded the island. Hating the Geilltian imperialists almost as much as the Tangoi on the other islands, they raised Prince Owynn to the status of a hero. He may have been astonished to learn that Nebelish invaders took him as their inspiration. After five years, Albert the Short defeated the last Geilltian Chieftain, and signed the peace treaty at Ralthangarle. When he left the ruins, the island of Geilltia became Ayrdland, and Albert its first king.

"It's possible Albert and Sonidar signed the treaty on this very stone," Deofoyl said, waving to the remains of their supper. "As an Ayrdishman, I wish my country folk had a consciousness of their own history."

The sun since set, and the stars emerging in the cold blue sky, they sat around the stone by lantern light. Aura looked at the "Valley." She cast numerous barrier spells herself. They were one of the first things apprentices learned. She always saw through hers. This one defied all her training and belief. Not only was it impenetrable to her vision, but it covered thirty square miles. If the emotional power of one woman healed a child nearly cut in half, then the combined feelings of an entire order could perhaps change the landscape, at least through solid illusion.

"Well, enough dry old tales," Deofoyl said. "Now, Miss Lockhaven, am I correct in assuming your favorite color is red, your favorite animal is a cat, you prefer gold to silver, and oak to ash?"

"How did you –" Aura began.

"For the past four days, I've listened to your every word," Deofoyl said, grinning. "I needed the information so our people could get to work. The order is going to bestow four gifts on you. Three of them are being crafted at this very moment. We are going to give you a ring, a staff, and a cloak. Oh, don't worry. Feel no obligation. If you accept our offer, then they will serve as your emblems of office. If not, consider them as gifts from friends. The fourth is in here," he said, opening his bag. "Somewhere. I know I have it. Aha!" He pulled out a small silk purse, and handed it to Aura. "King Edgar's coin is only good in his realm. In ours, you will need the contents of that purse. No doubt, you will wish to purchase something, if nothing other than our fine cheeses."

Aura opened the purse and held it so the light of the lantern next to her shone into it. She counted five gold pieces, stamped with a woman's face and the word Cygfran. So that's what the goddess queen looked like. The purse also contained ten silver pieces, with the image of Ystlena on them. Finally, she counted fifty copper pieces, with another woman's face, and the name Damaskarose.

"Who is Damaskarose?" Aura asked, holding up one of the copper coins.

"Princess Fayella founded the enchanters, but Damaskarose turned us into a formal order," Deofoyl said. "She was our first Chancellor, and our most powerful member. She created the Valley of the Mystic Moon, turning Vancinus' barren canyon into our home. Sagacius never mentioned her to you?"

"Not that I recall," Aura said.

Deofoyl looked off into the distance. He stroked his beard and frowned. "Now, that man is peculiar. I would have thought he would mention her almost every day." He looked at Aura with an expression of awe. "Damaskarose was Sagacius' teacher. She was also his mother."

Chapter Eleven

THE FULL MOON rose over the end of the vale, transforming the River Phant into a ribbon of quicksilver. Aura felt a note of expectation as she watched the pearl rise in the sky to its throne overhead. No doubt the fabled Sons of Trahern, and the Princess Fayella, saw a similar moon centuries earlier, as they stood on the same walls, looking down the length of Owynn's Vale. She nodded to the moon, and said a prayer of grace to Cygfran. Deofoyl joined her at the wall.

"The castle serves as our carriage house, and as our eastern gate," he said. "Pedyr protects it from nosybodies. Most people of Castlebury call Pedyr the ghast of Ralthangarle. He does enjoy his job." Pedyr overheard Deofoyl and laughed. "From here, we walk. Well, Miss Lockhaven. It is time. Are you ready?"

Aura thought about her life up to that moment. The sudden twists and bends in her path led her to stand on a crumbling legend, about to enter another. At age eight, she thought she would always be her father and sister's little shadow, the pest of Hartshorn. Children that young never thought about tomorrow. At age eleven, her world consisted of neverending rain, stench, and spiders. Tomorrow only held more of the same for her. At seventeen, she faced one chore after another and a perpetual onslaught of lessons. She was just too busy to consider anything other than the moment before her. Now, she tingled with anticipation of the next minute, the next hour, the next day.

Moments like these, when unsure girls traveled with warriors and powerful magicians, and stepped into magical realms, only happened in tales. She stood on top of one of the most mythical spots in Ayrdland. Next to her, stood a woman who stepped out of her father's tales of adventure in faraway lands. On her other side stood a man who led a mysterious magical order. While nearly every town had its wizard and every village its witch,

Aura never expected to meet one, much less be taught by one. Yet, she had been. Now, she herself would take his place as the town wizard. The wind blew her hair and dress behind her, as if she belonged to a tale. This was the stuff of stories, not the life of a tavern owner's daughter. Aura tugged on her sleeve, scuffed her sole on the stone, and caressed her face. She was awake and everything felt real.

"I've been ready my whole life," Aura said. "I just never knew it until now."

She turned around to see Elisabeth holding two lit torches. The Captain handed one to Deofoyl, who said, "Then, Miss Lockhaven, follow me."

Aura followed Deofoyl into the doorless entry of the northern tower, with Elisabeth behind her. They crossed a wide, empty chamber, to a wooden door. Even in the torchlight, the planks looked gray with age, the studs and hinges dull red. Elisabeth held Deofoyl's torch as the Vice-Chancellor threw his weight into the wood. With creaks of protest, the rust-caked iron hinges gave way, and the door opened enough to allow the three to enter the stairwell beyond.

"The stairs are more sturdy than they appear," Deofoyl said, entering the stairwell. "One of Pedyr's tasks is to keep them in repair. Another of his tasks is to keep that door from opening with any ease." He rubbed his shoulder and said, "Some days, I think Pedyr takes his assignment too seriously."

The stairs, a constant spiral of creaking wood, descended down a stone shaft. Moss clung to the stone walls, and tags of dried resin hung from the treads overhead. Yellow light from the torches flickered on the moss. Aura grimaced at the close, dank air. Every twenty feet, they reached a landing marked by another grayed wooden door with rusted hinges and studs. Something brushed against Aura's face. She lurched to her right. The wispy broken threads of a spiderweb danced in the air. Before Aura could whimper, she felt a feathery movement on her cheek.

"Get it off!" she screamed.

Flailing, she banged her hip against the stair railing. The wall before her tilted back and became the high, dark arch of the ceiling overhead. She felt nothing beneath her feet, and only the rail under her hip. That did not bother her. The scramble of the feet on her face did.

"Get it off!" she screamed louder as she felt the rail slip from beneath her.

Her eyes shut tight, Aura shrieked and slapped the air as she began falling. She barely felt the hand on her wrist, or the sudden tug pulling her back onto the stairs. She sank to her knees and screamed louder. Thousands of feet covered her face and her body. They rooted through her tangled muddy hair. They worked their way under her tattered, too-small blue dress. They bit her on the cheek, on the stomach, on the breasts.

"Get it off," she sobbed as tears gushed from her closed eyes.

Elisabeth jerked the cellar spider from Aura's face, and flung it out into the void of the stairwell.

"Captain, that was a living creature," Deofoyl said.

"It was an enemy," Elisabeth snarled.

Aura flung her arms around Elisabeth's legs and pressed herself close to the Captain. She breathed in heavy gasps as the terror attack subsided, keeping her eyes shut for fear of opening them, only to see a spider in its web inches from her nose.

"So ... much ... for ... my ... courage ..." she said through clenched teeth.

"We all have our fears," Elisabeth said.

Aura opened her eyes and released Elisabeth. Wiping the tears from her face with her kerchief, she said, "I think you've repaid me."

Elisabeth smiled. As she helped Aura to her feet, she said, "One spider hardly equals six rapists, Aura."

"It wasn't on *your* face!"

They continued their descent, but in a different pattern. Deofoyl held his torch higher, to illuminate any further spiderwebs. There were plenty. Elisabeth walked next to Aura, between her and the wall. Nearly every twelve feet, she thrust her torch into a web to either drive the spider back against the wall, or kill it outright.

Aura counted two hundred steps, and almost as many whimpers, before they stood on solid stone. This time, the door opened without even a squeak, and they entered a round room. Sixteen niches lined the walls. In each niche sat the crumbled remains of a wooden statue, long since reduced beyond human form by beetles, worms, and mites. Aura thought this must be the castle's chapel, Owynn's shrine to the Gweryn. An emblem of the sun marked the floor on the left, standing for the Dyddau, the children of Day and the gods of forests, while a crescent moon graced the floor on the right for the Tywelch, the children of Night and the gods of magic.

Beyond the chapel, they entered a wide chamber. Twenty pillars soared up into darkness. The flickering torchlight hinted at the vaulted ceilings overhead. To the left, twin doors led to the outer chamber. To the right, ten steps ascended to a platform, and a stone chair. Moonlight drifted through the windows at the top of the room, striking the chair and filling the empty chamber once again with the feeling of hope and magic.

"Owynn's throne," Aura whispered, as if even that defiled the sanctity of the chamber.

For a moment, the darkness lifted. Once again, the chamber filled with the light of chandeliers overhead and candelabras set against the walls and torches in sconces. The stillness crumbled under music as a fiddler, lutenist, and flautist tried to lift the spirits in the castle. The pillars and vaults echoed with the tromps of boots and the rattling of armor from dozens of warriors coming and going. Owynn, proud and defiant, issued orders from his throne. Glowering next to him, the Battle Prince relayed those orders, turning them into solemn commands to his captains. On the other side of the throne, the mysterious Night Prince conferred with the Dark Princess, scheming another sorcerous way to confound the imperial forces approaching from the east. Aura always imagined Princess Fayella as an adult, but in this fleeting vision, she was a mere girl, no older than she herself that late autumn day when Sagacius found her begging in the street of Hartshorn.

Deofoyl turned toward the throne. Once again, stillness became the music of the chamber, antiquity its monarch, and dust its numerous warriors. The slaps of leather soles against stone echoed in the chamber as Deofoyl led Aura and Elisabeth up the stairs to the throne. Pausing at the chair, he placed his hand on the horn of the unicorn decoration at the top.

"It is said that Fayella built this as an escape route when she led the rebellion. We've added some improvements," he said. Twisting the horn, he said, "Iortha."

With the scrape of stone against stone, the throne slid to one side, revealing another staircase beneath it. Without a word to either woman, Deofoyl stepped into the hole and descended into the darkness. Aura followed, down into a small chamber fifteen feet square. The tallest in the group, Aura's hair brushed the roof. She glanced around, scanning for spider webs, only breathing when she saw none. Once Elisabeth joined them, the throne slid back into place.

"Behind us lie the ruins of Ralthangarle," Deofoyl said to Aura. "Anyone can walk about them, provided they get past Pedyr. From here, the route is secret, and extremely dangerous. Stay close to the Captain and myself." He turned to the wall closest to him, examining it with his torch. He frowned. "I need to leave the Valley more often than I do. I'm having trouble locating the door latch."

"Allow me, sir," Elisabeth said. She reached past him and pressed against a stone three feet from the floor. The stone slid into the wall. As it did, a section of wall to Aura's left opened, revealing a room beyond.

"How did you find it?" Deofoyl asked Elisabeth.

"It's the only stone that isn't covered in dust," the Captain answered.

Aura followed Deofoyl into the next chamber. As Elisabeth entered behind her, the light of her torch struck a figure against the wall to Aura's right. She turned toward it, and shrieked. The corpse of a man lay fastened to the wall by thick chains. Alive, he must have stood over seven feet tall.

Even shrunken by time, his arms looked bigger around than Aura's legs. Dried flesh clung to his face, contorted into a scream of rage. The empty eye sockets poured fury toward her. A long, black ponytail, still braided, draped over his right shoulder. A hole gaped where his heart should have been.

Elisabeth swung her torch toward the figure and said, "How dare you startle this lady, you cad!"

"Who is that?" Aura asked.

"He was an ogre, until Titania skewered him," Elisabeth said. "We saw no point in wasting his carcass." She chuckled. "He seems to be having the desired effect."

The chamber led to another stairwell. Instead of using cut stone and wood, the builders carved this one into the granite itself. They descended twenty feet. Then, the light of Deofoyl's torch vanished. He stopped as the stairs ended into nothing. Only darkness appeared before him. Aura looked over his shoulder, trying to see anything beyond him.

"What do we do now?" Aura asked.

"We jump," Deofoyl said. He leapt into the chasm, and vanished.

Before Aura could say anything, Elisabeth threw her arm around her waist. Pulling her tight against her own body, the Captain jumped into the darkness. Aura began to scream, then her feet struck solid stone. She stood in another room, a rough square cut into the rock. Smirking, Elisabeth released her. Stunned, Aura looked around. The jagged staircase stood at eye level.

"An illusion," Deofoyl said. "Again, it would appear to be effective."

"You could have warned me," Aura mumbled.

"Would that have been as much fun? Now, don't move."

Flames shot from the walls on both sides. Aura flinched, but refused to duck or even scream. The fire licked her clothes. She felt no heat and smelled no smoke. Holding her hand out, she let the cold flames dance around her fingers.

"Another illusion?" she asked.

"You learn quickly," Deofoyl said. "This one could kill, if you responded as if it were real."

The flames died to nothing. Deofoyl turned to a wooden door set in the wall opposite the stairs. Opening the door, he held up his hand to block Aura and Elisabeth. He nodded, counting one, two, three, four, five ... A triple scythe swung from a pivot, arching across the room just beyond the door. It struck a bale of hay tied to the wall.

"Some things are not illusions," he said. "Captain, remind me to ask Pedyr to oil that trap. It's supposed to swing on a count of three."

The new chamber was a long corridor of cut stone, illuminated by pumpkin sized crystals set in sconces. The crystals cast cold yellow light down onto the dark floor. Between each sconce stood a white marble statue, twelve on each side. Each featured a man in full armor, holding a three foot sword to his chest. Intriguing, Aura thought, wondering who the statues represented. As they proceeded into the corridor, Aura saw a motion out of the corner of her eye. She turned to look. The third statue on her right turned its head to follow her.

Aura gasped. She stepped out of line and approached the statue. It raised its free hand and rubbed its chin. The statue cocked its head, as if pondering her the way she pondered it. Rubbing the hump in her nose, she took two more steps toward the statue. The statue placed its free hand on its hip, gazing down at her with what looked like curiosity on its stone face.

"Miss Lockhaven, stay where you are," Deofoyl said in a low voice.

The statue bent down, gazing at her with marble eyes. It blinked. When it did, Aura instinctively raised her right hand.

"Miss Lockhaven, no!" Deofoyl shouted.

The statue leapt from its pedestal. The floor shook as it landed on the stones. Before Aura could move, it raised its sword as if to strike. Aura prepared her throwback spell as the sword swung down. Steel met stone as Elisabeth stepped between them, blocking the statue's swing with her blade.

"We're in trouble now," Elisabeth said. She thrust her torch to Aura. "Take this. I need both hands."

Five statues stepped down from their pedestals. Aura did not need to turn around to know that others had done the same. The statues advanced, swords ready. Elisabeth flung herself in front of Aura, pressing the wizardess backwards, and away from the marble threats. Aura raised both hands. Deofoyl threw his arm across hers and lowered her hands toward the floor.

He said, "Whatever you do, do not use magic!"

"What do we do, then?" she asked.

"We run!"

Deofoyl grabbed her hand and pulled her toward the wall at the end of the corridor. Elisabeth ran behind them, turned to face the approaching statues. They reached the wall. All Aura saw was two of the sconces, set close together. The statues formed a semi-circle of death, and walked toward them as if time had no meaning.

Deofoyl grabbed both sconces. He shouted over his shoulder, "Captain! Keep them at bay while I open the door."

"Keep them at bay? I've never fought one, much less all twenty-four of these things. How do you expect me to keep them at bay?"

"Weren't you promoted to captain for your ability to improvise?" Deofoyl asked, putting all his weight into pulling down on the sconces.

"That was against ogres!" Elisabeth snapped. "May I remind you that steel is useless against charmed marble."

The sconces moved far too slowly for Aura's tastes. With each inch the sconces swung down, the statues took another step forward. If they could breathe, Aura thought she would feel their cold breath on her face. A part of the wall opened outward. Deofoyl grabbed Aura's hand and pulled her through the opening, with Elisabeth right behind them. The statues stopped their advance. The trio now stood in a room of utter darkness.

"I'm sorry, Lord Ashthorne. I think I did something wrong," Aura said.

"No, it is I who should apologize," he replied. "I should have explained that chamber when we entered it. The statues respond to your feelings. As long as you were merely curious, they were merely curious. The moment you became hostile, even in self defense, they became hostile. You should see how they respond to avarice and hate."

"No, she shouldn't," Elisabeth said. "It took Squad Two a full day to clean up that mess. Now, sir, at the risk of being impudent, please explain this chamber to her."

"Yes, you're right, Captain," Deofoyl said. He gulped. "This is a long corridor. It is the most foul of our various traps."

"I despise this chamber!" Elisabeth mumbled.

"In this chamber, you will see all your greatest fears unfold before your eyes. It is critical that you do not become separated from either of us. Always move forward. Do not try to run from what you see. That will only cause you to become engulfed by it and be lost to us. Men go mad in this room, if they live."

Aura swallowed. She knew her fears. They plagued her dreams. They crept from their closets in her soul from time to time. Deofoyl and Elisabeth saw one on the stairs with a mere spider. They almost saw another in her duel with the highwaymen. They did not need to see the others. Neither did she. Yet, to enter the Valley, she had to cross this room, and face whatever it held.

"I'm ready," she said.

Elisabeth said, "Like I said, you have courage."

Deofoyl took Aura by her left wrist. Elisabeth sheathed her sword, and took the torch from Aura. Holding it in her right hand, she took Aura's wrist with her left. With another gulp, Deofoyl started walking forward, into the dark. This was not so terrible, Aura thought. She had no fear of the dark. Often, she sat in the stone circle on moonless nights just to watch the stars.

A motion stirred to her left. Another statue? She turned to look. At the edge of the torchlight, she saw what looked like a severed hand. It moved. Then, she noticed that it did not have five digits, but eight. A spider! So, her first fear was spiders. She almost smirked. One spider, at that distance, presented no problem.

Two more spiders crawled into the light. Followed by two more. Then, a dozen. Aura gasped, and turned her head. More awaited to her right. As they walked forward, the torchlight fell upon more and more spiders. All types of spiders. Big green raft spiders. Brown hairy wolf spiders. Wispy cellar spiders. Quick jumping spiders. Spiders whose names she did not know, and had no wish to learn. As one, the spiders all began crawling toward Aura.

"No, no, no!" Aura shrieked. "Keep them away from me!"

"They aren't real, Miss Lockhaven," Deofoyl said. "Only manifestations of your fear. So is that! I'll see to you later, you fiend!"

"Damnation," Aura heard Elisabeth mutter behind her.

"I already killed you!" Deofoyl shouted.

"Get your hands off me," Elisabeth snapped.

The spiders faded, leaving only the light of the torches. Aura sighed. Real or not, that was too disturbing. The trio walked three more yards, then an image came into view on her right. She saw herself, as she was that moment, except her dress was red. She wore a long red cloak. Aura cocked her head to one side. Why should she fear herself as a wizardess? Then, she noticed that her image stood against a stake, bound to it by thick iron chains. Before her was a house. Aura smiled. She knew that house, with its red door and cheerful windows. It had been her home until the night of the fire. The door opened, and she saw her father. She almost called out "Daddy," but the house erupted in flames at that moment. A burning beam fell. Her father crumpled underneath it. Aura watched as her image struggled against the chains, but could not move. The flames engulfed her father as the wizardess at the stake screamed.

Aura knew what that image meant. She feared failure. She feared that despite all her training and knowledge and power, she would fail when someone needed her most. Clenching her left hand, she felt the stiffness of her scar. The Order of Enchanters held out hope that she could avoid seeing this image become reality. Whatever they offered, she vowed to learn it.

Turning her head from the flames, Aura saw a table to her left. On the table, she saw herself. She was naked and spreadeagled, her ankles and wrists bound to the corners by thick rope. A gag had been stuffed in her mouth. Six naked men stood around her, their intentions at the ready.

Aura inhaled a sharp breath. No, she thought. Not this. As she watched, she felt, on her own body, their hands groping her hips and breasts. She tried to squirm away from their touch. Elisabeth and Deofoyl tightened their grip on her wrists. No, she thought as one man climbed onto the table.

"No! Please get him off me! No!" Aura shrieked. Her shriek turned into a scream as she felt the violation in her own body. She felt the slap across her face. She felt the rip of her womanhood and the shredding of her soul with each thrust, as if what she watched happened to her where she stood. "Someone help me!"

"It isn't real, Aura," Elisabeth said behind her, in a shaking voice. "It isn't real."

"I will not succumb to you!" Deofoyl roared. "I will not become like you!"

"No, please don't let him seed me!" As Aura felt the rush of the man's lust erupting inside her body, she threw all her terror and rage into a scream. For a moment, the corridor turned white as searing light of all colors exploded around the trio. The darkness fled before it, as the light engulfed the table, the men, and the helpless woman.

"Dear mother of the goddess," Deofoyl said. "What was that light? That was no fear of mine."

"I saw it, too, sir," Elisabeth said. "My fear vanished. I was watching Titania and Osthryth being disemboweled. Now, I see only the two of you."

Aura heaved. She struggled against Deofoyl and Elisabeth's hands. She had to save herself, to get away from the next man who climbed upon the table. She opened her eyes, and saw only the faces of Deofoyl and Elisabeth in the light of their torches. Aura's groans turned into a sigh. It was over. The feeling between her legs faded.

They continued in darkness broken by torchlight, and silence broken by their footfall. The torchlight expanded, to show a chair. In the chair, Aura saw herself again. This time, she was clothed, but looked enormous. She was pregnant and ready to deliver. In her arms, she held a girl of about seven years of age. A boy of nine, sat at her feet.

"That will never happen," Aura said through clenched teeth. "I know potions to prevent that!"

"Just keep walking, Aura. You're doing fine," Elisabeth said behind her. The Captain did not sound fine herself.

As she watched, her image grimaced. Then, she dropped the child she held, doubling over in agony. The image screamed. Aura felt the pain within her own abdomen. It felt like a knife thrust into her gut.

"Mom," Aura whispered.

Aura gasped. She knew she did not much care for children. The taunts of those her own age still rang in her ears. She had also assisted the midwife on far too many occasions to ever want the agonies of childbirth herself. To know that she feared childbirth and children, however, was knew to her. She feared it because her mother died during it?

As she watched, the woman crumpled to the floor. She no longer looked pregnant. Another child entered the image, one Aura knew well. Herself. The child looked down at the woman. The child smiled. The child held a bloodied knife. Blood appeared on the woman's abdomen, and spread out, soaking the dress she wore.

"No!" Aura shrieked. "I did not kill my mother!"

Aura once asked her father if she had killed her mother. Henry Lockhaven held her close, and said, no. Aura asked if he hated her for the choice her mother made. Henry held her even closer and told her that

Aurora gave her life, and that choice made her more precious to him. She could not, however, deny the image before her. If she had not been conceived, then Aurora would not have had to choose between her own life and that of her child. Aurora Nightshade Lockhaven would still be alive.

"Mom," Aura said as tears poured down her face. "Mom. Please forgive me. I am so sorry."

"Miss Lockhaven, just keep walking," Deofoyl said, his voice trembling.

The image faded, leaving only darkness and torchlight. Aura breathed a sigh of relief, one that came with sobs and choked air. First, spiders. Then, failure. Then, rape. Now, fear that she killed her mother. What next? As if to answer, the light of the torches vanished. Aura froze as she felt Deofoyl and Elisabeth release her wrists.

"You let go of me," Aura said.

"No, we still have you," Deofoyl said. "At least I do."

"So do I," Elisabeth said.

Aura could not hear them. She heard nothing but her own breath. Raising her hands to her face, she saw nothing. She reached out to where Elisabeth ought to stand, and felt only cold air. She took three steps forward, expecting to bump into Deofoyl. Nothing.

"Don't you dare leave me here!" Aura snapped.

"She broke out of my grasp," Deofoyl shouted.

"I have her," Elisabeth said.

"Lord Ashthorne?" Aura called. Silence answered her. "Elisabeth?" Nothing.

Aura knelt, trying to feel the floor. Something supported her feet, but she could not find it. She gasped. She was alone.

"Please don't leave me," Aura whimpered.

When she lived in the barrel behind Ortha's bakery, at least she had that barrel. She also had the many folk who tried to help her, despite her uncle's threats. She also had Fulbert. Even though he slapped her and looked at her with lust filled eyes, he was something solid. Now, she had only black.

Aura leapt upright and roared, "Don't leave me! I can't bear being alone! You don't know what that's like. This isn't funny. You don't know what it's like not to have anyone in this whole world. Please don't do this to me."

Running forward, in the direction she thought Deofoyl took, she waved her arms, trying to touch the walls. To touch anything. Something solid. Something to remind her that she was not alone. When that failed, she ran the other direction. The blackness covered her. It smothered her. It felt like a clinging, wet cloak, one alive that crawled over her body and down her throat. Where was that place where she lay with the children? Those children were people. Where did those men rape her? They were people. Where were those spiders? They were creatures of some variety. Any of them could comfort her. If those men wished to seed her, she would give them her body with joy. Anything just to hear a voice, see a face, and feel a touch.

A voice? She thought some woman said, "Sir, she's like a madwoman. I need to hold her with both arms. I have to drop my torch."

Aura thought she heard a response say, "Do it!"

"She's heavy and she's strong. Find that door, sir."

Where were those voices? Voices came from throats. Throats had bodies and faces. Some invisible force coiled itself around her waist. It lifted her. She felt nothing on her body, yet something lifted her. At least, some thing was in this void with her. Perhaps, she could find it. She flailed with her hands, trying to strike whatever it was. Even if it were a monster, at least it would be a tangible being. It would be some life in this emptiness. Nothing. Her hands contacted nothing.

"Don't leave me! Please don't leave me!" Aura's screams melted into tears. She buried her face in her hands and sobbed. The darkness took her. Alone. All alone. Somewhere, she heard voices, so far away, so very far away. It was too late. They would never find her now.

"Sir! We're being attacked! They're bleeding all over Aura!"

"Captain! That's just a fear. There is nothing attacking you. Keep walking forward. Follow my torch. I see you both. We're almost at the wall."

"No. Aura! Sir, I can't hold her and wipe the blood off."

"There is no blood, Captain! Lady Lovejoy! Keep walking. I'm at the wall. Keep walking. Follow my torch."

"I'm losing Aura! The blood has eaten away her face!"

"There is no blood, Captain. Elisabeth! You're here! Stay back, Ekkehart! I am going to open this door."

Aura slowly opened her eyes. She tasted wine on her lips. Elisabeth knelt before her, a goblet in her hand. The Captain gave her a faint smile, one passed between sisters who just endured the same punishment. Deofoyl sat on a stool to their left. A keg rested at his feet. They were in a small chamber, well lit by torches.

"That is a most grueling trap," he said. "It is also quite humiliating."

"I seem to have found a new fear," Elisabeth said. Her smile softened. "Don't worry. I won't let them kill you."

Aura wondered who they were. It did not matter. Whoever they were, they were solid entities. Nothing could be worse than that feeling of being utterly alone.

"I had no idea my fears were so strong," Aura said in a weak voice.

"None of us do," Deofoyl said. "I thought I had conquered mine. I was wrong."

"Perhaps I am not a proper fit for your order, sir," Aura said. "If my fear is so strong, I could end up a disaster. I mean, if the enchanters base their magic on their emotions, what damage might I cause?"

Elisabeth snorted. "You ought to have seen my fears. I am going back to the Watcher's barracks, shake my squad mates awake, and pour a tankard of ale down their throats, just to prove to myself that they are still alive. Remember what I told you about courage? Please don't think I go into battle against angry, well armed ogres without desiring to urinate all over myself."

Aura smiled, at both the encouragement, and the silliness of the trilled Rs. The thought of Elisabeth reciting Ayrdish alliterative verse made her want to giggle, but the Captain seemed too serious to warrant what she may take as an insult. Deofoyl patted her on the shoulder. It was a reassuring pat, the kind Richard used to give her when she did something she thought stupid. He nodded to the Captain. Elisabeth handed Aura the goblet. She took it with relish.

"We originally designed that room so we could face and defeat our fears, but it proved to be overwhelming," Deofoyl said. "We rest here for a while. We are now below the barrier spell. Beyond this wall lies the Valley of the Mystic Moon. Its beauty is a refreshing tonic for what we just experienced. To reach the valley floor, however, we must descend a nine hundred foot staircase. So, we rest."

The Vice-Chancellor stood before a wall of solid granite, still bearing the pick marks from centuries ago. He said, "Miss Lockhaven, the Valley of the Mystic Moon lies on the other side of this door."

"I would ask what door, but somehow I think I know the answer," Aura said.

Deofoyl placed his left hand against the stone. He said, "Noctan portora onuman."

Aura blinked to clear her eyes as the stone beneath Deofoyl's hands began to swirl. The swirling spread outward until it encompassed three feet on either side. As it increased in speed, the stones turned translucent, then disappeared, leaving a round hole in the wall. Beyond, Aura saw open night sky. The Captain stepped through the opening. Looking around, she nodded, then motioned for Deofoyl and Aura to follow. The Vice-Chancellor paused, waving Aura to go through first.

As Aura passed through the doorway, Deofoyl said, "Miss Lockhaven, welcome to the Valley of the Mystic Moon."

Aura stood on a ledge next to Elisabeth. Deofoyl stepped through the opening, which closed behind him. Above them, one hundred feet of granite rose up to the sky, and the back wall of Ralthangarle. The moon and star light pierced the barrier spell with ease. Below, another nine hundred feet of cliffs dropped to the valley floor. A waterfall flowed from the side of the cliff to their left, cascading down over rocks to the silver stream below, where it wandered through the meadow, growing wider until it disappeared into the blackness of the forest beyond. The valley walls to the left and right continued to the horizon. In the middle of the valley rose a spire, vaguely pink in the light of the full moon.

"This is beautiful!" Aura said, with a gasp.

"Just wait until you see it by day," Deofoyl said. "You can't see our villages and farms from here. In the center is the city of Grahbale, our capital. That tower is the Grahtur, the Tower of Love. Well, we all have people to meet. Shall we?"

Deofoyl turned, and descended a set of steps carved into the cliff. In the moonlight, Aura saw her footing perfectly. She followed him, and Elisabeth took the rear.

Descending nine hundred feet of stairs was fairly easy. Still, Aura paused for breath several times, as did the others. Looking up the way she came, Aura hoped that the order installed a lift somewhere. Otherwise, going home would be a chore.

At the bottom of the steps, a woman greeted them. She held three dark horses by their reins. In the light of the moon, Aura guessed her age at seventeen, with shoulder length hair that looked brown. She wore a light colored tunic that barely covered her hips, and dark boots. From the belt around her waist dangled a three foot sword.

"Welcome home, Captain," the woman said.

"Thank you, Veronika," Elisabeth replied, taking the reins of her horse. She stepped into the stirrup, then swung into the saddle with the grace of a dancer on a ballroom floor.

Veronika handed the reins of the second horse to Deofoyl. The Vice-Chancellor smiled at her. Then, she climbed into her own saddle. Halfway up, her foot slipped from her stirrup, and she fell across the saddle with a huff. Her horse jerked, almost throwing her to the ground. With some effort, she managed to regain her footing, and pulled herself up. Even in the moonlight, the look of disappointment and disgust shone on her face as she glanced at Elisabeth. The Captain ignored her discomfort. Aura felt sorry for the girl. She knew all too well the feeling of clumsiness in the presence of those more seasoned.

"Well, Miss Lockhaven," Deofoyl said. "The Captain and I must leave you here. We have pressing business at the Grahtur. I've arranged for you to be met by Karyl and Karyn. They will escort you during your stay with us. Hmm. I wonder where those Kriger siblings are."

"Oh, Mister Kriger asked me to tell you that he was detained. He's helping Captain Baltarus with something," Veronika said. She dropped her head and mumbled, "I'm sorry. I forgot."

Elisabeth clapped her on the shoulder. She smiled, and said, "What are we going to do with you?"

"Keep me?"

"Oh, that is the direst of news," Deofoyl said. He mounted his own horse. He looked off toward the spire, and said, "Miss Lockhaven, you will be safe until your guides arrive. Feel free to wander about. Karyn will find you. She has the eyes of a hawk and the nose of a hound." He looked at her. "I will see you from time to time, whenever I am able."

Then, Deofoyl nudged his horse forward. Elisabeth and Veronika fell in behind. Aura watched as the three broke into a canter, and vanished into the forest.

Chapter Twelve

AURA FOLLOWED THE River Phant a short way until she stood in a meadow of heather. The moonlight rippled on the surface, broken and swirled by the current. She imagined the silver dancing upon the dark blue water as frolicking undines. Perhaps, they were. She longed to see one. Her magical eyes had never opened, allowing her to see beyond what others saw. A trout broke the surface, snatched an unseen insect, and splashed back into the river, startling her.

Everything felt so peaceful and serene, as if her best dream came to life around her. The lapping of the river on the shore blended with a low thrum that told her the river was much deeper than it looked. From the forest came the calls of nightingales. Overhead, the moon poured down its radiance, as if to caress the entire Valley.

She was here at last, the Valley of the Mystic Moon. Sagacius had been secretive enough about it. Now that she was here, it was more beautiful than she expected. She could not wait to see it during the day. She wanted to explore the forest, but despite Deofoyl's assurances about Karyn Kriger's senses, she doubted her own in a dark forest she did not know.

As she stared at the forest, a spritely form emerged from the woods, moving toward Aura. She narrowed her eyes as she recognized the form as that of a woman. A naked alabaster woman with an ethereal glowing light in her right hand. Even at the distance of fifty feet, she knew that figure. Nocturna. Aura placed her hands on her hips, frowned, and waited.

"You!" Aura snarled, when Nocturna was five feet away. "Are you spying on me again?"

"Oh, no, silly," Nocturna said, walking up to Aura. "I haven't watched you since the night we talked in front of your rather unfriendly door. I'm here because Karyl asked me to keep you company. He's looking for some lost girl in Grahbale. I don't know how one becomes lost in Grahbale. It isn't very big. I hear Colebury and Welcaster are much larger, but I've never been there. I'm just Nocturna, and don't know much about geography. Tee hee. Karyl will be along directly, I suppose."

"You're lying. I saw you seven nights ago, by my outhouse."

"Would I lie to you, Aura Lockhaven, whose name is longer than mine?" Nocturna looked at the ground. She put her finger to her lips, and mumbled, "That wasn't me. That was Ferne. I was replaced by someone a little less likely to get caught."

"Who sent you?"

Nocturna looked up at Aura, with her usual bright smile. "I told you, Karyl. Karyl Kriger. You know, Karyn's little brother. Tall, trim, and oh, so handsome. Karyl, that is. Not Karyn. Although, I suppose she's quite beautiful herself."

"No, I mean, who sent you to watch me at home in Hartshorn?"

"Oh, I'll never tell." She put her finger to her lips again. "Besides, I forgot. That was so long ago."

"It's only been three weeks!" Aura snapped.

"Well, silly," Nocturna said, beaming and waving her hands. "Much has happened in that time. I had to have my hair cut, get my nails varnished, there were parties to attend, and feasts to eat, and I had to have my clothes pressed. Oh. I'm not wearing any clothes. Tee hee."

Yes, Nocturna was definitely more daft than a barn full of loonies. Aura sighed. She may as well keep company with the little nymph. Whoever wanted her watched no doubt already knew of her presence in the Valley. As she pondered what to do next, she heard a high-pitched trill from the trees to her left. A startled "eep" escaped her mouth.

"It's just an owl," Nocturna said.

Aura had heard plenty of owls. Two barn owls lived in the woods just to the north of her home, and sometimes moved into the house's garret in the winter. Every night, she heard the calls of tawny owls. This one sounded like a tawny, so why did she jump at a familiar sound? Aura thought about her situation. The experience in Ralthangarle lay only a few hours behind her. She stood in a meadow in a place she had never visited, at night. She waited for a stranger with a naked nymph who spied on her and had no common sense. That would make anyone nervous.

Nocturna slipped her hand down to Aura's, and led her away from the river, into the wide meadow. Aura looked around to determine their direction. Ralthangarle and the cliff lay to her right. That was the east, so they walked north. The nymph hummed, as if she took a night time stroll with a friend.

Aura relaxed as much as she felt she dared. Nocturna seemed pleasant enough, when not prowling about the house watching her bathe. She remained on guard, just in case the nymph led her directly to the unseen person who wanted her watched. In the center of the meadow, Aura spotted an equestrian statue, its slender rider sitting slumped as if thinking. Odd place for a statue, she thought. Then, the rider's cloak billowed in the breeze.

Before she could collect her thoughts, the rider clucked and the horse walked toward them. The horse was the largest destrier Aura had ever seen, not only tall but broad across the chest and back. Under the light of the full moon, the horse's shadow reached her long before the animal did. Even in the moonlight, Aura could see the man's mane of black hair fell straight to his shoulders and he took great pains with his impeccable moustache and goatee. He wore a cloak over a dark clothes and boots. Around his neck and bouncing against his chest lay a silver pendant with a dark stone in the center. Nothing hid the massive sword that dangled in its scabbard from his saddle. The rider stopped his horse in front of the two women.

"I know you," the rider said to Nocturna in a deep voice fitting of a town crier.

"You should!" Nocturna said. "Most men don't forget a dance with Nocturna." Aura noticed the wide grin on the short woman's face, but heard the taunt lingering in her words.

If Nocturna's tone meant anything to the rider, he did not show it. He shifted his glance to Aura, and added, "I don't know you. This moon casts an ill shadow. This is no night for two women to be out for a stroll, and one of you a virgin at that."

"Virgin? One of us? Oh, silly, silly boy," Nocturna said. "You know for a fact that I'm no virgin, or did you forget last Tyrfin?" The rider's glove squeaked as he tightened his grip on the reins. "Oh, did I hurt your honor?" Nocturna threw her hand over her breast in a dramatic sweep and said, "I know, the very thoughts of sharing bodies with *me*!"

The rider harrumphed. "I was drunk."

Nocturna nodded toward Aura and added, "This is Aura Lockhaven, whose name is longer than mine. She is a visitor from some place called Hartshorn that I think I visited. If she's a virgin, she won't be for very much longer."

"What?" Aura asked, turning to Nocturna. She wanted to ask what exactly the nymph meant by that comment. While Sagacius said the order had grown lascivious, she did not expect to be the recipient of anyone's physical attention. She turned slightly pink at the idea that at some point in her visit to the Valley she might be seduced. The rider's presence made her keep the question to herself. She cleared her throat. "That's my business alone."

"She means she's been lain, so there," Nocturna said, sticking out her tongue to the rider.

Aura groaned and buried her face in her hands. Obviously, she knew she was not a virgin. Sagacius knew it, too. He served as friendly ears for both her raging tirades and broken hearted sobs following her experiences. The three men who took her also knew it. No one else did. What happened in bed was not a subject for public discussion, even in Hartshorn where folk cherished bedpleasure as much as their next meal, despite the protestations of the High Temple. Apparently, the people of the Valley had other ideas about topics of conversation. They also knew what certain phrases meant. At least, at night, no one could see that her cheeks matched her hair.

The rider fingered the point of his goatee with his left hand as he regarded Aura. His face lay hidden in his own shadow, but Aura could feel his gaze. She felt exposed, as his eyes lingered over every inch of her body. Her dress no longer felt sufficient. She eyed the sword hanging from the saddle. The moonlight reflected off the silver hilt and pommel, casting long shafts of brightness down the dark scabbard. The rider dropped his right hand to the sword, caressing the hilt with his index finger. A shiver passed through Aura. She understood the gesture. If the rider planned to do more than look at her, she doubted if she could cast a spell faster than he could draw that thing. While she believed she could outrun the rider, and reach the safety of the forest, she held no such hope against an ancient palfrey, much less a destrier the size of the one four feet away. Better to let the rider enjoy his visual feast.

The rider sighed. It was not the sigh of lust, or desire, or even weariness. It was the sigh of disappointment. "So, you're the visitor," he said. "I heard you'd be entering the Valley tonight. You look like something they'd get. Heavy in the chest, light in the head."

"That was rather rude!" Aura snapped.

"My strength is steel, not manners," the rider said. "But you are light in the head. You best learn how to keep fit company. Otherwise, I'll be rescuing you in the next fortnight, and we have enough fools in this Valley as it is." The rider clucked to his horse, and walked toward the forest, then broke into a trot.

Aura wanted to spit. She wanted to hurl oaths and curses. She wanted to throw a stone. She wanted to break her vow and fire a spell of at least significant violence into the retreating cloak. The volley of words tied around her tongue as fury washed over her. Not sure what to do, Aura chose not to do anything. She savored the rage, and let it recede on its own, instead of grounding herself with peace and calm. As soon as the rider vanished into the forest, Nocturna stuck her tongue out in his direction. Then, she turned around, bent over, and smacked her buttocks with a loud whack. The ensuing boisterous flatulence caught Aura off guard.

When she stood up, Nocturna said "Drunk, indeed! He had no brewer's droop that night, I assure you! He took me three times. Three times! If he didn't want me, he could have hired someone. We do have harlots, you know. No, that's right. He doesn't like opening his purse, only his britches! Indeed! See if I share bodies with him again, no, no, no!"

"The first woman I meet in the Valley is naked. The first man I meet is a son of a bitch! Who was that?" Aura asked.

"Baltarus, the captain of our guard. They're our constables. Oh, he's a churl with a cocklebur caught in his codpiece right enough, but he's serious about his job. They all are. I think they're just bored. All they do is break up tavern donnybrooks and arrest people who share bodies in the street under the sun. But if you're ever in trouble, just look for a man wearing a cloak the color of the sky. That's their emblem." Nocturna rubbed her chin and muttered, "Now what was silly old Baltarus doing out here all by himself? There's no tavern nearby. Why isn't he looking for that missing girl?" She shrugged and added, "No matter. Any of the men with blue cloaks can get you out of trouble faster than you can say my name, and you can say Nocturna pretty fast. Noc·tur·na. There you go. But probably not as fast as you can say your own name. Aur·a. Or is it Au·ra?" Nocturna cocked her head to one side and stared at Aura. "Why do you have one less syllable in your name than I do? That isn't fair!"

Oh, merciful heavens, Aura thought. This nymph changed subjects faster than she *could* say her own name. She also changed her mind faster than that. She looked at Nocturna. The nymph still looked enraged and hurt. Aura smiled. She learned the hard way that the recipients of insults were often the nicest and sweetest people. If a boor like Baltarus dishonored Nocturna, then perhaps the nymph was as innocent as she claimed.

Aura held out her hand and said, "Shall we be on our way?"

Nocturna giggled and grabbed Aura by the hand. "Yes, we shall. We've loitered long enough. Come, come. Much to do. Much to see. Come,

Aura Lockhaven. Well, you have a surname, and I don't, so you have five syllables to my three. That still isn't fair! But, enough. Come, come!"

Nocturna drew Aura deep into the meadow, toward the forest on the other side. At the edge of the meadow lay a thick sheen of silver. Nocturna squealed in delight.

"Oh, look, a pond!" Nocturna said. She grabbed Aura's arm and shook it. She beamed with a silly grin. "Don't you just want to go for a swim? Don't you just want to dip your skin in that water under the moonlight? Especially after Baltarus undressed you with his eyes. Oh, I could tell, yes, I could." Nocturna's grin faded into a sad frown. "You do swim, don't you?"

"Well, yes," Aura said.

"Don't tell me you bathe in a dress! I know you don't under that thing that pees on you, but how about in a pond?"

"No, I don't bathe in a dress," Aura said. "I bathe naked like anyone else." She looked at the pond. "Now that I think about it, a bath does sound good."

She had not bathed in days, other than using the quaint sponge and basin provided by the inns where Deofoyl's carriage stopped. Before she could say anything, Nocturna grabbed Aura's hand and led her to the pond. She skipped and hummed as they approached the shore. Aura broke into a jog to keep up with the nymph.

"La, la, la," Nocturna sang. "We're going swimming. We're going swimming. Aura Lockhaven from Hartshorn and Nocturna from wherever-she's-from are going for a dip. My name is longer than yours now, so there. La, la, la. Ladies going swimming." She giggled. "Isn't this fun?"

Nocturna released Aura's hand and ran into the water. When the water reached her hips, she dove headfirst underneath. Then, she emerged and floated on her back. Aura removed her dress, folded it, and laid it on a boulder. It needed a washing, but that could wait until day. Then, she removed her boots, and stood on the shore. She sat her foot into the water. It felt warm, warmer than she expected. Still, she held back.

"Well, come on in," Nocturna shouted.

"Are you sure there isn't anything in there that will grab me? I mean, it is water at night," Aura said. She never swam at night. She grew up hearing tales about slimy things in the Gourdvine, creatures that did nasty things to men and even nastier things to women. Testing those waters and those tales lay beyond the threshold of her courage.

"Oh, you don't believe that old superstition!" Nocturna said. "Balderdash to all that. That is just so much tommyrot concocted by mean old men who do not want women enjoying themselves. This is too small a pond for catfish large enough to eat you. As for tentacles that will reach into your nether regions, I don't think they exist. If they do, may they find me and may they be huge! There may be a perch or two that will nibble your toes, but that's all. Come on in."

"Well, why not?" Aura said.

She waded out into the pond. The water felt like none other she had experienced. She was accustomed to the brisk chill of the Gourdvine, and the almost disgusting warmth of the farm ponds around Hartshorn. This felt more like an invigorating bath. It tingled her skin. She wanted it to cover all of her. When the water reached half way up her thighs, Aura dove in.

She dove until she touched the bottom of the pond. Stretching out her long arms, she used her own version of a breaststroke to propel herself as far as she could under the surface until her lungs began to ache. Then, she surfaced. Nocturna floated on her back about twenty feet away, humming to herself and staring up at the moon. Mischief filled Aura. The desire to do something she had not done in twelve years consumed her. The last time she did this, Ester was still alive, and she did it to her sister in the Gourdvine in front of smirking onlookers. She sank into the water until only her nose and eyes remained above the water. Creeping toward Nocturna, she calculated the distance. When Aura was within five feet of her prey, she submerged without a sound.

Spotting the white hair underwater was easy. It hung down like a waving, glowing mass of silver moss. Aura grabbed two handfuls of

Nocturna's hair and pulled. Even submerged, Aura heard the nymph scream. The water around her erupted in chaos. When Aura thrust herself from the water, Nocturna stood up to her waist, hair in her face. She sputtered and spat, and glared at Aura.

"She vixen!" Nocturna growled. "There shall be payback, you tall breasty wench!"

"Do your best," Aura said. She threw herself onto her back and using long strokes propelled herself to the opposite side of the pond.

Aura and Nocturna chased each other around the pond. They grabbed each other's ankles, hair, and whatever presented itself within easy reach. They pulled each other under. They splashed water into each other's faces. They laughed, sang, and floated underneath the moon. Nocturna pointed out the constellations to Aura. They did look different to her, more spectacular, more real than ever before. The Axe Man almost moved as he chased the Lion across the skies. The Nine Sisters sang a song of joy as they danced across the heavens. Several perch nibbled Aura's legs. She tried to grab them with her hands, and Nocturna almost drowned herself laughing. When Aura said she still felt dirty, Nocturna held her hands together. Then, she handed Aura a coin sized wafer. It smelled like lavender and lathered like no other soap Aura had seen. When they felt exhausted, and Aura felt clean, they walked out of the pond and stood on the shore.

As Aura removed her towel from her bag, Nocturna frowned. "You don't need that." She clapped her hands together, and waved them across Aura's body. "Foop, foop, foop! There."

Aura felt herself. She was dry. Even her hair was dry, fluffy without any tangles. Before she could ask how Nocturna did that, the nymph touched her on the nose. "It's time for me to go," Nocturna said. "Toodles, Aura Lockhaven whose name is longer than mine."

With that, she vanished. Aura stood alone on the bank of the pond, surrounded by heather, trees, and singing nightingales.

"What a strange creature," Aura said.

"Astute observation," a masculine voice said behind her.

Chapter Thirteen

AURA SHRIEKED AND whirled around. She threw her right arm over her breasts and her left hand flew to her womanhood. Whatever joy she experienced earlier vanished. Now, she felt exposed with nowhere to hide but the pond. She feared that Baltarus had returned, to do more than just look at her. What she saw did not help her feel better. Three feet away stood a man and a woman.

The top of the man's head reached the tip of Aura's nose. In the moonlight, the sinews of his chest and arms stood out against the shadows they cast on his alabaster body. His hair appeared white. He did not have that ethereal glow, so he was human and not Fae. In his left hand, he held a staff with a crooked head, on the tip of which hung a lantern. The yellow glow of candlelight fell on a somber face with no hint of emotion.

The woman stood just taller than Aura's shoulder. Her hair and skin also appeared white. The belt around her chest did little to cover her full breasts, and the one running down from it between her legs barely covered her womanhood. She placed her hands on her hips and chuckled.

"Merciful heavens!" Aura shouted. "Who in the name of the gods are you?"

The woman laughed. She said, "I'm Karyn Kriger. We apologize for being late."

"I am Karyl Kriger," the man answered in a measured voice. "Why are you covering your body?"

"Because I'm naked! So are you, you creep!" Aura snapped. "She's clothed, if I can call it that."

Karyl said, "I am wearing boots and a loincloth." Aura looked below the man's chest for the first time. In the lantern light, she saw something that looked like a small plaid scarf, held in place by a belt around his waist.

Narrow and short, it hardly seemed large enough to cover his nose, much less his important area. "I am appropriately attired for my position."

Karyn added, "I wear more because I'm cold natured. Many of us in the Valley don't wear even this much." She grinned, or it looked like a grin in the moonlight, a broad expanse of teeth responding to a bit of welcome news. "You must be Aura Lockhaven." Karyn grabbed Aura's right hand, ripping away her attempt at minimal modesty, and pumped it. It was the exuberant and firm grip she expected from a lad who just won an archery tournament. "We've heard so much about you." She nodded to the man standing next to her. "Please don't let my brother scare you."

"Why should I endeavor to frighten her?" Karyl asked. Like his sister, he rounded his vowels and stretched them a little. Otherwise, he spoke in a southern Ayrdish voice. Aura thought they may have spent their childhood somewhere else before moving here. Unusual, but charming.

Karyl also shook Aura's hand, turning it so he took her by the fingers with his thumb. It was like a lord greeting a lady. She glanced from one to the other. The Krigers looked enough alike in the moonlight. From there, all similarity vanished. Karyl was formal, almost grim, while the bubbly Karyn stood grinning at her. With an imperceptible shrug, Aura asked, "May I get dressed now?"

"Don't let us dent your pewter," Karyn said.

"Why should we restrain you?" Karyl asked.

No similarity whatsoever. Aura pulled on her boots, then buckled them. Then, she pulled her dress over her head. As she laced the bodice, Karyn looked at her and cocked her head.

"There's enough material in that thing to make ten outfits," she said.

"If you made tanginis, yes," Aura responded.

"That's what most women wear in the Valley."

Aura paused with her bodice halfway laced. The tangini top covered the lower half of the breasts, while the bottom part covered the womanhood and buttocks. The rest of the woman was bare, save for the corseted laces holding the pieces in place. Only Coadics continued to wear them daily. Everyone else on the Forested Islands reserved them for athletic events. Sagacius once said that Aura's modesty may fill an eyedropper, if she added enough water. Still, the idea of walking into Hartshorn with that much skin exposed left her speechless.

"You have much to learn about us, Aura," Karyn said. "May we call you Aura?"

"Yes, please do."

Karyl waved to his side. "Please walk with us. Our home is not far from here."

Karyl and Karyn turned without a sound and disappeared into the trees. Aura ran to catch up with them. It was like chasing a cat. The glow of the lantern vanished behind a tree, then reappeared, then vanished again. She smashed her head against a branch before she fell in behind the Krigers. The lantern cast enough light around their feet for Aura to follow, and Karyl's height protected her from more headaches.

"Please walk beside me," Karyl said. He nodded to his left. "I shall cast more light." He held his free hand up to the lantern and said "Phosta."

As Aura stepped beside Karyl, the candlelight intensified. She saw the trees around her now, no longer lingering in the shadows to ambush her. The light of the lantern continued to grow until Aura thought she could read by it. In the new light, she recognized the bark of the trees as that of oaks and the lower shrubs as laurels. These trees felt friendly, as if they welcomed her into their world. In other forests, she often spent a few minutes calming the trees before they accepted her. Enchanters must harvest trees, she thought, but these seemed content knowing that they would continue to live on as houses, furniture, and tools.

"Ah, here we are," Karyl said.

They emerged from the forest into a clearing. In the center of the clearing sat a small one-story half-timber and stone cottage with a high-pitched thatch roof. She smelled the aroma of oak in the smoke drifting from the chimney. Several shrubs lay by the arched door, but in the darkness Aura could not tell what kind. Smiling at the homey sight, she followed Karyl and Karyn up the wide stone path from the forest to the house.

Karyl held the door open for Aura and she stepped inside the house. She gasped once her eyes grew accustomed to the light. She expected a tiny, quaint living room. Instead, the inside of a great hall greeted her. The cathedral ceiling stretched high over her head, held in place by massive timbers with carvings of dragon heads at their tops. Six iron chandeliers hung down, lighting the room as if by day. Comfortable chairs sat in a circle in front of a fireplace big enough for a man to sleep in without curling up. Over the fireplace hung two crossed axes and a round wooden shield with a raven painted in the center. Shelves filled with jars, scrolls, and books lined one wall, while long tapestries covered the others. The cottage was tiny outside, with only one story. This room took up at least two stories. It was the best illusion Aura had ever seen.

Karyl snuffed out the lantern's candle with his fingertips and propped the staff against the wall by the door. In the light of the living room, Aura looked at the siblings. Without the shadows cast by the moonlight, Karyl did not appear to be as brawny. He looked like a man who swam miles every morning. Karyn looked like a sculptor's model. She saw that both had shaggy flaxen colored hair and almost pink fair skin. Their blue eyes looked like ice.

"Skols!" Aura shrieked. She threw herself against the wall, extending both hands toward Karyn and Karyl. She narrowed her eyes and growled, "Stay where you are. You will not sell me as a bedslave. I should alert King Edgar to your presence on our island."

Karyn looked at her brother and said, "She called us Skols. I think we've been insulted."

"It is not the first time," he replied, with no expression on his face. "Aura, Karyn and I are Frystings. There are two islands in the north. Those of us from Frystun have pale blonde hair and light blue or gray eyes. Those who live on Skoldun have dark blonde hair and dark blue or gray eyes. There is a massive amount of difference between us, although our peoples are related. Frystings are traders and explorers, not pirates. A Skol would indeed sell you as a bedslave, although if we were Skols, Karyn would have already ravaged you."

"Humor is my line of work, brother," Karyn said with a smirk.

Aura's hands flew to her face as she fell numb with horror. Slowly, she sank to the floor until she rested on her heels. What had she done? She assumed the worst of the Krigers, just because of the way they looked, just because of a vague visual similarity between Frystings and Skols. How was that not unlike being called a Geilltian because her mother gave her Coadic green eyes and auburn hair. Sagacius had informed Rupert that he could tell the difference between a Coadic and a Geilltian, if he tried. Well, she could tell the difference between Frystings and Skols, if she tried. Frysting longships docked at Hartshorn every day. She knelt in the very boots of those who turned their heads to her just because of a Tangoi generality that made her look vaguely like the enemy of her people, the Geilltians. She knew what it felt like to stand in Karyn and Karyl's place, all too well. Now, she knew what it felt like to stand in the place of those who looked at her with prejudiced eyes. She hated the feeling.

"Dear Cygfran, I'm a bigot," Aura whispered.

Karyn crossed the floor of the great hall and knelt in front of Aura. She took the young woman's trembling hands in her own, and asked, "Are you all right?"

"I am far from being all right," Aura mumbled. "I am so sorry. Please forgive me."

"For what?" Karyn asked, smiling. She lifted Aura to her feet. "Come. You must be hungry. At least, you must be thirsty. I know I am."

Aura still trembled and felt disgusted with herself as she walked with Karyn towards a door in the far wall. She followed her into the kitchen with Karyl behind them. She thought the kitchen more suited for a manor than a cottage. Marveling at its size, she inhaled the aroma of bread, bacon, and onions. Aura realized she was hungry. Karyl motioned toward a table long enough for twelve people.

"Please sit down," Karyl said. "I shall prepare you some supper."

"I'll get the ale. What kind do you like? We have fine Ayrdish ale that will put hair on your chest, sweet Nebelish ale that will give you dreams of dragons, and our Frysting ale that will knock your skull right off," Karyn said.

"I'll take the Frysting ale," Aura answered, mostly to ease the bitter taste in her mouth left by her prejudice. How better to learn about a people than to sample their drink?

Aura sat down at the table so she could see the whole kitchen. Karyn busied herself filling three tankards from a rack of kegs set against the wall. Karyl selected a small knife from a long rack and sliced sausages from the roll of links hanging from its hook. He placed them on the preparation table next to a block of cheese and a loaf of bread. As he worked, Aura looked around the kitchen. On the inside, it was as large as the entire house on the outside. The fireplace behind her dwarfed the one in her father's old tavern. She had not realized that the night had grown chilly until the warmth of the fire struck her back. Slabs of beef and pork hung from hooks against the far wall. The preparation table took up more room than her dining table back home. Were those butcher knives on that rack, or did the Krigers collect swords? Aura knocked her knuckles against the table. It felt solid.

"Are the living room and kitchen illusions?" Aura asked.

"No," Karyn answered. "Both are quite real."

"How did you fit such big rooms inside such a small house?"

Karyl answered, "Real estate spell."

Karyn sat a tankard of ale down in front of Aura. She liked its honey flavor, as if mixed with mead. Then, Karyn handed her an orange orb. It felt dry, a bit soft, and fleshy in her hands. She asked, "What is this?"

"It's an orange," Karyn answered.

"I know it's orange, but what is it?"

"The color is named for the fruit. Our teachers did a favor for a Sollantine count once, and ever since, he sends them crates full of these. Our teachers like to share the wealth."

Aura raised an eyebrow. If the color meant anything, it ought to taste delicious. She raised the orange to her mouth. Just as her teeth touched the skin, Karyn shouted, "Stop!" She jerked the orange from Aura's hand and thrust her thumbnail into the rind.

"Oh, I can see you're going to be trouble," Karyn said, peeling the rind away.

Aura sat fascinated as Karyn peeled the orange. This was new. No one removed the skin of fruit. Seeing the thick rind with its white interior, she realized she almost made a bitter mistake.

A cat jumped up onto the table at Aura's elbow. The size of the creature startled her. A brown tabby with long glossy hair and a bushy tail, he was three feet long from nose to the tip of his tail, and had to weigh twenty pounds. The tufts on the tips of his ears and the thick ruff around his neck gave him the demeanor of a forest hunter. He sauntered up to Aura and head butted her elbow. Purring loud enough to shake the table, he meowed at her in a demanding voice.

"Ah, I hear Dreki has introduced himself," Karyl said without turning his head.

"You named him Dragon?" Aura asked.

"You will understand when you see him hoard his toys."

Aura scratched Dreki's head. The cat plopped down on the table, and rolled over on his side. He grabbed Aura's hand with one paw and pulled it to his face. She giggled as he rubbed his nose over her knuckle.

Karyl sat a pewter platter of cheese, a slice of bread and cut up sausage on the table in front of Aura. Karyn shooed Dreki from the table as she sat the orange, now divided into wedges, next to the platter. The cat hopped onto a chair, and assumed the posture of a sphinx. Since Karyn went to all the trouble of skinning the orange thing, Aura thought she best start with it. The wedge exploded in her mouth in a sweet and tart burst. It was wonderful. That is, until she bit down on something hard. With as much dignity and grace as she could muster, considering Karyn watched her with a grin, Aura stuck her fingertips into her mouth. She removed a pip. This orange was a lot of work.

After another wedge of orange, and more fingerfuls of pips, Aura moved to the cheese. The familiar bite of Ayrdish cheddar roared through her mouth. She smiled. It was every bit as good as those from Cheddarport or Vine Haven.

"Do you mind if we ask you a few questions as you eat?" Karyl asked, sitting at the table. Karyn joined him.

"Only if you mind that I answer with my mouth full," Aura said.

"You should have seen Karyn as an apprentice," Karyl said. "I have never heard anyone eat soup."

"I'm going to kill you," Karyn sang, glaring at her brother.

"One of our tasks is to explain the order to you, so you will comprehend the people you will meet and can make a well informed decision about joining us," Karyl said. "We understand that you were taught by Sagacius."

Aura hurried to swallow the piece of sausage before saying, "Yes."

"That's impressive," Karyn said. "He's a legend. If you're anywhere half as talented as his last apprentice, you'll gain a reputation with us, too."

"That's assuming I join," Aura said. "Master never told me about any of his other apprentices."

"I've only met three. The man I'm courting, his brother, and the apprentice before you. Oh, are they dreamy!" Karyn sighed with a grin on her face.

"You believe all men belong in your dreams," Karyl said, raising his tankard to his lips.

Karyn cut her eyes to her brother and said, "All but one."

Aura chuckled. The Krigers reminded her of Richard and Ester, bantering at the dinner table. She thought about assuming the role of Henry and bellowing, "Stuff it in a bottle, you two. You're going to give

Aura the wrong impression." That was the point in the evening when Ester grabbed Aura's arms and Richard dug his fingertips into her ribs. Guessing Karyl and Karyn knew Deofoyl's tickling spell, or worse, she held her peace, and just smiled.

"Did either Sagacius or Lord Ashthorne explain the nature of our order to you? Did they explain how we use our emotions?" Karyl asked.

"Yes," Aura said. Mumbling her words around a piece of bread embarrassed her, but it tasted too delicious for her to rush. "But only a sentence or two."

"What is magic, Aura?" Karyn asked.

Aura took a gulp of ale to clear her mouth and said, "What is this, my first day as an apprentice? Magic is changing your circumstances to correspond with your will. It is visualizing a desired outcome, putting your will behind that desire, and using your vitality to bring it to pass. The incantation is a focal point that pushes your will out into the world. Any number of channels may be used; spells, rituals, candles, incense, potions, food, water, ale. The important things are the release of vitality and the seriousness of the magician. In most cases, magic takes a long time to manifest. It must incubate, like an egg. In special circumstances, such as a duel, a magician can push his vitality out by forcing his will into solid form. Then, it has instant effects." She paused. Looking down at the tankard before her, Aura mumbled, "Magic is giving a little girl her life back."

"That may be one of the most complete answers I have ever heard," Karyl said. "My compliments to Sagacius for his training. Vitality has a limitation. If exhausted, the magician will die. The emotions have no limitations. They exist at full force at all times until the person decides to put them to rest. Love is the most powerful of them all. We use our emotions much as the Aitians use their curved glass to magnify words and the planets. We aim our emotions, our lens if you will, at our vitality and our will. They serve to magnify our vitality and will beyond anything imaginable. We are quite exhausted after lengthy spells and rituals, but it feels like only a hard day's work."

Karyn said, "We also use the other emotions. Sometimes we need lust. Sometimes joy. Sometimes we need anger or loyalty." She cut her eyes to her brother, and added, "Even tolerance for your little brother."

"You best tolerate me, elder sister. You cannot cook. I pity your future husband," Karyl said.

"I'll marry an innkeeper!"

"Apparently, I have a powerful lens, as you put it. I just don't know how to aim it," Aura said.

"Our power comes with a price," Karyn said. "Because our emotions are so well tuned to the lute of magic, we cannot practice some forms. Few of us divine. Our feelings cloud the results. None of us dare contact spirits or celestial beings. Many of those things feed on feelings and would see us as a feast. We have to leave the room if a sorcerer conjures a jenn. Working with the elements presents a problem. If we contact a fire drake while we're angry? Whoo wee! You're already an initiated wizardess, so you may have a slight advantage over most of us, already knowing how to divine and how to work with the elements." Karyn cocked her head. "You're a wizardess. Why on earth do you want to be an enchantress?"

She looked down at her left hand. A smile spread across her face as she said, "The power I have isn't strong enough. I want to defend the defenseless, help the helpless, and give hope to the hopeless."

"Ah, Sagacius taught you Damaskarose's old motto," Karyn said.

Aura cut her eyes at Karyn. They grew wide with astonishment. "What did you just say?"

"That was Damaskarose's motto. We only heard it once a week. We were taught by Lord Tyrus and Lady Naurelia, the Eorl and Eorless t'Ardora. Lady Naurelia was taught by Damaskarose. The full motto says *Remember to defend the defenseless, help the helpless, and give hope to the hopeless. That isn't just our sacred duty. It's our greatest joy.*"

Aura said slowly, "I said that to Master the day we met. It's my dream. It's something I live by. I only heard of Damaskarose this very afternoon." She looked down at her tankard as a lantern lit inside her mind.

A sense of unease spread through her. She remembered a moment of the day she would never forget. Sagacius said, *You also remind me of someone. I just can't place the name.* She also recalled the astonished look on his face when she first mentioned her dream to him. Even Deofoyl looked shocked when she repeated her dream to him. Aura now had an idea of who she reminded Sagacius of, and she did not like that idea. "Please tell me what Damaskarose looked like. The image on her coin is vague. What did she really look like?"

"Very few in the order knew her. She died one hundred and sixty years ago," Karyl said.

"That's impossible, not if she taught my Master. He isn't that old."

Another lantern lit inside Aura's mind. The sense of unease grew. Sagacius had to be older than one hundred sixty, if Damaskarose taught him. If he were the age of the typical new initiate when she died, then he would be at least one hundred eighty-two. She thought of the potion Sagacius took every morning for his unnamed condition, and how he looked for a few minutes afterwards. Deofoyl said something about Leynda's age, implying she was much older than she ought to be. Aura cut her eyes at the Krigers.

"You've discovered a longevity potion, haven't you," Aura said. "Even if it doubled your lifespan, that would be enough. You mixed it with either a youth potion or a glamour spell. You're much older than you look, aren't you?"

A brief flash of what looked like fear shot through Karyl's eyes. A peel of thunder shook the window. Dreki howled and bolted from his chair, running from the kitchen. Aura glanced up. The sky had been clear only half an hour earlier. Karyn put her hand on Karyl's arm, and whispered something to him that Aura could not hear. He closed his eyes and breathed in slow breaths. Karyn kept her left hand on Karyl's arm. She waved her right in Aura's general direction. Aura saw her lips move.

Karyn looked at Aura and said, "Don't ask questions that we can't answer."

"We can tell you to ask Lady Naurelia about Damaskarose," Karyl said, opening his eyes. His voice sounded even more measured. "You are going to spend several days with her. She will teach you how to harness and release your feelings. That is enough for tonight. I cannot speak for my sister, but I am fatigued. It is close to midnight. You must be fatigued as well, especially if you passed through Ralthangarle."

Exhaustion slammed into Aura as if someone threw a sack of wheat against her chest. She nodded and almost sank against the table. Between the long trip, the ordeal of the chamber of fear, and these revelations about her master, she wanted to do nothing but sleep for a full day.

"Come," Karyn said, standing. "We have a room ready for you."

With unsure feet, Aura followed Karyn into the great room, to a staircase in the far corner. Aura started climbing the stairs with difficulty. By the time she reached the top, Karyn supported her by the waist and almost dragged her down the hall to her room. She noticed little about the bed chamber in the light of its single candle. Karyn helped her out of her dress and boots, and let her flop onto the bed. After four nights in inns, the soft down mattress felt wonderful. Karyn said sleep well, then left.

Aura stared up at the high vaulted ceiling. As she closed her eyes, one word remained in her mind. One word she knew she would encounter if she drew a line between herself and Damaskarose. One word that Sagacius mumbled thrice and made Deofoyl almost choke. One word she wished would just go away.

Nightshade.

Chapter Fourteen

BASED ON THE shadows, the time looked to be seven of the sun. The three windows of Aura's room faced west. She stood at the middle window, watching the shadow of the house retreat from the wall of red and black oaks just beyond a small yard. Other than the woods, she saw nothing of the Valley. The trees, taller and more majestic than any she saw in Lodwynnshire, were enough. Aura always thought trees were creatures who simply did not travel very far. These proved it to her, their branches swaying in the morning breeze like the hands of dancers. From the forest, songs of families of red finches and chip-a-woos drifted toward the house.

Aura turned from the window, and faced the wall behind her. With a bow, she greeted Golau, the god king, the ruler of day. Continuing her bow, she touched her toes and held the pose for a full minute. Then, she stood upright and stretched toward the high vaulted ceiling. As she bent backwards, she wondered why Gweryn worshippers greeted Golau by facing the sun, when they all knew the Sun was the god king's grandfather. The peculiarities of religion, she thought, holding her arched pose for another minute before returning to an upright position. With her morning ritual complete, she walked to the low table at the foot of the bed. At some point in the night, either Karyl or Karyn washed and pressed her dress. It now lay folded neatly on the table. Her boots looked clean, too. She smiled at the kindness of her hosts.

Like the downstairs, her bed chamber enjoyed the effects of the real estate spell. If not for that spell, the chamber may be big enough for a tiny bed, a table, a chair, and enough room to knock her knees against it all. Instead, it looked large enough for six beds, and the bed sufficient for three people. It was the most magnificent bed she had ever seen, with a post at each corner that towered up over her before turning into rich carvings of dragon heads. Instead of a typical plank headboard, the bed backed up to a fully carved image of a Frysting longship, complete with twelve sailors and sail. She checked the mattress. It was supported by ropes like any other mattress, but filled with something other than down and straw.

She still felt clean from her bath the night before, so Aura saw no need to ask the Krigers if they had a tub. The basin and sponge on the table by the window sufficed. She bathed, keeping her face turned from the silver mirror. As she did, her mind drifted to troubling thoughts.

Aura was not bothered by the possibility that she resembled Damaskarose, at least in the face. There couldn't be enough faces to go around to all mortals, so the gods must have to borrow old faces from time to time. She was also not bothered by the idea that perhaps Sagacius took her as his student, and gave her a home, based on that resemblance. It was an unwritten law of magic that apprentices always honored their masters throughout their lives. If she ever encountered an orphaned boy who reminded her of Sagacius, she would do the same thing. She was also not bothered by the idea that her dream was word-for-word identical to Damaskarose's motto. Truth was truth, and if all people were connected to each other by the element Spirit, then why could that connection not flow backwards through the ages.

It bothered her that Sagacius kept it all a secret. For ten years, he never said a thing. Sagacius had been most insistent to know everything about her family. Aura told him about the Lockhavens. She knew nine generations from herself back through the tales and songs to the day that lumbering tree of a man roared from the woods and waged havoc with the Skols. All she knew of the Nightshades were scraps of tales told her by her father. That had been typical enough. Most Ayrdish upon establishing any form of relationship ask the usual questions, where do you come from, who was your father, who was your mother, are we second cousins thrice removed? Sagacius never returned the favor. She only learned he had a sister less than a week ago, and finally heard his mother's name the day before. Why had the old man never told her about Damaskarose, especially if she was his mother? If Aurora Nightshade had been an enchantress and the Chancellor of a magical order, Aura would have bragged about her every day. Had Damaskarose been a tyrant? Not if she had her image on a coin. She heard that the first thing the Ayrdish did upon the death of Wilbur the Angry was to melt down all the coins to remove his face from before their eyes.

Then, there was that word. That name. Nightshade. It would be just another word if it was not also her mother's maiden name. Aura knew her maternal grandparents' names. Garreg and Glynis Nightshade died in Coadia during a plague, the same plague that drove their young daughter Aurora to Ayrdland and safety. Other than that, she knew nothing. What unseen twine of time tied Garreg to this legendary enchanter? Did any twine tie Nightshade to Damaskarose? Aura loved strings, especially those on fiddles and in tapestries. She hated invisible strings. They usually came with spiders.

By the time Aura finished her mental grumbling, she had pulled on her boots and dress, and sat in the window brushing her hair. The bed chamber would answer none of her questions. She was not even sure the Krigers would, but she could ask.

Aura found her hosts in the kitchen. Karyl sat on a stool before the massive oven, watching a small cauldron bubble. Three eggs bobbed in the boiling water. Karyn stood before the table, glaring at three mugs of tea. She looked as if she wanted to cast a spell on them to hurry the steeping. Dreki lounged on one of the ale kegs, watching as if he owned the kitchen.

"Good morning," Karyn called. "Did you sleep well?"

"Good morning to both of you. I slept wonderfully," Aura said, setting her bag on the floor next to the chair she occupied the night before. "May I ask you a question?"

"You may ask, but as you found out last night, we may not answer," Karyl said.

"Who is Nightshade?"

Karyl turned on his stool, and blinked. Karyn cocked her head and looked perplexed. She asked, "How did you become a wizardess without knowing about nightshades? I thought you were a bunch of nature magicians. Don't you people borrow ideas from the druids and witches? We have rows of nightshades out back. Black, emperor's, enchantress', purple, evening, sorcerer's, smoking, as well as mandrake, henbane, potatoes, tomatoes, and eggplant."

"I do know about the plants. So, you don't know a man named Nightshade?"

"I know a man named Mandrake! I'm courting him. Or he courts me. It all depends on whose hands move first," Karyn said, putting a seductive purr into her voice.

"Elder sister, perhaps our guest does not wish to know about your nocturnal activities," Karyl said.

Aura felt vaguely satisfied, for the moment. Karyl and Karyn's faces betrayed no indication that they had ever heard of Nightshade. If the Krigers knew about him, they were good actors. She chose to believe they told the truth.

"You don't know what you're missing," Karyn sang. She placed her hand on Aura's shoulder. "Now, Aura dear. Keep your gauntlets off Mandrake. He's mine. His brother Manfred is unattached. However, he's out of the country. Such a pity. You'll no doubt still be here on Haemmont 1, and to indulge in every Parin activity, you'll need a consort." Karyn arched an eyebrow and smiled with the last word. Aura understood the meaning. She blushed, but could not deny that the idea pleased her. "Speaking of which," Karyn continued. She picked up a small blue bottle from the table and handed it to Aura. "Drink this. All of it."

"What does this do?" Aura asked, taking the bottle.

"Well, with our emotions raised to such levels, we're somewhat ... free with our affections. That's the polite way to say it. Oh, lute picks, we like being lain. You'll want to leave the Valley with a skull full of knowledge, some new clothes, and we hope a new title, but nothing more. That potion prevents a man's seed from taking root inside you."

"Are you expecting me to be lain!" Aura said with a gasp. Her face reddened. The idea did please her, but began to terrify her. Karyn saw her face, and giggled.

"Aura, always expect everything. That way you will never be caught unprepared," Karyl said.

Aura drained the potion into her mouth. Some of it tasted familiar. Some of it did not. She felt no lingering tingle of magic on her tongue. It was pure herbs, and a touch of Cailliac lifewater, the sort of potion she often brewed for brides and the town midwife. Karyn said, "It's good for two full moons."

"It lasts 56 days? I want to know the recipe."

They ate a breakfast of boiled goose eggs and sausage. Aura tried to stifle her chuckle. Heavy on the garlic, light on the sage. The Krigers also liked Aitian red pepper, which forced Aura to down three mugs of tea, the last two without waiting for them to steep.

When they had finished eating, Karyl stood and said, "Karyn and I have been called to the western end of the Valley on an unforeseen errand for Lord Ashthorne. He sends his regrets that you must travel alone today, but this cannot be avoided."

"You should be safe enough without us," Karyn said.

"Don't worry about my safety," Aura said.

Karyn snorted. "Now, I'm worried about your arrogance. You have heard of our order's nickname, haven't you?"

"The Order of Nosybodies?"

"The Order of Lust Magicians," Karyn said, grinning.

"The Lust Magicians? They're a whimsy order. They're a fabrication of the sorcerers. That order doesn't exist," Aura said. Karyn said nothing. "Please tell me that you're just pulling my hair." Karyn still said nothing. "Oh, merciful heavens! You're serious."

Karyn rolled her eyes toward the ceiling and whistled. Aura groaned. Every time Sagacius gathered with his alchemist, druid, and wizard friends, someone started a bawdy hour of tall tales with *Did you hear about the lust magician who ... ?* The witches were rumored to have a whole book of lust magician jokes. Sagacius had said the enchanters had grown lascivious. Perhaps the witches thought that was funny. She looked at her left palm and mumbled, "Hartshorn, I hope you're worth all this."

"Aura, we have discovered that the best way to build our vitality –" Karyl began.

Karyn held up her hand and silenced her brother. "Karyl, it's growing late. We have somewhere to go, and Aura does, too. Lady Naurelia will explain anything she needs to know."

"Yes, of course, elder sister," Karyl said. He looked at Aura. "Please gather your things." When Aura swung her bag over her shoulder, he said, "Excellent. Please follow me."

Karyl led Aura and Karyn out the kitchen door and down a stone path through the gardens. Aura wanted to take time to look at the various herbs and flowers growing in neat beds, but Karyl walked like a man in a hurry. At the end of the path sat the stable. Stables in Hartshorn were usually made of interwoven branches, although some folk built them from logs or planks. The Krigers' stable was built from stones, with a thatched roof. Aura expected it to be as big as a tithe barn inside, but it was a simple affair with three stalls on each side.

Karyn stepped into the first stall, which housed a palomino courser mare. Aura followed Karyl past the second stall and its black destrier stallion. He entered the gate of the third stall, and led a bay palfrey stallion out into the open.

"His name is Blister," Karyl said. "He is yours for the duration of your visit to the Valley."

Aura let the horse smell her palm. "Will I get blisters from riding him?"

"Blister is the Frysting word for lightning, and he does live up to his name. He has five gaits, and you will believe you are riding upon the air itself."

Karyl eyed the row of saddles on their rack. He selected one with thick padding and placed it on Blister's back. Then, he pulled the bridle over the horse's nose. Aura noticed that it did not have a bit. Before she could ask, Karyl said "Blister responds well to leg commands." Karyl led Blister out of the stable, with Aura following. Karyn already stood outside, holding her horse and the black destrier by their reins. Karyl motioned for Aura to climb into her saddle.

She looked at the saddle, and balked. She rode plenty back home, but always in trousers. Women rode in dresses all the time, but Aura had never watched them mount. If other women figured out how to sit in a saddle while wearing a dress, then she could, too.

Karyn understood her predicament and said, "Laugh about my clothes again."

Aura cast her a wry look. She glanced at the mere strap that barely covered Karyn's essentials, little of her buttocks, and none of her thighs. Then, she looked at Karyn's hard leather saddle. Aura thought, *say that again, tonight.*

Putting her left foot into the stirrup, Aura stood. Holding the short pommel with her left hand, she inched the right side of her skirt up with her right. When it cleared her knee, she swung her right leg over the saddle, and found the other stirrup. So far, so good. Standing in the stirrups, she raised her skirt to mid thigh, then sat down, adjusting the cloth under her and around her. It still bound her legs, but she had freedom of movement. Splitting the seam to above the knee would help. That could wait.

Aura inhaled. She loved riding. The view from the back of a horse stole her breath. Everything looked much more grand five feet off the ground. She felt Blister's soul reach for her own. The stallion wanted to be friends. She loved feeling one with another creature. The feeling of such power between her legs made her smile. She chuckled at the sensuality of that thought. She chuckled again, remembering that she lost her maidenhead to a saddle when she was fifteen.

She needed every inch of tight thigh muscle to ride a horse like this. Aura pressed with her right leg. Blister stepped in a semicircle and moved with the gracefulness of breeze around the yard. With a slight tug of the reins, the stallion halted next to Karyn and Karyl. This horse was subtle. Any any sudden and dramatic shift of her body may send Blister into a full gallop.

As Aura tied her bag to the pommel, Karyn handed her a scroll. "This is a map of the Valley. It's five years old, but we haven't built any new bridges. I don't think."

"Today, you travel to Dallington. Mayenne is carving your staff, and needs to meet with you before she finishes it," Karyl said. "Ask anyone for directions to her workshop. Travel through the Forest of Passion due north. You will find a path that leads to Gnessa where you will find a road west. Take it to Dallington."

"That's stupid! Travel north, then west? Aura, just cut across country, through the forests and fields in a straight line. It's shorter," Karyn said.

"That may be, elder sister, but roads do not knock riders from saddles. Tree branches and angry farmers do."

Just as Karyl said, she exited the forest and found a path. Wide enough for two riders, or a wagon, it appeared to be well traveled. The numerous stones packed into the hard clay spoke that at one time, it may have been paved. Glancing upwards, she deduced the time at nearly ten of the sun. Aura barely nudged Blister with her knees, and he entered a smooth lateral amble that allowed her to relax and enjoy the countryside.

Ahead of her, she saw the northern wall of the Valley, a tall expanse of gray granite dotted with patches of evergreens. She snickered at the idea that the valley had been a barren gorge that grew only rocks. The stones had long ago been gathered to form the straight fences and rock walls that separated fields of barley, millet, and spelt. Others formed the low barns that stood next to trim cottages. Windbreaks of poplars and laurels lined some of the fences, and a few clumps of oaks and meadows of wildflowers broke the chessboard of the fields. A pheasant perched on the wall by the road, watching her pass as if she and Blister were just two forest animals out for a morning stroll.

Gnessa occupied the vague space between village and town, too large to qualify as one and too small for the other. With its conglomeration of Tangoi and Nebelish architecture, Aura thought it was charming, in a strange way. It seemed like a good place to stop. She let Blister rest with a bucket of oats and another of water, while she enjoyed two tankards of ale at the tavern. As she drank, she watched the patrons. Most looked like ordinary Ayrdish people. Some wore next to nothing, while a few brave souls walked around naked. The less dressed wore cloaks and carried staves.

Of course, Aura thought, sipping her ale. While she could bless a candle, she did not know how to make one. While she could charm a ring, she knew nothing of smithing. While she could brew ale, she never took the time to learn how to grow barley. The home of a magical order needed as many craftsmen, merchants, and farmers as Hartshorn did. Those who wore little must be enchanters and enchantresses, while those who looked like anyone else were, well, everyone else. As patrons walked by, they nodded to her and smiled. She looked at her dress. Most of the other women wore trousers.

"They probably think I'm a traveling merchant," she mumbled into her tankard.

The road to Dallington was paved with cobblestones, and wide enough for two wagons to pass with ease. Even at a leisurely pace, she expected to reach the village by noon. The high northern wall of the Valley now loomed to her right, with forests and isolated houses between it and the road. To her left lay mostly pastures of goats, sheep, and cattle.

Around eleven, Aura passed a long stone wall next to the road. As she thought it an odd place for a wall, she noticed the outlines of windows toward the top. Looking closer at the wall, she noticed half the stones at the bottom were blackened. Those toward the top looked split as if by chisels in the hands of giants. In the weeds and tall grass surrounding the wall, she saw the remains of a path leading beyond it. Curious, she turned down the path.

The wall continued down the path, lower and more shattered than that along the road. In the side she now faced, she clearly saw the doorway, wide enough for two people to pass without touching. The third wall continued up, unscathed, except for its missing shutters and roof. If there had been a fourth, all that remained was the shell of the destroyed fireplace and toppled chimney. It had been a building at one time. Some force, greater than a mere fire, reduced it to rubble.

She dismounted. Tying Blister to a bush, she stepped through the doorway. The wind whistled low and lonely as it blew against the corners of the walls. No weeds or grass poked through the floor, clay hard packed through years of feet. Several demolished tables and chairs, their wood turned green with moss and gray from rot, lay scattered about. Long timbers, blackened from fire, leaned against the walls where they fell from what must have been the second story and roof. A pewter plate lay near one of the tables, along with some tankard fragments and one still intact wine bottle. Before its destruction, this must have been a tavern or an inn.

You will see the scars for yourself, in ruins and smoke stains on walls. This was a relic from the war. Something compelled her to kneel and place her hand on the ground. She did, and felt waves of sadness radiating from the hard soil. The ground remembered. The building remembered, even if its only song came from the wind blowing by the ruined corners.

Behind the building, in the shade of an old oak tree, split down the middle by what looked like lightning, Aura saw four stones standing over four low mounds of grass. She walked out to them, and recognized them as graves. A fifth stone, smaller than the others, lay on its side behind a short mound. The grave of a child. The stones held no names or dates. The lack of flowers told her that no one even remembered the graves were here. Only the torn oak and the shattered building knew, and they held their silence.

Aura knelt at the head of the child's grave. She dug in the dirt and lifted the small stone into place. Standing, she sighed. She walked back inside and retrieved the wine bottle. The cork dissolved in her hand. She returned to the graves and poured the contents of the bottle over them.

"I'm so sorry," she whispered.

Chapter Fifteen

AT THE OUTSKIRTS of Dallington, Aura stopped the first passerby she met, and asked for directions to Mayenne's shop. The man kindly pointed to the other end of the village. She couldn't miss it. A staff hung over the door.

Dallington was pure Ayrdish village. Being a port, Hartshorn had gradually adopted some foreign architecture, especially along the river front where Aura saw Tangoi, Frysting, and even Flumantine influence. Not Dallington. Nearly every building, from house to hall, was built of a stone first story with a wattle and daub second story, held together by thick oak beams that stretched up into a thatch roof. Most wore either white or cream colored plaster. Aura smiled as she rode through the village. Signs over the doors announced the cheesemaker, the butcher, the cooper, the cobbler, the tailor, several taverns, and other typical shops.

Like most Ayrdish villages, Dallington spread out along one road, with a few houses scattered down alleys. A wide green sat in the middle of the village. On the other side of the green, three buildings side-by-side stood out as if they did not belong. The first, made of logs, looked spindly. The second, a square of stone, boasted a high pitched roof capped with a tower and a circle with four golden balls set in it. The third looked like a small but ancient classical temple. At first, Aura pondered the buildings, but then, light dawned on her. They were houses of worship. The spindly log structure must be a temple to the Wealdenda, the faith of old Nebeland and the Frystings. Of course, the classical temple belonged to the Towering Ones, they of ancient Karanth. The one in the middle must be Pendurist, the faith of pure balance. She had never met a Pendurist, much less seen one of their temples. The Iricanists all but wiped them out as heretics.

Speaking of which, Aura scanned the village and saw no sign of a temple of Irican. Now that she thought about it, Gnessa did not have one, either. Cringing, she looked at the sky. Not a cloud in sight. So, Baniar could not smite the village for its lack of faith. Could he? She snarled at herself for the momentary superstitious backlash of her old religion. Three remained, but she doubted if the faith of old Glasenya drifted this far east, and Rationalism remained in Aitia. How about the third? Behind the three temples, she spotted a grove of oaks, with a table stone in the center. She smiled. That would be the temple to the Gweryn.

The last house in Dallington was a small two story affair, with a long annex attached to the side. Sure enough, a staff hung over the door. The house sat back far enough from the road to allow for a small yard with several hitching posts. Aura tethered Blister, and knocked on the door.

With the thud of an iron bolt thrown back, and the creaking of hinges that begged for oil, the door opened. A tall man filled the doorway, glaring down at Aura with a mix of irritation and curiosity. His pale skin and white hair contrasted with his black tunic, waistcoat, and trousers. If he had one crease in his face, he had fifty.

"May I help you, miss?" the man said in an even voice.

"I'm Aura Lockhaven. I'm here to see Mayenne about my staff."

"Please come in."

The man held the door open for Aura. She stepped into the foyer. The man shut the door behind her, bolting it. Aura's eyes adjusted to the dim light inside the house. A short hall ran from the door to the back wall and the wrought iron spiral staircase leading to the second story. To her right, Aura noticed a wide arched single door that she guessed opened into the annex. On the left lay three closed doors. Above her hung an unlit chandelier, also of wrought iron. Despite the appearance of the man at her side, whom she guessed was Mayenne's valet, the house felt warm and inviting.

The man gestured around him and said, "Please wait here. I will tell Milady that you have arrived."

The man disappeared through the door on the right. Aura heard him mumble, followed by a feminine reply. A petite woman appeared in the door. She was average height, with black hair lined with silver, and deep brown eyes. Aura guessed her age at 45. She wore a leather apron over a short blue linen skirt tied over her right hip. Aura thought the woman would be beautiful if she smiled. As she thought that, the woman grabbed Aura's right hand in both of hers and squeezed.

"You must be the visitor Lord Ashthorne told me about. I am so happy to meet you," the woman said, with the enthusiasm of a butcher carving a routine piece of pork. "I am Mayenne."

"I'm Aura Lockhaven of Hartshorn," she said, introducing herself.

"Your timing could not be better," Mayenne said. The continental lilt to her voice sounded familiar. "I was about to have lunch. Please join me. You must be tired."

While Mayenne did not smile, her wide eyes sparkled in an almost childlike enthusiasm. Aura relaxed, and smiled. Food did sound good. "Thank you. It was a rather long ride." As Mayenne led her to the last door on the left, she asked, "You wished to meet with me before you finished my staff?"

Mayenne held the door open, and Aura stepped into the kitchen. Compared to the Kriger's manorial house, Mayenne's seemed almost cramped. The kitchen reminded Aura of her own, except far more ornate, with the walls decorated by intricate woodcarvings of life in a faraway village. Recognizing the art as Flumantine, she also recognized Mayenne's accent. She reminded herself to watch her manners. Graciousness carried significant weight with the cultured Flumantines.

A fireplace with a beehive oven took up one wall, with mugs hanging from hooks on the mantel. A small table with four chairs sat in the middle, surrounded by shelves of cooking ware and food. She smiled at the aroma of fried bacon, sauteed onions, and fresh bread. Mayenne motioned to the table. Aura sat down as Mayenne removed two mugs from their hooks and placed them on the table. She admired the handiwork of the mugs, looking as if someone inlaid daisies into the clay before glazing it. Mayenne added dried leaves from a clay canister to the mugs, and then grabbed an iron

kettle from the spit in the fireplace. After she replaced the kettle, Mayenne
sat down across from Aura.

"Give it a minute to steep," Mayenne said. "I use Aitian tea but I also
add rose petals and dried elderberries. Yes, I wish to speak with you. Most
of my customers are people that I already know. An enchanter who broke
his staff being foolish. An enchantress who learned new spells and so needs
a new staff. A freshly initiated apprentice ready for his first. You, however,
I don't know. I am not comfortable just handing you a staff. That could,
how do you say, be disastrous."

Aura looked at the face as frozen as the flowers on her mug. "I can't
tell you how excited I am to be getting a staff."

"Have you ever had one?"

"I butchered a tree branch once."

Mayenne's eyes smiled for her. "You should have seen my first attempt.
The element of Wood is still angry with me."

Aura cast Mayenne a look of surprise. Wood was not one of the seven
elements, at least not those of the magicians of Sareth. Wood belonged to
Earth. In the back of her mind, she recalled hearing that magicians in the
western continent of Arantia recognized other elements, including that of
Wood. So, Mayenne knew a different form of magic, other than that of the
eight magical orders. This could prove to be an interesting staff.

"My old friend Lord Ashthorne informed me about you. To a point,
that is," Mayenne said. "You are a certified wizardess, no? That is different
from an enchantress. An enchantress is elegant, stately, refined. A
wizardess is organic, graceful, if somewhat unruly. It is like comparing a
carved marble column to a tree. Even if you join our order, you will always
retain something of your old. I was once a sorceress, and still work with my
will. So, you require a different type of staff, one that is more, how do you
say, natural. To know that, I must talk with you. It should not take long,
perhaps the remainder of today and tomorrow. You may assist me."

"I've always heard that making your own tool puts yourself into it,"
Aura said.

Mayenne held her cup to her lips. "Believe me, child. You will do more than just that."

The man in black stepped into the kitchen. Mayenne introduced him as her butler, Tyfford. Without a sound, Tyfford filled two tureens with beef and barley soup, and sat them in front of the women. After placing a loaf of still warm bread on the table, he bowed to Mayenne, and departed. They ate in silence, Aura enjoying every bite. Even if the meal was traditional Ayrdish, it was flavored with the spices of Flumance, giving it an exotic taste. After they finished, and enjoyed another cup of tea, Mayenne stood.

"Well, it is time for you to choose your staff," she said.

"Choose it?" Aura asked.

Aura followed Mayenne to the annex. The barn of a room smelled like wood, leather, and oil. She inhaled a deep breath, allowing the aromas of craftsmanship to take her back to her childhood, when she pestered the tanner, cooper, and cabinetmaker in Hartshorn, telling them of her most recent dreams while playing with the tags of wood shavings that hung from their benches. A rack of cured branches and hewn logs took up one wall. Green branches dried from hooks set in the rafters. Wood shavings filled a barrel next to the workbench against another wall. Racks and shelves of chisels, mallets, and planes hung on the wall above it. A treadle lathe sat next to the workbench. Mayenne walked to a set of racks beyond the lathe. Most racks held what Aura took to be blanks, slickened and polished. She led Aura to the far rack, where twelve staves stood, all ten inches apart. Unlike the others, these were branches simply skinned of their bark, aged, polished, and allowed to remain in their natural shape.

She waved to the rack and said, "In my meditations, Dariath often gives me visions of staves. I make them in advance, never knowing for whom they are meant. These are the ones I saw I should leave as found."

"I know the Gweryn, the Wealdenda, and the Towering Ones. I've never heard of Dariath. Who is he?"

"*She* is a Phrathian goddess, my matron," Mayenne answered. Aura expected a rebuke for mistaking the gender of a beloved deity, but none came. "Dariath has helped me since I was but young. All of these staves appeared to me in visions. One of them is yours. Even I don't know which. It is up to you to decide. You will know. Go on, touch them."

Staring at the staves, Aura thought she was in another meeting of the Midlands Poet's Society. The collection of druids, wizards, and witches from six shires met once a quarter to talk too much, eat too much, and drink too much. As Sagacius' apprentice, she was usually invited to join, mostly to polish the staves and fetch the next round of ale. The last meeting at Nightstead occurred at Sagacius' home and ended with a smashed chair, two broken tankards, and a hangover that lasted all day. She smiled, knowing that at the next meeting of the Society, she would be considered a full member.

Tall enough for Sagacius, the first staff was too twisted and knobby for her tastes. She dismissed it immediately. The second one, the white wood of rowan, looked more at home in the hands of a queen than a working enchantress. The third caught her fancy. Aura ran her fingers down the deep grains of maple, but felt nothing from the wood. The fourth, a charming poplar staff, also left her with no feeling. The fifth, however, surprised her.

Aura removed the staff from the rack and held it in both hands. It was as long as she was tall. Golden brown and glossy with coats of linseed oil and turpentine, it ran in a gentle twisted taper from the tip ending in a head shaped like an open mouthed cat with two long fangs in the upper jaw and two shorter ones in the lower. The staff seemed weightless in her hands, as if made from air. It felt warm and tingles ran through her hands. She had heard of the phenomenon of items calling their owners, but never experienced it before. She knew. She just knew.

"This one," Aura said. "It feels right to me."

"Then, that one is yours. It came from an oak planted by Damaskarose herself. You have heard of her by now?" Mayenne asked.

"Yes," Aura answered, somewhat uneasy that this staff came from a tree planted by her, of all people. Sagacius had better not ask. He just better not.

"Let me have that now," Mayenne said, taking the staff from Aura. "I have much to do to it before it can properly be called a staff, much less yours."

Mayenne led Aura to her workbench. She laid the staff on the bench before turning to Aura. The staffmaker regarded Aura with puzzlement in her eyes. After staring at her until Aura felt uncomfortable, Mayenne said, "I'm trying to place your nationality. Your verdant eyes and russet hair indicate Tangoi. You're too tall for a Tangoi, however. Even the Garranians are small people. In fact, you're the tallest woman I've ever met, other than Lady Etheria."

"My mother was Tangoi. She was from Coadia. My father was Ayrdish. I inherited my height from his ancestor."

"Oh, you're a halfbreed."

Aura bristled. Reminding herself to control her anger, she tempered her voice. "I've heard that term applied to sheep, goats, pigs, cows, horses, dogs, and cats. Never to a woman. I've been called ... other things ... but never halfbreed."

If Mayenne noticed Aura's irritation, she made no sign. "It's quite the common word in Flumance. I meant it as no insult, just a statement of fact. You incorporate the best, and worst, of both. The Tangoi are natural magicians. The Ayrdish are stubbornly independent. Well, child. Which do you wish to embody in your staff?"

"I am Ayrdish," Aura said, standing a little taller.

"Yes, you are," Mayenne said. Her eyes twinkled. "Well, that means your staff receives a ball, and one of crystal, not of metal." She eyed the crystal spheres on a shelf to the left of her workbench. "Now, which color? Which stone?" The staff maker looked at Aura with deep curiosity in her eyes. "What sign were you born under?"

"Erasto," Aura said.

"The sign of the lovers. That's active Earth. So, your color is green. Yet, you look red to me."

"Red is my favorite color," she said. Sagacius said the same thing, that she looked like a red, thinking it was her hair. There was more to it than that. Her eyes gave her an aversion to green. Blue was too commonplace and yellow too bright. Purple was best left to the king, eorls, and thegns. Orange looked horrid, and black, white, and gray lacked the life she craved. Brown made for decent clothing and wonderful dirt. She just liked red, and thought she knew the reason. "I was born on Parin, Haemmont 1. I understand that those of us born on the quarters and cross-quarters of the wheel of the year often inherit the traits of the signs at ninety degree angles to us. That would be the two Fires."

"You have my pity, child," Mayenne said, her eyes gleaming with humor. "That explains why you have a red aura, Aura."

So, Mayenne saw her aura. She had never seen any, especially her own. That skill remained closed to her. A red aura. She expected hers to be the emotional blue or the calm green. Red meant she was passionate, sensual, impetuous, temperamental, prone to try anything once, and often ended up in trouble. She sighed. That sounded too familiar.

"This one, yes, this one," Mayenne said, lifting a sphere from the shelf. She handed it to Aura. "Hold it and tell me what you feel."

It was larger than a man's fist, but not as large as a baby's head. Crimson and transparent, she saw through it, although it turned the world upside down. In the center, flaws created clouds of scarlet. As Aura watched, the clouds seemed to swirl, ever so slowly.

"It's beautiful," Aura said. "It feels warm, like a peach picked right from the tree. What is it?"

"It's called a stone of the sun. It's the most pure one I've ever found." Mayenne took the sphere from Aura. "Be careful with it. The stone of the sun is a passion stone. From what I see, you really don't need much assistance."

Aura's right fingers found the pocket of her left sleeve, feeling the ruby inside. People kept giving her passion stones. Were they trying to tell her something?

Mayenne set the sphere on her workbench. She lifted the staff with adoration, and placed it into the vice at the front of her bench. Using her right thigh, she clamped the vice shut. Then, she took the sphere and laid it against the teeth of the cat. Motioning over her shoulder, she said, "Hand me that mallet. The one with the leather around the head. Yes, thank you."

She began tapping the sphere. "You should have no problem fitting." Tap. "Go in." Tap, tap. "Do not be stubborn. Oh, you are the stone of Ayrdland, are you not?" Tap, tap. "Do not force me to lose my temper in front of my customer." With every tap, Mayenne's accent grew thicker, until she erupted in a volley of Flumantine commands. Aura knew Flumantine, and listened closely. Then, her eyes wide, she threw her hand over her mouth. Not sure if she should blush or turn away, she stood frozen by the words streaming from the staffmaker's mouth. Flumantine oaths were more colorful, and more direct, than any in Ayrdish.

Wanting to improve her skills, and also to have some fun with the staff maker, Aura asked in Mayenne's native tongue, <Is it to fit going to? Is anything there that I may do?>

<You speak Flumantine? I apologize for my words. Your accent is terrible, child! Although, your grammar is perfect. Too perfect.> Mayenne continued to tap. <Your Ayrdic language is Nebelic. You people speak as if chiseling stones. Why the rush? When we speak Flumantine, we say our consonants as if we make love to them. Try to say them as if you are placing them ever so gently into the mouth of your lover with your tongue.>

Aura had no experience with her tongue and lovers, but she thought she understood the concept. <You mean, like this to speak? Am I correctly it to speaking?>

<You learn quickly, child. Although dispense with the formal temple diction.> With two more taps, she stood upright. Over her shoulder, she

said, "I understand. I spent five years learning not to say in Ayrdish, please what is the placement of the sun?"

"What time is it," Aura said, chuckling.

"You have an illogical language," Mayenne said, shaking her head and waving her hand. She released her thigh, opening the vice. Lifting the staff up, she said, "However, you have a beautiful staff, no?"

With the sphere in place, it no longer looked like a cat with his mouth open. The staff now looked like a musical note carved from wood and stone. Light from the far window struck the sphere and shot throughout the workshop. The flaws inside danced. Mayenne laid the staff on the bench. She pulled a box from the shelf and dumped an assortment of iron caps. After rooting through them, she selected one. With three taps, she drove the cap onto the tip of the staff. "To keep the wood from chipping on cobblestones," she said. After asking Aura to put the iron caps back in their box, Mayenne pulled a strip of leather from a rod on the wall. With quick movements, she laced the leather around the middle of the staff, forming a grip. "So that it will not slip from your hands." Finally, she took a wide gold band from a box, and fastened it to the staff, just underneath the head. "That is not just to make it look pretty."

She motioned to the shelves behind Aura. "Hand me those small boxes, would you? The ones labeled R, O, and B, but not the ones labeled G, A, or K."

Aura did as she was asked. Lifting each, the wooden boxes rattled, as if filled with rocks. She set the boxes down in front of the staffmaker. Mayenne selected a small mallet from the tool rack over the bench.

"Your full name is Aura Lockhaven, is it not?" Mayenne asked. "No middle names? You Ayrdish are so stingy with names. We Flumantines usually have eight. Now, be quiet. You do not want me to make a mistake."

Mayenne returned the staff into the vise and clamped it shut. Fishing in the box labeled R, she removed a small stamp. Placing it against the gold band, she smacked it three times with the mallet. Setting the stamp back inside the box, she pulled out another stamp and repeated the process. She did the same with two stamps from the box marked O and the one marked B.

"There," she said, returning the mallet to its place. "I stamped your initials into the gold band. Once in runes for your father, once in oghams for your mother, and again in Bellician for anyone who cannot read the old letters. With any luck, this will keep someone from taking your staff by mistake in a tavern."

"I don't intend to keep my staff far from me," Aura said.

"You're a smart woman. Now, let me see if it wants anything else."

As Mayenne reached for it, Aura noticed the staff resting in a cradle over the work bench. The staffmaker lifted it with the care of a mother holding her infant. A head higher than she was tall, the staff looked made from mahogany or some other dark exotic wood. The well worn leather grip needed a replacement. A golden set of eagle's talons held a crystal globe on top as the head. Inside the globe, white light gently twirled.

"I take it that is your staff," Aura said.

"You presume correctly," Mayenne said.

Mayenne held the staff in both hands and closed her eyes. She inhaled and exhaled. As she did, a smile crossed her face, the first Aura had seen. The twirling light accelerated, spinning inside the globe. It smacked against the sides of the glass, as if it wanted to escape. Without opening her eyes, Mayenne reached for Aura's staff with one hand. Touching both staves, the staffmaker's smile widened into a grin.

"Yes, that is it. That is perfect," Mayenne said. Mayenne removed her hand from Aura's staff and opened her eyes. She continued to smile. "May I touch you?"

Aura nodded. Mayenne extended her hand and placed it on Aura's shoulder. Faint tingles raced through her as the staffmaker tightened her hand. With a loud gasp, Mayenne ripped her hand from Aura and fell back against her bench. She gripped her staff tight against her chest. The white light bounced from side to side in the globe, demanding its release.

"My goddess!" Mayenne shouted.

"What! What's wrong?" Aura asked.

"You ... have the strongest heart I've ever experienced. It's as if you're ... pure emotion, pure feeling. Your love ... your sensuality ..." Mayenne tore herself from the bench and strode across the workshop, still clutching her staff to her chest.

"Is there anything I can do?" Aura asked.

<You can stay where you are!> Mayenne snapped in Flumantine.

<Yes, my lady of the house>, Aura responded in the same language.

Mayenne huddled in the corner of the shop, looking like a defeated warrior cradling her broken spear. She trembled and her teeth chattered. Aura heard her mumble in her native tongue, <No. Not again. I promised ... no!> Aura stood where she was, by the bench. She wanted to help, but Mayenne's command still rung in her ears. After two minutes, Mayenne stood straight and turned around. Her impassive face showed no trace of any distress.

"I apologize, Aura," she said. "Some of us, how do you say, feel the emotions of others far more strongly than we would wish. Your feelings overwhelmed me. I am fine now." As she walked toward Aura and the workbench, she added, "Well, your staff is complete. For now."

Mayenne returned her staff to its cradle. Then, she took Aura's and laid it on a table in the middle of the workshop. She gazed down at it with a loving look, then said, "Tonight, we will bond the staff to you in a moonrise ritual. For now, I must rest. Please feel free to explore Dallington. If you need anything, just ask Tyfford. He will care for your horse."

With that, Mayenne turned and walked from the shop, leaving Aura standing in a pile of shavings.

Chapter Sixteen

AURA HELD THE lantern, leading Mayenne into the field behind her house and workshop. Mayenne clutched her staff in her left hand and Aura's in her right. The path led to a circle of low stones nestled in a clearing. The thick grass felt cool underneath her feet as she walked. Mayenne declared that this ritual must be performed skyclad, so both women were naked. Instead of clothes, Mayenne bedecked herself with jeweled arm and leg bands of gold, and a necklace that reached her shoulders and down between her petite breasts. When they arrived at the circle, Mayenne asked Aura to light the torches, one at each of the eight sarsens. She did so, using the lantern's flame. Mayenne set a bag of tools on the ground by her feet. The two women stood in the center of the circle, and began the ritual. Mayenne faced east while Aura stood opposite her, facing west.

Mayenne looked at Aura's hips and said, "You do not appear to be on your moon's blood."

Aura stiffened. She growled, "I wouldn't be standing here skyclad if I were!"

"Don't be testy, child. It is the best way for a woman to bond with her staff. I have an alternative. Shall we begin?" Holding both staves to the darkened sky, Mayenne shouted, "I call upon the great goddess Dariath. I invite you to attend our circle. Please grant us your power as I transfer this staff to its owner."

She began chanting in a language Aura did not understand, rocking back and forth as she did. The skin on Aura's back prickled. This was a sorcerous ritual. Mayenne worked a magic Aura did not know. The air pressed against Aura's body. The flames of the lanterns flickered. The ground trembled beneath her feet. Droplets of moisture struck her cheeks. The gold on Mayenne's body glowed. Light inside the globes of both staves glimmered. She called upon all six elements. Aura felt a tugging inside herself, as if an unseen hand caressed her heart. She called upon even Spirit. The staves shook in Mayenne's hands. Even her own element of Wood. The fine hair on Aura's arms stood up. She remembered western sorcerers believed in the element of Flesh. They also separated ... as she thought it, the rocks in the circle creaked ... Stone from Earth. Mayenne lowered her own staff and with Aura's still raised, continued to chant.

Then, she handed Aura her staff. As Aura took it, Mayenne said, "Place it against your womanhood. Not in it, just against it, so that it fits against you snugly."

"Why?" Aura asked.

"There are three doors into your soul. The first is your eyes. They are useless for this. The second is your mouth. Saliva is weak. The third is your region of pleasure."

Aura did as she was told. It felt peculiar. Mayenne grabbed the head of Aura's staff, looked to the sky, and held her own staff aloft. She shouted in the unknown tongue. Flames shot through Aura's womanhood. She felt penetrated. This was not that of violation, however. This was that of pure desire. It felt wonderful. Aura gasped as longing and pleasure erupted in her body. She moaned as an unseen phallus sent her deep within herself.

"What are you doing?" she stammered.

"This is necessary, child. This will bond you with your staff."

While this felt spectacular, she held a staff, not a man. She stood in a stone circle, instead of lying in bed. Someone was with her, watching. She said, "I am not comfortable with this, Mayenne."

"You want your staff, no? Then, enjoy and be happy you are not a man."

Aura closed her eyes and tightened her grip on her staff. The three men who took her never did this. They satiated their lust in her and departed. If this were a man, she expected to feel his caresses all over her, hear his own moans of pleasure, and taste his desire on her lips as he kissed her. As her wetness poured from her body and covered the staff between her legs, she barely heard the instructions to raise her right hand, palm out. Instinctively, she obeyed. Fire shot through her hand. Aura shrieked. Looking at her hand, she saw the red gash, pouring blood. Mayenne stood next to her, holding a bloody hawksbill knife.

"What are you doing with my blood?" Aura shouted.

"It is my way. You would rather have a fine magical tool that obeys you than a walking stick, no?"

The ground shook. The air rushed by her. Rain fell from a cloudless sky. The torches roared. The light in the crystal ball erupted. The gold ring just underneath the head looked like molten metal. Aura merely nodded.

"Place your hand on the staff and hold it tightly," Mayenne said.

Aura did so, trying her best to grab the wood with her slippery, bloody hand. As she did, she continued to press the staff against her loins. Pain and pleasure mingled inside her. Mayenne touched the globe of her staff to Aura's. The white light in her sphere smashed against the sides, demanding its release. Mayenne grinned and began chanting again.

Mayenne reached into her bag of tools and pulled out a chalice and a small pouch. Cradling her staff in the crook of her arm, she dumped the contents of the pouch into the chalice. Flakes of herbs and ground resins fell into the golden cup. The incense exploded into clouds of smoke. Aura frowned, as much as she could nearing climax. No fire, no charcoal. It just exploded on its own. It smelled floral, tart, bitter, smoky, savory, and nauseating. It smelled like roses, sage, and stockings that had not been washed in a year. It smelled like temples and graveyards. Mayenne held the cup aloft and shouted in her foreign tongue. The smoke billowed into the rain. Then, she held the cup underneath the head of Aura's staff, smudging it while continuing to chant. Aura had lit plenty of incense and performed smudging, but never like this. Between the rain, the pleasure, the pain, and a touch of trepidation, she shivered. All made her want to scream. She bit her lip.

As Mayenne stepped back from Aura's staff, she faded from view. She felt blood from her hand and moisture from her loins ooze into the shaft. In turn, it pressed against her sending shivers of ecstasy throughout her body and pangs through her right palm. A figure appeared where Mayenne had stood. Aura saw herself made of wood, with a red crystal head. She and the staff were one entity. The elements continued to roar around her, and the chanting grew louder.

All fell silent.

Mayenne stood before her, clutching her own staff to her chest. The white light inside the globe slowed its spinning to a crawl. The smoke from the chalice was gone. The rain had ceased. Mayenne sighed. "That is your staff now. It has willingly accepted you." She looked at Aura's hips and said, "You may remove it at any time."

The ritual left its memory, as shivers of delight raced up and down Aura's back. She looked at her hand, ready to cast a healing spell. She saw no blood. Not even a trace of the cut. She cast Mayenne a cold stare, and hoped she never experienced this form of magic again.

Mayenne's face remained impassive. In the now dim light of the torches, her eyes danced with merriment. "I told you that I was a sorceress, no? That ritual creates a more firm bond that simply leaving it in the light of a full moon. Now that your staff is yours, let us find out what it does."

"You mean, you don't know?"

"I never know what my staves do until after I pass one to its rightful owner. Its purpose is between the two of them. Most are reservoirs of power." Mayenne clutched her staff tighter. Her eyes narrowed. "I feel that yours is different."

"To tell you the truth, I'm not sure what any staff does," Aura said. "Master only held his, or leaned on it when he was drunk."

"Let's find out what it does, together. The light is better inside the shop."

Mayenne picked up the lantern and led Aura to the house. Back inside the workshop, Aura dressed while Mayenne returned her staff to its cradle. She put a chair in the corner of the room. Then, the staffmaker led Aura to the center of the shop. Pointing to the chair, she said, "Let's discover what your staff does. Hold it in both hands. Move the chair and let's see how the staff responds."

Aura held the staff in front of her, holding it around the leather grip. She faced the chair. This was different. Usually, she cast spells using the palms of her hands to direct the outflow of vitality, focusing it with her fingers. On occasion, she used her whole body. This was the first time she ever worked through a tool. She saw the chair through the head of the staff and concentrated on it.

"Kinetika," she whispered.

She nearly dropped the staff as heat poured from her hands. Her vitality tore from her body and poured into the oak. The wood in her hands trembled, almost wrenching itself free from her grip. The head glowed bright red, nearly blinding her. A shaft of light shot from the sphere head and struck the chair. It shattered into splinters.

<I said move the chair, not destroy it!> Mayenne snapped in Flumantine. The light inside the globe of her own staff slammed into the glass sides.

"That's what I cast," Aura said, lowering the staff and looking at the shards of wood lying across the floor. "That was a movement spell, and I didn't put much will behind it. The chair was just supposed to move three feet."

"That is remarkable," Mayenne said, rubbing her chin. "Your staff magnifies your power. It increases your emotions. Much like Aitian glass turns the sun's light into a burning beam. That is a first for me. Here. Let me have that."

Mayenne took the staff from Aura. She walked to the workbench and sat it down. Aura followed her. She looked down at her staff and wondered how much power she held. Her mind drifted back to Lodd and Sire Thaddeus. She mumbled, "Just how powerful am I?"

Mayenne looked at the staff, then at Aura, then back at the staff. Even though her face remained impassive, she licked her lips. Turning to Aura, she said, "You should practice with it. What would have been a mere movement with your hands becomes a destroyer through your staff. That makes your staff dangerous until you get to know it, and it knows you. It would be impolite of me to let you leave without instructing you in its use, after all."

"Merciful heavens, you're right," Aura said. "I want to help people not hurt them."

Mayenne leaned back on the workbench and stared at Aura. Even though her face remained unmoved and devoid of all expression, Aura saw something in the staffmaker's eyes. She saw intense hunger, the kind she usually saw on the face of a cat stalking a mouse. The look vanished before Aura could think further of it. The staffmaker said, "You have a beautiful soul, child. You live up to your name. You are luminescent."

Aura smiled at the compliment. "What color am I now?"

"A very bright red."

"What about yours?"

Mayenne held up her hand, and looked. Her face still remained devoid of emotion, but the globe of her staff glowed. Fear crept into her eyes. "I am gray today."

"What does that mean?" Aura asked.

Mayenne whirled to face her workbench. She ripped her staff from its cradle. Gripping it to her chest with both hands, she said in an strained but even voice, "That is for me to know, and with any good fortune, you to never find out!"

"I'm sorry," Aura whispered. "Please forgive me. I was just curious."

"It is not your fault," Mayenne said, not turning around. She muttered, <No, please. Not with this one.>

Aura noticed a shift in the staff maker. Still naked, her back bulged with rippling muscles. She seemed to grow taller and thicker. For a moment, Aura thought that Mayenne fought against some invisible foe, but she decided it was just the physique of a woman accustomed to labor with iron chisels, tough mallets, and a stubborn lathe. This was the body of a woman who bent wood to her will.

The staff maker ran her finger down the length of Aura's staff. <So much emotion, such strong feelings>, Mayenne mumbled.

"Pardon me? I didn't hear you," Aura said.

"I said, you are going to stay a few days," Mayenne replied, still looking at the staff on the bench. "I cannot let you leave with your staff until you learn to control it. You could easily kill someone while trying to help. If you don't control the magic, then the magic will control you. You can practice with your staff in the field behind the house. You cannot harm boulders." Mayenne turned around. Her face showed no feeling. "Well, I am somewhat weary, and I am sure you are, too. I've a room prepared for you at the top of the stairs. Get some rest. We will practice with your staff in the morning."

Aura couldn't sleep. Mayenne graciously offered her a comfortable room with an even more comfortable bed. Not as ornate as Karyl's, it still made her simple affair in Hartshorn look like mere sticks. The silk sheets and thick mattress did nothing to calm her mind. So, she sat on the windowsill, letting her right leg dangle out into the night air. Down the road, lights of candles, lamps, and fires glowed behind the windows of Dallington's homes. Glancing up at the moon, she guessed the time to be around nine. The taverns ought to still be open.

She needed a drink. The staff downstairs troubled her. It magnified her power. But how, and by what number? While advanced mathematics was her greatest weakness, she understood simple arithmetic. Her hand cast a spell of one. The staff cast a spell of twenty. The question was, what numbers lay in between, and how were they arranged. Twenty times one, ten times two, and five times four gave her the same answer. So did two times ten. That was a completely different problem than ten times two. Who held the ten, the staff or the magician? Did the staff magnify her power by twenty, or did it merely double her latent ability? If the latter, then where in all the gods did that ability come from.

A nightingale sang in the distance. On this night, he sounded lonely. He sang for Aura. She felt alone, sitting in the window, looking out. She knew every part of her body, from her full chest and hips to the bulge of her too-fond-of-ale belly to her long legs. She knew her face with its green eyes, bushy brows, humped nose, and full lips. She no longer knew the woman who lived in that body and behind that face.

"A wizardess can't heal a punctured liver," she muttered. "A wizardess can't heal a broken heart. A wizardess can't shatter a chair. I did all three." She had thought compassion saved Lodd and Sire Thaddeus. Compassion did not destroy a piece of furniture. That had been pure force, from somewhere inside her. The only feeling she had for the chair was curiosity about what her staff would do to it.

A cry of distress interrupted her thoughts. Aura looked out on the town. Everything seemed peaceful. No, that cry came from within the house. It sounded like a woman. Mayenne must be in trouble.

Aura leapt from the window. She picked up the lamp and stepped out into the hall. No lights shown underneath the doors. She heard mumbling from downstairs. The lamp cast a grim glow on the spiral staircase as she tread her way down. The workshop door lay open and lantern light flickered out into the hall. Aura crept close and peered inside. Mayenne sat naked on the floor with her back to the door. The lantern before her cast an unholy halo around her body. She sobbed and rocked back and forth, mumbling, <No, no, no. Please!>

Aura took a step forward into the workshop. A hand on her shoulder stopped her. She gasped and spun around. The lamplight carved dark shadows into Tyfford's cadaverous face. His blank eyes bored deep into Aura's own. She shivered.

"What are you doing here?" he asked in his monotone voice.

"I heard a cry. I wanted to help," Aura said.

"You may help by returning to your room."

With that, Tyfford stepped into the workshop. He closed the door behind him, leaving Aura alone with her lamp.

Chapter Seventeen

AT DAWN THE next morning, Aura practiced with her staff in the field behind Mayenne's shop. She began with the movement spell, sending a twenty pound stone hurtling across the field. She fared no better with her second attempt. After twenty minutes, she learned how to subdue her will and control her vitality to make them roll only a few feet. Then, she tried her more powerful dueling spells. Her first throwback spell shattered a boulder. By mid morning, she had learned to control that spell and moved on to the others, trying them all save the one Sagacius made her promise to never use except to save her life. Those were not as successful. The Shield of Golau knocked her onto her back, and the Hammer of Kregg split a boulder, felling the maple tree behind it.

The once peaceful field now looked like a place of battle. Smoke rose over the fallen trees, smashed stones, and torn up ground. Can't harm boulders, eh. Taking a rest, Aura sat down on one of the few undamaged stones. She pulled the kerchief from her sleeve and dried the sweat from her forehead and cheeks. Then, she tied her hair into a ponytail with the red ribbon. Several locks clung to her still wet face in stubborn disarray.

As she rested, she regarded her staff. After so many spells, especially dueling spells, she expected to be exhausted. Instead, she only felt fatigued. She thought that perhaps with her staff, she could cast more powerful healing spells like she had for Lodd without endangering herself. How would that spell work through her staff today? She wondered if she would heal Lodd in a second, or crush his body. The arithmetical problems from the previous night returned. Who had the larger factor, the staff or the magician? By how much was this staff magnifying her power?

Mayenne stood by, watching in silence. She wore a short sleeveless blue robe, belted around her waist. She leaned on her staff like a cripple, her face more impassive than before. Even in the sunlight, the light in the globe of her staff glowed. It no longer danced inside. Now, it consumed the entire globe, bathing it in mist.

"You are doing quite well, child," Mayenne said. It was the first time she spoke since they stepped out into the field hours earlier. "At this rate, you may earn my permission to depart tomorrow. It will take days, even weeks, before you are ready to use your staff on a living person, but practice as you travel."

"Thank you," Aura said. "I think it's more tiring to control my will and feelings than it is to cast the spells."

"Hmm. Control your will. Control your feelings," Mayenne said. She licked her lips and mumbled, "I don't know that I want you to do that."

"Pardon me?" Aura asked.

"I said, it's time for breakfast."

The cold goose tasted good, especially with two goblets of Mayenne's Flumantine wine. After they ate, the staffmaker led Aura to her workshop. Mayenne took Aura's staff from her and placed it on the work bench. Over her shoulder, she said, "I think that's enough practice for one morning."

"Thank you," Aura said. "That was rather tiring. Although, I'm not as tired as I should be, given the spells I used."

"That is not a surprise to me," Mayenne said. She returned her staff to its cradle, and mumbled, <I'm so sorry, old friend.> She turned to face Aura, with a shocking smile on her face. "There are other things you should practice now."

"What do you –?" Aura asked.

Aura fell silent as Mayenne untied her robe. She let it fall from her shoulders and hang on her elbows before it fell to the floor. For a moment, Aura thought Mayenne was just getting comfortable. The workshop did seem hot. Then, the way she undressed dawned on her. Before Aura could say anything, Mayenne walked toward her.

"I want you, Aura Lockhaven," she said.

The naked staff maker walked toward Aura, taking slow heel-to-toe steps and allowing her hips to sway. Mayenne looked at her through dark eyes shrouded underneath thick lids. Aura knew that look. She had seen it on the faces of her suitors as they undressed her. It was the look of hunger and desire. Aura did not know what surprised her more, Mayenne's sudden sensual longing or the fact that the staffmaker possessed that feeling at all. She seemed so unemotional most of the time. The look that Aura saw was no mere flicker. Mayenne's eyes smouldered with the flames of the need for conquest. Her face burned with pure lust.

Aura did not feel like being conquered. Stepping backwards, away from Mayenne, she bumped into the table behind her. Before she could turn around and bolt for the door, Mayenne stood in front of her and placed her hand on Aura's shoulder.

"Oh, merciful heavens," Aura said. "Uh, Mayenne, uh, that breeze doesn't billow my cloak. I ... I prefer men."

"I prefer men, too, Aura," Mayenne said, purring like a cat. "But your feelings have aroused me. Your aura entices me, child," Mayenne said, caressing her lips with her tongue. She narrowed her eyes as anger shot through them. "You do want your staff, no?"

"I do, but ... Last night overwhelmed me. Mayenne, I'm terrified of this," Aura stammered.

"Just relax," Mayenne said, caressing Aura's cheek.

Her fingertips felt cold against her flesh. Aura gulped. It appeared she had no choice. Trembling, she raised her hand and returned the caress. Mayenne's face felt even colder. Without warning, Mayenne tore herself away. She ran to the opposite side of the shop, sobbing. Backing herself into the corner, she stared at Aura with terrified eyes. She shook with such force that one of the staves fell from the rack and clattered on the floor.

She shrieked, "This is wrong! This is so wrong."

"Mayenne," Aura said, taking a step toward the staffmaker. "I'm confused. Do you want me or not? What do you –"

"You arrogant tart!" Mayenne snapped. "You don't understand what I'm talking about! You don't understand anything!"

Aura withered under the weight of Mayenne's rebuke. She stepped back and bumped against the table.

<I can't,> Mayenne said. She grabbed her hair and screamed, <I can't!> Throwing her weight against the wall, she cried in deep moans. Tears poured down her face. Her chest heaved from the exertion of what Aura guessed to be some sort of sorrow or confusion. "I can't ... I can't ..." she whispered. Mayenne closed her eyes. "I can't ..." Then, the sobbing ceased. The tremors stopped. She stood up straight. Wiping the tears from her eyes with the back of her hand, she stared at Aura with the look of hunger again. She smiled. "I can't help myself."

Dear Ystlena, Aura thought. This woman either showed no feelings at all, or showed them all within ten seconds of each other.

"I want you, Aura Lockhaven!" Mayenne said, advancing toward Aura with more determination than desire in her steps.

"You've said that before. I'm nervous, but I'm still here," Aura said. She reached for the laces of her bodice. "I suppose I should get undressed."

"There is no rush. It is not your body I crave. It never was."

"It isn't? Then what –"

Mayenne stood before Aura. Her smile widened. She placed one hand on Aura's shoulder and the other around her waist. She said, "I want your heart!"

Mayenne pulled Aura to her. Before she could say anything, the staffmaker pressed her lips to hers. Her tongue forced its way through Aura's lips and found her own. Aura squirmed to free herself. This was too sudden! This was disgusting! How about a nice, tender kiss to start? How about ... Aura felt nothing. Her shock disappeared. Her disgust vanished. Her surprise melted. She felt nothing. It was as if all her emotions just ceased to exist. Mayenne's tongue continued to explore hers, and as it did, she felt less and less inclined to pull away, or do anything else.

Mayenne released Aura's mouth. She still held her close, their chests pressed against each other. She panted in deep breaths of pleasure. She closed her eyes and moaned in a way that Aura thought sounded like the throes of pleasure, but she could not remember that tone for some reason. Aura wanted to caress the staffmaker. At least, she thought she did. Her hands refused to move. What did she feel? Did she feel anything?

"That was some kiss," Aura mumbled.

"Just wait," Mayenne said.

Aura looked up into Mayenne's face. At first, she thought her eyes betrayed her. After all, Mayenne just gave her the most powerful kiss of her life. She blinked a few times. No, her eyes did not deceive her. Mayenne's own eyes were entirely black.

"What the –" Aura started to say.

Before she could utter another word, Mayenne kissed her again, pressing her lips tight onto hers. Her tongue found Aura's again. All Aura's feelings faded into nothingness. All she knew was that kiss, a cold fact that existed in her mouth and on her lips that held no more delight or interest for her than a speck of pollen on the windowsill.

Rationality took its place as her dominant thought process. Cold hard reason replaced her usual bubbling cauldron of feelings. She had heard of this. What was it again? An old legend surfaced in her memory, one she heard from templegoers long ago about a demon seductress. Aura pulled her face from Mayenne's. The staffmaker held her even tighter. Despite her height and weight advantage, Aura could not tear herself from Mayenne's arms. She was not sure she even wanted to.

"I know what you are. You're a succubus!" Aura said, in the voice of someone sight reading a book aloud seen for the first time.

Mayenne cackled. "If I were a succubus, I wouldn't care about you. They steal the souls of men, no? To steal yours, I'd have to be an incubus, and then I wouldn't be simply kissing you. I am a balakalat."

"A balakalat," Aura said. She thought she should be terrified, but all she felt was mere trepidation. "The balakalat is a fable."

"Do I look like a fable to you?" Mayenne asked. "Let me show you reality again."

Again, Mayenne kissed her. Again, Mayenne's tongue forced its way inside her mouth and pressed against her own. Again, her feelings subsided to almost nothing. Aura's legs buckled under her. She no longer had the desire to stand. Struggling with Aura's weight, Mayenne stopped kissing her.

"Stop it," Aura mumbled. "You're draining me."

"That's the whole idea, child. You are so delicious."

Mayenne settled Aura on the table. She strode around the workshop, touching everything; her tools, her bench, the staves. Aura thought she should run while the staffmaker was distracted. Yet, she did not want to. She watched Mayenne with the cold detachment of an apothecary examining a man with ague. She tried to force her will into her legs but even that seemed to have fled.

As Mayenne fondled her staves, she said, "I have never experienced such feelings before. Is this how you see the world? Such wonder! Such amazement!" She sighed. "I am truly sorry, old friend. I know what I promised you, but this is all your fault, really. You never should have sent her to me. There are other staffmakers in the Valley." Looking at Aura, she said, "Don't worry, child. Your feelings will return in an hour or so. At least, I hope they do. I plan to feed on you for quite some time."

Aura realized what Mayenne meant to do. She had no desire to be anyone's feedbag, much less a desire to have her emotions drained on a daily basis. Exerting all her will, she stood up and held out her right hand. She thought in a way she never had before, with cold logic and calculating destruction. The almost malignant rationale of her thought would have terrified her, if she could feel terror. Her plan was so simple. All she had to do was fire one powerful throwback spell, knock Mayenne unconscious, grab her staff, and flee.

"Tenthatora," Aura said.

Nothing happened. Her hand remained as impassive as her own face. Only earlier that very morning, she cast five such spells. Aura slowly curled her fingers into a fist and drew her hand to her chest. She always believed that will was the key power behind magic. Now, she began to believe that, at least in her situation, emotion drove will. Without emotion, will was impotent, and impotent will created impotent magic.

"It is difficult to work magic without any feelings, no? I know, child. I know," Mayenne said.

Aura needed something to compensate for her subdued soul. Her staff! If her staff magnified her power to the point of shattering stone, then perhaps it would magnify whatever remained enough to render Mayenne incapable of any further attack. The staff lay ten feet away, on the workbench. Before she could take a step toward it, Mayenne jumped in front of her, cutting off her approach.

"I'm sorry, child, but I can't let you have that staff."

Aura considered punching her way out of the ordeal. That required more emotion than magic. She had never hit anyone without first experiencing fear or fury, and those emotions seemed so alien to her. Before she could decide on any course of action, Mayenne grabbed her and threw her to the table. Straddling the stricken Aura, she kissed her. As Mayenne's tongue ravaged hers, whatever remained of Aura's feelings subsided into an empty void. Then, her vision followed, leaving her mind in darkness.

Chapter Eighteen

AURA OPENED HER eyes. She lay on wood. This was not her bed, she thought. What happened. Did she drink too much and pass out on the floor again? She called her master, only no words left her mouth. She heard nothing but a muffled mumble. Her mouth refused to open. She reached for it, but her hands did not work. They were nailed to her back. Who? What? Glancing at her feet, she saw the leather straps binding them together. As clarity returned to her mind, Aura felt the leather straps around her wrists and those across her cheeks. Someone had bound and gagged her. She tried to sit up, but fell onto her side.

"You have returned, no?" asked a woman behind her. Mayenne walked around the table and stood in front of Aura. She was still naked. The head of the staff in her hand glowed and pulsed. She smiled, a look that sent shivers down Aura's body. "I've never had prey faint before. That was interesting. Unfortunately, that cut off the flow of your emotions. Based on your baleful expression, I'd say they have returned."

Aura remembered what happened. The balakalat drained her emotions enough to make her lose consciousness. She tried to scream. Nothing but an intangible mumble penetrated the leather mask across her mouth. She strained against the straps binding her hands. They refused to budge, biting into her wrists.

"I apologize for the straps and the gag," Mayenne said. "I'm not silly enough to let you speak with your emotions at full power. I know what you're capable of doing to me, even without your staff. I certainly don't want you to leave."

Mayenne leaned down until her face was inches from Aura's. She eyed the staffmaker with suspicion. At least, with the gag in place, Mayenne couldn't kiss her and suck out her feelings. She glanced at the staff in her hand. That thing empowered her somehow. Aura glared at her, wishing incantations could be thought, and not just spoken in old Karanthek. If they could, then Mayenne would be a smouldering cinder.

Mayenne smiled and said, "Aura, you don't realize just how special you are. You don't just have a gift. You *are* a gift." She caressed Aura's cheek. "You don't know what it's like to not feel, to never delight at a sunset, to never thrill at the sight of a man's body, to never pause at birdsong, to never savor the taste your food, to never smile at the scent of a rose. You wake up every morning with all those things, and to you, they are life itself. For me to have them, I have to employ artificial means. I would almost rather die than to do what I am about to do to you, but I cannot help myself." Mayenne licked her lips. "You see, we're going to be together. Forever. I'm going to, how do you say, put your heart inside me."

Aura squirmed on the table. She was not about to allow herself to be sacrificed in some ritual. The straps dug into her wrists and ankles, but she fought against them. They refused to yield. She screamed, but only a muffled murmur of protest escaped the leather that covered her mouth.

"Oh, not this organ," Mayenne said, placing her hand on Aura's left breast. "Your soul. I'd rather move my soul into your body. Oh, the staves I could create if I had your arms and your hands! But I don't know that spell. The one I am about to perform is dark enough."

"Milady, this is risky," Tyfford said.

Aura had not noticed him in the room. She looked upside down, behind her. He stood behind the table, near the rack of aging woods. Even from her flipped perspective, she saw his impassive face, regarding her as just another piece of beef to roast.

"I know, but I need access to her mouth and womanhood," Mayenne said.

"It isn't just untying her, Milady. I have been listening to the whispers of messengers. Aura was due in Ardora today. They grow concerned. I believe some are on their way here."

"Once Aura is inside me, I can handle Karyl and Karyn Kriger combined!"

"I refer to Lady Etheria and Lord Ashthorne. Their power is unequaled in all your order. One of them alone could kill you. I expect they will appear in tandem."

Mayenne sighed. "I considered that, Tyfford. Deofoyl is my friend. Let us hope he is dumbfounded enough to let me slip away. As for that blonde guttersnipe ... I think I can run faster than she."

"We should have stripped her. This dress is in your way."

"I can't think of everything, Tyfford."

"This should be performed on the night of a new moon, Milady."

"You really are a dour old man, no?" Mayenne touched Aura's cheek. She smiled the smile of the weary. "I hate to do this to you. I really do. I'd rather untie you, give you a nice fattening feast, join you for too much wine, and in the morning, send you off with your staff. But I can't. I can't! You don't know what it's like to live without your own feelings. How could you?"

Mayenne held her staff in her left hand. The light swirled inside, bashing against the glass globe. She lifted the hawksbill knife from her workbench. In a slow arc, she cut herself over her left breast. As the blood oozed from the wound, Mayenne slapped her hand across the incision. She threw her head back.

"Dariath ontu mayal parma cor," she shouted. "Nefta haif do ma nact. Cy'ur fral intu ma. Nee so! Unct so! Ana so! Mut! Cy'ur gen hanata covo. Ontu mayal parma cor!"

Aura shivered as she heard the words. She did not recognize the language, but she knew evil when she heard it.

Mayenne trembled. She shook as if she had a fever. Her ears lengthened into proud points. Her eyes turned from black to milky white. Her canines erupted into fangs. Thick blue ooze poured from her skin, covering her from her neck to her knees. The globe of her staff lit like a star, casting the workshop into white light.

In a voice like that of a man with the ague, Mayenne shouted, "Ganga pro nicti pratha ma! Ick lanatar sandalo trace. Dariath, ta mo re! Dariath, ta mo ra! Dariath, ta mo notor! Ontu mayal parma cor!"

The trembling ceased. Mayenne stood straight, more muscular and thick. The incision over her heart was gone. The blue ooze hardened into scales. A substance like mucus dripped from her fangs.

"You are an abomination, Milady," Tyfford said with no expression.

"Thank you," Mayenne growled. She looked at Aura, and said, "Now, I am a true balakalat."

She nodded to Tyfford. The valet walked to the end of the table, and unbuckled the straps binding Aura's feet. As soon as her feet were free, Aura squirmed. Tyfford put his hand on her chest and shoved her down onto the table. Dammit, but this skinny old man was strong. Her protests turned into a gurgle.

Aura's breath quickened as Mayenne crawled onto the table. Setting her staff down, she grabbed the hem of Aura's skirt with both hands. In one long motion, she ripped the right seam up to the bodice. Then, she threw the material aside, exposing the lower half of Aura's body. Parting Aura's legs, she knelt between her knees. Then, she leaned forward until her hand lay just above the leather gag. Mayenne nodded again. Tyfford unbuckled the gag. Before Aura could say anything, Mayenne clamped her hand over her mouth and pushed her head back against the table.

"I apologize, Aura," Mayenne said. "I'm going to enter you now. There are three doors into your soul, and your eyes are still useless. I must enter the other two. It is the only way for me to siphon you into me. Oh, but your aura has flames of black in it tonight. Anger? Hatred? Fear? That is unworthy, child. Try not to think of it as a violation. Try to enjoy the last thing you will ever experience with your body."

Mayenne thrust Aura's thighs apart with her own. She clamped down harder on Aura's mouth. With a roll of her eyes, something thick shot from her mouth, snakelike, black and dripping saliva. A similar thing, not unlike the sex of a stallion, erupted from her womanhood. Mayenne shifted her hips and the balakalat's "manhood" inched closer to Aura's womanhood. The staffmaker lowered her face to Aura's. She felt Mayenne's hot sticky breath.

"No, don't ravage me," Aura tried to scream. Her words turned into a groan against Mayenne's hand.

Even without Mayenne's hand over her mouth, she could not have issued the needed Karanthek incantation. All languages fled before the memory of finding Ester laying in the alley. It if happened to Ester, then it could happen to her. The slime on Ester's body, which she knew now to be spent semen, the lifeless stare from her cold blue eyes, the dead fists clenched in anger. That was all she saw. Her breath quickened as the grip of terror descended upon her. Her body erupted in cold sweat. No, now was not the time for a terror attack! Now was the time to think, to find a way out of this! She was about to be ravaged to death just as Ester had been.

Aura closed her eyes. Think, Aura, think. She remembered a similar situation, when she was eleven, in a field outside Hartshorn. The sixteen year old boy she only knew as Nubbin tried to rape her. What had she done then? She recalled laying on her back with her legs apart, his manhood dripping with desire only inches from her own body. Yet, she remained unviolated. What had she done? What had she done! Think, Aura, think!

She remembered. Aura's eyes flew open. She rocked her hips backwards, and drew her knees to her chest. Mayenne looked at her in surprise. Before the balakalat could react, Aura slammed her feet together. Her legs exploded with the force of muscles accustomed to lifting logs and kegs, extending to their full length. The heels of her boots crashed into Mayenne's face. Mayenne's staff flew from her hand. Her head snapped back. She tottered on the edge of the table, then vanished over the side.

That released Aura's mouth. She felt Tyfford stirring behind her. She sat up. Opening her hands, she aimed in his general direction and shouted "Tenthatora!" Her anger and fear combined to propel the throwback spell from her palms with greater force than she was accustomed to feeling. The recoil shoved her to the edge of the table. Based on the grunt she heard, and the clatter of wood against stone, she hit her target. Mayenne lay on the floor, not moving. Aura turned to look behind her. Tyfford lay still against the wood rack, beneath a pile of logs and branches.

"What blasphemy is this!" Aura said. She pivoted until she sat on the edge of the table. Free from imminent ravaging, her mind returned. She said the Karanthek for untie. The leather straps fell from her hands. As she rubbed her numb wrists, she muttered, "Gods smite this. I'm going home!"

Standing up, she felt her heart pound. She gasped for breath. The terror attack had taken its toll. She needed to center and calm herself, but that would have to wait. She spotted her staff laying on Mayenne's workbench. All she had to do was grab it, find her bag, and bolt from the house before the two on the floor awoke. Forget the bag. She could replace a hair brush.

As Aura reached for her staff, she heard the word "Fahtah!" Before she could turn her head, the bolt of force smashed into her shoulder. She spun around and collapsed against the table. Mayenne stood at the other end, glaring at her with her white eyes. As Aura regained her senses and stood up, Mayenne dashed to the workbench and picked up Aura's staff.

"Stay away from me!" Aura snapped, raising her hands.

"I have no intention of approaching you," Mayenne said. "Not yet."

Walking backwards, with her left palm extended toward Aura, she sat the staff in the corner of the workshop, the furthest point away. Then, she walked to the door and threw the bolt. Aura gulped. She was trapped inside the workshop with a hungry balakalat. At least the things that erupted from Mayenne's mouth and womanhood had receded, for now.

"If you want your staff, and if you want to leave, you have to fight me for both," Mayenne said.

"What did you say?" Aura asked.

"I said, I challenge you to a duel!"

The smile began as a twitch at the right corner of her mouth. It slowly spread across her lips until it ended on the left side as a grin. Aura's eyes twinkled. The fear of her near ravaging faded. The terror of almost losing her soul vanished. The horror of being locked in a room with a monster fled. She felt only excitement. Her first duel! After this, she would be a wizardress indeed.

"I accept!" Aura said. "I must warn you that I was trained by a duelist. Master taught me everything I know."

"Did he teach you everything *he* knows?"

"Why don't you find out?"

"By Dariath, but you are an arrogant tart!"

Mayenne cast the first spell. She waved her hand through the air and said "Plarg!"

That wasn't Karanthek. It must be Phrathian. Aura had no idea what to expect from a sorceress who knew western magic. With her solid white eyes, she also could not see where the balakalat looked. She found out both as she felt the slap across her face from an unseen backhand. Tightening her left hand, she snapped "Garoth!"

The invisible fist struck Mayenne on the chin, snapping her head back. She fell backwards. Mayenne clenched her fist and shouted "Vantar!'

Aura doubled over as a blast of force smashed into her stomach. She glared at Mayenne and decided that if she wanted a fistfight, she would use her real hands. Apparently, the staffmaker thought the same thing. Mayenne closed in, moving between Aura and her workbench. Aura stepped back, bumping into the table. With a snarl, Mayenne said, "Ongko!"

Aura discovered what the word meant when a wall of solid air smacked into her. She flew back against the table. The table tilted, hovered on two legs, then tottered over on its side, sending her sprawling on the floor next to Mayenne's staff. Aura shook her head. Using the overturned table as a shield, she raised her hand and shouted, "Tenthatora!"

The throwback spell caught Mayenne in the stomach. With a loud growl of pain, the staffmaker flew back against her workbench. She fell to the floor as the bench followed her, sending mallets, chisels, gemstones, and gold trim flying. Aura stood up and grinned. So, the balakalat was not adept in a duel.

Mayenne moaned under her bench. With slow deliberate movements, she crawled out from under it, righted it, and picked up her tools. Aura considered firing a spell into her back as she worked, but hesitated. That would be dishonorable, she thought. She stood transfixed, watching Mayenne restore her bench with the care of a mother tending to her baby. Even with the pointed ears, the tangled mass of hair, and the blue scales, Mayenne still looked every bit the craftsman and artist. When the last gemstone was back in its place, Mayenne whirled around. Saliva dripped from her fangs and fury radiated from her white eyes.

<No one messes up my workbench!> she snarled. "Now, I'm angry."

"Do something about it," Aura said.

"Oh, my," Mayenne said. "When I called you an arrogant tart, it was a terrible understatement."

"Sifir Kregg," Aura shouted.

A translucent mallet, the Hammer of Kregg, shot from Aura's palm. Mayenne almost sidestepped it. The hammer struck her in the shoulder, sending her into a spin. She collided with her workbench, again. Without looking, the balakalat aimed her hand in Aura's direction.

"Pasknat!" she said.

The fishnet opened a little early. It caught in the air. Aura stepped aside and watched it settle on the table, and then dissipate. Nice one, she thought. Just a little premature. Mayenne turned to face Aura, rubbing her shoulder. Sagacius warned Aura never to use the same spell twice. Her opponent would anticipate it. Still, she thought that perhaps Mayenne was not as good as she appeared. The fishnet showed her weaknesses. Perhaps she would not guess this one, and it was Aura's best dueling spell.

"Tentha –"

Aura never heard Mayenne's incantation. She felt the blows across her face. It felt like someone hit her with a series of stones. Whatever it was knocked her against the wall. Aura shook her head to clear it and felt her face. Nothing felt broken, but a trickle of blood oozed from her nose. Before she could stand, another Phrathian word sent the table scooting across the floor. It slammed into Aura, pinning her to the wall.

Mayenne stood with her arms folded, watching as Aura tried to push the table back. "Tell me, child. Did you meditate this morning? Did you converse with your gods? Did you spend time caressing the elements? No, you did not. At dawn, you flew down the stairs like a boy after a new puppy. You are unprepared to fight a duel with an apprentice, much less me."

Aura managed to squirm out from behind the table. She stood on shaking legs. Gulping, she admitted that the staffmaker was right. She was being arrogant. She had spent every morning preparing for more lessons or the crafting of luck charms. It never occurred to her to face each day as a fight for life. This was no practice drill against a friendly teacher. The balakalat meant to kill her.

"I just want to go home," Aura stammered.

"We shall go there, together. Remember, child. It is your soul I want, not your body. You just need to live long enough for me to siphon your soul. I don't care how much I break you in the meantime. You really should not just stand there, unprotected." Mayenne raised both hands and yelled, "Sirtius sata rath!"

Aura saw what looked like a Flaming Dragon shoot across the workshop toward her. Except, this dragon looked western, a long snake like creature with huge teeth, instead of the Ayrdish curmudgeon with wings. It consumed the space between the two opponents. This spell was new to her and she was not sure how to counter it. Her instinct took over. Her hands flew over her chest on their own and words shot from her mouth.

"Agis aspidar!" Aura shouted.

The Shield of Golau rose before her just as the fiery head reached her. It exploded on contact with the translucent sapphire colored plane. Flashes of yellow and red blinded her. She felt the heat around her, singing her arms. That was too close, Aura said to herself. She decided to keep the shield raised, not knowing what Mayenne was about to launch next.

"Nice counterspell," Mayenne said. "But you really should have extended it to the floor."

Aura glanced down. The balakalat was right. The shield stopped at her knees. Before she could enlarge the shield, Mayenne shouted "Stipes!" A log smacked into the side of her left leg. She sprawled to the floor. That broke her concentration and the shield vanished.

"Dammit," Aura muttered, pushing herself up on her hands.

"You do have a red aura, Aura," Mayenne said. "You're not thinking. Control the magic or it will control you! Let me tell you what a gray aura means. It means entrapment, suffocation! It's malaise!"

Aura shook her head. She fought a seasoned professional who knew dark magic and used strange incantations. Mayenne no doubt knew ancient spells that Aura could not counter. As if fighting a soul-devouring monster who had tried to rape her was not enough. Control the magic? How? She couldn't even tell what spell came at her until it struck. She glanced at her staff, then at the door. Wanting both her staff and to flee, she thought Mayenne might have just given her an opening.

Aura stood. She clenched her left hand, feeling the stiffness of her scar. Defend the defenseless? Help the helpless? Give hope to the hopeless? Mayenne didn't fit any of those categories. If anything, Aura felt like the defenseless, but it was worth the effort. "You don't have to live like this. Let me help you."

"An Ayrdish woman telling me what to do? How hypocritical," Mayenne said. "Nath kata tod!"

A pair of unseen hands grabbed Aura by the torso. Fingers closed around her waist. They lifted her from the floor by a foot. Reaching down, her own hands felt them, yet she could not see them. The hands began pulling her toward Mayenne.

"What further blasphemy is this?" Aura asked.

Chapter Nineteen

WHEN THE HANDS had pulled Aura within two feet of Mayenne, they stopped. The staffmaker smiled. She reached out and touched Aura on the cheek. Aura shivered under the freezing fingertips.

"You are a terrible wizardess, no? You fight a duel unprepared. You do not treat your gods with seriousness. You do not treat me with seriousness. Do you even know how to defeat a balakalat?" Mayenne purred as she spoke. "There is a way, but it's much too late."

Mayenne nodded. Two more invisible hands grabbed Aura. They reached underneath her torn dress and lifted the skirt above her hips. With a twist of her head, the appendage erupted from Mayenne's mouth. A shift of her hips, and the second one emerged from her womanhood. The one that should be her tongue reached for Aura's mouth. The other crossed the space between the women. It reached for Aura's hips.

"No," Aura whispered. "No," she said. "No!" she shouted.

Cold sweat engulfed her body again. This was too close to the prior attack. She still had not recovered from the first one. The workshop faded from view, replaced by a hot alley in summer. Mayenne changed into the body of Ester, twisted and broken. The aroma of woodshavings transformed into the stench of death and mud.

All her fear coalesced inside her. It came together in her chest, and erupted out her mouth. Aura threw her head back and screamed. The air in the shop grew white. Mayenne grunted. The hands around her waist tightened, threatening to crack her ribs. Beating against the unseen fingers, Aura gasped for air. She screamed again, and the hands faded. With nothing to support her, she fell to her knees on the workshop floor. Mayenne supported herself on her bench. Blood flowed from her broken nose, and oozed from one of her swollen eyes. If it was possible, worry etched itself into her scaly forehead.

"What did you just do?" she snarled.

Nothing, Aura tried to say. The word turned into a choking noise in her throat. The alley was too hot! No, it was a workshop. That was not Ester. It was a monster trying to kill her. She tried to remember her list of dueling spells, but the fear jumbled her Karanthek. She gauged the distance to the balakalat's body. Mayenne was still stunned by something, some unseen attack. Time to get physical. That worked before. It had to work again, before she lost all thought to the onslaught of panic.

She glanced around, trying to focus on the room. What could she throw at Mayenne? Noticing the shelf of tools, she thought about levitating the mallets toward the back of her head. No, too complicated. Besides, what was the word for levitate again? This needed to be simple and fast. She spotted Mayenne's staff on the floor next to her. It had an iron tip similar to her own. At least, it was a stick. Aura grabbed the staff, and holding it in both hands, thrust it forward like a spear. The iron tip jammed into Mayenne's stomach. With a shriek, the staffmaker slipped to the floor. She held her abdomen, and writhed.

<Dammit, that hurt!> Mayenne snapped in Flumantine.

Aura needed to center herself. She needed to calm down. She needed more time to recover from the last terror attack. Her mind refused to grant her the time. Her heart beat inside her chest, and the roar of blood rang in her ears. Sweat poured from her skin. The smell of mud changed into the smell of smoke. No, Aura thought. Not now. Mayenne climbed up the workbench, supporting herself. Legs sprouted from her body. Eight of them. Her mouth changed into mandibles. Panic consumed Aura. With a scream, she dashed across the workshop and threw herself against the door.

Pounding against the door, Aura cried, "Let me out! Let me out of this alley! Please get me out of this barrel!" She grabbed her hair. Why didn't anyone help her? Where was that Mr. Old Man who just knocked out Fulbert? She needed him. The heard the drone of children taunting her. Snake Eyes, Snake Eyes.

Now, Aura felt thousands of tiny feet crawling on her body. They weren't there, she told herself. It was just her mind. Still, she slapped her arms, legs, hips, chest, trying to knock the spiders from her. Wide eyed with terror, she looked around the workshop. The huge spider stood ten feet tall, laughing at her. With another scream, Aura bolted toward the window.

Halfway across the workshop, Aura heard the strange words. Something grabbed her and threw her to the floor. Her face smashed against the stones. Her arms pulled behind her back. Something snake like wrapped around her wrists and ankles. Immobilization and the hard floor knocked some of the panic from her. The spiders faded and the workshop returned to normal. Panting, and trying to clear her mind, she looked over her shoulder. Her hands were bound by thick ropes, ropes that also bound her feet. Aura struggled to free her hands, but the ropes tightened, cutting into her skin. Then, she lay her face on the stones. She had nothing left. That attack drained her. Perhaps she had no remaining emotions for Mayenne to use.

The staffmaker was right. As a wizardess, a nature magician, she knew to meditate on the elements every morning. Just five minutes was all they desired. Still, they had helped her in the past. She knew them and they knew her. Perhaps, they would be merciful today.

"I call upon Air, the spirit of the east. Please help me," Aura mumbled. "I call upon Fire, the spirit of the south. Please help me." Mayenne sighed. "I call upon Water, the spirit of the west. Please help me. I call upon Earth, the spirit of the north. Please help me." Mayenne walked toward Aura. "I call upon Light, the spirit of above. Please help me. I call upon Metal, the spirit of below. Please help me." Mayenne stood by her. "Please give me your strength and wisdom." Mayenne knelt by Aura. She whispered, "I call upon Spirit, my center. Please don't fail. Please don't fail."

"They cannot hear you, child," Mayenne said.

Mayenne grabbed Aura's shoulder and rolled her over onto her back. Aura lashed out with her feet, trying to kick the balakalat. Mayenne laughed and straddled Aura's legs, pinning her to the floor. Aura wriggled underneath Mayenne, trying to gain her freedom. Mayenne settled her weight down on Aura's legs, growing heavier as she did. The balakalat grinned, drool pouring from her mouth and dangling from her fangs. The scales on her skin glistened in the light seeping in through the windows.

"I can still consume you with your legs tied together, Aura," Mayenne snarled. "I wonder what it will be like to experience that temper of yours. What caused that explosion of fear? You almost rendered me unconscious with your scream, no? I shall practice that."

Mayenne shook her head and the thick dripping tongue extended. The second appendage shot from her womanhood. Again, she felt the fear take tangible shape within her and begin its climb to the surface. Her breath shot from her nose in a rapid staccato. Not a third terror attack within the same hour! The last time she had three in one day, she remained paralyzed in the alley behind Ortha's bakery for twelve hours. This time, after exhausting so much vitality fighting, she knew her heart would stop. Aura controlled her breath, inhaling and exhaling in deliberate slow beats, willing herself to remain in the moment, if not calm.

Sweat beaded on her forehead. The bodice of her dress turned dark with perspiration. Her efforts to control her breath collapsed. Aura had no choice now. She had to use *that* spell. Sagacius forbade her from ever using it unless she faced a dire situation. What could be more dire than facing violation with intent to drain her soul. *Do you vow to only use your power and office to harm another as an act of self defense or to defend someone else?* She had so vowed, and now her own life lay inches from ending. If the balakalat did not kill her, the next terror attack would. Her last attempt with the spell almost killed her master. Aura doubted if she had enough vitality remaining to kill Mayenne. Gulping, she hoped she had enough left to knock the creature unconscious.

Closing her eyes, Aura mumbled, "Forgive me, Master."

She opened her eyes. Mayenne leaned forward to press her tongue into Aura's mouth. That shifted her weight, taking some of it off Aura's hips. Ignoring the two appendages, hoping to control the rising terror, she tightened her muscles and pushed up with her legs. She lifted off the floor enough to make Mayenne move. Aura wrenched herself to her left, twisting and ignoring the deep bite of the ropes. She rolled over onto her stomach. Mayenne still straddled her legs, but sat upright to catch her balance. The balakalat sighed as Aura extended her hands in her direction. The ropes cut even deeper and Aura stretched her fingers and raised her hands off her body.

Aura forced herself to remember the incantation. Hurling all her growing panic into her voice, she imagined Mayenne embodying her burning father, her dead sister, and hundreds of eight-legged beasts. The staffmaker became the living personification of fear of being alone, fear of rape, and fear of spiders. As her terror roared from her heart and down her arms, she shouted, "Theto karino!"

Aura thought the skin peeled off her hands as her vitality shot into her fingers. A burst of white light crackled from each fingertip. Ten small blasts merged in the air beyond her palms, forming two long arcs of zigzagging movement. The air around Aura shimmered as the two larger bursts of energy met beyond her body. The room shook with the roar of lightning through sky as the Divine Thunderbolt spell came together into one, ripped through the space between the two combatants, and crashed into Mayenne's chest. Aura heard the balakalat scream, a thick raspy growl oozing saliva. The electrical shock poured through Mayenne's legs into her own. She shrieked as her body shook from the current of her own spell. Dammit, Mayenne was grounded to her!

Aura felt nothing. No weight. No feeling of thighs against her own. Only waves of tingles and numbness as the solid light subsided. Only the weariness she felt from launching the most powerful offensive dueling spell she knew. Only the emptiness she experienced when the terror attacks devoured her. The third one, still in its infancy, began to subside. Controlling her breath until her mind cleared, Aura rolled over onto her side and looked toward her feet. Beyond her, on her back, lay the silent form of the balakalat. A tendril of smoke rose from between Mayenne's darkened blue breasts.

Aura looked at the ropes holding her reddening hands, and with her last vitality, said, "Lyna."

The ropes holding her dissolved. Between her fight with Mayenne, the deep fear of the terror attacks, and using the Divine Thunderbolt, she was exhausted. The backlash from her last spell did not help. Her legs were still numb. Her arms resisted her efforts to move them. Raising herself on her hands, she looked around the workshop. She wanted to run away, but crawling away would have to suffice. She saw her staff, but it lay too far away to reach. Then, she saw Mayenne's. It lay five feet away. Aura thought if she could reach it, she may be able to climb up on it and use it as a crutch to limp out of the house.

Pulling her body across the floor seemed to take an hour. Her waking legs screamed their fury at her. Jolts of pain shot through her thighs and shins, the after effects of the shock from her own spell. Aura cursed herself for being stupid. She was, indeed, an arrogant tart. Aura finally crossed the short distance to the staff. She grabbed it and gripped it in both hands. Jamming the tip against the stones, she managed to sit up. Some feeling returned to her legs, but not enough to support her weight. Using her arm strength, she climbed hand over hand up the staff until she stood upright. Her right leg worked. Her left leg did not.

"A Divine Thunderbolt? Aura, that's a killing spell," Aura heard from behind her.

With more effort than she wanted to expend, Aura turned to face Mayenne. She leaned on the staff. She gulped. She could barely stand. How could she continue to fight? All Mayenne had to do was cast one little spell.

As Mayenne sat up, she started to say "It's a good thing you are exhausted or I'd be –"

Mayenne slowly stood, gaping at Aura. Mayenne looked shocked, worried, even terrified. She saw the monster's throat work. Mayenne pointed to Aura.

"That's ... that's my staff," Mayenne said.

Aura looked at the staff. It had just been a convenient weapon then a crutch. Inside the globe, the angry white energy shot around, as if trying to break out. Aura glanced back at Mayenne. The balakalat stood still, as if unsure of her next move.

"Aura, that's a powerful weapon. Please give it to me."

Aura glanced at the staff and back at Mayenne, as the balakalat said, "If you give it to me, I'll give you your staff and you can go in peace. I won't attack you anymore."

Aura thought that as soon as she turned her back, Mayenne would attack her again. She knew the staffmaker craved her soul. She would be damned if she herself be devoured. She glanced back at the staff. Mayenne feared her own staff. Aura thought she did not need energy or another spell. She held all she needed right in her hand. This was not about winning a duel anymore. This was about survival.

Putting all of her weight on her strong leg, Aura held the staff over her head as if it were an axe. She looked at the floor. She heard Mayenne scream and saw the balakalat lunge for her. Gripping it as if her life depended on it, she threw her weight behind her shoulders and arms and hurled the head down on the stone floor. The globe clanked, then shattered.

The blast of escaping energy threw Aura to the floor. The white globs shot through the workshop, as if dancing in joy. They expanded into hundreds of beams of light, racing around each other, around Mayenne and Aura. Then, they darted out the open windows, streams heading for some unseen freedom. That is, all but the brightest and largest. It shot around the room, then hovered between Aura and Mayenne. It trembled as if consumed by fury. Then, it threw itself onto Mayenne, and vanished inside her.

Mayenne trembled where she stood. The tremble turned into violent shaking. She threw her head back and roared, a scream that deafened Aura. It sounded like a lion thrust through with a spear. Aura covered her face and threw herself against the floor. Mayenne's scream gathered, and then rose in pitch until it sounded like a woman in labor. Then, silence.

Aura peeked from under her arm. Mayenne teetered on her feet. Her skin looked normal. The points on her ears had vanished. Her teeth looked like anyone else's. The white eyes faded back into brown. Then, Mayenne fell onto her face. She lay still. Aura could not even see her back rise and fall with breath.

Aura crawled to the overturned table. Using it to stand, she wobbled on unsure feet. Her left leg worked, but it still refused to take her weight. Her staff stood in the far corner, on the other side of Mayenne. With a sigh, Aura let it go. She would find another staff. Aura turned to the door of the workshop.

"Is it over?" she heard a voice whisper behind her.

Aura slumped against the table. She turned to look at Mayenne. She had nothing left in her, not even the strength to punch Mayenne in the face. For a moment, she thought about throwing herself across the workshop. If she reached the workbench, she could grab a chisel and plunge it into her own heart. That would at least deny Mayenne her soul. The staffmaker lay on her stomach, propped up on her elbows. She looked at her trembling hands. Then, she looked at Aura.

"Is it really over?" Mayenne asked.

"I ... I just want to leave," Aura said. The staffmaker gave her a weak, faint smile that made Aura shudder. Another blasphemy. She took a step backwards, nearly tripping as her heel caught on the stone floor.

"What have you done to Milady, you bitch!" Tyfford roared from behind her. She forgot all about him. Tyfford bore down on Aura with his hands clenched like claws, his mouth twisted in a snarl, fury pouring from his eyes.

"Tyfford, no!" Mayenne gasped.

Tyfford jerked his attention from Aura. Spotting Mayenne on the floor, he ran to her and knelt by her side.

"Are you all right, Milady?" He pointed toward Aura and snapped, "I will kill her if you but command it!"

"No, Tyfford. Aura freed me. Please contact Lord Ashthorne –"

"I already know!" a voice boomed. Aura turned as quickly as a stone. Deofoyl stood in the doorway, his hands on his hips, glaring into the room. The smashed door, its bolt wrenched from its fastenings, lay open. She never heard it. Two men in blue cloaks flanked him. Behind him stood a man Aura did not know. With a short hair, a thick chest and a jutting jaw, he looked like a human bulldog. Next to him stood Elisabeth Lovejoy. "Didn't you think I'd know as soon as you awoke the balakalat, Mayenne?" He rubbed the ring on his right index finger. "You promised me you'd never do that again!"

"I never will," Mayenne said. She looked at Aura. A faint smile crossed her lips, and sincere gratitude filled her eyes. She mouthed, "Thank you."

"You two," Deofoyl said, motioning to the guards. "Help Mayenne to a chair. Be gentle. Walter," he said over his shoulder. "Cover them, just in case. I don't trust her right now." The two guards and the third man nodded and entered the room. Walter glared at Tyfford. The butler stood back as the guards lifted Mayenne by the arms. Walter watched, standing with his palms open, but at his sides.

Deofoyl motioned to Elisabeth. "Captain Lovejoy, take Miss Lockhaven to the nearest tavern. I have some idea of what she's been through. Help her recover. Pour ale down her throat if you must. Then, personally escort her to Ardora." He glanced at the torn skirt of her dress. "Take her to Elenora, and tell her I'm paying for it. I'll meet you at Chester's."

Elisabeth nodded, and stepped by Deofoyl. As soon as the Captain's arm was around Aura's waist, she collapsed against her. Her right leg ached and her left screamed. Trembling, she wanted to sob, but not in front of Elisabeth. "My bag ... it's upstairs ... " she croaked.

"Walter, take Tyfford upstairs to fetch Miss Lockhaven's bag," Deofoyl said. As the two men departed, Deofoyl walked across the workshop. He picked up Aura's staff, still resting in the corner. He caressed it a moment before handing it to her. He placed it into her hands, and gave her a reassuring smile. "I believe this one is yours, Miss Lockhaven. It looks like you. I apologize for this. Usually a staff making isn't so involved."

Walter returned, following Tyfford. The butler handed Deofoyl Aura's bag. He handed it to Elisabeth. "Captain, I'll take care of Mayenne. Please get Miss Lockhaven out of here. I believe she's seen enough of a staffmaker's shop for one day."

Chapter Twenty

THE RAIN FELL in sheets, turning the streets of Ardora into a treacherous mix of slick cobblestones and sticky muck. Thick drops of water smacked the glass of the windows in Chester's Bawdy Bard Tavern. Peals of thunder rattled the door, only to echo off the walls of the Valley and return. People streamed through into the tavern and brushed the water from their bare shoulders. A serving girl stood by the door, handing the patrons coarse towels to dry themselves. Others ran by the tavern, huddling their arms to their chests, as if that would keep them dry.

Aura sat at a table letting the warmth of the kitchen dry her hair and finishing her first ale of the afternoon. She drank three in Dallington before she felt ready to mount Blister. She remembered little of the ride to Ardora. Even ripped, her dress clung to her legs. Her injured leg screamed. Through her tears and pain she knew Elizabeth had to lead her on Blister. Even now, her left leg cramped. She kept it straight underneath the table. Elisabeth sat next to her, keeping quiet.

Cradling her arms over her chest, Aura shivered. She felt as if she sat inside a giant upturned cauldron made of frosted glass. People drifting by seemed as but shadows, faceless and of unsure shape. Their voices were a din of soundless noise, like echoes from across the street, trying feebly to pierce a curtain. The curtain lay inside her own mind. The only thing that penetrated the frosted glass and the curtain was the distinct form of Mayenne. She appeared as a full balakalat, yet quivering as if made of soft suet, visible at the outermost edge of Aura's eye. When Aura jerked her head to look, Mayenne vanished, only to reappear across the room, always just at the threshold of Aura's vision.

From behind the curtain, Aura heard a voice. It was her own. It told her that this was the same place her mind fled the day Uncle Cedric cast her out into the bitter winter drizzle. Drifting from awning to shop to barrel for three cold, wet days in a black fog almost gave her the ague. That had been a simple riverfront town. This was a magical realm where a monster had almost killed her. She had to pull her mind out from behind the curtain now, before the mental cloth became a wall of stone. Closing her eyes, and using every shred of remaining will, Aura gripped the edge of the chair seat. Inhaling and exhaling, she slowed her heart beat. She grounded herself to the chair, and to the floor. Wood. Wood was a simple gift from Earth. It gave itself to the axe and tool willingly. It was a friend. Wood saved her life, in the form of Mayenne's own staff.

She opened her eyes. The haze seemed less dense now, more like gauze and not glass. Voices were distinct. Pushing her mind through the curtain, she forced herself into the present, and away from Mayenne. Aura looked around the tavern, deliberately focusing on every detail. Staves and paintings of enchanters and enchantresses hung on the dark walls. Candlelight danced through the thick smoke drifting from clay pipes and the kitchen oven. A bard sat on a stool playing a lute and singing some song that Aura did not recognize. She only caught every third word but the song sounded like it heralded the laying of some woman by some man who desired her so much he was willing to fight dragons to reach her.

While Elenora repaired her dress, Aura wore a borrowed tunic. White and sleeveless, with only one shoulder, and a short skirt that barely covered her hips, Aura felt at home with Chester's customers. Some wore tanginis made from leather, silk, linen, and some shiny material she could not identify. They came in red, yellow, blue, black, purple, with one bold man wearing orange. The woman closest to her had sewn sapphires into the tiny thongs that tied around her bare hips. Some of the women were bare breasted, but most wore the tangini top. Others wore everything such as robes that belonged on a 1,500 year old statue of a Karanthek god, while others wore modern trousers, waistcoats, and bodices. A few customers wore cloaks, and many had staves that rested against their tables.

She had never seen a wider range of red, blonde, and dark hair, all set in a fine collection of hairstyles. A few women wore their hair long and free like she did, but most wore the fashions of the continent. She noticed Flumantine falls, Nebelish buns, Frysting braids, and the baffling style of the Aitians. Some women wore what Aura remembered seeing on Bellician statues, a formal weave around the head. Half of the men wore beards, a few had moustaches, and some were clean-shaven. One man looked like a Bellician, with short hair chopped close around the head. All of the people were fair skinned, with just the first pink blushes of spring tans showing.

That is, except for one tall man in the corner, laughing with another sporting a red beard. The tall man wore a long purple cloak over what looked more at home on a Beryt charioteer. He held a staff in one hand, and a tankard in the other. His height and attire was not what caught her attention. The man looked like a statue carved from obsidian. Aura had heard of Farians, the people from the continent to the south, and always wanted to meet one. It never occurred to her that the order accepted members from outside Sareth, but his staff said they accepted all.

She continued to look around the tavern, until she stopped upon seeing the man sitting at a small table in the corner by the window. Her blood ran cold. In the gray light streaming through the window, Captain Baltarus' beard and hair looked even more impeccably groomed. In the tavern, he looked out of place in a leather jerkin over a light gray shirt and trousers. In one gauntleted hand, he held a tankard while the other caressed the amulet around his neck in languid strokes. In the light, Aura saw that it was silver with a polished onyx in the center. He smirked as he eyed her with the gaze of a wolf sizing up a fawn.

Aura jerked her head back to her tankard. Seeing him startled her fully into the present. As she shuddered under Baltarus' continued stares, she drained her ale. She sighed, and signaled Chester for another pint of ale. She liked his ale. It was heavier on the hops that she was accustomed to, with a faint taste of honey and roses.

"Here you go, miss ... uh," Chester said, setting a pint of ale down on the table in front of Aura. Chester looked like a man cut from the finest leather and sewn together using sunshine for thread. She liked the way he smiled and his face broke out in amused wrinkles. He wore a simple, dark brown keld, in the traditional Garranic fashion. Dark brown, just like her father wore. Brown hid beer stains. She liked Chester already.

"I'm sorry, miss," Chester said. "There are people who are bad with faces, and people who are bad with names, and I'm bad with both!"

"Aura," she said. "Aura Lockhaven. I'm not from here."

"Ah, you must be the visitor from the central hill area. I heard you'd be headed this way."

"News travels fast," Aura said.

"This is a tavern. My currency is gossip," Chester said, winking to her.

As Chester turned toward the kitchen, she looked back at the Farian. He stood, doubled over and clutching his knees, his howls of mirth echoing around the tavern. She wanted to know more about the man, and the Captain of the Watchers seemed the perfect source of information.

"Excuse me, Elisabeth, but who is the Farian in the corner?" Aura asked.

"That is Leonikas dur O'tan. He's a member of the council. He is our expert on shamanism. I believe he is from Thanatondora."

"I thought Thanatondora was a fable."

"Does Lord dur O'tan look like a fable to you?" Elisabeth asked.

The answer was too close to something Mayenne said just that morning. Aura shivered. She drew her arms around her chest. The frosted glass cauldron threatened to descend upon her again. Elisabeth looked at her, and gave her a comforting smile. She put her hand on Aura's shoulder.

"I understand the feeling," she said. "My corps is charged with defending the Valley from outside enemies. Mostly, we fight monsters. I understand all too well the feeling of facing a threat who isn't human."

Aura closed her eyes. She trembled as she said, "She was going to ... she was going to ..."

"Don't think about it. She was going to, but she can't. She can't because of you. I told you that you had great courage."

"I was just lucky," Aura whispered.

Elisabeth snorted. "Somehow, I doubt that. I've been around magicians most of my life. What you call luck today seems to me to be the result of wise choices made yesterday."

The door opened as another thunderclap shook the windows. Deofoyl Ashthorne stepped into the tavern. Soaked as if he just climbed out of a lake, his blonde hair lay plastered to his scalp and streams of water poured from his beard. The serving girl handed him a towel. He took it with a nod of gratitude. After wiping his face, hair, and shoulders, he returned the now drenched towel to the girl and thanked her. He lifted his left foot, pointed at it, and smiled the sheepish grin of the apologetic. The girl laughed. Deofoyl spotted Aura and waved to her. He walked toward her, leaving muddy footprints across the wet plank floor.

"Captain. Miss Lockhaven, it is good to see you looking more yourself," Deofoyl said.

"Good afternoon, Lord Ashthorne," Aura said.

Deofoyl grinned and took the chair next to Aura. He motioned to Chester and held up one finger. "Thank you for taking care of Miss Lockhaven, Captain." Elisabeth just nodded. He glanced at Aura. "I also owe you my gratitude for helping Mayenne."

"Helping her?" Aura said, choking on her ale. "She almost killed me!"

Chester brought Deofoyl's ale. He took several swallows, then set the tankard on the table. Clasping his hands in front of him, he said, "You did something for her that she feared to do for herself, and I did not know how. You freed her from her own curse."

"All I did was fight for my life."

"In that fight, you did something unexpected. Mayenne was once a powerful and highly respected sorceress in Flumance. She has a problem, however. She can't feel, not like you and I. Oh, she can see, touch, taste, and hear like any of us, but the sensations mean nothing to her. It's as if her soul doesn't fit in her body. That's enough to drive anyone mad." He lowered his voice. "And it did. In her madness, she severed her soul from its poor chalice of flesh, and encased it in a chalice of crystal."

"Her staff," Aura said.

Deofoyl nodded. "That enabled her to cast a curse on herself, transforming into a balakalat, the soul vampire of Glasenya. The souls of others became an obsession for her. By devouring them, she felt and enjoyed life. She kept fragments of their souls in her staff to feed her own. Mayenne's actions caught the attention of the Knights of the Holy Torch, who in turn caught Mayenne. They offered her a bargain. She became a ferret. Do you know what a ferret is, Miss Lockhaven?" When Aura shook her head, he said, "Pray to all your gods that you never encounter one. They are magicians who help the Knights track down other magicians. They are good at what they do, and Mayenne was the best. In exchange for her help in locating other magicians, she was permitted to devour the victim's soul, but not all of it. The Knights wanted the victim to feel the flames of death."

"Why is such a monster living in the Valley?" Aura whispered.

"That is my question, too," Elisabeth said. "Sir, my corps is charged with protecting the Valley from monsters, and if you knew one lived with us then why –"

"I thought she had changed," Deofoyl said, raising his hand. "Despite her ways, Mayenne did, and still does, have a powerful conscience. She fled the Knights, wandering Sareth looking for a cure. She ran into me. Perhaps that was an ill-timed fate, if there is such a thing as fate. I brought her here, thinking I could help her gain some feeling. Are we not an order based on the magic of the emotions? She promised me that she would never transform into a balakalat again."

Aura took several gulps of ale. She could still feel the invisible hands around her waist and see those things erupting from Mayenne's mouth and womanhood. Deofoyl said to her, "Mayenne won't tell me what, but there is something about your soul that overwhelmed her. It was like asking a drunkard to guard the wine cellar. When you destroyed her staff, you returned her soul to her body, thereby destroying the balakalat curse. You also freed the fragments of the other souls to go to the afterlife. Perhaps, now I can help her." He narrowed his eyes, staring deep into Aura's own. "Mayenne wonders how you defeated her. Every curse has a condition that will counteract it, and the condition on the balakalat curse is the hunter must perform an act of kindness. It must be performed within two suns of the battle. That grants someone the power to defeat the balakalat. Did you perform such an act?"

"No, I didn't," Aura said. Oh, yes, she did. She remembered the grave behind the ruins of the tavern. That fell within the required two days. The Law of Reciprocity, one of the fundamental laws of all magic, stated a good deed returned a good deed, and a foul deed a foul. She had never seen it act with such force. She chose to keep that to herself. "That is a horrible tale, sir."

"Yes, and it is only a tale. If you heard the whole of it, you would tremble in bed for three days. I certainly did."

"I'm sorry, sir, but your order is not what I expected."

"You expected us to be enchanting and this to be the land of enchantment, didn't you," Deofoyl said with a weak smile. "That is why we need you, Miss Lockhaven. A few who do not know who we are may remind us of who we were."

Aura wanted to tell Deofoyl she almost decided to go home, but her thoughts were interrupted. "I see you are still alive, visitor from Hartshorn," a voice said from across the table. Aura glanced up into Baltarus' mocking eyes. She forgot he was in the tavern. A wave of cold dread passed through her. He wore the faintest of smirks, and his eyes gleamed with predatory hunger.

"Captain Baltarus," Deofoyl said. "Why wouldn't Miss Lockhaven still live? I assure you that she can handle herself in a tight situation."

"Glad to hear it, sir," Baltarus said. "I wouldn't want our guest to come to any harm." Aura doubted every word of that. The captain leaned over the table and said in a low voice, "There was another abduction. Here in Ardora. Last night. Like the previous two, she was released."

"This is getting out of hand," Deofoyl said, returning the captain's murmur.

"Captain Baltarus, my squad has a standing assignment, but second, third, and fourth squads are unassigned. If you'd like, I can ask the Marshall if they can assist you," Elisabeth said.

"I can handle abductions, Lovejoy," Baltarus said. He cast Elisabeth a cold stare, looking her up and down, and lingering just a moment too long on her chest. "I can't handle ogres. We'd all sleep better knowing the Watchers watched the Valley walls."

"You could use Vivianne's eyes and nose."

"Dancer's sword is better where it is," Baltarus said.

"She has a point," Deofoyl said. "At least, borrow Vivianne Dancer. That woman –" The Vice-Chancellor interrupted himself as Baltarus shot him a withering look. "Yes. Lord Balkefor is rather picky about mingling Guards and Watchers. Very well. I have Karyn and Karyl searching down in Praterhall. I'll ask them to come here instead. If they turn up anything, I'll have them let you know immediately."

"Keep a close eye on that apprentice of yours, too. She's the age this girlsnatcher seems to like."

"Beala is perfectly safe," Deofoyl said, his voice cold as ice.

"Glad to hear it." Baltarus stood up straight. He bowed to Deofoyl, nodded to Aura, and offered nothing to Elisabeth. Aura felt Elisabeth's own cold return. She thought that any love lost between the two captains may fill a single drop of rain. With a flourish of his cloak, Baltarus turned to the door and stepped out into the downpour. Aura felt like she breathed for the first time in two minutes.

Aura looked at Deofoyl. He no longer smiled. He looked into his tankard with the frown of a man carrying more than he liked. Without taking his eyes off his drink, he said, "I apologize for that conversation, Miss Lockhaven. Order business. After that, I suppose our order is even less what you expected. We seem to have a criminal on the loose. It is nothing to be concerned over, however." He looked up at her. With a twitch of his eyes and his mouth, he dispelled whatever worry momentarily gripped him. "Well, let us change the subject. How do you like this weather?"

"That, sir, is a terrible cliché," Aura said.

"Not to a gardener. I can hear my vegetables and herbs singing all the way from Synclyr. I hope this rain continues tomorrow."

"Won't that make tracking the criminal more difficult," Elisabeth asked.

"Oh, that's right. Why am I overseeing this affair? Am I not but a gardener?"

"You're in command because Lord Balkefor is the titular head of the Guards and Lord Balkefor answers to the Vice-Chancellor, which would be you, sir," Elisabeth said.

Deofoyl just stared at Elisabeth. "There are days, Captain ... " The faintest of smiles crept into Elisabeth's lips. Deofoyl sighed. "Did I not change the subject of this conversation? Yes, let us keep it changed. Now, Miss Lockhaven, I could use the assistance of a nature magician. My moonflowers are invading my potato patch."

Chapter Twenty-One

WHEN THE LATE afternoon sun turned gray, and the downpour showed no signs of stopping, Aura decided to spend the night in the tavern and continue to Ardora Hall in the morning. After seeing her room paid, Elisabeth departed. Chester gave her the third room on the left, upstairs. Dropping her bag and staff on the floor of the tiny room, she removed her boots. Leaving the tunic on, Aura plopped onto the bed. The ordeal of the morning overtook her, and she fell asleep to the sound of rain beating against the glass window.

She awoke to black darkness and a terrible cramp in her left leg. At first, she did not know what was wrong. As she rubbed her leg, she remembered why it ached. It had stopped raining while she slept. Her mouth felt dry. Her stomach growled. She wondered at the time, and hoped that Chester's kitchen was still hot.

Sitting up on the edge of the bed, she made out the dim image of a candle on the table next to her. For a second, she wanted to reach for the tinderbox in her bag, but forgot where she left it. Aura cursed herself for never being able to learn the ignite spell, the ability to start fires with a snap of her fingers. She found her bag quickly enough by snagging her foot on it, which in turn, caused her to slip on her staff, then trip over her boots. Snatching the boots from the floor, she put them on in the dark. Then, she picked up her bag, so as not to leave the ruby unattended, She left her room, and shuffled down the hall. Gripping the banister in one hand, and using her staff as a crutch in the other, Aura limped down the stairs.

Aura ordered a simple meal of stew made with barley, beef, and peas, and a tankard of ale. The stew smelled better than it looked, and it looked better than most tavern stews. Evening stew had been Ester's specialty, so Aura knew how the dish was prepared. It was made from yesterday's roasts, thrown into a pot with a shovelful of grains and vegetables, and left to simmer over the fire all afternoon. She forced herself to eat it, more for her leg than any emptiness in her stomach. While the aroma reached her nose, the flavor did not reach her tongue.

Her whole being ached. Not just her body, and more noticeably, her leg. Her soul ached as well. Only that morning, she faced a nightmare turned flesh, one that touched her body and breathed into her face. She faced rape. She faced death. That evening, she sat at a table, picking at a pea with a spoon, only by sheer accident. Seeing the stew reminded her of Ester. Thinking of Ester reminded her of finding her sister's defiled corpse, one moment of horror that left her with a dread of the same fate. The dread grew into a nameless terror that lived in her heart, as she discovered two years later when Nubbin tried to ravage her. Three times in her fight with Mayenne, that unconquerable fear of being raped overwhelmed her. It almost destroyed her. Which had been the greater monster, Mayenne or fear?

She drained the bowl of stew, not even feeling its warmth in her throat. After ensuring that Chester would still be serving ale late into the night, Aura left him three coppers. She limped to the door and stepped out into the night. It was only seven, a night shrouded by the dark clouds lingering overhead. She stopped on the flagstone sidewalk, and breathed deep. Thick sheets of damp mist crept down the street and clung to the edges of the buildings. The cool and moist air, chilly but invigorating, felt good to her leg. The world after a rain came alive in vibrant passion, as if it wanted to bloom and grow in ways that it could not during a bright day. She decided to explore Ardora. Perhaps in the misty night, she could find some beauty, and in the beauty, some solace.

The road curved to the left. On one side of the street, the tannery still operated. The tanner and his apprentice tacked a hide to their wall. On the other side, the blacksmith worked into the night. Red flames raced from his forge like the breath of a dragon. Yellow sparks shot up into the black of the Ardora evening from his anvil as he pounded on a scythe. The mist glowed from the fires of the smithy, like clouds of lightning bugs dancing with fairies. Aura paused for a moment to investigate the street lamp. Hartshorn had them, but those were simple torches. This one had been set in a sconce with a mirror to cast twice as much light. It tried in vain to cut through the deep fog, only to have its light thrown back.

The doors of the next shop lay open, its tall windows bright with the light of lanterns inside. Elenora kept her promise, working feverishly into the night to repair Aura's dress. Aura decided to pay the seamstress a visit. Elenora, a short woman of thirty with brown hair, stood at a table with two of her apprentices. The prominent bulge in Elenora's abdomen said that Aura's dress would be her last for a few weeks. The seamstress cringed and rubbed her belly.

"Another kick?" one of the apprentices, a girl of thirteen, asked.

"I can continue to wear this tunic, if you'd like to go home," Aura said, entering the shop.

"Not at all. You're just in time. We just added the last stitch," Elenora said. With a wink, she added, "Even if he decides to come tonight, my girls specialize in emergencies." She nodded to the other apprentice, an older girl. The apprentice lifted Aura's dress from the table and held it up. The girl was not quite tall enough to clear the hem from the floor. "Try it on."

Aura took the dress and stepped behind the screen. Within a minute, she had removed the tunic and slipped into the dress. Looking down, she examined the ripped seam. She smiled, then looked at the other side. Her smile widened. She saw at least one thing about which to feel happy.

"I love the alterations," Aura said, stepping from behind the screen.

"Captain Lovejoy told me that you had trouble riding," Elenora said. "One seam was already open, so I just opened the other one to the hip. We finished the edges, of course. That skirt had enough material for me to add a panel behind the split on both sides. No one will notice, unless you run."

"I won't be running tonight," Aura said, rubbing her left leg.

After ensuring that Deofoyl had already paid for the repairs, Aura stepped out into the foggy night. She paused underneath a street lamp to transfer the ruby from her bag to the pocket of her left sleeve. There. That felt better. With her bag over her right shoulder, and her staff in her left hand, she limped out into the road.

She followed the road into a circular courtyard. The buildings that lined the courtyard were the round type, made of stone with thatch roofs, typical of older Ayrdish villages. Most of them looked like civic buildings instead of shops or houses. Aura wandered into the center of the courtyard. A statue caught her eye. Surrounded by four lamps sat a marble man and woman sitting on a table and facing each other with their hips touching. Aura blushed as she recognized that as the position of the Great Rite.

The statue beckoned to her. Even though carved from cold stone, the couple had something she did not. They had each other. Aura had no one. Elisabeth and Deofoyl had duties elsewhere, leaving her alone in an unfamiliar town. Deofoyl had not even apologized for sending her to a known killer. At least he apologized for Karyl and Karyn's absence, and promised to correct it.

Six benches surrounded the statue. Aura chose one underneath a young maple. She sat down, and leaned her staff against the bench. The mist played in the light from the lamps, and covered the statue like the thinnest of silk sheets. Aura had witnessed the Great Rite several times at high ceremonies. One of the highest sacred rituals in the magical world, she saw it performed on stone altars, at midnight under the full moon, and shrouded in shadows cast by torchlight. Never were those ceremonies as brazen as this statue.

Everything that formed the man, the high priest, joined with everything that formed the woman, the high priestess. It was more than passion. It was a tremendous blending of bodies and souls in a magical act of immeasurable power and devotion. The vitality created carried the strength of ten separate people, and was afterwards poured into the coven, or into the earth to bless others. Few actually performed the Great Rite, preferring the symbolism of the high priest inserting the ceremonial dagger into the chalice held by the high priestess. The ceremonies Aura witnessed left her with deep curiosity and a deeper ache in her loins. The position baffled her.

All her times in bed had been on her back, a mere five minutes that left her feeling sticky and empty.

Empty. That was what Aura felt even now. After the events of the morning, how could she feel anything else. The mist compounded the emptiness. In the thick air, Aura heard nothing but her own breath. It even masked the footfall of the couples that walked by the statue, on their way somewhere, oblivious to the Great Rite, or the stranger sitting in their presence. Like silent specters, they floated upon the cobblestones. It was as if they were as ethereal as the mist. Who was the ghost? Those who walked by, or the visitor, huddled on her bench in the shadows. Aura felt alone, separated from all those around her, by an invisible force. A familiar tremor grew in her right hand. She grabbed it with her left. Now was not the time for an attack of her greatest fear of all.

To take her mind off the fear, she looked at the oversized lovers on their marble couch. Deliberately, she pondered all the things she thought when she saw a painting or statue or illumination in a book. Who were the models? Who was the artist? What were they doing now? How long did it take to carve the statue? From where she sat, the statue looked perfect. Oversized, but perfect. It was as if the artist simply transformed the couple into stone. That must have required weeks, if not months, to finish. Feeling a bit more calm, Aura returned to other thoughts.

She felt alone and empty. She also felt another feeling she didn't like. Bitterness. Some land of enchantment! In one morning, in one creature, she faced more horror than in two years as an urchin combined. At least the people of Hartshorn had been under the iron-fisted threat of Uncle Cedric, and many had been kind despite it. The only threat hanging over Mayenne was the one inside herself. Deofoyl knew good and well what Mayenne was. He also knew good and well who Aura was. Yet, he still put the two of them together, without anyone to watch and help either. That had been careless. It was like throwing a starving dog and a wet cat into the same cage and telling them to behave.

Aura looked at her left palm. In the flickering yellow light of the torches, struggling to pierce the mist, the scar stood out in eerie relief. She traced it with her right index finger, a line of thick leathery skin beginning at the top of her palm underneath her little finger, crossing her hand to the index finger, then down to the base of her thumb, and over to the side of her hand. It formed a rough letter C. C for clumsy. C for catastrophe. She tightened her jaw. C for collision with monsters. C for careless Vice-Chancellors. C for ... C for ... C for compassion. She was here to learn how to develop and use compassion to empower magic to help others. She clenched her fist.

"No, I will not be bitter," Aura whispered. "I'm better than that."

Placing her palms on the cold granite bench, she closed her eyes. Breathing deep and slow, she grounded herself to the stone. With each exhalation, she released bitterness into her arms, and down to her hands, where she poured it into the bench, and out into the earth itself. Then, she forced emptiness to follow. Loneliness clung to her bones like sinew. There was nothing she could do about that.

Feeling slightly better, she looked back at the statue. It didn't look terribly old, but the couple was no doubt elderly by now, if not dead. Perhaps they had been lovers in life, but probably just a man and woman the sculptor hired for a few weeks. Either way, their embrace looked far more passionate than directed by the needs of mallet and chisel. The shroud of mist transformed the statue from a stone depiction of what must be a sacred subject for the Order of Enchanters. In the moisture laden fog, it became a couple so enthralled with each other that they ignored the eyes upon them.

Aura's imagination took her away, turning the marble couple into real people. They had each other. No matter what one faced that day, he or she could turn to the other. *I fought a balakalat today, darling. Well, you should have seen the nasty captain of the Guard who insulted me. Where is he? I'll punch him for you. I already sent him to the infirmary. Tell me about your soul vampire.* People who faced each other in the fires of passion, like the couple in the statue, usually faced the winds of pain and horror side-by-side.

A faint smile crossed Aura's lips. One day, she wanted to be held like the man held the woman in the statue. She wanted to be enveloped in the arms of a man who saw only her, who wanted her so much he did not care if the whole world watched. Mayenne had not been that different from Jack, Roderick, and Cecil. They all only wanted a part of her to satisfy their hunger. If a monster wanted her soul, then a man surely would. If a lust filled boy wanted her body, then a man surely would. She wanted the man who wanted her body and the man who wanted her soul to be the same man. She wanted him to want everything about her, even her green eyes. Not someone who wanted to be with her in bed, but someone to watch the sunrise every morning with her and talk her awake over the first mug of tea. Best of all, someone who was a friend to stand with her against future monsters. Someone to defend, as well as to defend her, and to remind her not to be such an arrogant tart. Such a man had to exist, perhaps even in the mist of Ardora. The day began under the worst of conditions. It ended with her injured, but alive, and with plenty of reasons to look forward to tomorrow morning. For the first time that day, Aura felt a touch of lightness in her heart.

Aura stood, and picked up her staff. She winced as a spasm shot through her leg. While the cool mist soothed the ache, it also stiffened the injured muscles. Her leg felt as if encased in an iron cast. It was time to walk. Looking around the courtyard, Aura felt a little confused. Six streets poured from the center of town like vines creeping up a tree. The town had no plan. It just grew out from the center. It became even more confusing as the streets vanished into the creeping mist. She looked back the way she came to make sure she could find the Bawdy Bard. Just follow the stone woman's buttocks, she thought. Turning around, she decided to explore the street furthest away.

It curved to the right. Here, the buildings looked more modern, built in the last fifty years, square with tile roofs. She remembered that parts of the

Valley had been destroyed in the war. Ardora must have suffered similar devastation. Any sound her feet made on the wet cobblestones disappeared into the fog that swallowed the town. She was grateful for the lamps. All she had to do was follow each yellow patch of mist.

The shuttered windows of the shops told Aura that they were all closed for the evening, but she read the signs as she passed each one. The Cheese Place. Grace's Herbs. Ardora Crystal and Stone Company. Enchanting Tailoring. Mikal's Staff Repair. Randolf's Mice and Rats brought a smile to her face. She wished that Ardora Books and Scrolls was open. Looking up, she saw the yellow flicker of candlelight in the windows of the second stories and guessed that the shopkeepers lived above their stores.

Aura heard something to her right. At first, she paid it no mind. The thick mist dampened the sound and disguised it. Probably a tipsy tavern patron trying his best to walk home. Perhaps even someone struggling to lift a heavy crate. She heard it again as she passed the opening to an alley across the street. It sounded like a scuffle. "No, please, let me go!" a young woman said. The voice came from down the narrow street. Aura inhaled a sharp breath.

No one had been present on the wharves when the Flumantine boatmen grabbed Ester. Only circumstance had allowed Aura to survive that very morning. Now, another young woman needed someone. That someone stood in the light of a lamp, with only a shroud of fog and the distance of a street's width separating the them. The stroll through Ardora had restored Aura's spirits enough so that she felt ready to tackle a potential ravager. Then, she blanched. What if the woman faced a horror of the magnitude of Mayenne. She shook her head. The assailant was probably a man. Men had loins, which in turn, were vulnerable to experienced knees.

A torch glowing in the mist turned the opening to the alley into the black mouth of a cave. Aura dashed across the street as fast as her leg allowed. The fog had not seeped into the alley. She saw mostly crisp darkness, but could make out a few shapes and shadows, highlighted by the light bouncing off the mist overhead and the lamp over her left shoulder. Ten feet into the alley, she saw a man and a woman. The man had the woman backed against the wall. He held her left hand and stuck the point of a short sword to her throat.

Aura clenched her teeth. She knew only one reason that a man would hold a sword to a woman's throat. This was not a lover's spat. Tightening her grip on her staff, she stormed down the alley, ignoring the throb in her leg.

"What's going on here?" she shouted.

"None of your business," the man said. In the faint light, she could tell the man was her height, with a short beard. He wore a cloak of some kind, but that was all she could identify. "Just having a talk with my girl, here."

Aura glanced at the woman. She could see her better, a girl about fifteen years of age. In what little light flowed over the walls of the buildings, Aura noticed the obvious fright on the girl's face.

"What's your name?" Aura asked.

"In ... Ingrid," the girl said.

"My name is Aura. Is it true, Ingrid? Do you belong to him?"

"Be careful how you answer, my sweet," the man said.

The tight shadows and hint of light on Ingrid's face told Aura all she needed to know. The girl even smelled like fear. She tightened her grip on her staff and tensed her arms.

The girl glanced from Aura to the man and back. She closed her eyes and screamed, "No! Please, help me!"

Aura did not give the man a chance to respond. Swinging her staff upward, she caught the underside of his sword, knocking it clear of Ingrid's throat, and out of his hand. As the man backed away, Aura stepped in front of Ingrid. She slid to her left, to be between the man and his sword, too.

"I think you better leave," Aura said, raising her right hand.

"Fuck yourself with a wine jug!" the man growled.

"I don't like your attitude," Aura said. She saw Sagacius' sword at her chest. Like Cecil, this man was probably a nomagian. Magicians knew ways of seducing women and manipulating them into bed. Ways that did not involve blades. Still, Ingrid thought she was in some sort of danger, and that meant Aura could use all the magic she wished. That is, she wished she could use magic. Feeling deep within herself, she felt only enough restored vitality to cast one throwback spell. Any more than that, she may faint from exhaustion. She felt strong enough to beat him with her fists, or strike him with her staff, for at least a few minutes. That should be enough. Not wanting to kill the man, and still uncertain of how to use her staff, she lowered its head toward the ground, and aimed her right hand toward him. She shouted, "Tenthatora!"

The throwback spell shot from her open palm. The bubble of force sailed across the open space and struck the man on the chest. He fell back a foot, but remained standing. Aura gasped as the bubble returned to her. Unable to believe what she saw, she hesitated too long. It smacked her in the chest. The rebounded throwback spell knocked the wind out of her and threw her from her feet. With a loud huff, she fell onto her back. Lying on the stone alley floor, she tried to catch her breath.

"You idiot!" the man said. He snickered and held up an amulet. In the darkness, all Aura could see was an equally dark circle. "This is a countercharm. No magic in the world can touch me!"

Aura pushed herself up on one hand, trying to breathe. The whole sky crashed down on her. It was much too soon after the duel this morning. The throwback spell exhausted her vitality and being struck by it almost ripped her physical strength from her body. The man sauntered to his sword and picked it up. He stood over Aura and set the point of the sword in her cleavage. Her staff lay three feet out of reach. Still stunned by her own spell, she doubted she had the strength to knock the sword away from her chest before the man plunged it through her into the stones underneath. She looked up at the man, his face shrouded in shadow.

Begging for mercy probably would not help, she thought. Neither would spitting curses.

"I really want to kill you right now, but I have more important things to do," he said. With a laugh, he lifted his sword and turned to Ingrid.

Aura's breath still came in jagged heaves. Damn fool girl, she thought, trying to rise. Why hadn't she run? The man grabbed Ingrid by the wrist and half dragging her, started toward the alley entrance.

Aura rolled onto her stomach and rose to her knees. Grabbing her staff, she used it to stand up. Her breath returned, she inhaled deeply, and then whirled to face the retreating man and Ingrid. He may be immune to magic, but probably not a physical attack. Holding her staff over her head like a spear, Aura limped down the alley, gaining speed with each step. If the man heard her clumsy feet slapping the wet cobblestones, he did not turn around.

Aura struck the man in the back of the head with the iron tip of her staff. The man released Ingrid, and staggered forward, into the light of the lamp.

"Dammit!" he shouted, whirling around.

In the lamplight, Aura saw him. His shoulder length hair and beard were blonde. He wore a light colored shirt, a dark leather jerkin, and leather gauntlets. The amulet was silver with a dark stone in the center. His clothing looked familiar. So did the amulet. The man rubbed the back of his head with one hand, and gripped his sword with the other.

In the lamplight, she also saw Ingrid. If she was fifteen, she just celebrated her birthday. Fear consumed her young face. Her brown hair clung to her scalp and beads of perspiration seeped down her cheeks, mixed with the tears that flowed from her wide brown eyes. Her pink dress was muddy and torn at the left shoulder. Just in time, Aura thought.

Aura stepped in front of Ingrid. She raised her staff, gripping it in a quarterstaff fighting stance, overhand on the right and underhand on the left. He had steel. She had oak. This fight may last three swings before he cut her staff in two. If she was lucky, Aura thought she could stab him with one severed end before he skewered her. That is, if cut oak penetrated leather.

Over her shoulder, she said to Ingrid, "When he fights me, run!"

"Where?" Ingrid asked.

"Anywhere!"

"What about you?"

What about me indeed. Tightening her grip on her staff, Aura moved her right foot back and slid her left foot forward. She shifted her weight onto her good leg. Her stomach began to tighten. This was stupid, but she would not let this man have Ingrid. Perhaps the leather grip would soften the blows. Perhaps his sword was dull. Perhaps he would just beat her to death with the flat of the blade.

"Well, if you want Ingrid, you have to fight me for her," Aura said.

The man regarded Aura. His mouth tightened into a grim slit. The sword in his hand moved an inch. Here it comes, she thought. *Remember, Ingrid, run! Do not look back!* The man jerked his head to his left as five laughing men poured out of a shuttered shop. They held bottles of wine and howled at an unheard joke. Aura wanted to shout to the men, but her mouth went dry.

The man looked away from the laughing throng and snarled, "This ain't worth it!" Sheathing his sword, he turned and strode away. Aura almost fell to her knees as she sighed in relief. She glanced to the passing men and silently thanked them.

As the would-be abductor passed into the light of the next lamp, Aura saw his cloak. It was the color of the sky.

Chapter Twenty-Two

"THAT IS A serious accusation, woman!" the man roared.

Aura stood in the center of a cramped room in the back of the Bawdy Bard. Smoke from the fireplace, the aroma of cooking pork, and the laughter of the breakfast patrons drifted underneath the shut door. She wanted to be out there with the smoke, aroma, and laughter. She wanted to be anywhere but where she was. Four flickering candles in iron sconces and a lone lantern on a table struggled to light the windowless room, casting grim shadows across the equally grim faces of the seven other people in the room. Aura knew six of them. Karyl and Karyn stood behind her. Deofoyl hunched in front of her, cradling his arms across his chest. Baltarus glowered by the door, Leonikas dur O'tan leaned in one corner, and Ingrid huddled in a chair in another. She found out who the seventh man was only a minute earlier, when he stormed into the back room with Baltarus trailing him like an obedient dog.

Two inches shorter than Aura, Lord Balkefor, the Eorl of Grahbale, still could have broken her with one hand like a dry cornhusk. He looked like a bear in boots. Brown hair billowed behind him like a short cloak and his brown beard fell to his hairy chest. All Aura saw of his face were the furious dark eyes and the white teeth behind his snarl. For clothes, he wore short leather breaches similar to those worn by the gladiators of old, and held in place by a wide leather belt with a gold buckle. The black boots strained under the flexing of his calves as he walked. His muscles rippled with rage as he strode right to Aura and yelled. Aura gulped as she saw the two thick leather straps across his bare chest, straps that held twin battleaxes to his back.

Balkefor tore the lantern from the table and shoved it toward Aura's face. He bellowed, "How dare you accuse one of Captain Baltarus' Guards, one of *my* Guards, of being a abductor. I know who you are. I'll not have that sort of talk from an outsider!"

"Outsider!" Leonikas growled. He stepped away from the wall. "I will not have that sort of talk from a member of the council. We are more civilized than that."

"Gentlemen. Leonikas, please. Calm down, Lord Balkefor," Deofoyl said, waving his hand at the eorl. "Miss Lockhaven did not accuse anyone. All she did was state what she saw." Deofoyl glanced at Aura, and added, "Please tell Lord Balkefor and the captain what you told the Krigers and myself. I am sure that Leonikas would like to hear it, too."

Telling Karyl, Karyn and Deofoyl had been easy. Balkefor intimidated her. It was not just his physical size. He wore authority as if it were a chainmail hauberk, and the knowledge of that authority as if it was a morningstar in each hand. Every eye locked on her as she stood, waiting to give her answer. Even Ingrid sat forward to listen. Balkefor held the lantern closer to Aura. The cloak of shadow that hid her vulnerability had just been ripped away.

Aura gulped again as she nodded. With her right fingers, she found the ruby in her left sleeve pocket. It reassured her. She said, "I saw a man with blonde hair over his ears and a trimmed beard. He was about my height. He wore a sky blue cloak and a dark pendant, just like Captain Baltarus is wearing now. He had a similar jerkin and similar gloves. He held Ingrid by the wrist and had a three-foot sword pointed at her throat. I fired a throwback spell at him, but it bounced right off and struck me."

Baltarus put his hands on his hips. He sighed and fingered the medallion around his neck. "That sounds like one of my men, all right."

"If you don't trust Miss Lockhaven, then how about Ingrid?" Deofoyl turned to the girl in the corner. "Miss Ingrid, do you have anything to add? You were the intended victim, after all."

"No, sir," Ingrid said. "It's just as Miss Aura said. Except before he grabbed me, he asked me if I was a virgin."

Baltarus rubbed his forehead. "Just like the last three," he said.

Balkefor snapped, "What do you mean, just like the last three?"

"Why bother you with the nighttime habits of randy stable boys? You hired me to deal with them. A month ago, someone grabbed a girl in Grahbale. Dragged her across town to the old burned out temple. Her attacker asked if she was a virgin. When she said no, he let her go and disappeared. It was dark. She didn't see his face or clothes. A few nights ago, the same thing happened. Same outcome. Karyl helped me since I was at the western end of the Valley. That was the night I met her," he said, pointing toward Aura. "Night before last, it happened here. Things like that happen. Boys get drunk, grab girls ... You're absolutely sure about the cloak?"

"It was the color of the sky."

Balkefor turned on Aura. "How could you possibly tell what he was wearing? It was dark! Are you part cat?"

Aura felt her anger rise. That was one question she never expected to hear in the Valley of the Mystic Moon. Sagacius said that no one would pay any attention to her eye color. Her lips trembled for a second. Then, she realized he meant a feline ability to see in darkness. Besides, how could Balkefor see her eye color in the flickering candlelight, unless he himself were part cat. Anyway, Deofoyl had green eyes. She tried to relax, but her irritation lingered in her throat and escaped with her answer.

"The lamps were bright and I'm not colorblind," Aura said, a little more forceful than she wished.

"Don't you take that tone with me, woman! Remember your place!"

"Miss Lockhaven's place is here, telling us the facts," Deofoyl said. "It would seem that she caught the first glimpse of our abductor, something that even your Guards have failed to do."

"I won't have that tone from you either, Ashthorne!" Balkefor snapped. "Remember, you hold your chair at the will of the council."

"If the council wishes my chair, it can have it. That is, if you can find someone stupid enough to sit in it. No? I didn't think so."

"It could be an imposter," Baltarus said, looking at Aura. Balkefor whirled around. Aura sighed. At least that lantern was out of her face. Baltarus did not flinch or even look at the Eorl. "Cloaks are easily made. I don't know where he got the amulet, but I'm sure a jeweler could make one that works the same. A countercharm that blocks incantations." The captain smirked. "You people know more about that than I do. But it makes sense. No woman would suspect a Guard of harming her. She would walk right up to him. Perfect ploy." He looked in Aura's direction. "You aren't as light in the head as I thought. At least, you have good eyes. You've given me a new place to look. For that, I thank you."

He still looked at Aura as if he wanted to either devour her in bed or devour her on a trencher. At least, Baltarus offered her a brief bob of the head that she took at a nod of gratitude. That was the first sign of humanity she had seen in the captain.

"There you go, Lord Balkefor," Deofoyl said. "Our villain could easily be someone disguised as one of your Guards. Are you satisfied?"

"No, I am not satisfied. I won't be satisfied until the girls have been found and this criminal swings from the end of one of my charmed ropes. I am certainly not satisfied by the testimony of an outsider."

Leonikas stormed across the room and stood next to Aura. "That is twice you have used the word outsider. There had best not be a third." He spoke with no hint of malice or even a growl. Yet, his even voice conveyed a sense of raw power that he alone knew. Aura shivered. She had some idea of what a shaman could do. Leonikas glanced at Aura, then back at Balkefor. "I shall stand with our visitor. I believe her."

"Leave it to an ... otherwordly type ... to support another otherwordly type. What do you plan to do if I don't agree?" Balkefor asked. "You aren't in your land anymore, Farian. You're in mine."

"I'm in *ours*. Would you like me to summon Lady Naurelia? This is the shire of the t'Ardoras, I believe. Let her decide who has true authority in her city."

"Gentlemen, please," Deofoyl said. "Save the bickering for the council chamber. We have a serious matter before us, and the first light has shone upon it."

"Yes, by a stranger to the Valley," Balkefor growled. "How convenient. We all know how trustworthy strangers are."

"Now *that* is a serious accusation!" Deofoyl snapped.

It occurred to them all that Balkefor just accused Aura of the very crime she had witnessed and thwarted. Not just this one, but probably others as well. She recalled all too well being sentenced for a crime she did commit, and did not want to face the possibility of something similar for one she did not. The cold stare and firm set of Deofoyl's mouth told her that she would not have to beg her innocence. Leonikas hand on her shoulder only encouraged her further.

"I am sworn to protect this Valley and its inhabitants. I do not know this woman. What else am I supposed to think? Who else am I supposed to suspect?" Balkefor asked.

"Yes, the handmaiden did it. Blame the commoner."

"I told you, Ashthorne, don't take that tone with me. I am an eorl!"

"Tell that to King Edgar. I doubt he'll be impressed," Deofoyl answered. Aura thought she heard a faint chuckle in his voice. She distinctly heard the snort of derision from Leonikas. "Miss Lockhaven has been busy for several days. All but for a few hours during one day, she has been with someone. She was with me for four days before that. Would you like to speak to Captain Lovejoy? How about Mayenne? How about any number of shopkeepers. Can a woman her height go unnoticed? Better still, why don't we contact Miss Lockhaven's master. I'm sure you'd love to talk to Sagacius, again."

"Sagacius? The Trollslayer was her master?"

Aura stifled her snort, and hoped her smirk did not show. Balkefor was already angry, and she did not want him to think she mocked him. Certainly, she thought Sagacius had the power. He felled an ogre once. Trolls, however, did not exist. They were just stories to frighten children and keep them from wandering into the forests. Dragons existed. She had seen their footprints. She had seen an ogre with her own eyes. Trolls? She had no idea that enchanters were superstitious.

In the yellow light of the lantern, Aura thought she saw Balkefor blanch. His eyes widened just enough for her to notice. Apparently, the pseudonym Trollslayer meant something to Balkefor. Good, Aura thought. She did not like this eorl, and if she held a slight advantage against him through her association with Sagacius, so much the better.

"Now, I do suspect her," Balkefor said. "Who better to be a criminal than the apprentice of an assassin?"

"You can't prove that!" Deofoyl said.

"Only two men can blow a hole in someone's chest with a Divine Thunderbolt, and I know where Tyrus was when it happened. I'm surprised to hear you defending Sagacius, considering he killed your master."

Aura cut her eyes toward Deofoyl. This conversation proved interesting, and in ways she did not like. Sagacius had admitted he had killed other magicians in duels, but only after begging them to surrender. Those killings had been in the line of duty and to defend his own life. Assassinations were stealthy murders, and she doubted that anyone with Sagacius' lofty morality could attempt one, much less succeed. She kept hearing things about her master that she did not like.

"Wolfstone killed himself through his own actions. If Sagacius was involved, which I highly doubt, all he did was carve Wolfstone's name on the gravestone," Deofoyl said.

"As assassin is an assassin, even if he did kill a rabid dog. I had no love for Wolfstone, I grant you that, but he should have stood trial for his crimes, not have had his heart and lungs blasted out while he drank lifewater up in Caillia. Who else could have gotten that close to Wolfstone? You could have, but you were drunk, crying yourself sick because you had been named Vice-Chancellor. Sagacius remained neutral in the war. Peacekeeper, he called himself. More like backstabber! He's also a wizard,

Ashthorne, and we all know how treacherous that bunch is! They steal from everyone. So, what did he teach *this* woman?" Balkefor asked, nodding toward Aura without looking at her. "How many bits of larceny does Sagacius have up the sleeves of his fancy robes? Do you think it's a coincidence that this woman chose to visit our valley at the same time the girls started disappearing? It takes a criminal to breed a criminal, and I think the one we seek stands in this very room."

With each sentence, Aura's anger rose until her emotional scales tipped close to rage. The sneering tone of his voice, dripping with self-importance and oozing superiority made her grit her teeth. She clenched her fists during his accusations of her. Accusing Sagacius and insulting the Order of Wizards was more than she could tolerate.

"My master is no murderer!" Aura snapped. "He certainly did not send me here to abduct women!"

"I told you to remember your place!" Balkefor roared. "You will not speak to me in that tone of voice! You will not speak until spoken to!"

Aura tried to hold her tongue. She told herself to mind her manners, that this was their realm, that she was still a visitor. However, she could not. Henry Lockhaven always told her to say what she thought at all times, as long as it was respectful. This man did not warrant respect. He insulted her master and he just ordered her to obey him, treating her like some vassal in an old story. Her rage flew from her mouth before she could stop it.

"Who do *you* think *you* are?" Aura shouted back. She put her hands on her hips and took a step forward. "No one tells me what to do or say. I have never bent my knee to any man or woman. I am Ayrdish, and we yield to no one! And let me tell you, Mister Lord Balkefor, sir. *You* will not speak to *me* in that tone of voice. Who are you to tell me to bow and curtsey and kiss your ring? Are you a god that I should? I will not tolerate your insults of my master any further. Since he is not here to defend himself, then I shall!"

Aura heard the simultaneous gasps from the Kriger siblings behind her. Deofoyl arched his eyebrow. Baltarus winced and turned his head. Leonikas took a step backwards. Ingrid lurched in her chair and tried to draw further back into the corner. Balkefor's already angry face transformed into a mask of wrath. His eyes narrowed to slits of black flame and his grimace split his beard in half. Balkefor raised his hand. Aura saw the backhanded slap coming. She braced to receive it, refusing to duck or scream when it landed. She would take it like a Lockhaven, and no vow would prevent her from retaliating. The slap stopped halfway to her face, held back by Leonika's left hand.

"If that hand flies again, *Milord*, I will remove it from your body!" he said, his voice even but laced with menace. "That is not a challenge. It is a promise."

Deofoyl said, "I concur with the councilman's actions."

Balkefor jerked his hand free and snapped, "The council will hear of this at the next meeting!"

"I shall tell them first. Lady Etheria won't appreciate you threatening bodily harm to our guest."

"Yes, protect Etheria's little pet!"

"She's *Lady* Etheria to you, *Milord*," Leonikas said.

Balkefor whirled. As he strode from the room, he shouted to Baltarus, "Don't you have something to do?"

After the door slammed behind the eorl and the captain, everyone in the room sighed. Deofoyl put his hand on Aura's shoulder. He looked at her with a serious gaze. "That was not the wisest thing you could have done, Miss Lockhaven. I am afraid you just made an enemy. *Lord* Balkefor is not a forgiving man. You almost issued a challenge to a member of the council, and that is a very serious offense. We have a law dating from the end of the war that forbids that sort of thing." Then, he grinned. Squeezing her shoulder, he said, "But I could not have said it better myself!"

"Yes, that was more courage than wisdom, miss," Leonikas said. He grinned. "But it was well done."

Deofoyl removed his hand from Aura's shoulder and said, "I am sorry you had to witness that. Our war still rages. He is right, though. We all have something to do. Karyn, I would appreciate it if you accompanied Miss Lockhaven to Ardora Hall. If she got a good look at our culprit, then our culprit no doubt got a good look at her. Once she is at Ardora Hall, she will be safe enough. Karyl, would you escort Ingrid home, and see that she is safe? Cast a few barrier spells on her house if you feel it will help. Leonikas, thank you for being such a good friend. And I ... I think I'll have a few pints of ale before I return to the Grahtur and tell Lady Etheria what I heard."

Leonikas held back as the others left the room. He took Aura by the arm and led her out into the tavern. In the light of the main room, Aura could see the councilman better. He didn't look as tall. He stood shorter than Aura by an inch, but made up for it in his broad shoulders. His eyes were as black as jet and his skin radiated health. If he ever knew pain or sorrow, his chiseled face did not show it. Raising his free hand, he ordered a tankard of ale for her. As she sipped it, he said in the most exotic and charming accent Aura ever heard, "We have not been properly introduced. I am Leonikas dur O'tan of Faria and now of the council. I am officially one of your sponsors."

"You probably already know this, but I'm Aura Lockhaven of Hartshorn." They shook hands. He had the firm handshake of a man of confidence and self-knowledge.

"Like yourself, I am not originally from this Valley or this order. I despise the term outsider, but it is true. I am partial to those like myself." He smiled. "Someone needs to be. So, if you have need of anything, just call upon me."

"How do I do that?" she asked.

"That's right. That does present a problem." He smiled. "I will just have to ask Lord Dirt to correct that."

"Lord Dirt?" Aura asked. "Who is Lord Dirt?"

Leonikas grinned. "You will know when you see him."

Chapter Twenty-Three

AURA HAD NO time to bathe before Deofoyl's frantic pounding on the door of her room woke her at dawn. Between the fight with Mayenne, the ride to Ardora, and falling in the alley the night before, she felt sticky and smelled like sweat. Her breath reeked of the ale she downed to ease the pain in her leg so she could sleep. Two nasty stains from the spill in the alley the night before blotched the back of her dress. A fine way to meet a noblewoman.

Leonikas made sure she was all right, paid for another tankard of ale, then departed. That left Aura alone with her thoughts. If nothing else, Aura learned one thing from her duel with Mayenne. Never start the day unprepared. She sat at the tavern bar, massaging her left leg. It still cramped, but held her weight. In exchange for weakness, her knee and ankle now bent in slow, grudging movements. As she massaged her leg and sipped her ale, she silently prayed to each of the Gweryn in turn, asking for their blessings and guidance, and wishing them a fine day. Then, she spent two minutes thinking about each of the elements. She saved Light for last.

An amazing element, Light. The other five, she saw easily. Even Air appeared as smoke or as a cloud. Its rush through leaves was readily spotted. Light, although all around during the day, and near candles and fires at night, was only visible as lightning. Some thought Light merely an extension of Fire, but that did not explain the raw and solid form that hurtled from a storm, or that she cast from her hands into Mayenne's body. In that form, Light saved her life. It also left her crippled. She flexed her right hand and felt inside herself. Not enough restored vitality to cast a healing spell. If the day required more than her basic throwback spell, she may as well surrender immediately. Perhaps the injury would heal itself. Perhaps not. She thanked Light anyway. The ache in her leg reminded her that she was still alive.

Karyn appeared at her elbow. "Our horses are ready." She looked Aura over from crown to feet. Frowning, she said, "I knew you'd be trouble. You look terrible."

"I feel terrible," Aura said. "Is the Eorless of Ardora anything like ... him?"

"Balkefor? They despise each other. If you angered Jimmy, then Lady Naurelia will be your best friend."

"Jimmy? His name is Jimmy?" The name Jimmy belonged to a happy boy playing with a ball, not a bear wanting to rip off a woman's head.

"James Balkefor, the Eorl of Grahbale, titular head of the Guards and the Watchers, and the Valley's resident pisspot. Come on." Karyn jerked the half full tankard from Aura's hands. She gulped it down, and smacked it on the bar. "Let's go."

Aura and Karyn left Ardora in silence. The alternations in her skirt made riding easier. Even her left leg ached less today, and she had no trouble controlling Blister. They rode to the center of town, and turned right, toward the east. After yesterday's rain, this part of town smelled like mud, straw, and horse. Or, did she smell herself? Karyn kept her face straight ahead, but Aura watched everyone and everything, always on the lookout for a cloak the color of the sky. It didn't help that every tenth enchanter preferred light blue. At least, none of them had blonde hair or the same type beard. She thought that any halfway intelligent abductor would have changed clothes by now, and perhaps even shaved. A man with the same color hair made her jump, but he was at least two inches shorter than the man she saw, and rotund.

Ardora ended without warning. One moment they rode on cobblestones with houses on both sides of the road. The next, they rode on clay streaked with cart ruts and surrounded by forest. Munching on grass at the side of the road, a stag and a doe ignored the two riders as if they were but squirrels. Aura relaxed, but still maintained her vigilance. Highwaymen preferred jumping out from behind trees, and the oaks that surrounded them were wide enough to hide several men, much less one.

"Here we are," Karyn said. Her sudden words, coming after ten minutes of silence, made Aura jolt in her saddle. Karyn turned off the road. Ahead of them, a narrow path of well packed clay led back into the forest. Two eight foot high standing stones marked the entrance to the path. "I'll go with you. Lady Naurelia will be angry if I don't at least stop in and say hello."

The path emerged from the forest into a wide meadow of well maintained grass, bordered by heather and lupines. Against the forest stood a carriage house and a tidy cottage that any farmer in Lodwynnshire would have been proud to call home. In the center of the meadow stood a great manor unlike any Aura had ever seen. As long as any temple, its wooden walls were painted blue and adorned with knotwork carved into the planks and gilded gold. Windows rose from the floor to the ceiling of what must be the first floor, and filled the gables facing south. The columns supporting the shingled roof were shaped like trees still in their bark. Drawing closer to the house, Aura realized that the columns were living trees and that their branches and leaves formed the roof. The manor was built inside a grove.

What struck Aura the most were the doors. As tall as the wall, they looked engraved with solid gold lettering in a language that she did not recognize. The letters were oghams, but she could not decipher the words. The language was older than Tangoi, as if from the time of Owynn and Fayella. Perhaps older than that, if letters existed from the dawn of time. Then, she saw the woman standing in front of the doors and the house became a mere backdrop.

Aura thought she was a clothed statue until she moved. The woman wore a tight purple blouse, shoulderless on the right, with a long bell sleeve on the left, and a matching wrap around skirt, tied over the hip on the left, but hanging down to her knee on the right. On her wrists, upper arms, thighs and ankles, the woman wore bands of gold, almost the color of her skin. She was barefoot, her toenails and fingernails painted sky blue. Aura could not tear her eyes off the woman. She looked like liquid bronze, flowing in the afternoon breeze, and her golden hair fell down her back in thick waves. With full breasts and hips, accentuated by an impossibly narrow waist and powerful thighs, she embodied artists' comparisons to an hourglass. The woman's hooked nose and red lips gave her a seductive air. Her eyes looked like topaz, dominating the morning and cutting through Aura's heart with an inscrutable gaze.

The woman smiled as Aura and Karyn stepped onto the fieldstone curbing in front of the door. Karyn walked right up to the woman, who threw her arms out. They embraced with a squeal.

"Welcome home," the woman said, in a pleasant, but unfamiliar accent. "It is so good to see you again." The woman turned to Aura and said, "You are the visitor?"

Aura paused, not sure what to do. Did she curtsey? Did she bow? She decided to take her usual direct approach to good manners. "I am Aura Lockhaven of Hartshorn," she said. "I am honored to meet you, Eorless."

The bronze woman laughed. She laughed so hard that she doubled over, clutching her stomach with one hand and her mouth with the other. Aura felt angry and humiliated. When the woman gathered herself, she stood back up, still chuckling. Aura wanted to slap her, but she did not think that was an appropriate action to take with nobility.

"Oh, my," the woman said. "Oh, please, Mistress. I am not the Eorless of Ardora. I am Miriam, her handmaiden. Thank you for assuming that I was nobility. I have not been so flattered in years."

Aura tried to smile and said, "Uh, you look like royalty."

Miriam smiled and held out her right hand to Aura. As Aura took it she said, "Welcome to Ardora Hall. Milady is expecting you. Please come in." Looking at Karyn, she added, "You will join us for luncheon?"

"I can't, Miriam," Karyn said. "I have pressing business. I will stop in and slap the old girl, though."

The fourteen-foot tall door opened for the three women as they approached, held in place by a short man. The man looked to be nearly forty years old, his once black hair turning iron gray. While he struggled to maintain the impassive visage of the well groomed servant, the laugh lines on his face betrayed him. Shorter than the three women, and with a bit of a pot belly, he wore a short, sleeveless white tunic and knee sandals more in keeping with the balmy climate along the Sea of Aradakar.

"Mistress Aura, this is Juhnn," Miriam said. "He is Milady's valet. If you have need of anything, just call for him. His wife Lurna is our cook and their daughter Banya takes care of our cleaning. That frees me to assist Milady with her ... how should I phrase it?"

"Her more dangerous toys," Karyn said.

"Spoken with all the tact of a Frysting," Miriam said with a snort.

"Retorted with all the subtlety of an Aitian."

The two women giggled, and Aura followed them into the house. She stepped into the foyer and stopped. Trees wrapped in ivy grew up from holes in the floor, swept to the ceiling, forming the columns. Their branches provided the supports for the rooms overhead. The chair in the corner looked less carved from a tree than it looked as if a tree took on that form because it wanted to. A small fountain set in the wall trickled down into a silver bowl. At the top of the fountain lay a silver carving of Dalen, the Gweryn god of forests.

"This is magnificent," Aura said.

"Come, Mistress," Miriam said, taking Aura by the arm. "There will be plenty of days to admire the house. Milady expects you."

"Don't call me mistress," Aura said, staring at the ceiling. "I'm just a commoner."

"She calls me that, too," Karyn said.

Miriam led Aura through the door into another room, cavernous and open to the second floor. More trees rose from the floor to form the six columns supporting the ceiling. A table for fourteen sat in the middle, with tapestries of ancient bards and druids gracing the walls. The handmaiden guided Aura through the room to the stairs at the other end. As she reached the stairs, Aura looked through the other door, into a room that opened onto a veranda. In the center of the room stood a marble statue of a man.

"Who is that?" Aura asked.

"Never you mind," Miriam said, stepping up onto the first tread of the stairwell. Miriam tugged on Aura's arm, dragging her away from the open door and the statue. "Please follow me. Milady is in a good mood. She is so excited about having you here. She misses teaching. I have not seen her this happy in years. For that alone, Mistress, you are my friend. Don't worry about addressing her as Eorless. She is in an informal mood."

"I heard that, Miriam," a darker voice shouted from upstairs.

"I apologize, Milady. I was just telling Mistress –"

"Never mind that," the voice shouted again. "Just bring the wench up here. I need her! Do I hear Karyn? Tell her she never writes."

"You never visit," Karyn shouted. "I swear. You could deliver the oranges in person, you know. The last time I looked, you had legs."

Aura followed Miriam up the stairs. Live saplings formed the stairs, trained to grow in the direction of handrails and steps, with planks laid across them. Running her hand along the banister, Aura felt the love and joy radiating from the trees.

Miriam stood at the door at the top of the stairs and motioned for Aura to enter. Bright flashes of light shot from a table against the far wall. When Aura's eyes adjusted, she noticed a short woman in a knee length skirt that once had been white. She had the figure of someone who enjoyed her food. She had shoulder length black hair and stood at the table, with her arms raised. The flashes of light came from her hands, and a stream of mumbled Karanthek poured from her lips. Aura stepped toward the woman, and smacked her face against something hard, something metal. Aura took a step back and looked at her assailant, a large iron disk attached to a pole that dangled from a hook in the ceiling.

"Forgive the mess," the woman said without looking at Aura. "That's a pendulum to a new type of clock. If I can ever figure out how to make it work."

"Mistress, if I may introduce Lady Naurelia, the Eorless of Ardora," Miriam said.

"How do you do, Milady? I'm –"

"Yes, yes, I know, I know!" Naurelia snapped. "You're the visitor from Hartshorn. Believe it or not, I once visited your town. Nice place. Forgive my rudeness, but I can't take my eyes off this cauldron for one second. Oh, I am so close!"

Aura looked around the room and guessed it was Naurelia's workshop, but she had never seen anyone's workshop look like this. At least thirty candles illuminated the room, and the window stood open behind the workbench. Against one wall lay what Aura thought was a desk, what little she could see of it from the piles of books, scrolls, and magical tools that overwhelmed it. Along the other wall lay what appeared to be someone's attempt at making a gristmill out of iron parts, along with children's toys fashioned out of pewter. If that were a forge, it would never work. It lacked a bellows. What was that funny looking giant metal box with the gears pinned to it? Not only did she see the pendulum hanging from the ceiling, but also giant batwings made of goatskin, and several long, thick columns made of iron. Tall glass cylinders of bubbling potions connected to each other by glass tubes covered Naurelia's workbench. Blue flames shot up underneath the cylinders, but Aura saw no wood, only little metal pots. Aura looked at Naurelia again, and noticed the straps behind her neck and around her waist. She wore a leather apron.

"Aura, be a dear, and hand me that tincture of silver," Naurelia said, pointing to her right.

"Uh ... where is it?" Aura asked. All she saw was the funny iron box.

"Oh, forgive me, Mistress," Miriam said. "The shelf of ingredients is behind the computation machine."

"The comp – The what?"

"It's about to get interesting around here," Karyn sang.

"It's a way to figure out mathematical problems fast. Neither of us is very good with numbers," Miriam said.

"Miriam," Naurelia snapped. "Stop telling our weaknesses and just move the machine again!"

"Not good with mathematics?" Aura said. "I came to the right place."

"Wait until she explains why the calendar is off by an fourteenth of a day," Karyn murmured.

Miriam shoved her shoulder against the box. Karyn leaned against the door frame and yawned. Frowning at the guide, Aura decided to help Miriam. Leaning her staff in the corner, and dropping her bag to the floor, she took a position to Miriam's left. She gritted her teeth, expecting to feel pain in her leg. The box moved without much effort. As the box slid across the floor, Aura noticed a huge shelf behind it full of bottles, pots, jars, and boxes.

"I didn't know iron was so light," Aura said when they finished moving the box. "Did you cast some sort of levitation spell on it?"

"No, I put wheels on it," Naurelia said.

Karyn grinned at Aura and said, "Sucker."

Aura stared at the shelves. Tincture of silver? Which one! Miriam grabbed a tiny bottle and thrust it into Aura's hand. She held her finger to her lips and nodded toward Naurelia. Karyn continued to lean against the door frame, grinning. The guide apprenticed to this woman. Had every day of eighteen years been like this? Aura carried the bottle to the Eorless. As she handed it to Naurelia, she saw a device, like some sort of mask, over her face. It covered her eyes and gave her the appearance of an insect. Before Aura could ask about the device, Naurelia shot another blast of light into a cauldron on the bench in front of her. She pointed to the cylinder closest to Aura.

"Please add three drops to that mixture," Naurelia said. Aura tapped the bottle three times over the cylinder. With each tap, a liquid moon drop fell into the mixture. It bubbled with excitement. Naurelia reached for the knobs on the two glass tubes hovering over the cauldron. "Stand back. I don't really know what this is going to do."

Aura took three steps backwards as Naurelia twisted the knobs. Karyn grabbed her arm and pulled her to the corner of the room. The guide looked genuinely terrified, but too fascinated to bolt downstairs. Then, the handmaiden stepped in front of them and raised her arms. The mixing potion hissed in the cauldron. Steam rose around Naurelia, illuminated by the candles and the light from the window. White light engulfed the room, and Aura saw nothing else.

Chapter Twenty-Four

PHRASES IN KARANTHEK flew so fast that Aura could not catch them all. She saw something in the thick smoke that engulfed Karyn, her, and the workshop. It looked like a bubble of liquid glass emanating from Miriam's hands and surrounding all of them. Miriam twirled her arms three times, and the smoke condensed into a large ball between her hands. With a flick of her fingers, Miriam shot the smoke through the open window into the air.

Naurelia hunkered over her workbench for a moment, and then whirled around. Her black hair lay blasted back by the explosion in tangled disarray. What remained of her shredded apron did nothing to hide an even more shredded tangini top, her breasts, or the slight bulge of her belly, all blackened with smoke. She ripped the mask from her face and tossed it on the workbench. Soot covered her face, except around her eyes, giving her the appearance of a highwayman in reverse. Her brown eyes gleamed with triumph. She held up one hand and grinned.

"I did it! Oh, yes!" Naurelia shouted.

"You were successful, Milady?" Miriam asked.

"Of course I was," Naurelia said. "Why wouldn't I be?"

Miriam, Karyn, and Aura walked up to the Eorless. She held a small blue pill in her right hand.

"What did you do this time?" Karyn asked.

"This is dehydrated beer. Drop one of these in a pint of water, and it's an instant ball. Swallow a handful and you'll have a three day hangover. Take that, Percival!"

"Who is Percival?" Aura asked.

"He's the premier of the alchemists. We're always challenging each other. I suspect that next month, he will beat me. He thinks he can make a candle out of glass, the poor boy. That's how it works. One month, I win.

One month, he wins. Last year, he said I couldn't fly." Naurelia pointed to the batwings hanging from the ceiling and said, "But I flew two hundred and fifty-seven feet."

"Then you broke three ribs and your arm when you crashed into a tree," Miriam mumbled.

"Miriam!" Naurelia snapped. The handmaiden shrugged. Naurelia dropped the little blue pill back into the dry cauldron. She wiped her hands on what remained of her apron and said to Aura, "Well, I don't suppose you're here to learn about my mad inventions, are you? No, that's right. You're here to learn about ..." She cut her eyes at Miriam and gave her a helpless look.

"How to harness and release her emotions, Milady," Miriam said.

"That's right, yes, yes. Now, why didn't Karyn tell you that? It's her job. I shall have to speak to Karyn about informing you about your entire lessons. I can do that. She was my student. Wait until I see her again."

"You may take a good look at me now. I'm standing right here, you know," Karyn said.

"Of course you are, why wouldn't you be? Where have you been? You never visit anymore. Never mind! Why didn't you tell Aura about her lesson with me?"

Karyn threw her hands into the air and rolled her eyes toward the ceiling. Miriam shrugged. Naurelia ignored them both and waved Aura toward the desk. "While I clean up, why don't you start with a little light reading? Here. You will need this one, and this one, and no not that one, and this one, oh, this one is in Karanthek! Can you read Karanthek? Neither can I. Ah, this is a classic. And I wrote this one myself. And, how did this get in here? Miriam, remind me to clean this pile up one day. Now where is ... there it is."

By the time Naurelia finished thrusting books and scrolls and piles of parchment into Aura's hands, she had to peer around the side of the stack just to see. She held the stack below her waist and it still reached the top of her head. She always considered herself a strong woman, but her arms and back already ached under the weight of the paper. She doubted if her leg would withstand carrying this much. Miriam took half the stack from her. Aura thanked her with a smile.

"I warned you, Aura," Karyn sang.

"Miriam," Naurelia said. "Be a dear and escort Aura to the veranda. The light is better out there. Also, bring a bottle of wine. No, bring several. We will need lots of wine! I shall go bathe and join you shortly."

Karyn remained behind with Naurelia. Aura took the stairs one at a time, testing her leg with each tread. By the time she reached the bottom, sweat beaded on her brow. Miriam led her through the arch, past the statue, and out onto a wide veranda overlooking a meadow with a forest beyond. A man stood with his back to the door. He turned around as the women stepped onto the veranda. He dashed forward.

"Let me help you with that," he said, taking the stack of books and scrolls from Aura's hands.

"Thank you, sir."

The man stood as tall as Sagacius, with piercing blue eyes and a mane of blonde hair that flowed over his shoulders. He was clean shaven, which Aura thought a good thing. She tried to stop the smile that spread across her face as she looked at him. She felt her heart skip a beat. He had to be the most handsome man she had ever seen. The set of his mouth spoke of the hunter, while his eyes reflected the scholar. The slight puffiness of his cheeks revealed his love of ale, but his lean neck said he also practiced self control. His sleeveless white shirt, loosely laced across his chest, allowed the bulges of his arms to show. The charcoal gray keld did the same for his legs, and the Karanthek sandals only made his calves look tighter.

As the man sat the stack down, Miriam said, "Mistress Aura, may I present Master Manfred Rowanwand of Grahbale. Master Manfred, this is Mistress Aura Lockhaven, a visitor from Hartshorn."

Manfred stood up, and gave her a look of astonishment and pleasure. He took her hand, and raised her knuckles to his lips. Aura blushed.

"Aura Lockhaven," he said, releasing her hand. "I've heard much about you, but not nearly enough. We're practically family." When Aura gave him a quizzical look, he said, "We have the same master."

"You're one of Sagacius' other three students," Aura said with a gasp. Manfred gave her a slight bow. "So, your brother is Karyn's young man."

Manfred bellowed a laugh. It was the kind that started in his toes and did not end until Aura and Miriam were chuckling along with him.

"Young? Don't tell Mandrake that, or he'll burst his shirt laces. That is, if Karyn lets him wear a shirt."

"It isn't his shirt that gets in my way," Karyn said from the door. Aura, Miriam, and Manfred all groaned at the same time. Karyn smiled as she walked up to the three embarrassed people. She looked at Manfred and asked, "When did you return?"

"Yesterday," Manfred said to Karyn. "My ship caught a trade wind out of the North Sea. I thought I'd visit Lady Naurelia for a few days."

"The tavern has gone to seed without you. Mandrake can't cook."

Manfred smiled. "I'm glad at least someone besides me knows that."

Naurelia stepped out onto her veranda. Clean, Naurelia looked more regal than Aura thought upon first meeting her. In the light, her round features gave her the appearance of a classical statue brought to life. She wore a black gown, split over both legs and cut low over her bust, with angel sleeves, and covered in gold embroidery. The golden sash around her waist appeared to be woven with threads of the actual metal. Her still wet hair fell free to her shoulders.

She stared at Manfred for a moment, then said with a chill in her voice, "Mr. Rowanwand."

"Eorless t'Ardora," he replied, with even more of a chill.

"Will you be joining us for dinner?"

"I'd be delighted."

The most imperceptible of frowns crossed Naurelia's lips for the briefest amount of time. "Very good," she said, in the voice of the displeased. "Now if you will excuse us, I have much to discuss with my other guest. Please feel free to explore the grounds."

Manfred gave Naurelia a stiff nod. With more fluid nods to Aura, Miriam, and Karyn, he stepped into the house. Karyn gave Naurelia a hug, then took her leave. Naurelia motioned to the thick cushions.

"Please sit down. I heard about your little tiff," Naurelia said to Aura. "Both of them actually. If the legends of the balakalat are only half true, then you are blessed to still be alive. As for Balkefor, I wish I had been there. He was in my shire, after all. I'm not sure which was worse, so I want you to conserve your strength." After they sat, Naurelia said, "Allow me to properly introduce myself, I am Naurelia t'Ardora, the Eorless of Ardora."

"I am Aura Lockhaven of Hartshorn." Not knowing whether to stand and curtsey, or nod, or any other sort of protocol to do with nobility, Aura bowed as much as she could while sitting.

Naurelia stared at her for a long minute before saying, "Now, Aura, dear. I must ask you several questions. As Miriam will tell you, there are two Naurelia t'Ardoras. You already met the first, the daft inventor as they call me. The other is the Eorless who watches over her people."

The change was as direct as if one woman left the veranda, and another took her place. Naurelia's face grew serious. Her eyes turned darker brown as the sparkle in them switched from the mad dash of experiment to that of protective inquiry. She sat up higher, drew back her shoulders, and threw out her chest. An invisible cloak descended upon her, one of command and responsibility. Regality replaced frivolity. Aura had no delusion that the mind inside the Eorless' skull was no longer absent, and the brain no longer scattered.

"I am now the Eorless." Even her voice sounded like that of gravity and earned respect. The Eorless lowered her head enough to look upwards at Aura, in a slightly haughty, yet mostly curious, manner. Her expression was not that of disdain, but that of a judge learning facts. "I know why you are here, at least from the council's point of view. You accepted an invitation from us to examine the order and our ways. If you like what you see, then you will accept our invitation to join us. That isn't enough for me." She leaned forward. With a finger bent by an injury long ago, she pointed to Aura. "I want to know why Aura Lockhaven is here. What do you see in my order that strikes your fancy? This visit is no mere holiday for you, no, no. I know what Lord Ashthorne said, but I want to hear it from your own lips."

Aura stood. She didn't know if that was proper in front of a seated Eorless, but it seemed like the right thing to do. Her leg ached. Her mind ached even more. Crossing her arms over her chest, she walked to the edge of the veranda. She gazed out at the meadow for a minute, watching the butterflies enjoy the wildflowers. They were so fortunate. They were just butterflies, doing what butterflies do. She turned around and faced Naurelia.

"Eorless, if you had been in my sitting room last week, you would have heard my answer. I suppose you know about Lodd and my town's priest." Naurelia nodded. "I wanted the power to heal catastrophic illnesses and injuries without killing myself. I wanted to defend the defenseless, help the helpless, and give hope to the hopeless." She paused, expecting at least a gasp from Naurelia. The Eorless didn't even arch an eyebrow. "I still want all those things, but now, I'm not sure that's all there is to it. So much has happened. I've seen my fears. I've learned things about myself and my master. I've fought a living horror that I thought was just a fable. My staff ... " Aura looked around, but didn't see it. "Where is my staff?"

"Your staff is upstairs in Milady's workshop. Shall I bring it down?" Miriam asked.

"No, that's all right. I just want to know where it is. My staff is dangerous, at least to me." She rubbed the hump in her nose. How did she explain her staff? "I know there are rings that grant the wearer more power."

"The Chancellor and Vice-Chancellor's rings triple their power," Naurelia said.

"That's exactly what I mean. My staff magnifies my power, to a degree I cannot fathom. A simple movement spell shattered a chair." This time, Naurelia arched her eyebrow. "I didn't know I had that in me. Lady Naurelia, nothing cannot be magnified."

"That doesn't make any sense, Mistress," Miriam said.

"Yes, it does, Miriam," Naurelia said, sitting up straighter. "Aura is talking like me. Ten times nothing is still nothing. Power can only be magnified if power exists to be magnified. If you did not possess the power to begin with, then your staff would be a mere stick."

Aura nodded. "My staff is magnifying something I didn't know I have. I know magic is the manifestation of will and intention. I know that. But my knowledge is encyclopedic. If I need to heal someone, I consult the books until I identify the illness, then I consult other books to find the right potions, herbs, and crystals. That's how a wizardess operates. That is enough for things like blessing livestock or curing gout. It isn't enough for a life or death situation, and I've faced three since my initiation. I consider myself blessed to have survived one, much less all. I don't think my staff merely magnifies the words in my head, like a reading prism. There's something in me that I don't understand, something that helped me heal two dying people and kept me alive in the face of horror."

"I see," Naurelia said. She rubbed her chin and looked at Aura with an intense gaze. The furrowed brow and the flashing brown eyes spoke of someone calculating many possibilities at the speed of thought. "There is more. Yes, yes, there is more. Please tell me."

"I have strange memories. They're like shadows of dreams, the kind you think you remember while you're sipping that first mug of tea at sunrise. It's as if I'm standing outside my own body, watching. I see all my feelings, all my thoughts, and all my will combine into one mass and come out in the most dreadful scream. Things happen when that happens. Oh, merciful heavens! That didn't make any sense, but neither does that memory. I have no idea what it is. It's just there. I've had four such memories in my life. The first happened when I was ten. Since I was initiated, I've had three. I was initiated three weeks ago."

"That is very interesting," Naurelia said, still looking at Aura with that intense gaze.

"It sounds as if you almost faint, or are in that place between dreams and wakefulness when that happens, Mistress. It sounds like a trance," Miriam said.

"Yes, yes, that is exactly what it sounds like," Naurelia said, smiling at her handmaiden. "Excellent analysis, Miriam. That explains much. That makes perfect sense." Aura was happy it made sense to someone because it made none to her. Naurelia looked back at Aura. "Please continue."

"I understand that the only way to defeat a balakalat is to have performed an act of kindness for someone." She paused. What she had to say made her tremble. In a low voice, Aura said, "Lady Naurelia, only an hour before I arrived at Mayenne's shop, I poured wine over the unmarked graves of a family. I told them I was sorry. I even straightened a fallen tombstone."

"That was an act of extreme power, Aura. Extreme magical knowledge," Naurelia said.

"I don't have that knowledge!" Aura said, throwing her arms out. "I only did it because I felt sorry for them. I had no idea that it would save my life the next day." She shook her head and whispered, "That's what my life has been like since my initiation. It's one accident and one incident after another, and I have no idea how I'm doing any of them."

"I know exactly what that is. I know what you did at the grave, Aura. I think I understand your mysterious memory, and I have a hunch I know what your staff is magnifying. I could tell you, but I'd rather show you," Naurelia said.

"Why am I here?" Aura repeated Naurelia's question. She shook her head. "I don't know. I don't know anything about anything anymore. How can I tell you why I'm here when I don't know who I am. Lady Naurelia, if you had asked me on Bloomstead, I could have told you exactly who I was.

I was the newly initiated wizardess who would spend her days making luck charms for the clumsy, brewing lust potions for brides, and helping the constable find lost children. Occasionally, I would perform divination or consult the ancient texts for the mayor. Today, I don't know who I am at all. I am totally confused about myself, my ability, this strange power I have. So, I really can't answer your question. I'm not sure, but I think I'd just like to go home."

"I see," Naurelia said. She stood, and walked over to stand by Aura. As the Eorless, she seemed taller, yet still only reached the top of Aura's shoulder. "That changes things, a great many things." Naurelia looked out at the meadow. "You answered my question. I think I can answer your question."

"I didn't know I asked a question."

"You didn't, yet in not asking, you asked the most profound question of them all. What do you know about self-knowledge?" Naurelia asked.

"Apparently, nothing."

Naurelia smiled. "Based on that answer, you know more than you realize. You know twice as much as you think you know, which is four times what everyone should know, but only half of what they believe they know, and it's a thousand times greater than the average woman in Ayrdland, so think nothing of it."

"That didn't add up," Aura said.

"It most certainly did!" Naurelia snapped. She whirled around to face Aura so fast that Aura stepped back. The Eorless advanced. "Only a fool says she knows about self-knowledge, when she doesn't. You just told me that you are no fool. Congratulations, Aura, dear, you're ahead of the majority of people in this country. That doesn't mean that you aren't vulnerable. Oh, you are in no danger in my home, dear. Out there, however," Naurelia said, nodding toward the Valley rim. "If you don't know yourself, then you are vulnerable. Do you know Marsh the Elder's Axiom?"

Aura cast a faint smile. "Which part? The axiom states *If you know yourself better than anyone else knows you, then no one can control you.* The reverse corollary is *If you know someone better than he knows himself, you can control him.*" Aura sighed and looked at the ground. "You don't have to say it, Eorless. I see it clearly. Others have known me better than I've known myself. I've been manipulated. By my uncle, a rotten thief, three men who maneuvered me into bed, and almost to my death yesterday." She paused. "I was manipulated by my own arrogance."

"You admit that you're arrogant. You also admit that you're blind to the intentions of others. That's a good beginning, yes, yes. Marsh the Elder was a philosopher, but there is a reason his axiom is in the books of all magical orders. Self-knowledge is one of the highest forms of magic, if not the point of the pyramid. It is invisible armor. It requires constant asking of questions of one's self. So far, you have only made statements about yourself, but they show that you are ready to ask questions. You are ready to begin to armor yourself. You must. We live in a dangerous world, and our line of work puts us in the paths of dangerous men. Now, I suppose that someone as educated as a wizardess has heard of the concept of variable control."

Aura smiled. This conversation reminded her of many evenings spent in front of the fireplace, sipping ale, and discussing the philosophy of magic with Sagacius. "That's Valran's Law. *If one controls all the variables in a situation, he controls the situation.* It sounds good, but Valran was a mad hermit. His law is whimsy, Lady Naurelia. It's impossible to control all the variables. Even if they are known and fixed constants instead of unknown and changing variables, it is impossible to control them all."

"Of course it is, why wouldn't it be? Now, Aura, dear. What if you controlled one? What if it was a known and fixed constant, and under your control at all times?"

"I may not control the situation, but neither would the other person. I'd have a chance of winning, or at least escaping alive."

"That one variable is yourself," Naurelia said. She smiled at Aura. "You already did that very thing, Aura, dear. Your action at the grave transformed you into a known constant in your own mind, but a variable that the balakalat could not control. You knew more about yourself than she did, even though you didn't know it. That's why self-knowledge is so important. If you know more about yourself than anyone else does, you become a fixed constant firmly under your own control. You are your own secret weapon."

Aura considered her duel with Mayenne. For most of the previous day and all last night, she thought Mayenne had been right. She was an arrogant tart. Mayenne held all the power, and Aura had simply been lucky. In retrospect, perhaps Aura held more power than she thought, and Mayenne had been the arrogant one. The staffmaker thought she controlled all the variables, but three eluded her. Neither opponent had any idea that Aura's little ceremony at the grave activated the condition that could defeat a balakalat. Mayenne had no idea that Aura's soul would somehow cause her to slip back into her cursed state. If the tales were true, then as the balakalat, Mayenne was blinded by her own appetites and allowed herself to grow slovenly the longer the duel lasted. It sounded arrogant to say, but Aura had to admit that her survival had been a little less due to dumb luck. Still, her control, if she dared call it that, over those three variables had been accidental.

She stared at the meadow behind the house. A red fox sauntered from the woods, strolling across the grass as if he were the lord of the estate. No one had to ask the fox who he was. No one had to ask about what variable he controlled. Anyone who grabbed him would find out in a storm of teeth and claws. As Aura watched him continue on his way, she mumbled, "Who am I?"

Naurelia narrowed her eyes and gave her a knowing look. "Now, you are asking questions. Very good." She took Aura's hand and led her back to the cushions. Aura knew to sit after a noble had seated herself, but Naurelia insisted that Aura sit first. Miriam smiled at both of them. After she settled herself on her cushion, Naurelia returned to her upright posture. In her firm voice of authority, she said, "I know what you want, Aura Lockhaven. I know why you are here, in our Valley, in my home."

"I'm in no condition to answer a riddle, Lady Naurelia. You'll have to explain it to me."

"Aura, I am Naurelia, a student of Damaskarose, and the wife of Tyrus t'Ardora, the Eorl of Ardora. He is descended from the first family to settle in this valley after Damaskarose transformed it from a cleft of rock. His title is ceremonial, but it carries weight within the order. Until my husband returns, I am First Noble. The Chancellor leads the order, but First Noble leads the people. Even the Chancellor defers to First Noble, out of good manners. I say that not to boast, but so you will understand that I have the authority to offer you what I am about to offer you." She spread her arms wide. "This may look like a veranda to you, Aura. Yes, yes, why wouldn't it. Well, it is a veranda. Yet, it is not." She paused, a little longer than it took for her words to sink into Aura's mind. "It is a crossroads before you."

Aura began to feel the aches throughout her body from the day before, and the fatigue in her soul from that morning. A riddle she could not handle. A metaphor, however, sounded almost interesting. "What do you mean, Eorless?"

Naurelia smiled. "Your original purpose for your visit has been altered by circumstances beyond your control, yet circumstances that you changed to conform with your will. That tells me that you have great potential, not to the order, but to yourself. Not as a magician, but as a woman. Anything you do as an enchantress must be built on that foundation and that potential, yes, yes. So, I offer you a choice. You may return home, and after a duel with a balakalat, none would blame you. There would be no ill feelings between us. I would ask that you remain with me until your cloak is woven and your ring is fashioned. We wish to bestow them upon you, if for no other reason than we hold you in high regard. Or ..."

Naurelia let the conjunction hang in the air. Aura stiffened, waiting for the sentences that followed. The word *or* usually joined two absolute opposites. This or that. Black or white. Man or woman. Dualities, the philosophers called them. Direct opposites who tried to nullify each other. Sagacius trained her as a wizard, one who saw polarities, opposites that interacted with each other to create a new dynamic whole. Those were joined by the word *and*. This and that. Black and white. Man and woman. Go home or ... Go home and ... ? The terms of her visit apparently just changed.

Naurelia seemed to sense Aura's tension. She smiled. "Or, you could remain here, with a new purpose." She paused again. Aura relaxed a bit. "That of the Dyrgan."

Miriam gasped. Aura cut her eyes to the handmaiden. She held her hands over her mouth. Her topaz eyes twinkled with amazement. Still watching Miriam, Aura asked, "What, or who, is a Dyrgan? That sounds remarkably like the old Coadic word for discovery."

"That is because it *is* the old Coadic word for discovery. A Dyrgan is a rare person who undergoes a quest within the Valley of the Mystic Moon. In the old Ayrdic tales, such a person is known as a Seeker. Flumantine romances call them Questiara. Hero is the word used by the Karanthek legends. Frysting lore evokes the rather pedestrian term Forstata, or explorer. The quest of the Dyrgan, or in your case the Dyrgana, is not so grand as saving the world. It is a deeply personal search. Although, from what I understand, some Dyrgans have believed saving the world would have been child's play compared to their own searches. Each search is different, because the needs of each Dyrgan are different. To become a Dyrgan, one has to be possessed of both courage and foolhardiness. One has to have a specific purpose, a purpose that drives him or her forward on a special quest of discovery. I cannot tell you what you would face. Perhaps nothing more than your original purpose, a mere visit. Perhaps things that make the balakalat seem like a mewling kitten."

Aura sat up higher. This intrigued her. "So, my initial question, can the Order of Enchanters teach me to heal without endangering myself, would become a part of the larger quest?" Naurelia nodded. Good, Aura thought.

At least, that answer still lay on the platter of possibility. "What about the council's invitation to join the order?"

"Aura, dear, if you choose the path of the Dyrgana, it is a path with no short cuts, no side roads, and no way back. Your journey along that path will lead to either initiation or expulsion."

"If I become a Dyrgana, what would my quest be?" Aura asked.

Naurelia smiled. She looked at Aura the way a knowing mother looks at a confused child. She said, "Why, to find Aura Lockhaven of Hartshorn."

Chapter Twenty-Five

EVENING CREPT INTO the forest not unlike a man approaching the lover in his bed. Shadows caressed the oaks and maples, cloaking them with grayed and blued images of themselves. Night larks and loft swallows swooped low over the meadow, grabbing the last of the day's midges and flies before turning in. Crickets began their nightsong, making the air, still moist from the previous day's rain, feel cooler.

On any other night, Aura would have opened all her senses to inhale such an evening. Not this night. As she had all day, she struggled with Naurelia's offer. The Eorless told her to consider it until breakfast the next morning. All day, she vacillated, deciding to accept, then deciding to return home, then deciding to accept. By dinner, a delectable shepherd's pie eaten alone with a silent Miriam, she changed her mind for the sixth time. Looking out at the gathering darkness from the veranda, she whispered "Why be miserable?" Then, she limped to the stairs to her room to pack.

She didn't have much to pack. A bag, her staff, and the clothes she wore. Her clothes. She looked at the sleeveless red silk dress, clasped over her right shoulder by a golden broach, descending down over her chest, and tied by a long thong just over her left hip, leaving her left side and leg completely uncovered. Miriam loaned it to her while Banya cleaned Aura's stained brown dress. Even if the dress was too short, she liked the look, and felt like a priestess from some classical temple. Banya also cleaned Aura's boots, so the red sandals she wore matched the dress. Well, she would stay until morning at least. Not even her map showed her the way back to the Krigers' house in the dark. That gave her more time to think.

Aura plopped down on the bed and stared at the ceiling. "I came here to learn to control my feelings. They are anything but under control right now. I always failed at quitting, so why am I succeeding tonight?" She threw her hands over her eyes and muttered, "This is only getting worse. Why can't I make a decision?"

The room Naurelia loaned her was comfortable enough. The three triple candelabras filled the room with light, flickering on the branches that formed the high vaults overhead, and casting playful shadows in the leaves of the ceiling. Stuffed with the feathers of thousands of geese and ducks, the mattress invited her to spend the rest of the week sleeping. Miriam told her that the room once belonged to Naurelia's son Tyrelian, but he had since moved out and was currently with his wife and daughters, copying ancient texts in Aitia. If Naurelia was a grandmother, and her teacher had been Damaskarose, then she was nearly the same age as Sagacius. The mystery of the longevity potion could wait. The answer to Naurelia's offer could not.

"I don't want to quit," Aura snarled. She sat up. She always thought best under the shower. The calming effect of water flowing over her body, and a routine chore to occupy her hands, left her mind free to think. Perhaps a nighttime bath would do the same thing. She left her room and walked down the corridor to the bathing chamber.

Miriam had explained how everything worked. She had been to Welcaster and luxuriated in the old Bellician spas. Those were hot springs. She also understood the big tank behind her home that poured cold water over her. She had used quite a few bath tubs. Those were oversized tin pails filled with buckets of hot water. All she saw in the bathing chamber was a cube of marble, hollowed out and polished until it reflected everything in the room. Two brass pipes jutted up from the side of the tub, and curved downward into it, with latches on top. Two red towels hung on a rod on the wall opposite the tub.

Miriam said that the t'Ardoras had built a copper tank into the wall behind the kitchen oven. It held water that the oven heated. When she released the latches of the tub, hot water from the tank and cold water from the well mixed in the tub and one simply sat down and bathed. Water does not flow uphill, Aura thought, looking at the tub. Still, anyone who could make dehydrated beer could figure out how to defy the laws of nature.

Aura opened the two latches. She knew enough about bathtubs to know that she needed to mix the two at a temperature she liked. Not unlike mixing water from the well with water from the kettle to wash dishes. She jumped as two waterfalls poured into the tub. So, it worked like her indoor cistern. She smiled as she placed her finger underneath one waterfall. Nice and brisk. She squealed at the other one. That could make tea. Let them mix, she thought. Her left leg still cramped, and now her fight with Mayenne told in the rest of her aching muscles. She decided on a little more hot than cold. As she watched the two waterfalls, the water level in the tub rose no higher. Miriam said something about putting the stopper in the tub, whatever a stopper was. Aura looked around the tub and saw only a cork sitting between the two brass pipes. She picked it up. Then, she noticed the hole in the bottom of the tub.

"Miriam could have said put the bung in the keg," Aura said, shoving the cork into the drain hole.

Aura winced as she lowered her body into the full tub. It took only a moment for her to adjust. Her muscles thanked her for making the bath hot. Aura sank into the water until only her head remained above, letting the heat soothe her arms, legs, and back. This day began with a near slap by one eorl and ended with a luxurious bath in the home of another. Squares of soap, made from olive oil and honey, lay in a brass tray on the edge of the tub. Sniffing them, she detected lavender and sage. The perfect combination for tonight. She slathered herself from hair to toenails, letting the aromas remind her of peace and wisdom.

As she lay in the tub, she returned to her original question. Could the Order of Enchanters teach her to heal fatal injuries without dying? That question had rapidly been replaced by a shorter, but more profound question. Who am I? As if in answer, Sagacius' words crept into her mind. *You are important to the entire country of Ayrdland. You have the potential to write history.* That was a laughable statement. Important men, much less women, were not the children of tavern owners. People who wrote history were the children of priests, wizards, philosophers, knights, thegns, and eorls. Even in the largest town for three shires, the only man of any note to come out of Hartshorn was Squire Mullow, and his fame was that of the buffoon. She snorted. The idea that Aura Lockhaven could write history was as preposterous as a blacksmith becoming king.

She paused in her mental gripe, watching the water drip from the spout. The sound of water striking water reminded her of hammer striking anvil. Songs heard at home and in Lockhaven Tavern replaced Sagacius' words. He was an unlearned blacksmith, so the songs said. His name, as well as the name of the hamlet where he smithed, had been lost to historian and minstrel alike. After a bitter winter killed his wife and three children, he forged a gargantuan axe, then set out to slay Skols. He had no interest in saving Ayrdland from conquest. He only wanted to die a death with meaning. The harder the blacksmith fought for that death, the more of a legend he became. Finally, he stood alone at the gates of Vine Haven, facing a horde of Skols. He killed twenty that day, or five hundred, depending on the song and the drunkenness of the particular minstrel. The number didn't matter. He shattered the invading army, sending them limping back to their ships. The southern coast of Ayrdland lived in peace for a decade, and the hulking blacksmith earned the name the Lock on the Haven.

Aura looked at her hands. Her eyes traced the scar on her left palm. That was earned trying to save her father. She counted the calluses at the base of her fingers on the right. Those were earned grinding herbs with a mortar and pestle. In their own way, her hands were not unlike those of a blacksmith. Fire and work left their marks. If a blacksmith could write history, then perhaps the tavern owner's daughter could do the same in her own little way. Perhaps the orphan could be important to the one thousand people in Hartshorn. Perhaps the apprentice could matter to the wizardess she became.

That is, if she were willing to pay the price. Naurelia never mentioned the price of the quest, and Aura knew enough songs and tales about quests to know they never came cheap. Quests were about loss. What did Aura Lockhaven have to lose? She had only her growing reputation, a tidy home awaiting her when she returned, and a trusted friend and teacher. If she lost those, then that fear she faced at Ralthangarle, alone and running in the darkness, would become reality. She also had her life, and had come close to losing that, even before Naurelia offered Aura the role of the Dyrgana.

The bath had not helped. If anything, it only made her thoughts darker and deeper. At least, she was clean and her body felt relaxed. After she dried and redressed, Aura returned to her room. She removed the ruby from her bag, placed it into a small pocket on the right side of the borrowed dress, then limped down the stairs. The house lay quiet, and mostly in shadow broken by intermittent lanterns. She passed into the chamber that held the statue.

With no one around, she paused to look at it. It was life sized and perfectly executed. It caught a handsome man in mid stride, with a smile on his face and his right hand outstretched as if in greeting. Aura wondered who the model had been, and who the statue represented. Fortunate piece of stone, she thought. He had no decisions to make. With a sigh, she walked out onto the veranda. The stars had taken their place in the night sky. In the absence of the still yet to rise moon, they looked like salt spilled on black silk.

Still no closer to a decision, her thoughts continued to race through her mind. Why did she even hesitate? If this were just about discovering the truth of her power, and how to use it, she would say yes without hesitation. The foundational question of life was *who am I*. People went on pilgrimages to find out. They visited philosophers and priests to answer it. Some even went mad seeking the answer.

That was the least of it. This seemed like Valran's Law, except it worked. Someone else controlled almost all the variables, and the situation was her life. Some still unknown person sent two nymphs to watch her. A piece of oak controlled more of her power than she did. Her mother's surname, Nightshade, hung over her like a scythe ready to strike. Sagacius feared another name of equal poetic value, Brightstar. Then, there was Damaskarose and whatever resemblance Aura had to her. Everyone controlled all these variables about Aura, except one. That one was Aura herself, and apparently, not even she controlled it. If going home ripped those variables from the grasp of whomever controlled them, then quitting made perfect sense.

None of it answered the nagging question, *who am I*.

Aura pulled the ruby from her pocket. Sagacius gave it to her to help guide her. For the first time, she held it up as more than just a beautiful crystal. Perhaps, it had something to say about her decision. She peered deep into its facets. In the darkness of the yard and forest beyond, all she saw was the color of a rose, yet the thickness of blood. The facets reflected her own face back at her. In the red stone, she looked half way attractive. If the ruby had any guidance, it held its peace.

Aura heard footsteps behind her, clomping loudly on the tiles of the hall. They were those of a man deliberately wanting to be heard. She smiled as she was in no mood to be startled by someone trying to be quiet. This man had the long legged lope of a tall Ayrdishman. In fact, his footfall sounded like that of Sagacius. Before Aura could turn, Manfred Rowanwand appeared next to her, holding two tankards.

"You look like you need this," he said, handing Aura one of the tankards.

"Thank you," she said, taking it from him. The cool, smooth pewter felt good in her hand. Right now, the simple feel of a familiar metal reassured her. So did this man she only met that morning. He stood three feet to her left, straight as an oak, and about as sturdy. The lantern on the veranda wall behind him threw his face into sharp relief, accenting his aquiline nose. Aura smiled. She liked his face. It was more than that. It was as if ... she put her thoughts into a question. "Why do I feel like I've known you all my life?"

Manfred grinned. "In a manner of speaking, you have. I apprenticed to Sagacius for eighteen years. One doesn't do that sort of thing without acquiring something from his teacher. His mannerisms. His inflection. His thoughts. His view of the world. Even his favorite word."

"Egads!" Aura and Manfred said at the same time. Aura giggled while Manfred chuckled.

Aura took a sip of her ale, and almost spat it out. It didn't just bite her tongue. It ripped it from her mouth. Naurelia mixed her ale with lifewater, at what tasted like a ratio of three pints to one. The daft inventor was also a daft drunkard. She breathed a few times through her nose to muster enough air to swallow. The ale burned going down her throat, but felt warm in her stomach. Perhaps, she needed this after all. She took another sip, and said, "Lady Naurelia doesn't seem to like you."

Manfred snorted. "The Rowanwands and the t'Ardoras go back for generations. My great-grandfather was valet to Lord Tyrus' grandfather. Lady Naurelia and I love each other, but that doesn't mean we don't cross mental swords. On some days, we'd like to remove the letter N from *mental* swords."

"I take it she told you about her offer to me."

"Aura, there are six great halls in this Valley, if you count the ruins of Tallen Hall and the derelict of Damaskarose's castle. I've traveled the world. The only country in the continent of Sareth I haven't visited is Glasenya. The halls of knights in Flumance make the order's great halls look like cottages. Damaskarose's grand estate is a hovel compared to the castles of barons in Nebeland and counts in Bellicia. The ones in Arantia dwarf them all. I said that to say this." He waved behind him to the tall doors. "She didn't have to tell me. Ardora Hall is a small house, and nothing is secret in a small house."

"Good. Then, I may speak freely. I have to make a decision, and I'm not sure what to do," Aura said. She held up the ruby. Perhaps there wasn't enough light on the nighttime veranda for it to speak. Well, this man from

Grahbale could speak. She slipped the ruby back into her pocket. With a sigh, she said, "I really need to talk to Master, but he isn't here."

"In a manner of speaking, he is," Manfred said. "I'm pretty sure I know what the old man would say if he were standing right beside you, so feel free to talk to me. I had no idea that we'd meet, so I didn't reread Sagacius' letters to refresh myself on his newest apprentice. Besides, they're at home. My hinges are somewhat rusty when it comes to what Aura Lockhaven likes and dislikes."

"He wrote to you about me?" That was news to her. The man always wrote letters to people, but she never interrupted his privacy to ask to whom.

"He wrote to Mandrake, too. One of the unwritten laws of magic is that a master and apprentice always remain in contact with each other. I hope you don't think your apprenticeship is concluded! The old man will trail you like a badger for the rest of your life. You will hear far more than you care to know about his next apprentice, and you best tell him about yours. He's protective about all of us, you know. He would chastise me in ways that aren't decent to explain to a woman if I didn't offer you my ears. I can at least listen to you vent your bladder."

"Spleen," Aura said. "The phrase is vent my spleen."

"Yes," Manfred said. He rubbed his forehead and mumbled, "No one wants to hear anyone vent her bladder."

Aura stifled her snicker. Manfred offered to serve as Sagacius' surrogate ears. She would take advantage of that offer, and had no desire to insult him in the moment of a verbal mistake. Manfred was still a stranger to her, even if he and she were brother and sister in their craft through their apprenticeships to the same master. He was not quite ready for the needling she wanted to give him were he Richard. She liked this kind, handsome man with a delightful way of tying his tongue in embarrassing knots. He wanted to listen, and she needed to talk. She took several more sips of ale before asking, "What would you do if you were in my boots?"

"Aura, take a walk with me." Without waiting for her, Manfred stepped off the veranda and plunged into the meadow. Usually, Aura had to shorten her steps to keep up with a man. With this one, she could increase her stride. Usually, she loved stretching her legs to their full length. Not tonight, not with her left thigh and calf cramping with each strike of her heel against the ground. She didn't want to complain and ask him to slow down. "I love the night. There is little to distract my eyes, save for the stars. So, my ears come alive in ways they aren't in the day. Hear that owl? The crickets are singing for you. Ah, and those nightingales. Bats! My nose works better, too." He inhaled deeply as he walked. "Smell that? Lady Naurelia loves moon nightshade. It's a heady aroma. It mixes well with her roses. Why do I smell lavender and sage?" He sniffed in Aura's direction. "Oh, that's you. Sorry." He stopped at the edge of the woods, and turned to face the house. From this distance, it looked more quaint than grand. "As I said, this hall is a small house. We should be far enough away from the ears of the t'Ardoras. Miriam's are sharper than Lady Naurelia's. We may talk freely here."

"What was he like when you were his apprentice?" Aura asked.

"Are you changing the subject?"

"Perhaps," Aura said. She sipped her ale. "Perhaps knowing what he was like will help me make my decision."

Manfred laughed. "That's spoken like the old man. Well, Sagacius was the most optimistic, energetic man you ever met. Egads! He tried to work me to death. He ran circles around me, and I was at least fifty years younger than he was. Every day was also an adventure. Those were the times before the Watchers, so Sagacius and Lord Tyrus fought monsters all over this valley. When Mandrake and I were old enough, we went with them. Then came the war." Manfred fell silent for a moment. "Sagacius became bitter. He took the apprentice he had then, and left the Valley. I think he tried to find someone to kill him, because he tackled the Knights of the Holy Torch, saving witches from the pyre. He even spent six months in the Mellistenya Mountains. We only think Ayrdland has monsters. He may also have been hunting someone. He was vague about that. Mandrake and I feared for his life, but what could we say? Then, something unexpected happened."

"What?" Aura asked.

"He met you," Manfred said. He smiled at her. Even in the dark, she saw the warmth of his face. "You made him remember who he was. He calmed down and stopped chasing danger. You saved our master's life. Mandrake and I owe you a debt. You will always be welcome under our roof, and you will never pay for a drink or a meal."

"I made him remember who he was," Aura whispered. "Why couldn't he do that for me?"

"That, I cannot answer," Manfred said.

"What would our master say to me? What would he say about becoming a Dyrgana?"

Manfred frowned. He hesitated for a moment, as if weighing every word of his answer. Then, he rubbed his chin. "Well, I can only tell you what he said to me whenever I had to make a choice. He said, let my feet follow my mind and my mind follow my heart."

"That isn't very helpful. My mind and heart are warring with each other, and they're taking turns saying go home and stay." She sighed the sigh of the weary. "Why am I hesitating? Doesn't everyone ask who am I at some point? Not knowing could be dangerous."

"Especially when that someone blasted away the wall of a house with a flick of her finger," Manfred said.

"That isn't what happened!" Aura snapped.

"I told you this is a small house," Manfred said. "For some reason, the smaller the house, the more room a tale has to stretch. By the time I heard it from Juhnn, you fought a three headed squid with tentacles of lead and teeth of silver." He winked at her.

"There's no such ... " Aura looked at the sky. She held out her free hand. "That's it. I'm going home!" She turned toward the house. Then, she stopped. "No. If I don't know who I am, I may start believing stupid tales like that about myself." She drained her tankard. The ale roared down her throat. The fire in her belly felt good. "I'm staying. I'm ... oh, merciful heavens."

"Aura, it isn't that difficult of a decision," Manfred said. "I knew a Dyrgan. He didn't even go anywhere. He sat in a room rented from us, holed up with quills, parchment, and many questions. His quest was more a philosophical pursuit than anything else. He spent three months writing a blooming book. How hard is that?"

"I'll bet he didn't fight a three headed squid." She sat her empty tankard down on a boulder. "When I accepted the order's invitation to visit, it was as if they opened a window. On the other side, I could see the Valley and its members. Now, Lady Naurelia offers to hold a mirror to my face." She paused. "I hate mirrors."

"Why? If I had your face, I'd stare at a mirror all day," Manfred said. He turned away quickly. He mumbled, "I'm sorry."

Aura smiled. The compliment had been a gift, but turning away in embarrassment wrapped it with a ribbon of sincerity. She found her left hand moving to her uncovered shoulder. From there, her fingers traced a line down her bare side to her hip, then down her leg as far as she could reach. A shiver raced up her back. It was a nice shiver. For a moment, she imagined the feel of Manfred's fingers moving up her leg. She shook her head and chided herself. The three men who used her body and left her alone had been acquaintances from childhood. This man was still a stranger, connected solely by the coincidence that they shared the same master. Despite his kindness, taking any interest in him other than his advice was folly. Still, she thought his comment deserved a response. "That was sweet. Thank you."

Manfred cleared his throat. "Yes. Where were we? Right. Who are you."

"Who am I indeed," Aura said. She walked a few steps toward the woods, then turned to face Manfred. "I could give you my family lineage back nine generations on my father's side, a list of brewers and warriors.

I'm Ayrdish, and obviously, a woman. I've been daughter, sister, niece, orphan, apprentice, and now wizardess. All those are titles and attributes, except the last. Wizardess isn't just what I do, it's who I am. But that doesn't answer the entire question, does it?"

"Perhaps a little tale will help you, Aura." Manfred sighed. He set his tankard on the ground and crossed his arms over his chest. "There were four of us. Myles was the eldest, followed by Mandrake, then myself, and last our little sister Morning. Our parents built the tavern in Grahbale, and it was understood that Myles would inherit it. Being the good people that they were, mother and father wanted something better for their three youngest, other than building a tavern to rival Myles. So, they apprenticed us out to become magicians. Sagacius leapt at the chance to teach two boys at once, so he took Mandrake and me. Morning apprenticed to an enchantress in Praterhall. Then, our parents succumbed to old age, and Myles took the tavern. It turned out that Myles was not the ripest keg in the cellar. Within a year, he drank himself to death. Mandrake inherited the tavern and asked me to help. I've been there ever since. Despite eighteen years as an enchanter's apprentice, I knew in my heart that I was always a brewer."

"So, you aren't an enchanter," Aura said.

"Oh, yes, I am!" Manfred said. He smiled. "I hope you don't think I just brew ale and beer."

"You brew them as potions, don't you." It was not a question.

"My compliments to the old man. He taught you how to take 2/3 and 1/8 and a whole bushel of fractions and add them up into four."

"That's what a wizardess does," Aura said, smiling.

"According to most folk, we serve two flavors of ale and three of beer. However, each flavor has several varieties, depending on what the customer needs. Peace, love, joy, laughter. We even have one for lust that we serve on Parin and Tyrfin. We aren't going to let a customer leave with the same sour mood he entered."

"That's rather manipulative," Aura said.

"Is it? Is it manipulation to give someone something he already wants? All we do is hand him a key and point him toward the right door. He has to open that door and cross the threshold on his own."

"Lady Naurelia gave me a key and pointed me toward a door. I'm not sure I want to open it."

"Thank you for bringing me back to my tale. I said all that to say this. I always knew who I am. Perhaps, you do, too. Perhaps, you've always known who you are, but you forgot."

"How do I remember someone I've never been before? Manfred, I'm different from most people." She held her arms out. "Look at me." She noticed Manfred's expression. He took her invitation a little more serious than she meant. Even in the dark, she could see his eyes trying to tear themselves from her face and look lower. That pleased her. If the conversation weren't so serious, she would have walked up to him wearing a playful expression. Instead, she just walked up to him. When she stood close enough to hear his breath, she said, "If you haven't noticed, I'm rather tall for a woman. I am also the only person in my town with green eyes. I'm a wizardess. Every other woman in Hartshorn is a shopkeeper, farmer, or wife." With a sigh, she turned away. Over her shoulder, she said, "Now, I'm different even to myself."

"You might like these differences. How will you know until you meet yourself?" Manfred asked.

"That's a fair question. Perhaps I will love myself."

"Ah," Manfred said.

Aura cast him a cold glare. She had said more than she wished, and Manfred grasped every nuance of her meaning. He returned his own stare, one of knowing and understanding. He said nothing. Silently, she thanked him for his reticence. She also thanked him for his candor. Manfred's little "ah" shocked her into realizing part of her hesitation. Aura Lockhaven loathed Aura Lockhaven. No matter how many days passed, how many lessons she learned, how great her reputation rose in Hartshorn, she still felt the cobblestones, smelled the alley, and heard the name *Snake Eyes*. She blamed herself for the death of her father, and probably her mother. Despite this handsome man's verbal compliment about her face, and exerting all his will to keep from undressing her with his eyes, she still thought of herself as ugly.

Aura feared facing herself. Of all the fears that reared up in Ralthangarle, that one did not. If it had, she would have been lost inside the ruins. Perhaps, she wasn't even aware it was a fear at the time. She stared at Manfred and asked herself why she feared facing herself, of discovering who she really was. The answer came as soon as the question left her mind. She feared that once she learned who she was, her self-loathing would become hatred. Even worse, she may actually love herself, and that she did not know how to do.

Sagacius once said that he wished she could see herself as he did, and apparently, most of the townsfolk of Hartshorn did. She wanted to. Not long ago, she thought she could love the unlovely, meaning herself. That was sitting in her chair in her home, not when the possibility of having to do so actually presented itself. Could she love herself if she liked what she saw? Was it worth the risk? She could not answer, but perhaps someone else could.

"I'm going to ask you what I would ask our master," Aura said. "Do you think I should undertake this quest to find myself?"

"You're a wizardess, correct? That means the old man trained you to offer counsel to others. So, let's reverse our roles. Now, I'm the one who has to make this decision, and you're offering counsel. What would you say to me?" Manfred asked. He let his arms hang at his side, and assumed the countenance of a naive, eager young man who just came to her to ask if he would marry the girl next door. He even swayed side to side in anticipation of her answer.

Aura smiled. He knew how to play the part, right down to the wide eyes that blinked too much. Well, so did she. She crossed her arms over her chest. She tucked her chin in a bit, the way Sagacius did when about to hold forth with well researched and reasoned counsel. Locking eyes with

Manfred, she said, "I'd say become the Dyrgan. Undertake the quest. You have nothing to lose and everything to gain. If you fail, then you can still return home and resume your life, perhaps with more wisdom and knowledge. If you succeed, then all your dreams are open before you. Perhaps, you won't find yourself. Not in a matter of weeks. You will, however, have begun to search, and it's the search that is important."

Manfred smiled. He placed his hand on Aura's bare shoulder. Shocks of pleasure flowed through her at his touch. He said, "That is good counsel. Now, say those very words to yourself."

Aura's mouth flew open. He had trapped her with her own tongue. Manfred Rowanwand was Sagacius' student after all, and he had learned well. Her master did that once a month for her first two years. Every time she doubted magic, he somehow convinced her to turn her reasoning around until she ended up arguing against her original position. Like Sagacius, Manfred even used playful charades to lure her into the argument. Needing to think without seeing Manfred's face, she turned from him. The ache in her leg seemed but a faint echo as she walked with uncertain steps towards the forest.

Manfred was right. If she would say that to someone else, she should say it to herself. Could she? She had to. Truth was truth, no matter who said it and who received it. She had said it. Now, she had to receive it. Anything else would be hypocritical.

Her life opened before her. Henry Lockhaven always called her a dreamy-eyed little mystic. He said she always acted as if she came from a world full of wonder, and haunted by a memory only the ancient possessed. She wandered through town, pestering anyone who listened with her tales of barbarian warriors and sorcerers. The news from Welcaster about kings and taxes and wars bored her. Let one customer tell a tale about a dragon, and she sat in his lap and begged to hear it again. As a child, she played with her dolls. Where other girls pretended to be mothers with their babies, Aura ruled as the magical princess leading her army of wizards in defending her town from ogres and swamp boars. When other girls dressed in their sisters' clothes and played ball hostess, Aura grabbed her brother's sword and played thegn of the witches.

She always thought she would never have become a wizardess if her father had not died, and her uncle not kicked her out. Now that she recalled all those memories, she was not sure. Perhaps, the path of magic was the only true path open to her, and she would have found it regardless. There was such a thing as natural talent, and some people knew from the cradle what they wanted to do, or rather, who they were. Alvin the woodcarver sold his tables and chests to foreign shippers in Vine Haven. He started at age six, whittling a piece of wood just because he liked it. Frank the lutenist always said he couldn't stop plucking his father's hunting bow when he was a child. Brythony began her life's work by spending more time making clothes for her dolls out of scraps than she did playing with the dolls. Perhaps, Aura walked the path of magic from birth, and it had only been interrupted by those two years she spent as an urchin.

Manfred was partially right. She may not know who she was, but she knew who she had been at least, and she had forgotten. It lay buried underneath two years of misery. Two years, between the ages of ten and twelve. Yet, those two years nearly erased the ten that came before. Those two years also clouded the ten that came after. If not for those two years, she would not loathe herself. She would not think herself ugly, and she knew it. Those two years severed who she had been from who she became, and they still threatened who she was and hoped to become. Those two years still defined Aura Lockhaven.

The wind picked up, billowing Aura's dress around her. She knew that may expose her buttocks to Manfred, but if the man wanted to look, let him see all of her as raw and naked as she felt to herself. Yes, she felt vulnerable, but only vulnerable to the unknown lurking in her own mind. To the rest of the world, she felt as if she presented a facade of iron. It was time to face herself. If anyone else wanted to look, let them look at her the way she had to look at herself. Love her, step aside, or be damned. Naurelia offered her a chance to rewrite her definition, and perhaps remove the remains of those horrid two years.

You're a Lockhaven, you can do anything, her father always said. If she was a Lockhaven, she could face herself, find herself, and know herself. That facing, finding, and knowing would finally, with any luck and any hope, expunge the two years of stench and wretchedness from her heart. In the process, she should learn the way of the enchantress, and discover how to use the wild power inside herself. She had nothing to lose. Her home, her position, and her friend were safe four days away. They would receive a better, stronger, and wiser Aura when she returned.

Aura looked at her hands, the left one with its scar, and the right one with the fading apprentice's calluses. Lowering her left hand, she clenched her right. "What is magic but to give a young woman her life?"

"Pardon me?" Manfred asked.

Aura turned to face him. "Thank you, Manfred. You helped me make my decision. I accept Lady Naurelia's offer."

Chapter Twenty-Six

WITH THE SOFTEST caresses, he filled her with sensations of pleasure that left her breathless. His left hand pressed against the small of her back, drawing her toward him. The fingers of his other hand drew a line from her chin, down between her breasts, around her navel, and toward her ... Then the man faded into blackness, and his hands became a lump of down in the mattress and a wad of blanket between her thighs. Aura's sigh was that of a curse. That is, until she heard what awoke her.

The whitelark sat on the windowsill, peeking into her room in Ardora Hall. The smallest of the larks, from tip of his beak to the tip of his tail, he was no bigger than her fist. Yet, his presence filled the bed chamber. He peered right at her, and serenaded her with a rather loud, "Go chase a moonbeam. Go chase a moonbeam." She opened her eyes, and smiled at the bird.

"Good morning, little friend," Aura said.

His song changed to the more familiar, "Dance in the moonlight. Dance in the moonlight."

"You only come out by day, yet you sing about nighttime." The whitelark chuffed his feathers, and thrust out his black beard. Aura swore the bird winked at her. "The insects are tasty. The insects are tasty," Aura sang back to the bird. With another call to chase a moonbeam, the whitelark spread his pale gray wings, and flew off into the sunrise.

Aura felt better than she had in weeks. She rose and washed her face. Sitting on the windowsill recently visited by the whitelark, she brushed her long auburn hair, while thinking about her deities and the elements. Pulling the wad of hair from the bristles, she her hand out the window, and released the tangle to the breeze for any bird to find. Humming the tune of the whitelark, she limped across the room to her bag on the table. Today called for a bit of festivity. She dug to the bottom of her bag and found the small pot of eye makeup, made from clay and oil of willow bark. Having avoided mirrors for a decade, Aura knew how to rub the clay onto the lids over her emerald eyes without smearing it across her face. The color dampened the effect of her eyes, making them almost pretty in her mind. The brown dress, cleaned and pressed, waited on the table by the wardrobe. She pulled on the dress, then jerked her hair out from under the collar, and shook it free.

Still humming to herself, she nearly trotted down the stairs. At least she did until halfway down, when her left leg seized, almost throwing her to the floor below. Gripping the banister, Aura closed her eyes. As the cramp subsided, she became one with the wood of the stairs. Feeling deep within herself, she smiled as she felt almost enough vitality to cast a decent healing spell upon herself. Unless Naurelia mixed a regenerative potion in her ale, this was the result of a settled mind.

Aura found the Eorless standing in the chamber with the statue. She held a book in her arms, and talked to a young woman. The newcomer stood just taller than Naurelia, with skin as pale as snow, eyes so blue they looked black, and hair so black it looked blue. There was something oddly familiar about her face, but Aura couldn't decide what. She guessed the girl's age to be around twenty. Her dress, low cut and split up the sides to the hips, matched her hair and flattered her petite figure. Naurelia saw Aura approach, and smiled.

"Good morning. Aura, this is Beala Merton, Lord Ashthorne's apprentice. Beala, dear, this is Aura Lockhaven, a visitor from Hartshorn."

Aura extended her hand. Beala stiffened. The air in the room turned bitter, as if it suddenly became midwinter. She stared at Aura's open hand, without taking it. Then, her gaze rose to meet Aura's. The dark irises were bottomless pools of contempt.

"So, you're Aura Lockhaven," Beala said.

Beala's dry monotone of a voice cut through Aura like a surgeon's saw. It was not just the scorn that oozed from every syllable. The sound of her voice carried a low magical power that made Aura shiver. It felt as if icicles had been thrust through her heart. As a child, Aura sometimes played in the kitchen of her father's tavern by dropping snow on the hot griddle. The sound caused by Beala's voice in her mind was the same as that snow on that griddle. Aura lowered her hand. She struggled to maintain her smile as she said, "Don't believe everything Lord Ashthorne says about me. He probably exaggerates."

"Others do not," Beala said. She turned to Naurelia, and took the book from her. "Thank you for the loan of this book, Milady. I will return it when Master is finished. Have a good morning, Milady." She bowed to the Eorless. Then, without even a glance toward Aura, she turned and strode out the back door of Ardora Hall, her slippers making no sound on the floor.

"I do believe I have just been offered a shoulder carved from a glacier," Aura said.

"Beala has ice in her veins," Naurelia said. "Why wouldn't she? Lord Ashthorne found her nearly frozen to death in a snowdrift just outside Castlebury ten years ago. I don't think she fully thawed. In all the time I've known that child, I have never once seen her smile. But Beala has never been rude, either."

"I wonder who she thinks I am, or what she thinks I did to her. I've never met her before." She held her peace about thinking Beala looked familiar. The thought seemed like a fleeting glimpse of a dream from years past. Something from ten years ago, when she lived in the alley. But Aura would have been twelve, making Beala around ten. No, the familiarity belonged to an adult. It must simply have been a stranger in Hartshorn that she spotted as she went about her daily begging. She did not believe in mere coincidence, but decided that this had to be one.

Naurelia smiled at Aura. "Think no more about it. I will talk to Lord Ashthorne. Perhaps he can shed some warmth on the chilly subject. In the meantime, breakfast is ready. Afterwards, we will talk."

Everything looked brighter and tasted better. Aura tore into the breakfast of roasted ham, pear tarts, and fresh barley rolls. Divided between her appetite and her manners, Aura hesitated to ask for a second helping. Lurna decided for her by placing another slice of ham and another tart on Aura's trencher. As the second tart exploded in her mouth, Aura understood Naurelia's slightly corpulent figure. Lurna's cooking was addictive. If she stayed another week, she would gain five pounds herself. Glancing at Miriam, she did not understand how the handmaiden kept such a trim waist and muscular limbs.

Naurelia seemed in a better mood this morning. She bantered with Manfred, instead of trying to battle him with her mood. Both dressed more formally. The Eorless of Ardora wore a long black gown with silver brocade, with a full matching cloak, and an ornate medallion of brilliant silver shaped like vines intertwined around a cabochon of moonstone. The brewer dressed in brown shirt and trousers with a fancy waistcoat and neckerchief. Aura felt a little out of place in her simple brown dress. They pulled Aura into their conversation about brewing, how much hops to use, and which grains made better ale. Only Miriam ate in silence, staring into space as if concentrating on a future task. She wore a blue version of the dress she loaned Aura the day before.

Naurelia left the dining hall, as Aura, Manfred, and Miriam helped themselves to another mug of tea. They found the Eorless in the room leading to the veranda, standing before the statue and caressing its marble face. She turned with the cool countenance of someone expecting to be interrupted in the middle of an intimate kiss.

"Well, Aura, dear," Naurelia said. "Have you reached a decision?"

Aura cast a surprised glance to Manfred. Despite his assertion that Ardora Hall was small and that news travelled fast, he had kept his mouth shut. She looked back at Naurelia.

"Yes, I have," she said. "I accept. I wish to become a Dyrgana. I want to discover who Aura Lockhaven really is."

"Excellent. In that case," she said, placing her hands on Aura's cheeks. "Go on your journey of discovery, embark on your quest as a Dyrgana to find yourself. May your gods go with you and speed you on your way."

Releasing Aura's face, she added, "I will tell Lady Etheria, Lord Ashthorne, and Leonikas dur O'tan. They are your sponsors as a visitor. They will no doubt sponsor your journey. Especially, if I tell them to do so. Now, the rules of play have changed for you, yes, yes."

"How so?"

Naurelia smiled. "You are now in a rather nebulous place, Aura, dear. As a visitor, you were a guest from the outside. You were free to do as you wished. As a Dyrgana, you are practically a member of the order, so our laws are somewhat binding on you. Yet, you are not initiated, so you are little free to bend them to a point. The first and most binding, at least here in my home, is you have to respect me as First Noble." She chuckled. "Don't fret, I won't tell you to do anything. I will ask. I also won't ask you to do anything that I'm not willing to do myself, no, no."

Aura returned the smile. "I agree to that."

"Excellent. Well, why wouldn't it be excellent? The second important rule is no more shouting at Balkefor. As a member of the council, he outranks you, and we have stiff laws with stiff penalties for challenging a member of the council. Leave such remonstrations to myself, Lord Ashthorne, Lord Dirt, Lady Daphne, or Lord dur O'tan." She smiled in wicked delight. "We will all be more than overjoyed to put the old boar in his place on your behalf."

"I'd rather not have to see him again, so I certainly agree to that."

"Now, the first thing we are going to do is prepare you for your quest." She glanced at her handmaiden. "Miriam, I need my belt and mist box from my chamber. Join us on the veranda." Miriam nodded, and turned toward the stairs. Naurelia cut her eyes to Manfred. "You. Come with us."

"Me? What did I do?" Manfred asked.

"You were born," Naurelia muttered, turning and walking toward the veranda.

Aura followed her, flanked by Manfred. By now, the sun had cleared the forest behind the house, and the sharp shadows retreated into the trees. Red finches sang from the branches, announcing to the world that their eggs had hatched. A pair of robins stalked through the grass, looking for crickets. The four startled a whitelark, resting on the steps. Aura wasn't sure if it was the same that woke her that morning, but he looked at her before flying away.

Naurelia stopped at the steps. Aura stood taller than most women by at least four inches. As she grew, she developed a habit when talking with another woman, although she tried to break it. With no conscious effort, she looked at the top of Naurelia's head, and thought, *Your part is as crooked as a countryside path, Eorless.* Aura assumed that handmaidens tended to their mistress' appearances. Miriam seemed a bit slack in that regard. As absentminded as the Eorless was, perhaps her hair had been straight before breakfast.

"I notice you're limping more today than yesterday. So, no heavy magic for you. Your vitality is not restored yet. If it were, you wouldn't be limping. No, no, why would you? I have plans for that leg later. Leave the heavy magic to me for now."

"What are we going to do?" Aura asked.

"Before anyone embarks on a quest, he takes stock of his assets. His food, drink, weapons, clothes, horse, even his companions. Now, in your case, in a quest to discover yourself, you need nothing more than your heart and mind, yes, yes." Naurelia stepped closer to Aura. "You may not know who you are, but you know how you came to be. Perhaps not in your waking mind, but deep inside." She stepped even closer. "I am going to show you that. Knowing how you came to be standing here on my veranda, right now this very moment, will help you know where you are going."

Miriam returned, holding a small ornate blue box in her right hand. In her left, she held a belt with ten wands hanging in sheaths from it. Naurelia took the belt, and buckled it around her waist.

"I don't use a staff," she said. "I prefer wands, and I make them myself. Now, Aura, dear. You know more about yourself than you realize, but you don't know the language of your own self, so you're deaf to it. It is rather like an Ayrdish man trying to understand a conversation in Sollantine.

However, I speak fluent Sollantine, so that is not difficult for me." She ran her hand down her side to her hips. "Although, I'm hardly an Ayrdish man, now am I. Neither are you, Aura, dear. No one with eyes or ears would ever confuse you for a man, although you are rather Ayrdish. Er ... " Naurelia blinked a few times. She looked hopelessly at Miriam, and asked, "Where was I?"

"You were explaining to Mistress Aura that she knows more about herself than she realizes, Milady," Miriam said.

"Yes, yes, of course I was."

Aura pressed her toes tight against the soles of her boots to help stifle her grin. The brewer did not act fast enough. Manfred did nothing to hide his guffaw. That brought a quick, sharp, and if made of iron, deadly, glare of remonstration from Naurelia. When he returned to a more respectful countenance, Naurelia said, "Come with me. All of you." She turned, and walked into the back yard, followed by Miriam and Aura.

"I still don't understand why you need me," Manfred said, stepping off the veranda. "I do need to get back to Grahbale. Mandrake has probably poisoned half the town with his atrocious cooking by now."

"Then, you can heal them. Tomorrow," Naurelia mumbled. She stopped in the middle of the back yard, and looked up. "It is a beautiful morning. Most people prefer the Moon for what I am about to do, but for this, I need the Sun. The light of the Sun illuminates the mind, and we need for your mind to be unlocked to its full knowledge."

With a smile, Naurelia drew the second wand over her left hip. The wands Aura had seen were simple sticks, stripped of bark and smoothed. This one was as long as her forearm, intricately carved from ebony in shapes of clouds and birds in flight. Gold inlay wrapped the wand from tip to tip. A sunstone sat in the handle, while a clear quartz crystal rested in the other end.

Holding the wand in both hands, she drew it to her chest. Closing her eyes, she inhaled. Once again, Naurelia transformed. Aura had seen the barely sane absentminded inventor. For the past day, she had been the

Eorless of Ardora. Now, she became the enchantress in full possession of her power and authority in the magical realm. The air around her crackled with pulsing force. The feelings of love, joy, pride, loyalty, and even the dark ones of loneliness, fear, and anger washed over her as Naurelia opened the gates of her heart. Aura stood in the presence of one of the most powerful magicians in all Ayrdland, and she knew it.

Naurelia faced the Sun, and pointed toward it with the wand. "I call to the east, to the Spirit of Air. Welcome, and join us. Please grant us your power to know the mind." She turned to her right, and said, "I call to the south, to the Spirit of Fire. Welcome, and join us. Please grant us your power to know passion." Once again, she turned to her right. "I call to the west, to the Spirit of Water. Welcome, and join us. Please grant us your power to know the heart." Again, to her right, and she said, "I call to the north, to the Spirit of Earth. Welcome, and join us. Please grant us your power to know the body." Pointing to the sky, she said, "I call to above, to the Spirit of Light. Welcome, and join us. Please grant us your power to know wisdom." Pointing to the ground, Naurelia said, "I call to below, to the Spirit of Metal. Welcome, and join us. Please grant us your power to know the will." Holding the wand to her chest, she said, "I call to center, to the Spirit of Spirit, that which brings the six together to form life. Welcome, and join us. Please grant us your power to know ourselves." Turning with the sun, Naurelia drew an invisible line around the four people standing in the grass, coming back to where she began. "The circle is complete. As above, so below."

Manfred grabbed her arm. He looked afraid. "This isn't just magic. This is a blooming ritual! What are you going to do?"

"Remove your hand, sir," Naurelia growled. She looked down at his hand, staring at it until he did. "That's better. We are in sacred space now, and as you know very well, even that little act could upset the balance we have created." Looking him in the face, she said, "I am going to put Aura into a trance."

"Is that wise?" Aura asked. "Trances are shamanic. I thought enchantresses avoided the shamanic."

"You enter a trance every night, although you don't know it," Naurelia said. "It is that place between wakefulness and sleep, when you dream, yet you are awake enough to know you are dreaming. A trance is the doorway into the shamanic. It is the open flap to step beyond the veil. I go there all the time, but I never cross the threshold. I do hope you don't think I just come up with my inventions on my own! I see them across the door of the trance. I am going to take you to the door. On the other side, you will see the steps you took along the path that led you to this moment. That is, if you are willing. I won't do this without your consent."

"If it will help me know myself, then I am more than willing, Eorless," Aura said.

"Exceptional," Naurelia said. She waved to the grass. "Please be seated."

Aura breathed a silent sigh of relief. While she had never been in a trance herself, she knew many who had. They all entered trances skyclad. They said that clothing bound them too much to this material realm. She would have had minimal problem being naked before Naurelia or Miriam, but Manfred was a different matter. She liked him, and wanted to get to know him better, in a nice slow way. That nice slow way did not include suddenly thrusting her unclothed flesh into his line of sight. She sat down as well as she could, given the stiffness of her left leg. She drew the right one to her, but kept the other straight. Even so, the muscles argued with her.

Naurelia motioned to Miriam and Manfred. "Miriam, sit next to Aura and take her left hand. Manfred, take Aura's right. You two will be anchors, tethers to this realm in case something beyond the door tries to pull Aura through."

"Will that happen? Naurelia, I'm not comfortable with this," Manfred said.

"May I remind you that Manfred Rowanwand is not the Dyrgana."

Manfred sighed, and sat down on Aura's right. "I'm just protective of my friends."

"That is why we quarrel."

Miriam handed Naurelia the blue box, and seated herself on Aura's left. Naurelia sat across from Aura, and opened the lid.

"Most people enter a trance through meditation. As this is no doubt your first trance, I am going to cheat. I am going to guide you into it, and I am going to do so quickly. First, wear this."

Naurelia handed her a necklace of black cord, with gems dangling from it. Aura immediately recognized the moonstone pendant in the center, and the two blue tiger's eyes that flanked it. Based on the yellow speckles on pale blue, she guessed the next two stones to be leopard jaspers. The final stones, on the outside, must be kambabaras, the brown on brown striped stone of the shaman. She slipped the necklace around her neck. As she did, the slow pulse of the stones entered her. Her heartbeat slowed to match their rhythms.

"You responded quickly," Naurelia said.

Aura smiled. "I am a wizardess. I work with stones and plants."

"Then, you should like this," the Eorless said, handing her a small red vial. "It's a trance potion. I won't tell you what's in it. Otherwise, you probably wouldn't drink it. But trust me. It won't harm you."

Aura bolted the potion. She recognized the flavor of three of the herbs in the bottle. Each was medicinal, when used alone. Together, they were poison. Then, her head felt like it rocked from side to side. She knew that effect, from having accidentally eaten dreamer's spur. The lingering final note of sage brushed her tongue. The herb of immortality. So, Naurelia used sage to blend and ground the others, coaxing them to work together in beneficial ways. As Aura handed the vial back to Naurelia, she began swaying. She smiled in the loopy way of the drunkard.

"Miriam. Manfred. Take Aura's hands. She won't be with us much longer," Naurelia said.

"I think I'm going to fly," Aura sang. Last night, Manfred's touch thrilled her. As he took her hand, she barely noticed.

"Not yet, you aren't! No, no. There are two more steps."

Naurelia pulled a nosegay from the box. Aura recognized turnera, coughwort, synkefoyle, mugwort, and several dried pink roses, tied together with twine. Holding the nosegay in her left hand, Naurelia pointed at it with her right index finger. She said, "Kifon." The tip of the nosegay burst into flame. If Aura could have felt irritation, she would have frowned. She never could learn the spell to start fires.

Then, Naurelia reached into the box. She gently lifted a sphere of water sapphire the size of her fist. Smiling, she held it in front of Aura's face. She snuffed the fire on the nosegay with her breath, turning it into a smudging bundle. As the smoke billowed up, she held it underneath Aura's nose.

"Breathe the smoke through your nose."

As Aura inhaled, Naurelia continued. "Let its fragrance carry you to the door. As it does, look deep into the sphere. You will begin to see things. Visions. Let them tell you what you need to know. I will control the sphere, but not what it shows you. I will ..."

If Naurelia said anything else, Aura never heard her. If Miriam and Manfred still held her hands, they were made of air. She only knew the feeling within her, the feeling of seeing something beautiful and terrifying at the same time, much like she felt when she first saw the ocean.

In the mists of the water sapphire, Aura saw a shape. It looked familiar. It grew and solidified, into Lockhaven Tavern. She gasped. It even smelled like ale and roasting pork. She saw herself at age six, sitting behind the bar, with twelve straw dolls around her, and a big pile of sticks tied up with twine in the vague shape of a man. The sticks were a troll and the dolls her army of wizards sent to destroy it and save Hartshorn from calamity. A stately blonde girl of thirteen knelt by her. Ester! She looked so real.

"That isn't how you do it, Little Sissy," Ester said, picking up one of the straw dolls. "You're playing a boy's game. You're a girl. You're supposed to be the mommy and these are your babies."

"I don't want to be a mommy with babies. I want to do something im ... im ... portant, Big Sissy," Aura said, with a lisp. Had she lisped at six? She had forgotten.

"Our mother would say that having Richard, and you, and me was very important."

Aura looked at her big sister. "It was. For her. Not for me."

"Oh, you want to be queen. Well, Princess Miranda will be the queen, even if she isn't much older than you. Sorry."

"I don't want to be queen. The queen just sits in a big stupid chair all day and looks bored and stupid and all. I want to keep bad people from hurting good people," Aura said, with all the authority and conviction that only the young possess.

Ester hugged Aura and said, "Don't you ever change!"

Lockhaven Tavern again, and she was nine. She stuffed new candles into the candelabras on the table, making sure each sat exactly upright. No, that one wasn't quite straight. It leaned just a little.

"You're so persnickety," Ester said, wiping the table.

"If the candle is crooked, then the light will be crooked, and the customers will drink crooked ale," Aura informed her.

"That doesn't make any sense!"

"It most certainly does, Big Sissy. People can only have what they see, and they don't know how to see anything else but what they do see. I have to help them see it right."

A crash interrupted the sisters' bantering. Henry Lockhaven stood in front of the fireplace, looking down at the massive Locchaefen axe, laying on the floor. He wiped his forehead and cursed the huge weapon. Richard loped across the tavern, grinning.

"What's the matter, old man? You can lift twenty pound kegs all day, but a twenty pound axe bests you?" Richard asked.

"It weighs more than that!" Henry snapped.

Richard grabbed the axe in his left hand, his off hand, and lifted it with ease. He swung it around his head twice, then hung it back over the fireplace as if it were a mere feather.

"I could have sworn you said something, Dad."

"Show off!" Henry said, with a wide grin on his face.

Twelve, and waking up soaked in sweat. Another nightmare, of her father's death. She smelled the smoke, and saw the flames. Her left hand ached. Crawling from bed, she fumbled at the table until she found the small box of alchemists' firesticks. She still didn't know how these worked, but they worked. Striking one against the piece of flint, it burst into flames. She lit the candle, and dropped the firestick into the abalone shell on the table. Then, she reached for the smoke stained notebook of her father's tales. Opening it, she read his story of how the Sarethian Seven prevented the murder of the Queen of Phrathia. As she read, she heard Henry's voice again, that of a man turned giddy small boy recounting an adventure in breathless excitement. Feeling calm again, Aura closed the book, and looked around her.

The firesticks were the least of the miracles she saw. She pushed down on the mattress. Yes, she had a bed again. It was hers, all hers. Overhead, she saw the thick oaken beams supporting the roof, instead of the stars and clouds she had seen only a month earlier. She mashed her toes against the wooden floor, instead of cold and wet cobblestones. Caressing the wardrobe, she knew that inside hung her clothes. She now owned several shirts and trousers and a new pair of boots. That tattered old blue dress dangled from a peg in the kitchen as a dish rag. Running her hands down her body, she marveled that she was clean. Creeping to the door, she opened it. Across the narrow hall, she heard the deep snores of the town's wizard who took her in and gave her all this.

Aura walked to the window and threw open the shutters. She inhaled the brisk air. Outside, the snow fell in thick sheets that echoed in the silence of the night. It fell on the ground, not on her. She smiled at the first winter in two years that she was not cold. Once again, the sleeping time of the earth looked beautiful. Glancing up at the dark clouds, she saw the moon peaking out behind them.

"Lunambyra," she whispered, to the sorceress of the legendary free lance warrior band in her notebook. "I know you're dead. You have to be. You lived one thousand years ago. Queen Theda was helpless. She was defenseless. She was surrounded by her enemies. But you saved her. Mr. Sagacius saved me, like you saved her. I want to be like you!"

The room vanished, replaced by a field at the foot of Piper's Knob. Soldiers of Hartshorn's townsfyrd stood on top, clutching their spears, not knowing quite what to do with the sight below. Standing in the field, an ogre laughed at them. Seven and a half feet tall, with shoulders four feet across, he reeked of wet muck. He clutched an iron club that probably weighed fifty pounds. Several arrows, unable to pierce his skin, dangled from his waistcoat.

Seventeen year old Aura trailed only two feet behind Sagacius as the town's wizard strode toward the ogre. Sagacius had spent the previous year instructing her about most of the legendary creatures that she might face in the Forested Islands. She had heard about ogres all her life, but hearing about one and seeing one before her eyes were two different things. Ogres had been on Ayrdland long before the first men arrived. Most lived in pockets where they formed their own underground villages. Ogres were nuisances, slipping onto farms to steal sheep and raid barns. They were worse than wolves, but better than dishonest neighbors. Others, however, saw people the same way that people saw deer. Those stole children, whom they roasted that night. Those also stole women, whom they kept for sport, then roasting. This one must be one of those. Otherwise, he wouldn't be so close to Hartshorn. Ogres did not like the odor of people. Raw, that is.

"What do you want me to do, Master?" Aura asked.

"Stay behind me, Aura. Ogres are smart, cunning, and very, very fast," he said over his shoulder. "I'm going to try to talk to him."

"Talk. To *that*?"

"He's still a living thing, Aura. Now, if he attacks someone, including me, then he becomes a target."

Sagacius never had time to talk. He barely had time to sidestep the oncoming club before it struck him on the shoulder, sending him sprawling on the ground behind Aura. The ogre just became a target. Aura took two steps forward. She was not about to let the creature kill her master. With her left hand, she cast a throwback spell, followed by one from her right. If the ogre felt either, he showed no sign. Before Aura could cast the third throwback spell, the ogre lunged. She saw the back of his hand before her face. She woke up in her chair at the Big Hedge. Sagacius held a cold cloth to her broken jaw.

Twenty now, and picking yarrow on the side of the Morningstar Road. A scream interrupted her, a scream from the little farm house nearby. Aura dashed across the barley field to the front door. Jerking it open, flames and smoke met her. The odor of burning beams and carpet sent her to her knees, gasping. No mere nightmare, this. Too much smoke, and it was real. Her left hand exploded in agony.

Fighting the memory of her father's death, Aura crawled into the house. Beyond the thick smoke, she spotted a woman, cowering in the corner, holding her baby. Burning logs had tumbled from the oven, across the rug. The dry carpet and the drier wooden floor caught quickly, sending flames toward the walls and curtains.

Keeping the last of her sanity, Aura growled, "Why didn't the fool head for the damn door!"

On her hands and knees, she moved as fast as her memory permitted, inching across the still unburning parts of the floor to the woman. She grabbed the baby. Mustering all her remaining courage, Aura stood. She dashed toward the door. Once the baby was safe, she ran back for the woman. Finding her took time. The small one room house was full of smoke. She followed the screams. She pushed the woman out the door into the yard. Then, she looked down at the threshold. She lay on her stomach, and her back ached. Looking over her shoulder, she saw the beam laying across her hips. A beam that erupted into flames.

"No!" Aura shouted. She no longer saw that beam, but another. She saw Henry Lockhaven's shirt catch fire. She felt her hand burn as she tried to move the beam. Then, she looked up at blue sky, and Sagacius' worried face, as he dragged her out into the front yard.

Now, on the green in Hartshorn. A month ago, or was it three? A woman with green eyes knelt on the grass in front of her small cart of pots and pans. She could have been Aura, if she had red hair, and stood five inches taller. Aura narrowed her eyes into slits. The woman was Geilltian, the enemy of her people. They once held this island, then sold it to the hated Bellician Empire, and with it, the entire chain known as the Forested Islands. Now, they hunkered down on the small island of Warlden, lusting for the big island back. Then, Aura saw the fear in the woman's eyes. She also saw the stones, scythes, and knives in the hands of the mob around her. Without a thought, Aura stepped between the Geilltian peddler and the mob.

"Go home," she said.

"Get out of the way, Aura," a voice shouted.

"You're just like her!" another yelled.

"I'm Ayrdish, like you. My mother was Coadic," Aura said. "If you remember history, Coadia struck the first crippling blow in the wars that felled Bellicia. My mother's people gave us this land for our own when Nebeland forced us to flee. So, hear me! Yes, King Trahern sold Geilltia and the Forested Islands to the Bellician Empire, but that was 850 years ago. What has this woman to do with Trahern? She came here to sell things to you, not steal from you."

Aura spread her legs. She held her arms from her sides, hoping that increasing her physical size would stop any attack. "If you want to kill her, then you have to kill me first. But remember who I am. I am one of you. Despite my height and my eyes and my hair, I am still Henry Lockhaven's daughter. Would you really kill one of your own, just so you can kill a Geilltian?"

Stones fell from hands. Scythes lowered to the ground. Knives returned to sheaths. One by one, the people turned away, until only three remained; the Geilltian woman, Aura herself, and the one man she did not wish to see that day, Cecil Fowler.

As Cecil grinned, Aura's vision came back into focus. The shifting mist of blue turned back into the water sapphire sphere. Half the still smouldering nosegay was blackened. Miriam removed the necklace from Aura as Naurelia replaced the sphere into the box. Aura breathed deeply several times to clear her mind. She felt light-headed, giddy, nauseated, and cold. At least, for the first time in two days, her left leg did not hurt. In fact, she didn't feel it at all. The same could be said for the rest of her body. She stared blankly at Naurelia. The Eorless wore a tight smile, as if trying to mask great pain. Aura shivered. Manfred put his arm around her. This time, she felt him. With deliberate effort, she turned her head, and gave him as much of a smile as she could manage.

Naurelia exhaled, and her mask of pain dissolved. "Welcome back. Based on the shadows, I'd say you were gone almost an hour. Feeling cold is a natural part of coming back. It will pass soon. What you saw is for your heart alone. No need to tell me. Did the visions illuminate the steps you took to reach this point in your life?"

"I don't know," Aura mumbled. It took some effort to find her voice. "I remember all those visions. They are all good memories. I could have told them to you without the trance. Yet, none of them had to do with magic. Well, one did." She rubbed her jaw with a trembling hand, remembering that Sagacius spent the better part of that day healing her. "That is so odd."

"Is it really? Why should it be? Perhaps, you have been on this path all your life, and magic is but a convenient tool. Based upon what your master told me, that is true. A heart as powerful as yours doesn't just spring into being overnight."

With one hand, Naurelia closed the lid to the mist box. She raised the other to her chin. "Powerful," she muttered. Cocking her head, she looked at Aura as if she searched for something hidden. Aura watched Naurelia's mouth move. She spoke without sound. Reading her lips, Aura made out *there is one coming.* She tried to arch her eyebrow, but her facial muscles still did not have that much movement.

Miriam cleared her throat. She stared at the Eorless in terror. Naurelia paid her no mind. She pushed herself up to her knees, and reached across the distance between herself and Aura, moving as one approaching the statue of a beloved god in a temple. She knelt in the grass and looked Aura in the eyes for what seemed like eternity. Aura tried to judge what she saw in the deep brown eyes. Hope. She saw hope. With a slow movement of trepidation, Naurelia raised her hand to Aura's face. She brushed her cheek with her fingertips.

"The most powerful ..." Naurelia whispered.

Miriam cleared her throat again, a little too loud to be a mere cleansing of mucus. Manfred leapt up, and placed his fists on his hips. He glared at the Eorless, as if he wanted to cut her in half. A faint growl escaped his open mouth. Aura froze where she sat. She had heard those very words twice before. *Old words spoken by an old friend long ago. Old words believed by another. It was spoken to her, not you.* Could Sagacius' old friend and *her* be the First Noble who knelt on the lawn? They apprenticed to the same teacher, the great Damaskarose. If Sagacius was Damaskarose's son, then could –

Before Aura completed the thought, Naurelia mumbled, "Are you?"

"Am I whom?" She felt cold inside, dreading to hear one word from Naurelia. One name. Nightshade.

This time, Miriam actually said, "Ahem," and did so in the firm voice of a rebuke. Naurelia glared at her for a moment, then horror clouded her face. She nodded and stood up.

"You may eat luncheon at any time. Aura, dear, I suggest you eat early. Miriam and I have a plan for you afterwards. Now, if you will excuse me, I need to confer with my handmaiden." With that, she walked toward the house, with Miriam at her side.

Aura sat on the grass, watching them until they vanished inside the tall doors. "What was that all about?"

Manfred helped Aura to her feet. He looked at her as if one of them stood inside a cage, but she couldn't tell whom. He said, "I'm not sure you want to know."

Chapter Twenty-Seven

"CAN YOU HEAL her, or should I send for Erba?" Naurelia asked, her voice heavy with concern.

Aura lay naked on her stomach upon a table. It felt a little odd. Miriam and Naurelia remained clothed. This was no different from being examined at age nine by the apothecary for the goose pox, she told herself. Miriam stood over her, gently poking her left leg with her fingertips. Naurelia stood by the door to prevent Juhnn, and more importantly, Manfred, from suddenly barging into the room adjacent to the sitting chamber.

The room was as big as Aura's bedroom. Despite no windows, it was brilliantly lit by forty candles that filled the room with warmth and the fragrance of lavender and rosemary. Twenty bottles of various shapes and colors sat on a shelf opposite the table. The table itself was of oak, and highly polished. Aura forced herself to stare at her reflected face. Those damnably big and damnably green eyes shone back at her. If she found nothing else on this quest to find Aura Lockhaven, perhaps she could find reason to believe she was halfway beautiful.

Miriam ran her hands from the ankle of Aura's left leg up to her hip, then across her buttocks, then back down the inside of her left leg. She said, "Yes and no."

"You're talking like me, Miriam. Yes and no that you can heal her, or yes and no that I should call for Erba?"

"Yes, I can heal Mistress Aura. No, that you should call for Lady Erba."

"I would have appreciated a bit more pause between words," Naurelia mumbled.

"Although Mistress Aura's skin is healthy, the muscles underneath are burned." Miriam pressed her palms against Aura's outer thigh, forcing her to grimace. "The center of the injury is here. It is severe. It is as if someone

306

thrust her through with a nearly molten spear, without damaging the skin. The burns extend to her mid calf, and up into her hip, with a bit of injury in her lower back." To Aura, she added, "I am unfamiliar with this particular spell, Mistress, but you baked yourself like a ham. That you even walk is testimony of your will."

That had been a weak Divine Thunderbolt, too. She cast it with the last of her vitality. Rested and at full strength, she may have killed Mayenne and herself. No wonder Sagacius forbade her to ever cast it.

Miriam walked to the end of the table. Grabbing Aura's ankles, she held them side by side. Her right foot extended half an inch beyond the left. "Already, her left leg is shriveling. At this rate, her leg will be two inches shorter by the end of the month."

"You can heal me?" Aura asked. She rose up on her elbows to look over her shoulder into Miriam's face. Her stomach fluttered. What would the people of Hartshorn think if their healer were lame?

"Yes," Miriam said. She smiled. With a pat on Aura's shoulder, she walked to the shelf and picked up a blue bottle. "I have help. This oil is a healing potion."

"Which one is that?" Naurelia asked.

"The same one I applied to your back last year when when your solidified light exploded, Milady. The injuries are identical."

"The Divine Thunderbolt spell *is* solid light. I ought to know. Together with Aura's master, my husband invented it." Naurelia said. She sniffed and tilted her head back a little, jutting out her jaw. "I simply borrowed it for another purpose. Solid light may even replace candles one day. I just need to revisit the mathematics."

That was exactly what Nadula of Beryt said, Aura thought. *Just days before his experiment with iron vapors burned down the university of Tynthak.* So, this room was a healing chamber, made necessary by the experiments conducted upstairs. She lay back down. Miriam poured some of the oil on the middle of Aura's thigh, and rubbed some onto her hands. Aura gritted her teeth. This would probably hurt.

It did. Miriam's fingers dug deep into Aura's flesh. Fire worse than the actual spell shot through her leg, dashing toward her toes and racing toward her hip. She screamed and thrust her chest from the table. It took all her will not to roll over onto her back, and with her good leg, kick the handmaiden across the room.

"Endure, Mistress," Miriam said. "I must work the oil deep into your leg if it is to heal you properly."

"I know sometimes the cure is worse than the illness, but this is ridiculous," Aura snarled through clenched teeth.

Naurelia grabbed two chairs from the corner of the chamber. She thrust one underneath the latch of the door. Walking to the head of the table, she sat the other down, then perched on the edge of the seat. Taking Aura's hands in hers, she drew them toward her, forcing the wizardess to lie down on the table.

"Talk to me," she said. "It will take your mind off Miriam's hands. Surely, you have questions by now."

There were so many, but they all jumbled in Aura's mind as agony shot through her leg. She bit her lip and forced back the tear trying to form at the edge of her eye.

"You apprenticed to Damaskarose," Aura stammered. "What was she like?"

Naurelia smiled that of wistful memory. "She was wonderful. Damaskarose was the most powerful enchantress who ever lived. Her power came from her inexhaustible ability to love. Oh, she wasn't perfect. She had a terrible temper and I was on the receiving end of that many times." She frowned, that of mischief. "Dear goddess, but that woman was short. She could walk beneath my extended arm as easily as I could walk beneath yours."

Aura smiled, as much as she could with Miriam's fingers digging deep into her injured leg. "I realize that I'm taller than average, but that's remarkably short for an Ayrdish woman."

"Damaskarose was not Ayrdish. She was Geilltian."

"Geilltian! You have that trash in the Valley?" Aura exploded. Then, she recalled her initial reaction to seeing Karyl and Karyn in the light. With a mortified groan, she lowered her head to the table. "Forgive me, Eorless. I am so sorry."

"Not a surprising reaction from someone who is Ayrdish. I am Ayrdish myself, yes, yes, and eye some Geilltians with suspicion. The ones living on Warlden claim this island as their own, and refuse to accept that they forfeited it by selling it to the Bellician Empire. Not all, mind you. Here is a piece of history you may not know. The Tangoi never forget a betrayal. On the eve of Baron Reidwulf's voyage to claim this island, Coadia, Caillia, and Garrania were poised to attack. They never forgave their kinsmen for giving them three hundred years of brutal Bellician rule. They planned to slaughter Geilltia for its treachery, right down to the last dog and cat. Our invasion actually saved the lives of the Geilltians, and many are grateful. Of all the Geilltians I know, Damaskarose was the most content, happy actually, knowing that her former island was occupied by a million of Baron Reidwulf's Nebelish refugees."

"I apologize, Lady Naurelia. My response was beneath me. I have a wider streak of prejudice than I suspected. My father's mother claimed descent from Thegn Karlborn, one of Reidwulf's lieutenants. He was murdered by Geilltians. I guess I grew up hearing too many stories."

"As did we all."

As pain rocked her leg and back, Aura fought to put the next question into words. "What did she look like?"

Naurelia looked at the floor. The silence in the room was broken only by the sound of oil on flesh. She mumbled, "Her hair was the color of night. I no longer remember her face. Isn't that peculiar. I can't remember the face of my own mother."

Miriam cleared her throat. She needn't have bothered. It was too late. "So, my master is your brother."

Naurelia shot her a withering glare. "He told you!"

"No," Aura said, smiling. She left it at that. The members of the Order of Enchanters had their secrets, ones that they wished to keep from Aura. They forgot that while Aura Lockhaven had been trained by one of their own, that enchanter was also a wizard. Wizards knew what they wanted to know, and knew how to find out what they did not know. She botched numerous potions, fumbled charms, and forgot every fourth spell. The lesson she learned the best was how to ferret out facts. For five years, Sagacius spent evenings throwing riddles her way, sending her on treasure hunts, and playing hide and seek. He quit the night she knew Hartshorn was building a water clock, and he didn't, despite being the town wizard. Two years as an urchin living in a barrel behind the baker's shop gave her an ability that he did not have, the ability to hide in shadows and listen to the conversations of others. She had listened to, and remembered, the words of Deofoyl, Karyn, Karyl, and Naurelia herself. No need to let Naurelia in on her own personal secret. It may give her the opportunity to learn even more.

"Yes, that insufferable brat is my brother."

"I don't know how to say this without sounding insulting, but you don't look alike."

Naurelia smiled. "Well, we're both adopted." She glanced down to the corner of the chamber. "Damaskarose didn't have any natural children."

Miriam moved her hands down toward Aura's calf, forcing a wince and a groan from her. Aura felt grateful. The grimace hid the frown she cast at Naurelia. Her glance down was the telltale sign of a lie.

The Eorless seemed content to talk about herself now. "My real parents were Rodeck and Jenycka of Praterhall. My father had been Damaskarose's apprentice. When they journeyed to Caillia to cure a plague, they left me with Damaskarose. My parents failed, and died in the plague themselves. I don't remember them at all. I was just a baby. Damaskarose felt she owed it to her former student to raise me, so I became her daughter. When I was eight, a Pendurist priest from the continent visited. He had a six year old boy with him, whose family had perished in a war fought on the borders of Nebeland and Flumance. The boy had a natural talent for magic, so the priest left him with us, and Damaskarose adopted him, too."

"Sagacius," Aura said.

"Yes."

"If he had a natural talent, then he must have been a brilliant apprentice."

"Your master was a total buffoon!" Naurelia roared. "That man was more interested in wenching and pranking than in learning magic. He initiated at thirty, eight years beyond most men."

Aura smiled at the thought of Sagacius being incompetent, or foolish. Her smile turned into another grimace as Miriam's fingers dug into her buttocks. There were so many questions to ask. The most dominant one was about Nocturna. If Naurelia was Sagacius' sister, did she send the nymphs to Hartshorn? If so, why? What was it about the wizard's apprentice that attracted her attention? She knew the answer to the question did she look like Damaskarose was already lost. Naurelia didn't remember her mother's face, or that was what she said.

"I remember my father well," Aura said through clenched teeth. "Sagacius isn't my father figure. He's like an uncle to me. But he is my spiritual father and my father in magic. Why didn't he tell me about you, or Damaskarose? I would have liked to have known my spiritual lineage and met you long before now."

"My brother has his reasons," Naurelia answered, slowly. "I won't betray him."

Aura nodded. She groaned again, but this was the sound of relief. Miriam now massaged her lower back. She no longer felt her left leg at all. She wiggled her toes to ensure she still had a left leg. Lowering her head to the table, she nearly fell asleep as Miriam moved up her back.

Perhaps she did fall asleep. The next thing she knew, Miriam helped her sit on the edge of the table. Apparently, at some time, she rolled over onto her back. The front of her leg and hip glistened with oil. "Now,

Mistress. The best way for the potion to work is for you to walk. Tonight, I shall show you a way to hasten the results. For now, just walk."

"I've postponed anything else that you may do for today," Naurelia said. "It pained me to see you limp this morning. I imagine it pained you worse, yes, yes. Please spend some time strolling in the rose garden. I will send Manfred to accompany you. You two can argue over how to brew ale. Arguing is what he does best."

With tremulous steps, Aura left the healing room, walked through the gigantic sitting chamber, and down the hall. As she passed through each room, her smile widened. By the time she reached the veranda, she wore a grin. In only a few days, she had grown accustomed to the ache and cramp in her left leg. It no longer ached. She no longer limped. Her leg felt a little weak, but it didn't hurt. The left boot slid on her calf from the oil, and the left side of her skirt clung to her hip.

Aura found the rose garden by following her nose. It lay down a path of flagstones, behind a hedge of boxwood on the other side of the carriage house. Aura kept four small rose bushes behind the outhouse at home. They were wild ramblers she found in the Big Hedge, white with a pink blush at the tips of the petals. The t'Ardora rose garden filled two acres. Each bush was carefully trimmed, and covered with blooms. The array of reds, pinks, yellows, and oranges, interspersed with white, looked like a patchwork quilt spread on the ground. The hum of bees working the blooms filled the air.

Closing her eyes, Aura inhaled the deep aroma. Over the past ten years, she trained her olfactory sense to discern flowers by smell, and not just shape and color. The three Jennifer's spires looked the same, white and fuzzy. Each, however, had a different magical property. The only way to get the one that brought abundance of gold and not abundance of cattle was by scent. It was the same with roses. The more dominant the aroma, the more powerful the love potion. The more delicate the aroma, the more powerful the peace incense. From where she stood, Aura detected seven different aromas, from toss-me-into-bed-right-now to an-earthquake-won't-bother-me to this-will-make-a-fine-addition-to-mead. The combination drove all thoughts of magic from her mind, filling her with the simple enjoyment of sheer beauty. As she enjoyed her thrall, she heard footsteps on the path behind her.

"Well now, don't you look better than you did a little while ago," Manfred said.

"Thank you," Aura said, turning to meet him. "I certainly feel better."

Manfred put his hands on his hips and eyed her up and down. "I'm no artist, but that dress doesn't work out here. It's as dull as a witless minstrel. In this garden, you should wear a red silk gown. That would tie your hair in with the rest of you, from stem to stern." He paused, with his left hand at her breast height, and his right even with her buttocks. "Oh, dear, oh, that's terrible," he stammered, turning as red as the rose bush next to him. He quickly threw one hand up level with his eyes, and the other one toward the ground. "I mean, from scalp to sole."

Aura giggled. The more Manfred tied his own tongue, the more charming he became. If this was his idea of courtship, he succeeded in spite of himself. She decided to offer him a hand out of the hole he dug for himself. "So, you see me as preferring red, too?"

Manfred cast a weak smile of relief. "Red clothing to match your hair. Together, they would set off your eyes like emeralds. For your diadem," he reached up. "The whole sky. Red, green, and blue. Now, that would be a contrast."

"And you said you weren't an artist."

Manfred shrugged. "It's how mother set the tables in the tavern. Guess who had to wash the table linens." He poked himself on the chest. Aura slipped her hand inside his arm, and they began strolling through the garden. "It's good to see you walk without a limp."

"You have no idea how good it feels to walk without a limp!"

"Oh, yes I do. I was shot through the hip during the war."

"If you were in the war, then you must be at least seventy-five years old," Aura said.

"I'm eighty-one, last month."

"Your longevity potion is amazing."

"Who told you about that? It's an oathbound Order secret."

Aura gave Manfred a knowing smile. "I figured it out for myself."

"Since you already know about it, I won't be violating my oaths. If you're initiated as an enchantress, you'll drink it for yourself."

Aura paused to admire a brilliant gold rose next to the path. Manfred chuckled. She knew what that meant. Sagacius mock grumbled that walking with Aura one mile required two hours. She stopped to talk to every flower and bird she met. When her master wasn't with her, she talked to stones, too.

They continued on their way. It must have been the combination of the fragrances of the roses. Aura found herself saying, "I take it that you aren't married."

"No," Manfred said, with a snort. "I never have been, and probably never will be. With so many years available, those of us who marry tend to do so late, around age forty or fifty." He sighed. Gazing off toward the rim of the Valley, he said, "We really aren't all that enchanting, Aura. Most of us just float from one tryst to another, with no concern about what, or whom, we may leave in our wake. Most of our children are bastards, and we just don't care. Those of us who survived the war, remember what it was like before. We cared about everything. We loved everyone far too much to take a chance like that. So, we survivors tend to not marry. We can't settle with someone who is as shallow as a puddle on a hot day."

"I'm sorry, Manfred."

"Oh, don't be. It is what it is, and you're not responsible. Personally, I hope you join us. Someone like you may just restore the enchantment to being an enchantress."

"I'm not even sure I know what an enchantress does," Aura said. "How is her magic different from –"

She came to a dead halt. Manfred almost ripped his arm from her grasp, and stumbled before he could stop walking. Next to them, in the center of the garden, a rose bush covered fifty square feet of ground. Unlike the rest of the bushes, this one remained in its natural shape. It stood even with the top of her head. From its size, and the thickness of what she saw of the gnarled base, Aura guessed its age at nearly two hundred years. At first, the red blooms looked huge, but up close each bloom was actually a cluster of ten smaller ones, crimson with pink centers.

"A damasara," Aura whispered.

"Damaskarose took her name from this one," Manfred said. "I'm not sure where the K came from. I suspect she just found it laying on the ground between the sage and thyme."

"In the Garranic form of Tangish, the damasara is called damaskaron. Ancient Geilltian was similar to Garranic."

"Oh," Manfred said. "Now, why didn't the old man teach me that?"

The damasara was the sacred flower of the Tangoi. Aura had seen it in illustrations of books, but only dreamed of seeing a live one. Extinct on Ayrdland, it could only be found in the deep forests of Coadia, the crags of the uplands of Caillia, and in the royal gardens of Garrania. Gently, she caressed the velvety petals of a bloom close to her. The aroma transported her to another time. A time when men and women stood together to fight foes that threatened their homes. A time before the dreams of emperors and the schemes of Supreme Sires. A time when enchantment lay just underneath everyone's skin.

"Can you imagine the power of this rose?" Aura asked. She looked at Manfred as a girl talking about a new boy. "Rose petals make wonderful love potions. In a bath, they help sooth heartbreak. In an incense, they invoke peace. Eaten, they make your dreams come true. A damasara would give all those a power a mere mortal might not be able to handle. Just one petal, Manfred! An entire cluster from this bush would bring peace to Hartshorn for a month."

Manfred roared in laughter. "The difference between us is amazing. We were both taught by the same man. Yet, when Sagacius taught me, he was strictly an enchanter. By the time he found you, he was a tree-climbing rock-kisser. To me, this is just a pretty flower. To you, it's a magical tool of tremendous power."

"It isn't just a tool, Manfred. It's a friend. All plants are. They're friends and partners in helping make someone's life better." Aura gripped one petal between her fingertips. She whispered to the damasara, "May I have one of your petals?" The plant felt warm in her fingers, so she plucked the petal. She slipped into her sleeve pocket, next to the ruby. As Aura caressed the rose again, she said, "I've seen a damasara. I could leave the Valley today and feel my life is complete."

Manfred laughed. "You're adorable, Aura." When she gave him a quizzical look, he added, "I'm serious. You fought a three headed squid, and it almost killed you. It left you crippled. Most people who endure that have to drink an entire tavern to calm down. You? All you need is one rose bush."

She grinned. Between the sight of the roses, their intoxicating aromas, and the presence of a man who wanted to talk to her, Mayenne seemed years in the past, instead of a mere two days. She said, "That squid had five heads. I counted them."

"I can think of better things to do than breaking your leg, or whatever it was it did to you," Manfred said.

Aura looked at him playfully. She imagined his lips on hers. She imagined his arms around her waist. The words tore from her mouth before she could stop them. "Such as kissing me in this garden?"

Manfred frowned. "Do you always throw yourself at a man you only just met?"

Aura blushed. She looked at her feet. Dammit, that was too quick. "I apologize. I feel flirtatious. I don't know why. Maybe it's the garden. Maybe it's the oil Miriam rubbed into my leg. I didn't mean to offend you."

Manfred placed his finger underneath her chin, and lifted her head. He smiled, and said, "You didn't. I'm just cautioning you to be careful. You're in the Valley of the Mystic Moon, and the air here does that to people. It's permeated with centuries of love. We enchanters used to get so filled up on it that we'd have to go out into the world to share it, or we'd burst. You aren't familiar with it, so it will affect you like a tea drinker's first tankard of ale. Just practice some wisdom, or you'll find yourself out of that brown dress, and not because you're changing into a red one."

Aura looked Manfred in the eyes. She almost asked *and you don't want to see me out of this dress?* In her heart, she sensed that he did, but he practiced the very wisdom he just advised her to follow. He didn't really know her, despite Sagacius' letters. Besides, Manfred was a gentleman, and that question was one a gentleman did not answer. It was also a question a lady did not ask, especially on what amounted to a first stroll through a garden together. With a simple nod, she decided to heed his advice. Slipping her hand back inside his arm, they continued their walk.

She had to watch her words. Worse, she had to watch her heart. There was something about Manfred Rowanwand, a deep sense of comfortableness, as if she had known him all her life. That didn't mean she could be so familiar with him, or assume their budding friendship was anything but that. He was right. She didn't know him. Not really. He could be every bit the predator that Cecil was, or even Mayenne. She decided to simply engage him in safe conversation. "Did you know Sagacius and Lady Naurelia were brother and sister?" she asked.

Manfred whirled. He grabbed her by the shoulders and glared in fury. He shouted, "Who told you?"

His anger sparked her own. Jerking herself from his grip, she snapped, "I figured that out for myself, too! I'm not as simpleminded as you people think." So much for a safe conversation. Apparently, it meant more to Manfred than a way to pass the time. "From your answer to my question, obviously, you did know."

The fury melted from his face, replaced by cold resignation. "Yes, I knew. That's the bone stuck in our craws. Spiritual aunt and spiritual nephew don't always agree."

"Why didn't I know? Don't you dare say that Sagacius had his reasons."

"All right, I won't say it." Manfred sighed. "Aura, I really don't know the answer to that. Sagacius is my teacher, and if he chose not to tell you about Naurelia, or Mandrake, or Gordon, or me, or his family, or the Valley, or our order, I have to respect his wishes. Now that you do know, I'm a little more free to answer your other questions. I think."

"Gordon? Who is Gordon?"

"Dammit!" Manfred snapped. "Please forget that name, Aura. He was the apprentice after me, and the one before you. That is all I wish to say of him."

The idea of a pleasant stroll with Manfred was a thing of the recent past now. All the questions she had lost to Miriam's fingers returned. "Then you may answer another question. Manfred, who is Nightshade?"

"It's a plant. There's a bunch of them. My brother is named for one. Surely the old man taught you about nightshades."

Her sigh was that of disgust and weariness. "For the past month, I've been told a series of half-truths and riddles, especially when I ask about a certain name. I've had enough of them. I like you, Manfred. I like you quite a bit. I'd like to get to know you better. If I find out that you're hiding the truth from me, I won't appreciate it. Now, I'll ask again. Who is Nightshade?"

Manfred sighed. "Well, I don't suppose there's any harm. They are, after all, two of our biggest legends."

"They?" Aura asked.

"They. Long ago, when the order was still fairly new, there were two brothers. The older was Alfred, and the younger was Holbert. They were nicknamed for their appearances. Alfred was called Nightshade because he was dark and homely, while Holbert was called Brightstar because he was handsome and charismatic. Yet, their personalities were the opposite. Nightshade was kind, gentle, and loving, while Brightstar was arrogant, cruel, and tyrannical. They developed two different philosophies of magic, which over the years, grew further apart. They ended up fighting each other. If I remember right, a curse was put on both because of that, but I don't know the details.

"Anyway, their differences reached their apex during our great war. One side followed the philosophy of Nightshade, that of absolute obedience to the law. The other side followed the philosophy of Brightstar, that of unbridled power without laws. Essentially, selflessness versus selfishness, or legalism versus freedom, depending on your point of view. Our cataclysm was nothing but a battle between two brothers, even though they had been dead for more than a century." Manfred looked down at his hands. "The war is never far below the surface of our skins. We'd prefer the scars remain scars, and not reopen into running wounds."

"How did they die?"

"Beats the bung out of my keg. Old age, I imagine. Brightstar is buried in the Valley. No one knows what became of Nightshade. He left the Valley, and vanished."

"Do they have any descendants?"

Manfred was silent for a minute. "I don't know about Nightshade. No one does. As for Brightstar ..." He paused. "Our master killed his last descendant. Blasted his right arm clean off his body a duel. At least, that's what he told me. I wasn't present. I was in the infirmary, having that arrow dug out of my hip."

Aura frowned. The only time Sagacius mentioned the name Brightstar, he said the man walked away from the duel, even after losing his arm. If Manfred was not present at the duel, then perhaps he genuinely did not know Brightstar's true fate. Such wounds usually prove to be fatal. Sagacius had called the man he fought Brightstar. Yet, Manfred just said Holbert Brightstar died one hundred years earlier. So, his nickname became a surname. If it could, then so could another.

"My mother's maiden name was Aurora Nightshade."

"Oh, ho! That's what this is about. You think you're descended from Alfred Nightshade."

"No, but apparently someone else does," Aura said.

"If I were you, I wouldn't fret over trifles. The continent of Sareth is big, but there can't be enough names to go around to thirty-five million people."

"It would mean nothing to me if it didn't mean too much to far too many –"

A horse nickered. Aura turned toward the forest, while Manfred looked back toward the carriage house. The trees beyond the rose garden grew thick and lush. Too thick for a horse to graze with any comfort.

"We aren't that close to the paddock," Manfred said.

"It didn't come from the paddock," Aura said, pointing to the woods just beyond the edge of the center of the garden. "It came from there."

"How do you know?"

"I can locate a bird within three feet of his perch by his song."

"Either one of the horses escaped the paddock, or someone is trespassing. My gold is on the latter," Manfred said. "I better go shoo him away. If Naurelia finds out ... well, you haven't seen a vile temper yet."

Manfred strode down the path. Aura followed right behind him. Her leg twinged a bit, but not enough to cause her to limp. Abruptly, he turned down a dirt path that led between two tall pink rose bushes, and through an opening in the boxwoods. Beyond lay the forest of rowan and oak. Manfred slowed his pace, creeping into the trees like a cat. Unlike most men in the forest, Manfred made no sound as he stepped on the fallen leaves and parted the underbrush. Aura followed in his footsteps. The horse nickered again. Just ahead on the left.

As soon as Aura spotted the sky blue cloak of the rider, she grabbed Manfred's waistcoat. Throwing herself to the ground, she pulled him down on top of her. Clamping her hand over his mouth, she motioned him to be silent. She peered through the underbrush. No doubt about it. The rider was a Guard. He sat on his horse, scanning the trees as if searching for prey that vanished. Just as she feared. He had shoulder length blonde hair and a blonde beard. Manfred looked at her in absolute consternation.

Aura leaned as close to Manfred's ear as she could. She whispered, "Two nights ago, I fought him in an alley in Ardora. He was trying to abduct a girl."

She released his mouth. He whispered, "You've been drinking the dregs. He's a lawman."

Sushing him, she watched and waited. Manfred remained motionless beside her. The Guard stroked his beard, then turned his horse and rode through the trees toward the road to Ardora. Aura felt she could finally breathe. She said to Manfred, "Captain Baltarus thinks he's an imposter, posing as a Guard."

"Why is he at Ardora Hall?" Manfred asked, rising to his knees.

"I suppose he's after me," Aura said, standing. She looked into the forest, the way the Guard had ridden. No sign of him. In the thick woods, she didn't fear him charging her from behind. He didn't have enough clear room to maneuver that fast. Even the best rider would make a noise in the underbrush, or smash his head on one of the low hanging limbs. "I got a good look at him, and he got a good look at me. From what I understand, I'm the only witness to his crimes. Be honest. I'm difficult to conceal. All he has to do is ask for the whereabouts of the tallest woman in these parts." Aura lifted her skirt, and began working her way through the brambles and young rowans, toward where the Guard had sat moments before.

"What are you doing?" Manfred asked.

"I'm following him. Are you coming with me?" She searched the woods to satisfy herself that the Guard didn't wait in the shadows for her, then followed the path of bent brush his horse left behind.

"That's stupid, Aura," Manfred said, hurrying to catch up to her. "Those men are warded against magic. He has a sword and we don't."

"Thanks to him, I was accused of a rather serious crime. So was our master."

"Oh. Well, that's different."

The Guard picked the best route through the forest. His almost clear path would have remained unseen by Aura, until she followed it. From the vantage point of a saddle, he would have noticed thinner briars and wider spacing between trees. She and Manfred worked their way through the woods, watching the ground for hoof prints, and the way ahead for a waiting sword. They both breathed a sigh of relief when the trail led them to a wide clay road.

"Well, we lost him. There are too many prints," Manfred said. "He probably turned left, back toward Ardora. The right would take him to Tongren's Tower, and only a fool would go there. Of course, we're talking about a man disguised as a Guard who abducts girls. There's nothing foolish about that."

"Lovely," Aura mumbled. Ardora Hall no longer felt safe. The Guard had ventured too close for her comfort. At least, by night, the forest would be impassible for him on horseback, and probably afoot, too. The best course of action seemed to remain as close to Naurelia t'Ardora as possible. Not even an imposter would have the courage to confront the ruler of the shire, or so she hoped. With a final glance at the road, Aura turned to walk back into the forest, with Manfred at her side.

Chapter Twenty-Eight

THE PERSONAL LIBRARY of the Eorl of Ardora filled almost one entire side of the lower floor of the manor. Shelves of books and scrolls reached to the ceiling fourteen feet above. Several ladders leaned against the shelves, and four overstuffed chairs waited beneath candelabras for readers. Some Iricanist priests would pay dearly to have a library half this size. Others would burn it to the ground for the books it contained. Naurelia offered the room to Aura for her use and enjoyment, and as a comfortable place to rest her healing leg. For five minutes, she stared at the library, salivating as if over a fine roast. She didn't know where to begin, so she grabbed the first book that looked interesting, Makelstene's *Flowers of the Plains*. As she read, she heard voices in the hall outside the door. She recognized them both. They sounded angry.

"I don't appreciate this!" Naurelia rumbled. "You don't trust me with her."

"No, I do not," Manfred replied. "You've given me no reason to trust you. Your ritual this morning was dangerous. That girl has memories that don't need to surface."

"You talk like Gordon."

"If you were not Lady Naurelia t'Ardora, I would slap you for that comment," Manfred said, his voice full of menace.

Naurelia chuckled. "He and I still write each other. I'll tell him you said that. I'll also tell him that you're spying on me. Gordon, in turn, will tell –"

"That's hypocritical, Naurelia," Manfred snapped. "You sent two nymphs to spy on her, in her own home at that."

"I ... I did no such thing! How dare you accuse me of such! A t'Ardora does not spy. That is for the likes of ..." She paused. In a low, calm voice, she said, "I know who did. Come with me. This conversation is for behind thick doors and thicker walls. And I trust you will keep your lips sealed."

Aura laid her book in her lap. "That was interesting," she whispered, just in case they lurked in the hall outside the door. Manfred knew more about her than he implied. Well, Sagacius no doubt still wrote to him. She would have a nice talk with Mr. Old Man when she returned home. He wouldn't like it. The thought of Sagacius squirming in his chair brought a smile to her face. That would suffice for all the things he hid from her over the years.

In the process, the question of Naurelia's involvement in Nocturna's mission had just been answered. That raised another question. If Naurelia had not sent Nocturna and Ferne, then who did? For a moment, Aura thought about following Naurelia and Manfred, in hope of overhearing who the Eorless believed sent the two Fae. That was too risky. She would try to coax the information out of Manfred by tricking him, Sagacius style, in the morning. She returned to the book.

Aura lost track of time. The book was a poor Ayrdish translation of a fair Flumantine translation of a Nebelish sorcerer's drunken attempt to describe the herbal magic of Glasenya. Despite the interesting topic, the baffling sentences left her bewildered. It would have been better left in the original Nebelish. She could have translated that. Despite the butchered language, the chapter on the mystical uses of morning glory seeds was so fascinating she never heard the library door open.

"Aura Lockhaven of Hartshorn, you will please accompany me," Naurelia said.

Aura laid her book in her lap. The woman who stood before her was not the inventor, nor the Eorless, nor the magician. Naurelia had transformed once again, now into the high priestess. Her gossamer dress and cloak flowed around her thick body like black water. The silver crescent moon circlet around her forehead and the matching medallion dangling against her chest added to the gravity of her person, filling the air in the Ardora Hall library with somber heaviness.

"What have I done?" Aura asked.

"Nothing. Your presence is requested by someone whose authority greatly exceeds my own. I have instructed Miriam to postpone her lesson with you until tomorrow night. Come," Naurelia answered, with no trace of the usual distracted inflections.

Without another word, Naurelia turned and exited the library. Aura followed. Silently, they walked outside. When Aura entered the library, it was only midafternoon. Now, stars twinkled in the black sky overhead. Naurelia lifted a lantern that Aura had not noticed before. With a command, the candle lit by itself. They walked across the yard, and down a narrow crooked path through the trees. In minutes, they entered a clearing. Before them stood a stone circle of indeterminable age and indescribable majesty.

"This is magnificent!" Aura said, staring at the sarsens.

Naurelia smiled. "The second Eorl of Ardora erected it. The four tall stones mark the directions. The eight medium sized stones are for the spokes of the Wheel of the Year. The twelve small ones mark the first days of the months. It's a calendar, actually, and it's more accurate than it has a right to be. The circle also does something else. It creates phantoms."

"Phantoms? Do you mean it summons ghasts?" Aura asked.

"They are not ghasts. We simply call them phantoms," she answered, as if explaining that the sky was blue. "We don't really know what they are or how they are created. They are physical representations of people we remember, people we want to see again. Sometimes, they are people we need to see and hear. They are quite solid, and speak to us. Phantoms are more like life sized poppets with ties to the shadows within our souls, than chalices for spirits. Several places within the Valley create phantoms. This circle creates those we need to see and hear, and only when it wills." The Eorless lifted the lantern, and nodded to the gap between the stones. "It has so willed. You need to enter the circle, Aura. There is someone in there that you need to see and hear."

"Who is it?"

"That is not for me to know nor ask. The circle contacted me and called for you. This is part of your journey to discover yourself. Who you see and what you hear is for you alone. Once you enter, a veil will descend over the circle and I will see and hear nothing. When it is time for the phantom to appear, the torches will light themselves."

"This is all rather advanced magic, Eorless," Aura said.

"It is the magic of the land itself," Naurelia said. "I've nothing to do with it."

Heavy silence fell as Aura passed between the sarsens. She heard no crickets, owls, or anything else. Only her own breath. Aura walked up to the stone facing the south. She placed her hand on top of her head, then moved it forward. She stood five feet, eight inches tall. Based on where her hand rested, this stone was five feet, ten inches tall. Aura never could guess weight based on size, but this stone must weigh close to six tons.

She pondered where the Eorl of Ardora found it, and how many men it required to drag into place. Perhaps the Eorl performed the task alone, using an advanced form of levitation. Such things were possible, whispered in fable and scribbled on faded scroll. She thought about the simple stone circle behind her house. It had only four sarsens, one for each direction. This one had twenty-four, each with its own purpose. Parin drew near, Haemmont 1, the day of Ystlena, the day of Aura's birth. It marked the official first day of summer. She smiled at the thought of the shadow its representative stone would cast upon the ground on that day.

With an almost imperceptible hiss, the torches lit. They grew in intensity until Aura could have read with ease. Yet, while the flames were yellow, they filled the circle with cold blue light. The breeze blew by Aura's face, carrying with it a chill belonging to late autumn. Aura braced herself. Whatever, or whoever, was coming may not be pleasant.

"It's been a long time," a voice said from Aura's left.

She turned to face the eastern most stone. A woman leaned against it, her arms crossed over her chest. In the light of the torches, Aura could see enough color and details. Her black trousers were worn through at the knees, and ripped down the left thigh. Her blouse, missing the right sleeve, may have been white once, but now looked the color of old clay. Twine held closed the patch covered bodice. She wore one brown boot, and one black shoe, both with holes in the toes. Several gunny sacks, roughly sewn together with fragments of yarn, served as her cloak, knotted at the throat. Even though tangled, the woman's auburn hair showed clearly in the torchlight. Layers of grime on her face could not hide the hump in the nose and the green eyes. Her full figure strained at the bodice and trousers, sewn for someone about ten pounds lighter. Then, there was the woman's height, just shy the top of the stone, a stone Aura had measured herself.

Aura gasped. "You look like ... me," she said. Remarkable, she thought. Someone crafted an uncanny likeness, although she had not looked that ragged in ten years.

"I am you, but I'm surprised you recognize me, considering you never look at yourself in a mirror," the woman said. "I am Aura Lockhaven, daughter of Henry and Aurora, little sister to Richard and Ester, and niece to Cedric."

The voice sounded identical, just like the one she heard in her own ears whenever she spoke or sang. Mid-country accent, with its soft A, soft R, and hard L, with a touch of Coadic lilt learned from Ester who learned it from their mother. The similarities were just too remarkable.

Aura put her hands on her hips. "Who are you really?"

The double glared at her, and muttered, "All your brains settled into your chest. You know who I am."

Aura recalled an old story Richard whispered to her on nights when he wanted her to scream. *Ever notice how the girl in the mirror tries to get out, but you stop her by blocking her with your hand? Well, on some nights, Squirt, you aren't there to stop her, and she steps through,* he told her. The mirror image tramped about the house, causing mischief for which the real person would be blamed. She had not believed Richard, and only squealed to make him feel like a successful big brother. She even threw a blanket over the mirror and said, *If I can't see her, then she can't see our house to get in.* That made Richard stagger away, howling in glee.

In a land where balakalats roamed at will, however, perhaps a children's tale could become real. There was one way to find out. Aura dove to the ground, snatched a rock, and rolled over on her left side. She hurled the rock at her double's face. The other Aura's eyes flew wide. She reached across her face with her right hand, and caught the rock, only inches away from her nose.

"Nice," the double said. "If I were your mirror image, I'd be left handed. But I'm not a mirror image." The double chucked the stone over her shoulder.

Aura stood and backed away. Having proven that the double was no mirror image, she now faced two possibilities. Neither filled her with any joy. This could be a witch or wizardess employing a brilliant glamour spell. Those, however, had limitations. No matter the power or skill of the witch, a glamour spell could not change a person's height or eye color. She knew of no other woman her height, much less with green eyes. Glamour spells also did not change a person's sex, so this was no sorcerer disguised as a woman. Besides, that implied a deep conspiracy, and who was she to warrant that level of attention. That left the final possibility, and one worse than facing another balakalat.

The Nebels called them Dupfelgetten, double goers. They were demons who took on the form of a person they intended to capture and replace. Where the Dupfelgetten took the victim, and what it did to him or her, was beyond nightmare. A chain of thoughts raced through Aura's mind. Mayenne practiced western sorcery, from the heart of Phrathia itself. She could know such a demon. She may still lust for Aura's soul. Worse, the goddess Mayenne worshipped may now know about her and want her for herself. That goddess could have sent a Dupfelgetten. Such creatures, however, only looked like their victims. They knew nothing of them.

"Prove to me that you're me. Tell me something about myself that only I know, something not even Master knows," Aura said.

The double sighed. "Skeptical, aren't you? Very well. I'll humor you. Hmm. Well, anyone who sees you swim or bathe would assume you shave underneath your arms and between your legs. Most women do. Many men do, at that, even here in barbaric Ayrdland. Ever since Paratikus lan Attatar wrote his book of physik 1,500 years ago, shaving those areas is considered healthy. It smells better. It keeps lice and fleas at bay. You, however, don't shave. Because of some freakish Lockhaven trait, you have no hair below your chin. None. Our sister was like any other woman. Our father and brother, however, had nice beards, but bare chests, arses, and manhoods. That caused no end of giggles when they swam, not that anyone would have laughed at them to their faces. A good business deal is known as being *as smooth as Lockhaven's chest*, although since you grew those," the double paused and pointed to Aura's breasts, "that proverb has fallen into disuse."

"Son of a bitch," Aura whispered.

"We're girls, so that would be daughter of a bitch, and is that any way to talk about our mother?"

Aura narrowed her eyes, remembering what Naurelia said about the stone circle. "You're the phantom," she said.

"It took you long enough," the double said.

Aura looked at the stone circle. The flickering yellow flames of the torches reflected eerie pulsating blue on the granite, adding to the silence of the night. Some places called to certain people, but in a spiritual sense. This one specifically called for her, and used a high priestess as its medium. The earth and stones contained tremendous magical power, but not on this level. Aura stilled herself and listened. The power of the circle was palpable. She felt a low throb from the ground itself, clarified and magnified by the stones. It was as if she stood in the hand of a god holding his breath. Whatever it was, the circle created a duplicate of herself, yet dressed it in rags and covered it in dirt.

"Why would I need to see and talk to myself?" she asked no one.

"You talk to yourself all the time. Well, I'm here to talk back," the phantom said. The double stepped away from the stone. "You decided to undertake a journey to find yourself. Well, you are at the end of your journey. Here you are, in all your glory. Take a good look at Aura Lockhaven."

"You may be my phantom, and have my face and body, but the similarities end there."

The phantom snorted in derision. "You created me, inch by inch, threadbare garment by threadbare garment. On the first day of winter, twelve years ago, you began carving and painting me. Today, I'm your walking masterpiece."

The throb of the circle grew, until Aura felt it in her feet. Another veil descended, this time over Aura herself. The reality of the phantom grew more clear, while her sense of wakefulness evaporated. Her reason fled. It was like trying to think her way out of a dream from which she wished to awaken, but could not. She sensed she had to fight her way through this, to force herself back to the present. The only way through was the phantom.

"What do you want?" she asked.

"Everything you denied me." The phantom walked toward Aura, swaying her hips in rhythm to her words. She lowered her head, and looked up at Aura with sultry eyes, and a smouldering smile. "You wish to be an enchantress. An enchantress is beautiful. An enchantress is seductive. An enchantress uses the power of her voice. She bends a man to her will and makes him think it is his idea. At least that's what the legends say. You have everything an enchantress could want. As for me, do I look enchanting?" The phantom turned and walked away. Over her shoulder, she said, "I want to look like you. I want to be enchanting." She whirled and shouted, "But you won't let me!"

"I have no control over you. How can I? You're a phantom, a poppet tied to the shadows of my soul," Aura said.

"What do you think I just said?" the phantom asked.

Something about that made sense. Aura tried to piece the fractions together to arrive at the whole. The phantom didn't speak in fractions. This was a mere two plus two, yet Aura could only add them to seven. This was so obvious it blinded her. She had to fight, push through to find the answer. Her feet vibrated as the throb of the circle increased. The torchlight quivered. A tiny pebble fell from the southernmost sarsen. The circle wanted to tell her something, but she could not understand its language.

"You don't have the right to be an enchantress, or a wizardess, or to even think about helping the good folk of Hartshorn," the phantom said slowly.

"What do you mean?" Aura snapped. "I'm an initiated wizardess. I've earned my status."

"Oh, a wizardess is merely what you do. Now, as for who you are, that's a different story. The *who* disqualifies you from the *what*. I'm going to tell you *why*, and I shall be gentle. Permit me to refresh your memory." The phantom began walking around Aura, smirking. She made two full passes before saying, "Let's start with our mother. Aurora Lockhaven was the most respected seamstress in Hartshorn. She loved her husband. She had two wonderful children. Only two children is unusual, but that is what the gods wanted. Seven years passed after Ester's birth and everything was fine. Then, you decided to spring into her belly."

The memory of her mother flashed through her mind without any control. Her father told her the story. On the day Aura was to be born, Aurora Lockhaven hemorrhaged. The apothecary and the midwife couldn't stop the bleeding. They offered her mother a choice. They could save her by killing the baby, or save the baby by letting her die. They could not save both. Aurora chose Aura. With Aurora too weakened from blood loss to push the baby out into life, the apothecary cut Aura from her womb. Mother held child for five minutes before death took her. As she remembered her father's story, Aura stiffened. Her hands flew to her face.

"You know what I'm about to say. How delightful," the phantom said.

In that black pit of fear in the bowels of Ralthangarle, she saw it for herself. Aura Lockhaven had killed Aurora Lockhaven. Daughter had killed mother. Aura knew that wasn't the way of it. Her father told her several times that Aurora chose to give her life. That made her only more precious to him. Richard slapped her one day for insulting herself. *Never insult someone Mom died to save*, he roared. *You're worth this entire town to me!* Ester often told her that one of the reasons she loved her was she had hair like their mother. Yet, she just heard it out of her own mouth. She couldn't have killed her mother. Could she?

"No," Aura said. "That's wrong. That was Mom's decision. A child is not to blame for something that happens before she's born."

The phantom patted Aura on the shoulder and said, "You're stammering. That means you don't believe a word you're saying. Mother wouldn't have had to choose, and she would still be alive today, if not for you." Before Aura could respond, the phantom continued. "Now, how about our big brother, Richard? He adored you. He wanted you to be proud of him. Remember his words the day he was appointed captain of the townsfyrd? He said he was going to do great deeds of valor so you would brag about him. He could have retreated with his men that day on Rathstone Bridge, and it would have been honorable. He stayed on that bridge to make you proud."

"That's a lie!" Aura snapped.

"Is it?" the phantom asked. "Search your heart. Aren't you proud of him?"

Richard had been the captain of the Hartshorn townsfyrd for only four months. Selected more for his height and bravado, he proved to be a capable leader. He inspired the confidence of his men, and the entire town. Somewhere inside his barrel chest, he found stern discipline the whole family thought he lacked. That sent him out the door one foggy morning in summer, shouting for his men.

News reached Mayor Hunter's ears that two longships of Skols slipped by Vine Haven, and sailed up the Gourdvine. Their target was Hartshorn.

From there, they could spread out into the middle country, and possibly reclaim the kingdom they held for two decades in that part of Ayrdland. Richard and the townsfyrd met them on Rathstone Bridge. Overwhelmed, Richard ordered the townsfyrd back behind the town walls. To give them time to retreat, he stood on the bridge, slashing at any Skol that came close. He killed ten before they cut him down. In death, he inflicted enough injuries to force the Skols to retreat to their camp. He lay on the bridge, surrounded by dead foes, clinging to his sword, a smile on his lifeless face.

Aura stood on the walls with Henry. She watched her brother die. The big, blustery, wenching man who laughed his way through life proved to be an oak clad in steel. She never felt more proud of Richard Lockhaven. Neither did the town's folk. The next morning, their numbers swelled with carpenters, farmers, and several dozen women, the townsfyrd left Hartshorn in the dark. They attacked the Skols at dawn, shouting *For Richard Lockhaven and Hartshorn*. The few invaders who survived the fury of the Ayrdish forces fled down the Gourdvine, into the waiting spears and swords of Vine Haven.

"No! It wasn't like that," Aura said, shaking her head. "Richard died for Hartshorn, not for me." Now, she wasn't sure. Richard doted on his littlest sister, in a way he didn't dote on Ester. The eldest and youngest of the three siblings were almost identical in their humor and love of tales, leaving Ester alone in her aloof dignity. He had wanted to make Squirt proud of him. He may just have retreated behind the walls with his men, if she had not been watching. Just before he fell, he looked up at her, and grinned. Aura's stomach revolted. She wanted to vomit. Richard had died for Aura, just like the phantom said.

"Shall we move on to dear old Daddy?"

"No, please!" Aura said.

That night haunted her in her dreams. Like that woman she rescued from a fire, ten year old Aura huddled in the corner of the sitting room as flames engulfed the draperies, then the rug, the walls, the floor. She fled underneath the table. Moments turned into centuries as fire leapt through the house. One of the oldest dwellings in Hartshorn, the thick stone walls and heavy closed shutters kept the smoke inside. Fire devoured the elderly wood paneling and ceiling beams. Only one man heard Aura scream, a man who simply came home to have supper with his remaining child.

Grabbing her, Henry dashed to the front door. As he was about to step through, a burning beam fell on him. It knocked her out of his arms and into the yard. From there, the memory roared through her skull like a team of horses out of control. The sight of the timber. The smell of burning flesh. The sound of the flames crackling. The feeling of the heat in her face and on her hands. Her left hand searing as she tried to move the burning beam. Watching her whole world and life vanish in smoke and horror. Aura shuddered. A moan escaped her mouth. A tear tore from her eyes, and rolled down her trembling cheek.

"Henry Lockhaven was the wealthiest tavern owner in Hartshorn," the double said. "He ruled your town from his bar, and everyone loved him for his generosity and sense of humor. That is, until until that night. That, too, was all your fault."

"No ... I ... it was a new candle. There was something in it. It ... it just exploded and ... fire went everywhere."

"Why didn't you pull Daddy out of the fire, Aura? Why did you let him burn?"

"I didn't! I mean, I tried. I mean ... he was too heavy! I went for help, but when they arrived ... " Aura said, through gasps for air between tears.

"When they arrived, you thought you were the new tavern owner. Isn't that it?"

"No! I loved my father!" Aura said, wiping her face.

"You are such a liar," the phantom said. "He would still be alive if you hadn't been born. It's all your fault, Aura. You killed Henry Lockhaven."

Aura knew she didn't murder her father, but she did light that candle. She had killed her father, not through a deliberate act, but through her own prissiness. The phantom smiled. She looked at Aura in a way that made her shiver.

The phantom asked, "So, what about Big Sissy? What about Ester?"

"No! Please! Anything but that!"

Aura's worst memory forced its way to the forefront of her consciousness. Ester should have returned from the market long before. It didn't take two hours to walk to the green and buy a few apples. The family still mourned Richard, and the three survivors didn't like to be long out of each other's sight. Aura set out to find her. Maggie told her that Ester decided to buy fresh apples from the wharves. Aura went there. A few people said they had seen her, but not recently.

Then, in an alley, she found her. She didn't know why her sister was naked. She didn't know why she wasn't breathing. Ester was breathing only two hours ago. Her father slumped in a chair with his face in his hands after hearing the news. Four men brought Ester's limp body into the house and laid her on the table. She tried to comfort her father as two women prepared Ester for burial.

Constable Alvin heard from a dock hand that Ester had been with some Flumantine boatmen. He found one of the boatmen. From him, they learned what happened. Full of lust, the boatmen spotted Ester, wandering on the docks. They lured her onto their boat with a promise of tart pie apples. She refused their advances. They raped her. Not knowing what to do next, they strangled her. They dumped her body in the alley behind the sailmaker's shop. The boatman's trial lasted ten minutes. It was the only time Aura felt happy to watch a man hang.

"You were Ester's little shadow," the phantom said, sneering. "You followed her everywhere. Then one day, you told her that you wanted to grow up to be beautiful like she was. That thrilled Ester so much she told you she was going to the market to buy some apples and bake you a pie. She even tweaked you on the tip of your nose as she left that morning."

"Stop!" Aura snapped.

"She wanted your pie to be the best."

"Don't!" Aura shouted.

"Ester wouldn't have been at the riverfront that morning to be raped and murdered if not for you, Aura."

"Enough!" Aura screamed.

"It's all your fault."

"Silence!" Aura tried to say, but her voice caught in her throat.

"Ester would still be alive today, if not for you."

"Please ... please ... don't," Aura whispered, sinking to her knees.

"You killed Big Sissy, just like you killed all the others." She bent down until her lips brushed Aura's ears. "Uncle Cedric cast you out because he feared you would kill him, too."

Aura didn't try to stop her tears. They erupted from her eyes and flowed down her face. Cries of anguish tore themselves from her throat. Her breath reduced to ragged gasps. She didn't cry just for Ester, but for her father, mother, and Richard. She cried for them all. She cried for four months of anguish and grief, followed by twelve years of questions for which no answers came. For years, she wondered if she caused their deaths. Now, she knew. It had to be the truth. She had just heard it from her own mouth.

"Why are you doing this to me?" Aura asked, her words punctuated by sobs.

"You say you want to defend the defenseless and help the helpless. You can't. You have no right to defend anyone or help anyone. Do you know why?" The phantom paused. In the silence, all Aura heard was the faint hiss of the torches, and her own sobs. The phantom roared, "Because you're a murderer!"

"Please stop tormenting me. You've done enough," Aura mumbled. She collapsed forward onto her hands. Tears spattered on the grass.

"I am far from finished with you. You created me. I want so much to look like you, but you refuse. You murdered me, too! So, I've been waiting a decade for this moment."

"I would never create such a horrible bitch!" Aura shrieked.

"You still don't understand, do you," the phantom whispered.

336

The ground vibrated beneath her hand. She could almost hear it, not unlike the sound of stones turning in mills. She felt she should understand, but couldn't. Some force clogged her mind, preventing her from seeing what should be obvious. Yet, that same force compelled her to push into it, to strain for that understanding. It beckoned to her while it resisted her. She needed time to figure this out.

The phantom didn't give her time. "Look at me. Look at me!" she snapped. "Take a good look beneath the dirt and rags. You have luscious hair. That deep red with the brown cast called auburn. It glows in the sunlight. Your face is quite fetching. Certainly, you have a humped nose, but that makes you elegant. You will still be fetching when you're sixty. As for your body, it stirs lust in all but blind men. There is just one problem. Two, actually." The phantom pointed to her eyes. "Snake Eyes."

Aura's sigh came from the depths of her soul. She lowered her head, and crouched on the grass on all fours. Snake Eyes. For two years, she bore that taunt from children her own age, and a few adults. It didn't end after Sagacius took her home, although it ceased being said to her face. That is, until she became a woman and experienced the bed. After Jack took her, he called her Snake Eyes. So did Cecil. At least Roderick had been kind enough to merely say she had the eyes of a cat. All three had wanted her body, but not anything else. They especially did not want what her body could have given them. No man wanted a son with snake eyes.

"As if I want to be a mother," Aura whispered.

"I heard that." The phantom said. She shrugged. "It's just as well. You'd probably kill your children, too. Now, I've seen the way you look at Manfred Rowanwand."

Aura jerked her head up. A tinge of fury raced through her. She snapped, "Don't talk about him!"

"Oh, do you feel something for him more than just friendship? I don't think he returns the favor. Why do you think he refused your opening to kiss you this afternoon? Again, what man wants to mate with a snake? If he feels anything for you, it's just to sow his seed in you and pray for a crop failure. He could never love you. You don't even know what that word means."

Aura felt the jolt of the thought. She wiped her face with her sleeve. There was something about what the phantom just said. Everything came into focus. Then, it faded away. Two plus two almost just equaled five. That gave her enough room to feel a little more grounded.

She lowered her face to the ground. This time, it was not in surrender to the phantom's words, but in rebellion. She refused to let the vile double see her lip tremble. Manfred no doubt only wanted to be friendly. No man could ever love a woman so hideous, so filthy, so ragged. Aura froze in mid thought. She wasn't describing herself. She was describing the phantom. Something about that stuck in her mind. It was enough to give her a shot of courage.

"Don't mock my heart!" she snarled.

"You've done a good job of that, yourself. Now that I've told you the truth about who you are, I want to tell you about who you are not. You are not a wizardess. You're too incompetent. For ten years, you pestered Sagacius to teach you, but you never learned a thing. In fact, the reason you're here is so he could get rid of you. He's tired of trying to teach you."

The tinge of fury she felt moments earlier lingered. "Master said I was his best student ever."

"That is what he *said*, but he only said it because he didn't want to hurt your feelings. He's smart, but not smart enough to teach someone as dense as a stone. The truth is, he knew about Mayenne, and asked Ashthorne to send you to her, hoping you'd be killed."

The tinge of fury exploded into wrath. It flowed through Aura, consuming her. She bent herself upright, resting on her knees. No one questioned Sagacius in her presence. She already dressed down a high lord over something similar. She'd be damned if she took it from herself. "That is enough!" Aura shouted. "I've had it with you!"

"It is far too late for that, Aura. You made me. You made me a murderer. You made me ugly. You made me unlovable. You made me stupid. You set me up to be killed. I'm not leaving until you acknowledge that and realize you are just like me."

"What did you say?" Aura asked.

"I believe you heard me. We speak the same language, and I don't stutter," the phantom said.

The numbers clicked into place. The sum flashed into view. In her mind, it was if she heard the sounds. It was like the morning Mayor Hunter first pulled the lever, setting Hartshorn's new water clock into motion. The slight gush of water diverted from the Gourdvine flowed from the uppermost pipe, down onto the wheel, which turned another wheel, which moved the minute hand. The sloosh, clunk, thwack, and knock fascinated her. With the flow of water and the movement of iron, Hartshorn took its place in the Eleventh Century. With the realization of who the phantom was, Aura took her place in the present.

The phantom was not Aura Lockhaven. Yet, she was more Aura Lockhaven than even the wizardess kneeling on the grass facing her. The phantom was Aura's inner image. This abomination was how Aura saw herself. She was that dark view of herself that lingered deep inside her heart, always ready to erupt. She was a shade of someone that should have been buried a decade ago, but instead, had been allowed to grow up until she filled the fleshen vessel that walked the streets of Hartshorn.

Aura avoided mirrors, and not just because of her eyes. She feared that she would see the urchin, only older and filled out. Richard had been right. Because she never stood before a mirror, she had not been there to prevent the image from escaping. It escaped. It stood before her now, incarnated in the form of a mysterious phantom created by the standing stones.

The phantom was right. She did often feel she killed her family. She felt deep guilt over Ester. Perhaps no man could ever love a woman so tall and with such green eyes. But the phantom made a mistake. She reached for something beyond her grasp. While Aura conceded the phantom's claims about her family and lovers, she would never yield on Sagacius and her own magical skills. The old wizard saved her from a life of misery. He gave her a home and a purpose. She held his undying loyalty and friendship, and she knew it. He had also taught her everything she knew about magic, and set her on the path she now walked. Other wizardesses knew more, but they were older and more experienced. What she did not know, she would learn in time. The foundation of herself as a woman was built on quagmire, but that of Sagacius and her competency were built on granite. On those two things, she could stake her faith.

It was enough.

Aura stood. It was time to begin laying the shade to rest, starting with its phantom. She fingercombed her hair into place, and patted her face dry. Smoothing down her dress, she cleared her throat. She narrowed her eyes and glared at her other self. This didn't require magic. This required something more direct. It was personal, and it required pain. The throb of the circle came to an abrupt halt. The torchlight reflecting on the sarsens slowly changed from blue to yellow.

"I thought that was what you said. Thank you for saying it. You're right. You've spoken the truth to me, but it may not be the truth you think it is." Aura paused. "I know who you are now, and you're standing between me and what I want."

"It doesn't matter," the phantom said, shrugging.

Aura walked up to the double. "Permit me to refresh *your* memory," she said. She clenched her fists. "I lived in a barrel behind Ortha's Bakery for two years." She tightened the muscles of her arms. "Not everyone in Hartshorn was nice, especially some of the boatmen who docked at our wharves." She bent her knees. "I remained a virgin the whole time." She shifted her weight to her left leg. "It wasn't because I could run fast, either. Don't you remember how I did it?"

She waited until horror dawned in the phantom's eyes. Then, Aura belted her in the stomach with her left fist. With a whuff, the phantom doubled over. Aura threw her full weight into her right arm. She lashed out and up, catching the phantom underneath the chin. That blow put several boys on their backs, but they were young and only thought

340

themselves tough. Aura knew how much physical abuse she had received, and how much she could take. Two bitter winters spent in a barrel toughened her constitution. Years of cutting wood, digging herbs, lifting kegs of ale, and running to keep up with her long-legged master gave her strong muscles beneath the curves. Her own recent Divine Thunderbolt spell left her numb to lesser pain. The phantom would recover within moments, if given the opportunity. Aura had no inclination to give her that opportunity. In quick succession, Aura slammed her fists into the phantom's jaw. She pushed her back with each blow.

Minutes of anguish became years of fury. So, this was what she had to face. This was what the stone circle wanted to show her. She had to see a physical embodiment of how she saw herself. She hated what she saw. With each blow, loathing poured from her heart and into her fist, not at herself but at how she saw herself. It may take years to see herself as worthy of her home, her friends, and perhaps the attention of someone like Manfred Rowanwand. Until she could finally defeat that image, she would give it a beating she would never forget. Aura's hands ached. The skin split across the knuckles. Blood oozed between her fingers. She continued to pummel her own image, until the phantom stood against the western stone. The phantom weaved on uncertain feet, supported only by the granite behind her. With a shout, Aura threw a right cross at the phantom's face. It was a bit high. Her nose exploded in a cloud of blood.

Aura grabbed the phantom by the collar of her tattered blouse and slammed her against the stone. "Sometimes, flesh and bone are more effective than magic!" She smashed the phantom against the stone a second time. "You say I created you? Then, listen to me. I am going to destroy you. The artist has that right. I'm going to erase every brush stroke and every chisel mark, replacing them with what I want to see. That way, when I do look into a mirror, and I will, I don't see you!"

The phantom smiled. Blood oozed from her mouth, mingling with the torrent pouring from her nose. "I love it when you get your Lockhaven up. Tell me, can you maintain this attitude? Can you keep this resolve? I am you, but unlike you, I'm not restricted by the gulf between mind and heart. I'm nothing but pure perception and intuition, and what I perceive and intuit isn't blocked by what I think I know." She spat out a tooth, and wiped her bloody mouth with the back of her hand. Looking at Aura, she grinned. "You're going to need all this attitude and resolve. I know things that you don't. Trust me. You won't like them."

The phantom giggled, although with a throat full of blood, it sounded more like a gurgle. Then, she vanished, leaving Aura clutching air and staring at stone.

Chapter Twenty-Nine

NAURELIA LED AURA back to Ardora Hall. The Eorless said and asked nothing. Aura was grateful. She trembled as they walked, but couldn't tell if it was from fear, fury, or exhaustion. As they walked, Aura pondered the phantom. She had seen and faced the image of herself, one etched in her heart. It was beyond ugly. Hideous did not even describe it with any accuracy. Now that she knew, she could change it. She was so lost in her own thoughts, that she stood on the veranda before even realizing they had left the clearing with the stone circle.

"It is not for me to know what you saw, Aura, dear," Naurelia said, snuffing the lantern. "Based on your countenance, I take it that it was unpleasant. Feel free to wander about the manor to clear your head and think. Help yourself to the wine and ale in the kitchen. Just stay out of my private chambers and my workshop. Oh, also, I don't recommend that you walk through the rose garden at night. It lies outside the troll barrier."

"Troll barrier?" Aura asked, stammering as her mind returned to the present. "Surely, Lady Naurelia, someone of your intelligence does not believe in trolls."

Naurelia did not frown or smile. She simply said, "Good night, Aura. I will see you in the morning." With that, Naurelia entered the manor, and faded into the darkness of the house beyond, leaving Aura alone on the veranda.

Aura wanted to think about the phantom, and about how to erase the image in her mind. For that, she needed fortification. Entering the dining hall, she guessed that the kitchen lay through the door to the left. A single torch, growing dim in its dying fuel, cast enough light for her to see. She searched for the wine rack. Half the kitchen was a wine rack, endless rows of red, white, pink, and purple wines. She selected one that did not look too fine.

After opening the bottle, and sniffing it to verify that it was indeed wine and not an explosive tincture, she walked back toward the veranda. She passed the statue and paused. Twin candles in sconces cast a dimming yellow light across the room, sending an ethereal, yet almost creepy, shadow of the statue to the other wall. Since no one was around, Aura walked up to it. In a way, the statue was similar to the phantom. It was a copy of someone else, wrought over time, stroke by stroke. Unlike the phantom's artist, however, the sculptor had captured the essence of masculine perfection, instead of disfigured wretchedness.

Sighing, Aura stepped out onto the veranda. The torches extinguished, it lay in thick shadow, cut only by the light of the half moon. Forgetting to grab a goblet, she decided to do what she would have done back in Hartshorn. She drank from the bottle, tasting the sharp, yet sweet, flavor of grapes. She had chosen a fine red, finer than any she had ever tasted. Her father specialized in ale, beer, and mead, but had taught her something about wines. This one tasted like it had been pressed twenty years ago of the best grapes available. Rubbing the bottle, she felt no dust. At least, it was not an old vintage. Perhaps, Naurelia would not miss this one. Better still, Aura thought, perhaps this was a noblewoman's idea of garbage.

Sitting on the corner of the veranda, she leaned against one of the columns. Caressing its rough bark, she allowed her fingers to know the tree and not think about how it felt. She hugged it and smiled. Who thought about building a house inside a grove of trees, she wondered. Was this the Eorl's ancestral seat, or a new house? It was so hard to tell about trees. They held their age well and guarded their secrets even better. Even after ten years, the mighty oaks, maples, rowans, and larches on the Big Hedge still held their own counsel, but she could coax wisdom from them by climbing into their branches and listening. She listened now, to the tree next to her. It said nothing, only a faint whisper of expectancy. Young trees. They were so much like young men, always looking at tomorrow.

With another sigh, Aura drew the ruby from the pocket of her sleeve. Sagacius gave it to her to guide her. Tonight, she needed guidance. She asked it, "What can you show me?" The moonlight struck her face, reflecting her image in the center facet. She stared at the tiny, red-tinted image. In the stone, she thought she looked lovely. The ruby said nothing.

"How do people see me?" she asked. Again, all she saw was her own reflection.

"How should I see myself?" One more time, only her reflection.

"You aren't very helpful," Aura muttered, returning the ruby to her pocket.

Her fingertips brushed the damasara petal. She drew it from her sleeve. It had dried a bit in her pocket, giving it a leathery feel. As the moisture left, its power began to concentrate. She twisted the petal in her fingers, looking at it in the available light. It seemed to glow, even brighter than the ruby.

She knew four love potions. The first, she learned only so she could avoid it. That one made someone fall in love with the spellcaster. Manipulative, and prone to reversing itself, it lay in the realm of the sorcerers, and even they hated it. The other three prepared the spellcaster to give and receive love. It helped the spellcaster see herself as worthy of being loved. If she was on a path to discover Aura Lockhaven, one thing she already knew is that she did not feel worthy, but she wanted to. She especially wanted to feel worthy of her own love toward herself. Perhaps, this single damasara petal would help.

She couldn't help but think about Manfred. Her cheeks flushed as she thought about him perhaps a bit too much. He was everything she wanted in a man. He was kind, thoughtful, a good talker, and handsome. He was also considerate. She had thrown herself at him, and he resisted. Far too many other men would have seized the opportunity to kiss her, and lead her into the forest to do more than just kiss. Aura knew he wanted to do just that. It radiated out from him like heat from burning coal. Yet, he had put her safety ahead of his own desires. She liked that. Perhaps, however, Manfred was simply the one she wanted today, and not the one she needed for life. He may just be in her present as a friend, a surrogate counselor in

Sagacius' stead, and to set a standard for how she should be treated. That, she could live with.

"Little friend," Aura said to the petal. "Help me see myself as I am. Help prepare me for the man who will love all of me. Help prepare me for myself."

Then, she popped the petal into her mouth. She swallowed it whole. Sagacius hadn't taught her that. Every girl in Hartshorn ate the final petal at the end of the game "he loves me," except the flowers were daisies.

"Well, I'm going to be either so loving that I disgust even optimists, or so peaceful that a house full of balakalats won't scare me."

Voices behind her interrupted her thoughts, voices coming from the house. Choosing to ignore what sounded like an argument, she stared out into the clearing. Then, she heard her name. Two women talked about her. Aura stood up and crept toward the door to listen. She ducked behind the doorframe as two figures strode into the chamber housing the statue. Naurelia led Miriam, and from the stern way she entered the room, and her animated gestures, Aura guessed that the Eorless was not happy.

"Miriam, stop telling me what to do!" Naurelia snapped.

"I am just reminding you of your promise to Master Sagacius, Milady. You almost spilled the secret to Mistress Aura this morning," Miriam said.

Aura pressed herself against the exterior wall of the house, keeping all but the edge of her face hidden by the doorframe. She watched the two women with her right eye, trying her best to keep out of sight. If they were talking about her, then she wanted to know what they said without giving her presence away.

"I remember my promise," Naurelia said, spinning to face Miriam. "Do you think I'd betray my own brother?"

Aura pressed herself closer to the wall and made sure that she cast no shadow from the dying torches on the veranda. The last thing she wanted now was for Naurelia or Miriam to detect her. This sounded intriguing, if not odd.

"Milady, I know how you feel, but how do you know Mistress Aura is the enchantress of promise?"

"You've heard me say this a thousand times, Miriam. Damaskarose died in my arms. With her last breath, she said, *There is one coming who will be the most powerful enchantress who ever lived. The hope of the Order rests in her hands.* I know how powerful Damaskarose was," Naurelia said, caressing the extended arm of the statue. "Even now, I am only a tenth of that woman. I watched her teach Sagacius how to duel and she flattened him for twenty years, and he is our greatest duelist. Yet, Aura makes Damaskarose look like a mere stable lass!"

A shiver ran up Aura's back. How was that even possible, she thought. She was a wizardress, not an enchantress, at least, not yet. How could she have more power than the legendary Damaskarose?

"How do you know, Milady?" Miriam asked.

"I felt her, Miriam. I could not feel the end of Aura's great love for people. She has the largest heart of anyone I have ever met. You know of the people she healed in her hometown. You know she defeated a balakalat. This morning, during her trance, she pushed her visions into me, despite my efforts to shield myself from them."

"Perhaps you pulled those visions into yourself," Miriam said.

"Miriam, I do know the difference between a pull and a push. You know how strong my mental shield is, yes, yes. Yet, she still broke through it. I saw everything she saw. Aura said that none of her visions were about magic. If you had seen what I saw, you would know that every one of those visions was about magic. Aura lives for one thing, to help those who cannot help themselves. It doesn't matter if she uses a spell or her hands, her very being changes circumstances to conform with her will, and her will is compassion. Aura is still a novice to our ways. I imagine that in ten years, she will be a force of nature." Naurelia paused before saying, "Tonight, the stone circle summoned her."

Miriam gasped. "It summoned her? You did not send her there like you have all your students?"

"I did not. Aura is not my student. I am teaching her, but as a peer, not an apprentice. The circle summoned her, and it was most insistent. It only summons those it feels are worthy. Aura is most certainly worthy. In a manner of speaking, she outranks me. She is, after all, a Nightshade."

Aura bit her lip to stifle her moan. There is was, that name. It just had to surface. Why couldn't her mother have been named Smith or Branson or something common. Yes, Aurora Nightshade was a Nightshade, but that did not mean she descended from *the* Albert Nightshade. Manfred was right. There were too many people, and not enough surnames. Not everyone even had a surname.

"There is something else in her, Miriam. Something I have never encountered, something I cannot define. During her trance, when she pushed her visions into me, I briefly flicked her soul with my mental fingertip. It was as if I touched the face of a god."

"We know who her parents were," Miriam said. "I doubt if a brewer and a seamstress were gods in disguise. Besides, the gods no longer visit mortals."

"I was invoking a metaphor, Miriam!" Naurelia snapped. "Why wouldn't I?"

"That may not qualify as a metaphor, Milady," Miriam said.

"Never mind. It will take Aura some time to grow into her role. I could flay her with just one spell today, but that could change overnight. In time, she will defeat me with ease. All she has to do is learn to be who she is."

Who am I? Aura asked herself. Or, she thought she asked herself. When Naurelia and Miriam jerked their heads toward the door to the veranda, Aura realized she said it aloud.

"Miriam, where is Aura?" Naurelia asked.

"I heard her retire," the handmaiden answered.

"I can't feel her for some reason. I need you to feel for her."

Miriam stiffened. Aura saw her look right at her. She moved slowly to the left, trying to blend into the frame of the door, yet not let her motions be noticeable. Willing for Miriam to be blind to her presence, she held her breath and wished invisibility spells were real.

"Mistress Aura is right where she should be," Miriam said.

"Good," Naurelia said. "There for a minute –"

"All is well, Milady," Miriam said, turning to Naurelia.

Aura exhaled, making sure it remained silent.

Naurelia grabbed Miriam by the shoulders and said, "I touched her, Miriam! She is right here, under my roof! You don't know what that means to me. I've lived to see the manifestation of Damaskarose's prophecy."

"Couldn't Mistress Aura just be the most powerful enchantress you've met so far?" Miriam asked.

Naurelia hugged Miriam. As the Eorless pulled back, she said, "Oh, Miriam! I love you. And not because you are my most stellar student. I love your optimism, your courage, your sense of wonder. You are young, Miriam, and prophecies are not for the young. The young have tomorrow. They have dreams and hope. Prophecies are for the old, Miriam. For people who have only yesterday, for people whose dreams have become bitter nightmares, and for people who forgot the flavor of hope. They are for people like me. That prophecy helps me remember how to dream. Aura reminds me of the flavor of hope," she said.

Aura watched the Eorless walk up to the statue and kiss it on the lips. She heard Naurelia say, "Good night, beloved. I still have dreams and I still have hope."

Aura stared in disbelief. These people believed in trolls. They lived with a balakalat for years and never noticed. They believed strange prophecies. Now, they kissed statues, too.

"Excellent. Yes, yes. Aura *is* the most powerful enchantress who ever lived. That was prophesied, and no one can stop a prophecy. Not you, not me, not Etheria. Not even Aura Lockhaven herself. She is the most powerful enchantress who ever lived and I mean to see that she fulfills her destiny. I owe that to my mother."

Aura watched Naurelia and Miriam leave the room and mount the staircase. At the bottom of the stairs, Miriam turned and looked toward the door. Aura remained still. She was part of the door, one of the living trees that formed the wall. Then, Miriam ascended the stairs. She listened for the sounds from upstairs. One, then two doors closing in the darkness. Aura whirled and flattened her back against the wall of the house.

"Oh, merciful heavens! She thinks I'm some strange reincarnation or some fulfillment of prophecy," Aura said.

Sagacius hated prophecies. He read them to Aura, but always prefaced them with a warning not to take them literally. Her master had ordered her to read the Word of Irican. She loved looking at the magnificent illuminations on every page, although the language eluded her. Sagacius often translated it, and the prophecies terrified her. Too many cases of "do this or die" and "this will happen and you can't stop it." The prophecies of the Nebels and Aitians also terrified her. Too many gods treating mortals as little dolls on strings. Why bother having a will if you have no choice, Aura often asked Sagacius. At least the Gweryn had the decency to not spew prophecies.

Aura leaned back against the wall of the house. She closed her eyes. Inhaling and exhaling in slow rhythmic breaths, she pushed her anger down into her legs and out the soles of her feet into the veranda. When the last finger of the fiery glove of anger left her, she opened her eyes. Only she did not feel calm. A scent drifted underneath her nostrils. It was not the aroma of the roses or the evening nightshade. It was the stench of searing human flesh and burning wood.

"No, not now!" Aura said.

Trembling uncontrollably, Aura slid down the wall and sat on the floor. She pulled her knees to her chest and took several swallows from the wine bottle. Her hands shook as if from palsy, spilling wine across her cheeks. Tears formed on their own, drifting down the side of her nose.

Her terror attacks always began when the threats of being alone or living without a home presented themselves. The fight with Mayenne showed her that they also happened when she was threatened with violation. Neither had happened. This was different. This was as if she already lived back in the alley, sleeping in a barrel, and wondering if she would wake up covered in spiders. This was dread, the awful feeling of helplessness she once faced every day, trying to live in a situation beyond her control.

"No," Aura mumbled. "No! I refuse. I will not accept this. Naurelia believes what she believes. That doesn't mean it's true."

Aura closed her eyes, inhaled and exhaled, and willed the fear to leave her. The fear refused to depart. Instead, it grew stronger with each breath. The most powerful enchantress who ever lived. They were just words. Words could not hurt her. Dead women could not hurt her. No one could force her to be something she did not want to be. Even if that person held a sword to her throat, she still had the right to refuse. Then, all he would have would be her dead body. The most powerful enchantress who ever lived.

She was Aura Lockhaven. Naurelia wasn't woman enough to thwart her. Back home in Hartshorn, she frightened people with her eyes, and intimidated people with her height. She was no longer in Hartshorn. Perhaps these people could thwart her. They knew more than she did about their form of magic, while she knew so little. Glancing around to see if any eyes were upon her body, Aura felt exposed. She felt vulnerable. They did not care about her eye color or her height. They cared about other things. She was the Dyrgana, the searcher, the one who knew nothing. They had her. This madwoman had her and they both knew it. The most powerful enchantress who ever lived.

Dread turned into despair. She gulped from the bottle, sloshing wine over her face and chest. The most powerful enchantress who ever lived. Aura knew enough about herself to realize she could not spot manipulation. Three men manipulated her into bed with their words. Mayenne manipulated her by complementing her eyes. The men wanted her body. Mayenne wanted her soul. Naurelia wanted everything. How far would someone go to manipulate another to gain everything? The most powerful enchantress who ever lived!

Aura screwed her eyes shut before she saw spiders on her body. Trying to control her shaking body, she stammered, "I don't want to be the most powerful enchantress who ever lived!"

Aura took a deep swig from the bottle. She clutched the bottle to her chest and rocked back and forth.

Chapter Thirty

AURA BARELY SLEPT during the night, tormented by a neverending round of *the most powerful enchantress who ever lived*. When she did fall asleep, she dreamed. In her dreams, she stood stark naked on top of a mountain. She drove the Sun and Moon from the blackened sky. Flames poured from her fingertips and flowed down the sides of the mountain, toward a village at its foot. The flames consumed a house, drenching children in fire. At that point in every dream, she sat up in bed, gasping. Usually, whenever she had a nightmare, she awoke drenched in sweat. Last night, she remained as dry as sand. Even her perspiration was too terrified of the prophecy to show itself.

She lay on her side, with her knees drawn up to her chest, staring out the window. The night sky slowly changed to the color of blued steel. The first mockingbird of day sang. Soon, the t'Ardora household would stagger to life. Juhnn would go about trimming the lantern wicks and replacing candles. Lurna would prepare breakfast. Banya would drive any dust out of the manor. Miriam would do whatever she could to assist Naurelia in her tasks of inventing and caring for an entire shire. Manfred, although a guest, had his own routines in Ardora Hall, items of business that kept him out of Aura's sight for most of the day. As for Aura herself, she now faced her greatest challenge in recent memory. She had to comport herself in Naurelia's presence without even hinting that she overheard last night's conversation or knew anything about any prophecies. Until she recovered from the shock, she wasn't sure she wanted to admit such knowledge to herself.

Memories of the phantom would have kept her awake anyway. At least, the night would have passed without nightmares, unless she dreamed of losing her fight with herself. No matter how she turned that possibility around, she ended up either losing the fight with herself, or winning it.

There was no other alternative when fighting oneself. With that thought, she sat up. The sounds drifting up the stairs and through her door told her that she alone remained in bed. It was time to face whatever the day brought.

"I need an outrageous lie," Aura mumbled. She knew what she would tell Naurelia, and hoped the Eorless did not have the ability to detect falsehood.

Her left leg no longer ached. It worked perfectly. Her sleep deprived feet did not. She stumbled down the stairs, to find Naurelia standing on the veranda, reading a note. The Eorless looked up at Aura. Her smile faded into a frown.

"Aura dear, you look terrible," Naurelia said. "Your eyes are dark. Did you not sleep well?"

Aura swallowed. "No. I know you said what I saw and heard inside the stone circle was for my eyes and ears alone, but I need to tell you. I saw myself. I hated what I saw. It kept me awake all night."

"You faced your greatest enemy, didn't you?" Naurelia asked. Aura nodded. "That may keep you awake for a week. If it had been within my power, I would not have subjected you to such torment. It was all the circle's doing, and its wisdom is supreme. Well, I planned to teach you about intuition today, but I think that will wait. Yes, yes. As tired as you are, you may intuit too much, too little, or the wrong thing. So, we will do that tomorrow." She returned to the note in her hand. With a deep sigh, she said, "Besides, I myself am distracted."

Seeing the perfect opportunity to change the subject, Aura asked, "Is there anything I can do to help?"

"Not with this," she said, casually waving the note. "A basket weaver on the other side of Ardora sent this to me. His son is deathly ill, and wants me to come heal him."

"Would you like me to go with you?"

Naurelia cast her a cold glare. In an even colder voice, she said, "I am not going."

"You are sending someone else."

"I am sending no one," Naurelia said.

"But the boy may die," Aura said with a gasp.

"If he dies, he dies. What is that to me?" Naurelia sighed. "Aura, the basket weaver was expelled from the Order. He is an outcast. You think Geilltians are trash? We of the Order think outcasts are worse trash. If the boy dies, then that rids the Valley of one more piece of trash."

"I don't believe you!" Aura shouted. "He's a boy! What his father did doesn't concern him."

"Believe me or not, that is my decision. I would rather mate with a leper than visit an outcast. The sins of the father are upon the sons. That is the law of the Order."

Aura put her hands on her hips and glared at Naurelia. "If you won't help him, then I will."

"You will most certainly do no such thing, Aura Lockhaven!" Naurelia snapped. "You are practically a member of the Order and our laws are binding upon you."

"You said so yourself that I may bend them a little."

"This is not bending our law. It is breaking it."

Aura tilted her head back. She pulled herself up to her full height. Constraining her anger, she said, "I am willing to break the law to save a life."

Naurelia regarded Aura with an impassive stare. Finally, she said, "So be it. Go! The consequences are upon your head alone. You will find the basket weaver in a white cottage on the far side of the bridge over the River Phant."

Aura stormed up the stairs. Fury flowed through her. This was the Order of Love? Sagacius had been right. The Order was corrupted. Naurelia did not just apprentice to Damaskarose, she had been raised by her. How quickly one generation forgets the one that came before. That woman often said to defend the defenseless. A sick boy wasn't merely defenseless. He was innocent.

She slammed the door to her room open. Grabbing her bag and staff, she rushed back down the stairs. Phantom be damned. Prophecy be damned. A dying boy was more important than anything that she faced during the night. Laws be damned. If the Order cast her out for this, then she could return home with her head held high. At the bottom of the stairs, she collided with Manfred, and sprawled across the floor.

"Rushing off somewhere, are you?" Manfred asked, helping Aura to her feet.

"Yes, I am going to heal a sick boy," she said.

"Well, by the time you return, I will have departed. I was due in Grahbale yesterday. Someone has to save the town from Mandrake's atrocious cooking." He took Aura's hand in his and lifted it to his lips. She blushed. "It was a pleasure finally meeting you. I'm sure your quest will take you through Grahbale. When it does, please visit Rowanwand Tavern. Mandrake would love to meet you, too. Until then, I hope to see you again."

"I hope to see you again, too," Aura said, knowing that phrase meant more to her than it did to him. By the time she returned, she might be an outcast herself. If the Order did expel her, then perhaps Grahbale would make a good place to think before returning home. That is, unless Manfred shared Naurelia's view of outcasts.

"May your gods go with you, Aura Lockhaven," he said, ascending the stairs.

Blister's hoof beats changed from a thud to a clop as he stepped from clay to stone. Square cut granite formed the bridge, with its curve over the River Phant, supported by twin arches. The river flowed thirty feet beneath the bridge, in a deep gully of red clay and granite, its water dark brown, and seductive in deadly ways. A poll barge passed beneath the left arch, the crew leaning leisurely against the rails, letting the river itself carry them forward. A second barge followed five lengths astern. The men in the trailing barge shouted to Aura.

"Awa, look at the bonnie lass," one yelled, pointing up at Aura.

"Aye, and the girl's pretty, too!" another bellowed.

"I was talking about the girl!"

"You can't tell the diff'rence 'tween a girl and a harse, ya blind oaf!"

Aura chuckled as the first crewman's oaths echoed off the granite walls of the river. She returned the crew's greetings with a wave and a broad grin. From her left, Aura saw a small river cog heading upriver hugging the far shore. The sailors on the cog launched into a rowdy version of "Sassy Tavern Maid." The relaxing crew of the barge headed downriver responded with "Boatman's Chant." The cog captain's defiant roar of "We'll see who sweats on your trip upriver, you mutts!" echoed throughout the gully. Aura smiled. The boatmen of the Gourdvine were the same, full of strong muscles, strong pride, and later in the evening, strong ale.

On the other side of the bridge, Aura spotted her destination. A neat cottage stood by the side of the road, nestled in a grove of oaks, maples, and poplars. One story tall, with whitewashed stone walls, it lay behind a thicket of rose bushes. Its trimmed thatch roof looked new. Green shutters lay open. In front of the green door, a man sat cradling a limp six year old boy. The man rocked back and forth. Aura reined Blister toward the cottage.

The man spotted Aura and cried out, "Please, miss! Help me!"

"That is why I'm here," Aura replied, bringing Blister to a halt. Jumping from the saddle, she tethered the stallion to a post. Grabbing her staff, she ran to the man's side. The man looked to be in late 50s, his face withered with care and sorrow. His black eyes held no life. His blonde hair hung in limp strands against his sorrow ravaged face, mingling with his short beard.

"What's wrong with him?" Aura asked, kneeling by the man. She put her hand on the child's brow. The boy burned with fever.

"I don't know," the man said. "He complained of not feeling well yesterday. Today, he hasn't woken up. Please. Can you help my son?"

"Your son?" Aura asked. She expected the boy to be the man's grandson.

"A young wife to comfort an old man. She gave me a son," he said.

"Where is your wife now?" Aura asked. Her stomach tightened in anticipation of the answer.

"Away visiting her sister in Cheddarport. Please, don't let her come home to find her son dead."

Relieved that the mother still lived, she said, "Bring him inside."

The man held his child in his arms and led Aura inside the house. As neat inside as it was outside, the cottage smelled of wood and fresh bread. The few pieces of furniture in the sitting chamber looked clean and well placed. The man entered a small bedroom. The child's arms and legs hung from him as if broken. Laying him on the bed, the man arranged the boy's limbs, then carefully set his head on the pillow. The boy did not move.

Standing up, the man looked even more careworn, hunkered under a great invisible weight. His clothes of undyed linen hung on him as if cut for someone much larger. He looked down on his unmoving child with an expression of resignation. Aura knew that look. She had seen it on her own father in the month between Ester's death and his own. Leaning her staff against the wall, she sat down on the bed next to the boy, dropping her bag to the floor.

Thick sweat covered the boy's face and body like honey. Fever filled his sunken cheeks. His stomach bulged like that of a pudgy glutton. It didn't match his thin arms and legs, nor his neck. Aura frowned.

"What has this child had to eat?" Aura asked the father.

"Porridge, yesterday morning," the man answered.

"Before then."

"Lampern pie the night before last."

Aura made a face and turned to the wall. Not fond of any fish, she especially hated lamperns. They looked like eels and acted like maggots, burrowing into their host. Seeing a catch of them in Vine Haven, wriggling in the net like giant worms, was enough to last the rest of her life. The mere thought of putting such in her mouth made her want to vomit on the cottage floor. Then, she stiffened. Lamperns lived in the estuaries of rivers, near the coast. She never heard of them upriver. If they didn't live in the relative calm of the Gourdvine near Hartshorn, they definitely would not like the rushing Phant. The lamperns had to have been brought into the Valley from the outside, by cart or by foot, in the increasing heat of spring.

"Your son has food poisoning," Aura said, standing up. She walked up to the man. "Those lamperns were tainted. Lift your shirt, please." The man did as he was told. His stomach had begun to bulge in a way that also did not match the rest of his body. "You have it, too, but you may not feel it yet. You're much taller and older. By nightfall, you will be doubled over in agony."

"That's what I get for thinking I can cook," the man mumbled.

Aura turned back to the unconscious boy. She thought about using the same force to heal the child that she had with Lodd and Sire Thaddeus. That force still lay outside her control, much less her full knowledge. She glanced at her staff, leaning against the wall. One swift spell and this child would skip away singing. Then again, she had only used the staff to shatter boulders. The boy needed to be healed, not pulverized. Diseases were not like injuries. They responded well to the slower forms of healing spells and potions. The boy needed something Aura spent ten years learning to do.

"I don't suppose you have many herbs or stones?" she asked.

"What do you want with those?" the basket weaver asked.

"I'm a wizardess. I heal with herbs and stones."

"Oh, how quaint. The Eorless sent an old fashioned witch," he said, in a mocking tone. "Well, that might be better, considering the Order seems to have forgotten everything. No, I am a basket weaver. I have a few herbs for the stew, and the only stones are in the walls."

Grabbing her staff and purse, Aura said, "I'm riding into Ardora. I need a few things. Keep a cold, wet rag on his face. Also, bathe his feet. It will lower the fever. I will return as soon as I can." Seeing the concern on the father's face, Aura smiled and said, "Don't worry. I will return!"

Aura strode from the cottage, grumbling. Someone as powerful as Naurelia could have healed father and son within minutes. Fine. If the enchantress would not bend her rules, then the wizardess would. Stuffing her staff into the sling, she untethered Blister. She climbed into the saddle, and turned the stallion toward the road. Tightening her thighs, and leaning forward, Aura said, "It's time to live up to your name."

Blister nickered and bolted from the yard. Making the sharp turn onto the road at a fast trot, he almost threw Aura from the saddle. The stallion broke into a full gallop. Keeping one hand tight around the reins, she gripped his mane with her other. If she fell off, she might have to heal herself from a broken neck. Blister stormed across the bridge. If any of the barge or cog crews shouted a greeting, she did not hear it. Aura leaned further forward. Her hair flew behind her. On the other side, they shot past a farmer leading a cart full of melons toward Ardora. Horses grazing neighed as stallion and rider raced by the farm.

Slowing Blister to a fast walk, Aura entered town. The mixture of people, horses, and carts ambled along in front of horse and rider. A few passersby stared at the tall redhaired woman. Ahead, on the right, she spotted the sign for Ardora Crystal and Stone Company. Tethering Blister to the post in front, she entered the store. In most times, Aura would have spent an hour wandering around, touching everything, feeling the warmth and power of the stones. Today, she walked straight to the clerk and asked for his shelf of greenspar. He led her to a table of thirty crystals of different sizes and shapes.

She lifted each one, looking for the right feel in her hand. As she did, two men, wearing far too much gold and far too little cloth, walked by on the other side of the table. One said to the other, "I swear, it was up in Dallington. Itty bitty Dallington. This girl killed a dragon. That thing had claws like this and was covered in oily fur. Half lizard, half wolf, all ugly. Disguised itself as a staffmaker, can you believe it?" Dumbfounded, Aura watched the two men wander around the shop. With each word, Mayenne grew more bizarre. "I hear the girl was some witch from out of town. She roasted that dragon alive. Oh, they say she was six feet tall and had fire for hair." Apparently, Aura grew more bizarre, too. So, this was how tavern songs began.

"Oh, merciful heavens," she muttered. If the bard at Chester's sang about "The Redheaded Witch and the Dragon Bitch," she'd duck underneath the table. Until then, she had a son and father to heal. She returned to her work. She found a greenspar the size of her fist. Raw, and uncut, its glare looked like emerald fire. She felt a mild tingling in her left leg. If it sucked lingering infirmity from a healthy woman, it would certainly draw sickness from an ill child.

The stone cost Aura five coppers. She almost choked on the price, but she remembered her father. Henry Lockhaven bore the death of Richard with the grace of a man whose son died honorably defending his people. Ester's death destroyed him, reducing him to a ruin held together by the mortar of his remaining child. She did not want the basket weaver to face the same thing, so she plopped the coin on the counter and stuffed the greenspar into her bag. If she could buy a child's life for mere copper, it was coin well spent.

Across the street lay Grace's Herbs. Leaving Blister tethered in front of the crystal store, Aura entered the herbalist's shop. Again, on most days, she would have spent an hour meandering from jar to jar, sniffing the contents and letting her mind wander as the aromas tickled her nose. Today, she walked straight to the clerk and placed her order. She emerged a few minutes later, shy ten coppers, and carrying a bundle of black dwale, willow bark, Notting's Cap, Kensey spindle, and sage. Purple dwale worked twice as fast, but the shop had sold out of it. Black dwale would suffice. After dashing to the shop next door for a mortar and pestle, and to the wine shop beyond it, Aura returned to Blister, her bag bulging with new purchases. The mortar and pestle ought to be cleansed under the light of the full moon, or at least in salt water. Apothecaries didn't bother, and she had no time.

A few minutes later, a sweating Blister came to a stop outside the basket weaver's cottage. Aura hugged the stallion before dashing inside. The father had obeyed her instructions, bathing the boy's forehead and feet. He felt cooler beneath Aura's hand.

"I'm going to perform a ritual now and brew a potion," Aura said. "When a thing is named, it can be controlled. I know the name of the disease, but what is your son's name?"

"Maedyan. Mine is Misthyde," he replied.

Aura looked down at the unconscious boy and said, "Maedyan, hear me! You will live! You will awaken! You will feel much better!"

Placing her bag on the table next to the bed, she removed the bottle of wine, the stone, the bag of herbs, and the mortar and pestle. Then, she faced east. Spreading her arms wide, she closed her eyes. She sang out, "I call to the spirit of the east, to the spirit of Air. You are the breath in our lungs. I ask that you guide me so Maedyan may live."

She turned to her right, and sang, "I call to the spirit of the south, to the spirit of Fire. You are the spark within us all. I ask that you guide me so Maedyan may live."

Turning again, Aura sang, "I call to the spirit of the west, to the spirit of Water. You are the blood in our veins. I ask that you guide me so Maedyan may live."

Facing north, she sang, "I call to the spirit of the north, to the spirit of Earth. You gave us our bodies. I ask that you guide me so Maedyan may live."

Facing upwards, Aura sang, "I call to the spirit of above, to the spirit of Light. You are the vision in our eyes. I ask that you guide me so Maedyan may live."

To the final direction, Aura chimed, "I call to the spirit of below, to the spirit of Metal. You are the strength in our bones. I ask that you guide me so Maedyan may live."

Turning to face east once again, Aura looked up. "Great Adphyr, god of healing. I ask that you guide my mind, my heart, and my hands. Please, sir. Let Maedyan live."

She knew quite a few healing potions, but this boy required something special. Food poisoning worked fast. The potion needed to work faster. She had all the necessary ingredients to brew the most effective, and most disgusting, healing potion in her catalog.

"I need two cups, a lit candle, and a small shallow dish," Aura said to Misthyde.

The basket weaver returned with two clay goblets, and a saucer. He lit the candle on the table next to the bed with a broom straw held in the sitting room fireplace. Aura worked up a mouth full of saliva and spat into each cup. For once, her spittle made it past her lips without falling on her chest. Misthyde winced. Looking at the globs of spit in each mug, she wanted to wince, too. Yes, the most disgusting potion in her catalog. As vile as it looked, it would put her life inside the boy, her health inside his illness. Picking up the mortar and pestle, and the bag of herbs, she sat on the edge of the bed. She put four thick pinches of each herb, and eight of the black dwale, into the mortar. Then, she ground them into fine powder. Pouring the mixed herbs into the saucer, she divided them in half, then one half yet again. She poured the smaller portions into the two cups. Finally, she filled the cups with wine. Sloshing the cups counter-sunwise, she stirred the mixture as best she could without a spoon.

Lifting the two goblets over her head, Aura closed her eyes. She imagined her vitality as a ball of red light, pushing it up her arms into her hands and out into the cups. Maedyan is healed. Maedyan is healed! *Maedyan is healed!* She sang out, "Ekos entola plagos epolotha natara!" The cups shook in her hands as the potion bubbled from the heat of her vitality flowing into them.

She handed one to the basket weaver and said, "Drink this. It's all you need."

"But it has *stuff* in it," Misthyde said, whining.

Aura glared at Misthyde. She drew herself up into the full authority of the wizardess, squaring her shoulders and setting her jaw. Putting an edge into her voice, one she had heard from Sagacius more times than she could count, she said, "You wish to die. You wish for your wife to return home to find her son alive, but her husband dead. You wish for your son to be fatherless. If those are your wishes, then by all means, don't drink it."

Misthyde bolted the potion. Aura held the candle to the remaining powder in the saucer, until it caught. Blowing across the flames, she reduced the fire to mere sparks, which turned the powder into incense. She wrinkled her nose. Black dwale, when burned, smelled like a pile of unwashed stockings. Misthyde grumbled as she passed the smudging incense under his nose, and blew the smoke into his face. She did the same with the boy, blowing even more across his face, and down his body to his stomach. Then, she passed the greenspar crystal through the smoke. Setting the saucer on the table, she let it burn itself out.

Sitting on the bed, Aura lifted the boy's head. She poured the potion sip by sip into the child's mouth. Even unconscious, Maedyan swallowed. Laying his head back on the pillow, Aura reached for her greenspar. She put the crystal underneath the boy's tunic, on top of his stomach.

"Little friend, please draw the poisons from Maedyan's body," she said to the stone.

Then, Aura placed one hand on the child's forehead and another on the stone. She chanted, "Ekos entola plagos epolotha natara!" The heat of her vitality flowed through her arms and hands and into Maedyan. The child shook under the force of the spell.

The boy moaned. He opened his eyes. Looking at the basket weaver, Maedyan mumbled, "Daddy?"

"You did it!" Misthyde yelled. "Thank you so much!"

"We will celebrate in an hour," Aura said.

An hour later, Aura shouldered her bag and picked up her staff. Maedyan sat on the edge of the bed, his feet swinging in the air, sipping a cup of chicken broth while holding the greenspar in his other hand. Misthyde was nowhere to be seen. With a smile, and a final mussing of Maedyan's hair, Aura turned toward the door.

"Before you depart, join me for tea, Aura Lockhaven of Hartshorn," a man said behind her. The voice sounded the same, but the inflection was different.

Aura turned. Before her stood the basket weaver, but he had changed. No longer hunched in worry, he stood tall. Confidence flowed from his ferocious black eyes. His full hair framed a radiant face. The linen clothes now hugged a muscular body. Care and worry fled from him, transforming him into a powerful man still in his prime.

"How did you ... ? I never told you my name," Aura said.

"You didn't need to," Misthyde said. He smiled a crooked smile, cocked up on the right. His gaze bored through Aura, as if he read her every thought and feeling. "I know all about you, Dyrgana."

Chapter Thirty-One

MISTHYDE TURNED TOWARD the sitting chamber. Calling over his shoulder, he said, "Come with me."

Filled with curiosity, Aura followed. Misthyde led her through the cottage and out the back door. Behind the cottage stood a small hut of whitewashed stone with a tall thatch roof. Lazy smoke drifted from the chimney. Its neat red shutters stood open to the breeze. Lilacs and young garlic lay behind an iron fence surrounding the hut. Misthyde held the red door open for Aura.

Aura thought she entered a museum of magic. Lit only by the fireplace and the open windows, the single room of the hut was packed, leaving just enough room for them to walk. In the center sat two comfortable chairs, pulled up in front of a giant ball of blue crystal. Shelves of ancient books and even more ancient scrolls lined the walls. What shelves did not hold words held other items and tools. Skulls of bats, cats, dogs, wolves, and a few people lay between bags, sacks, boxes, daggers, crystals, pendulums, and wands carved from every recognizable wood, and many that were not. Several globes of the world cast in gold sat on small tables. The rest of the items that filled the shelves, tables, and floor, Aura had never seen in her life.

A map of the Forested Islands dominated one wall. Made from a four foot cross section of an oak tree, each island was carved from crystal. Ayrdland, the big island, with its prominent peninsulas and bays, was of amethyst. Just above it, due north, lay the small star shaped island of Warlden, cut from jet. Bloodstone formed the Eggs and Bennoft to the east of Ayrdland, with green jasper as diamond shaped Emerald just south. To the east, the second largest island, the jagged shape of Garrania, was of red jasper. Caillia, above and between the two larger islands, looked like a glob of wax formed from lapis. Looking like a bouquet of flowers, and carved from garnet, the island of Coadia lay below Garrania and east of Ayrdland. Pearls marked the locations of the capital cities, one on each of the four big islands. Aura smirked. A Geilltian would have placed a pearl in Warlden to identify it as an independent country, but as far as the Ayrdish and King Edgar thought, it was just another shire in their realm.

Aura wanted to stare at the map, but Misthyde beckoned her toward the fireplace. Baskets hung from the rafters on that side of the hut, while an incomplete basket sat on the floor next to a stool and a pile of willow splits. A table with two chairs sat next to the fireplace, a lazy fire dancing underneath a steaming kettle.

"I told you the truth," Misthyde said, leading Aura to the table. He motioned to one of the chairs. As Aura sat, Misthyde said, "I do weave baskets. It keeps boredom at bay. But I didn't tell you everything. I am a diviner. That is how I know about you." He patted the blue crystal ball. "I saw you coming."

"I understand that enchanters and enchantress tend to avoid divination. Was that why you were expelled from the Order?" Aura asked.

Misthyde chuckled. "I was not expelled. I refused my initiation. There is a final step that I found ... unnatural." He sighed. "Some diviner I am. If I had bothered to consult the oracle about my cooking, I may have seen to boil chicken instead of lampern."

Aura winced. Boiled chicken was almost as detestable as boiled lampern, or boiled anything else. Had this man never heard of roasting meat over a fire? At least, a chicken could be caught in the backyard, and would be fresh. "Well, you and your son have plenty of time to consult oracles about supper, sir." She looked around the hut. A wry smile crossed her lips. "You could have healed your son yourself. You were simply testing me, weren't you?"

Misthyde smiled. "That is for me to know, Dyrgana. And no, I couldn't have healed him. I wouldn't have sent for an enchantress if I could." He threw his arms wide. "Anyway, I brought you out here so that I could repay your kindness, in some practical manner. Whatever you wish. I doubt you need anyone to cast a spell for you, so how about a magical tool of some sort?"

"There is no need sir. I –" She interrupted herself. A diviner knew about prophecies. He lived on the edge of the same quill of destiny or doom that often inked scrolls of vellum frowned over by priests huddled in temples. Perhaps he could ease the torment of the thoughts that kept her awake all last night, and now loomed over her like an angry bear. "Actually, there is a way. What can you tell me about prophecy?"

The old man snorted. "I can't believe a seasoned wizardess, much less the Dyrgana, doesn't know about prophecy. I thought you people lived in dusty old archives."

"I've studied them, but only as lore and texts, to understand the beliefs of people I may encounter. I've never studied them as portents of the future."

"Ah. That does make a difference." He brushed his beard with his fingertips, and grinned. "Well, prophecies are not the grave peril that many think they are, yet they are far more dangerous than they appear. That conundrum is caused by people who put more faith in prophecy than it warrants. Prophecy is a mere shadow of things that *may* be. But far too many transform them into solid objects, so that the shadow itself casts a shadow, only now of things that *must* be.

"Very few prophecies are written in stone. The ones that are have been given by gods. There are fewer of those than priests like to admit. Most prophecies are written in sand, on the seashore. Those are given by men. They are given to those to whom they are given, and meant for no other, to dissolve with the winds and sea. Unfortunately, some people spend their lives attempting to hold back the tide of time, or the sea of chance, in vain efforts to ensure the fulfillment of a prophecy given to someone else. Others carve the words into stone, establishing them as divine writ, and changing the meaning somewhat simply by trying to render them permanent. That is when prophecy becomes dangerous."

Thrusting a gnarled finger into the air, he said, "It has been my experience that such divine writ and permanent prophecies lie along paths of great suffering, even those that promise a golden age, if such an age is possible. When someone tries to force them to fulfillment, suffering becomes great calamity."

"You aren't reassuring, sir," Aura said.

Misthyde frowned. He bent over Aura. With probing black eyes, he looked her in the face. "Who has prophesied over you?" he whispered.

"No one, but someone thinks I may be the fulfillment of an ancient prophecy."

His frown deepened. He growled, "The prophecy would be alarming enough, but to have someone else believe it concerns you would be terrifying. We need to talk." He walked to the cupboard and removed two earthenware mugs. After setting them on the table, he pulled a canister from another cupboard, and put three pinches of tea into each mug. "Don't worry, not all my larder is tainted."

Misthyde filled the mugs with hot water from the kettle. Aura closed her eyes and inhaled the aroma of Aitian black tea mixed with roses. The diviner returned the kettle to the fireplace. Then, he walked to a shelf near the stool and unfinished baskets. Fishing through the tangle of stuff on the shelf, he grabbed a suede bag the size of two fists, and returned to the table. Sitting down, he said, "I may need these."

Aura took a sip of tea. It tasted wonderful on her tongue. Simple, just like she brewed at home. Holding the mug in both hands, she stared down into the dark tea inside. Her face reflected back at her. For once she did not flinch, but forced herself to look at the green eyes, dancing in the tea. "Is there a way to prevent a prophecy from coming to pass?" she asked.

"A personal prophecy? Yes. Kill yourself." He waited until Aura glared at him. Misthyde cast her a crooked grin. "That does defeat the prophecy cold, but I don't recommend that course of action. You could discover the path along which the prophecy lies, and take another path. That course of action, however, is self-defeating. You end up second-guessing yourself all the time. It can also cause the prophecy to come to pass, despite your best efforts. If nothing else, you go raving mad. You can't walk forward too well if you're always looking over your shoulder for doom and gloom. No, I recommend that you continue as you are, continue being who you are. If the prophecy fulfills itself, then it fulfills itself, with no fault of your own. If it does not, then the one who believes it looks as a great fool."

"The one who believes it is no fool," Aura said.

Misthyde closed his eyes and sighed. "Lady Naurelia t'Ardora."

Aura blanched. "I did not say any names, sir."

"You didn't have to, and I know the prophecy of which you speak, Dyrgana. That did not require any divination, either." Misthyde opened his eyes. The black orbs bored through her. "You are not the first woman to visit me asking if she is the one. You won't be the last. The Eorless horrifies every woman who passes through her door with the same accusation. Suffer her. She will find another victim next week, some other poor girl that absolutely must be the most powerful enchantress who ever lived. That story never ends. It probably never will."

Aura sighed. She played with her mug, not wanting to say what she had to say. "There is evidence that she may be right about me."

"If you are, then you are," Misthyde said, shrugging.

"I don't want to be!" Aura shouted. "I came here to learn the power to help my town, not be some godlike being foretold in the past."

"Don't run from it, Aura," Misthyde snapped, jabbing a gnarled finger in her direction. "That would be the worst thing you could do. If you run *from* it, you may just run right *into* it."

He held her gaze, freezing her with his midnight stare. Aura gulped. The old man was right. Any direction she now took could carry her into fulfilling the prophecy herself. That is, if she really were the most powerful enchantress who ever lived. But if she didn't change directions, she could blunder into it anyway. She felt trapped. Aura tore her eyes from his and shook her head. This was stupid. The prophecy was given to Naurelia, not to Aura Lockhaven. Apparently, Naurelia had thought everyone fulfilled it. Aura was nothing new, and nothing special. Yet, it ate at her, like the lamperns had eaten away at Misthyde and his son, slowly poisoning them.

"Why can't I shake this?" she whispered.

"The very possibility frightens you," Misthyde replied. "Your reaction is perfectly normal. I advise that you don't take any action against it. I know enough about you to know that hiding inside your home, trying to avoid this prophecy, would kill you. You are much better off living your life to the fullest, in total spite of the prophecy. That way, if it does come to pass, you can spit it in the eye."

"That is what I want to do, but I'm scared. I don't want to be put into a cage because of some dead tart's words to someone else."

Misthyde slowly stood up. He glared down at Aura until she withered in her chair. With a slow growl, he said, "Damaskarose was hardly a tart, Aura Lockhaven. I suggest you never say that again, not in the Valley, where she is viewed as almost a goddess."

"Yes, sir," she whispered.

The old man smiled, and sat back down. "Well, why don't we see what the oracle says about you? That should put your mind at ease."

"You're going to look at my future," Aura said. "Will the oracle tell me if I'm this person foretold in the prophecy?"

"Probably not," he said with a shrug. "If nothing else, this is a good start for your quest to discover yourself. I know about that, too." He pondered her for a moment. "You are also no fool. Gullible, yes. Innocent, yes. Naive, yes. That is mere inexperience. It will pass in time. But you are certainly no fool. A fool would not ask the questions you ask. A fool would run toward the prophecy in some vain attempt to be powerful or unique. A fool would never embark on a quest to discover herself. Instead, a fool would go about her blind business, stumbling into chance encounter after chance encounter, wondering why her life was a failure. So, never assume that you are a fool, Aura. If you do, then you insult yourself."

"Thank you," Aura said. "That's the first thing you've said that's been reassuring."

Misthyde pulled the bag to his chest, and held it as if he held a kitten. "It is my turn to ask you a question. What do you know about divination?"

"It's one of my duties as a wizardess," Aura answered. "Divination is like your definition of prophecy. It simply shows shadows of things that may be, unless the person changes direction. Oracles only tell someone what he already knows, but doesn't know he knows it, which is really more than he knows." She paused. "I'm talking like Lady Naurelia," she muttered. She shook her head to clear it before she talked herself into a useless circle. "I use both runic and ogham tiles. As a Gweryn worshiper, I prefer oghams, but my customers are Ayrdish, and more familiar with runes. I perform simple divination, really. The questions range from Maureen asking if Jack will marry her to old Ben asking if his crop will be a good one. My master handled the important divination for the mayor and town."

"What do you tell them?" Misthyde asked.

"What the tiles show. Then, I give them practical advice. Jack won't marry Maureen if he doesn't know who she is. She needs to introduce herself. Ben's crop will be dismal if he doesn't fertilize his fields. He needs to pasture his cattle in the fields for a month. I let them think the oracle said that. Otherwise, they may not do it."

"You are a sound diviner," he said with a smile. "Then you are prepared for what the oracle will show you. The future is indeed like prophecy. It is written in sand on the seashore. You yourself are the tide and the wind. You may erase the writing at will. What the oracle will show you are possibilities that may come to pass if you continue along the path you walk. If you don't like what you see, change paths."

"I tell that to my customers all the time." She stopped. A horrifying thought crossed her mind. It was one she should have had long ago, and one she should be able to answer for her customers. "What if changing paths leads me to what the oracle shows me, instead of another direction?"

Misthyde shrugged. With a wave of his hand, he said, "Destiny is what it is, Aura. None of us can make any guarantees about tomorrow. None. Just remember that tomorrow only gives you the consequences of the actions you take today. So, make your actions good ones, and you won't need to fear tomorrow."

Misthyde closed his eyes. He inhaled deeply, and held the breath. Almost imperceptibly he rocked back and forth. As he did, he hummed. The air in the hut grew cold, and the light seemed sucked into his body. His rocking motion grew, and the humming intensified. With a rush, the air warmed and the light returned. When he opened his eyes, they had turned white. He now channeled the oracle itself.

He held the bag in the air. "I don't use runes or oghams. Oh, I can if you so wish, but they are far more limited than this method. I use the seer tiles of frozen Glasenya. It is a form of divination that, like their magic and everything else about that country, has been hidden away on the other side of the Mellistenya Mountains for a thousand years. There are fifty-five tiles, instead of the twenty oghams and twenty-seven runes. The oracle has a greater chance to talk to you."

He shook the bag up and down, then spun it sunwise seven times. Opening the bag, he held it out to Aura. "The series I will use is the basic life sequence. It will show you things that may be tomorrow, based upon your actions of yesterday and today, as well as things that the oracle knows about you. I am going to ask you to draw a series of tiles. Do not look into the bag. Pick the tile that seems right to your fingertips. First, draw one tile, and set it on the table."

Aura rummaged in the bag. The first tile felt like ice. The second burned her fingers. The third tingled in a pleasant way. She drew that tile from the bag. It was pink marble, and twice the size of her thumbnail. Setting it on the table, she saw that it lay face down.

"Now, draw two, and set them on the table." She did, resulting in another face down tile, with a tile showing a carving of the Sun, resting at an angle on top of the other. The old man arched an eyebrow. "Interesting. Well, we shall see what that tells us. In the meantime, draw two more." This time, she lay one tile face down, while the second depicted a set of deer antlers. Next, Misthyde had her draw three. The first, she placed face down, while the second showed a sword, and the third was of a staff. Then, he had her draw two more sets of two tiles. Both of the first set faced up, a chair and two girls hugging. The first of the next two faced up, showing a clenched fist, overlapped by one facing down. The final draw was one tile, which also came to rest face down.

Misthyde ran his finger along the table top, just below the tiles. Eying them one at a time, he said, "The tiles that face down speak of you. The tiles that face up speak of people who will intersect your life." He returned his finger to the first tile. "Now, this tile is face down. It is you, and it's place in the series is where you are today. Please, turn it over."

Aura did so. The face showed nothing. "It's blank," she said. "There's nothing there."

"There is everything there," Misthyde snapped. "This tile speaks of you, right now, where you are today."

"I'm nothing?"

"You're reading it wrong, Aura. No, you aren't nothing. You are everything! You are a clean piece of marble, waiting the sculptor and the chisel."

"Who is the sculptor?" Aura asked.

Misthyde grinned, aiming a knobby finger at her chest. His white eyes glowed. He said, "You are!"

Aura lifted her mug to her lips, but did not drink. She stared at the blank tile. Just yesterday, she faced herself, a horror that she had created. She promised that horror that she would destroy it. Today, she faced the proverbial empty book, waiting for the words. She held the pen. A shiver ran up her back. In her hands, Aura held the power of a goddess, the ability to create a woman in her own image. She just wished she knew what that image was.

Misthyde leaned back, and crossed his arms over his chest. Still grinning, he said, "I hope that lays to rest your fears of being Lady Naurelia's enchantress of prophecy. If you were, there should be an image on that tile. Instead, you are free to write your own life as you wish. At

least, as I read the sequence now. Let us see what the other tiles say."
Leaning forward, he shifted his gaze to the next two tiles. "Now, this is
perplexing. It is no accident that the Sun tile overlaps a tile speaking of you.
Turn that one over, and let's see what it is."

Aura did so. The tile showed a crescent Moon. "The Sun and the
Moon," she muttered. She finally took a sip of her tea. "I am the Moon?"

"Yes, so it would seem. That is even more perplexing. I've never had
anyone draw both the Sun and the Moon together, much less for this
position in the series."

"What is this position?" Aura asked.

"The position of mates. It is you and your husband. However, since the
Sun overlapped the tile representing you, it also speaks of a great
adversary."

She couldn't help a small grimace. "I'm going to argue with my husband
every day. Lovely."

"No, I don't think it means that, not like this," Misthyde said, shaking
his head. His long hair fell about his shoulders. "These are opposites, but
also complements. Sun and Moon," he said, pointing from one tile to the
other. "Day and night. Man and woman. Mind and heart. Reason and
feeling. Words and music. In almost every nation's lore, Sun and Moon
were husband and wife. However, if the Sun were your husband, the tile
would rest beside yours, not overlapping like it was." Aura jumped as
Misthyde smacked his palm against the table. He glowered at her. "Beware
the Sun, Aura. That star is no husband. It is your enemy. You will be
joined to him far more closely than you would wish. Like the Sun in the sky
fades the Moon, the Sun in your life could cause you to fade."

"But the Moon can eclipse the Sun," Aura said. "Despite the Sun's best
efforts, it must retire at night, allowing the Moon to shine brightly. While
the Sun remains fixed, the Moon changes shape. She controls the tides and
the seasons, something that not even the giver of light can boast." She
paused. "Nor prevent."

"Ah," the old man said, smiling. "Perhaps the Sun ought to beware of you." He rubbed his hands together. "So, the next position in the series. This tells where you will live. The hidden tile also represents you."

She turned over the hidden tile, revealing a castle. It rested next to the tile of antlers. Aura smiled. She knew the meaning of the antlers. "Hartshorn. I live in a town named Hartshorn. But a castle? Why would I ever live in a castle?"

"It is also you, so it is not just a place you live. Is there a castle near your town?" When Aura shook her head, he continued. "There are several in the Valley. They're all over Ayrdland. Now, if you removed to Welcaster, you would live in the shadow of the greatest castle of them all, that of King Edgar. I suspect that is what this tile means. In time, you may live in the capital city." He rested his hand on top of hers, and gave her a squeeze. "Don't fret over any of the meanings. Remember them. Ponder them. But also know that they are but shadows of things that may be." Aura nodded. "Now, for the trio. This reflects those whom you may trust. Turn over the hidden tile." It showed an axe. "Well, this is interesting. You may trust a warrior and a magician. Apparently, you may trust yourself." He looked at her. "You'd be surprised how many people do not have a tile representing themselves in this position. How fortunate for you. You are also a warrior, but of a different type from the sword. Either that, or you are a woodcutter."

Aura smiled. Elisabeth Lovejoy fit the description of a warrior she could trust. As for the magician, Manfred Rowanwand crossed her mind. So did Sagacius. The axe confused her. Certainly, she had done more than her share of cutting wood. That was what apprentices did. Her ancestor carried an axe. Perhaps this merely spoke of the Locchaefen's spirit, one that every Lockhaven hoped to inherit. When the old man offered nothing else, she turned her gaze to the next two tiles.

"A chair and two girls," Aura said. "What position are those?"

"People who will have profound influences upon your life," the man said. "That is not a chair, Aura. It is a throne. A king will affect your life.

Somehow. Ah!" He pointed back to the tile of the castle. "Now, this tile becomes a little more clear. King Edgar could ask you to serve on his council. Enchantresses have advised kings in the past. They make the best diplomats. If he did, you would certainly live in a castle."

"I am a loyal Ayrdishwoman. If the king asked me to serve, I would with all enthusiasm," Aura said. It was a lie. At least, she had time to build up her feelings toward such a moment.

Misthyde shrugged. "It could speak of Lady Etheria. The Chancellor is as a queen to us. That is more likely, as you will no doubt cross her path at some point." He looked up at her. "When that happens, remember your best manners. Lady Etheria does not suffer rudeness with any mercy. She also doesn't take no for an answer." He looked back at the two tiles. "As for the girls, that is the tile of sisters. Do you have a sister?"

Aura sighed. "Not alive."

"How about your mother?"

"She is dead, also."

"Oh, my girl. I am so sorry. Well, perhaps they reach out to you from beyond, but this probably speaks of a woman of great importance who will influence you. Lady Naurelia already has, but I think this tile speaks of someone of even greater consequence. You probably don't know her yet. Now, these next two tiles speak of your place in life. Turn over the hidden tile."

It was of a gravestone. "I'm a grave. I don't understand."

"You overlap the fist. The fist is the sign of evil," Misthyde muttered. He stared at the tiles for several moments, while Aura finished her tea. Finally, he said, "I believe this means you are here in this life to bury evil. If it were the other way around, and the fist overlapped your tile, we would stop right now. That would mean evil buries you. But this is promising, Aura." He frowned. "I hope. The final tile will tell me. Turn it over, please."

With hesitant fingers, Aura flipped the tile onto its back. It showed a crown. Misthyde sat silent for a full minute, staring at the tile. Finally, he muttered, "I am so sorry, Aura. I am so sorry."

"It's a crown. Why is that bad?" Aura asked.

"Because that tile shows you at the end of your path." He slowly looked up at her. His face was pure sorrow. "At the end of your path, you wear a crown. In the process, you fight evil. A king intersects your life. All that indicates that in time, you will wield tremendous power and influence. I'm sorry, but there may be truth to that prophecy after all."

Aura bolted to her feet, knocking over her chair. She bumped the table, sending the bag sprawling open, spilling tiles. The empty tea mug wobbled and fell over. The tiles in the sequence remained as they were, as if glued to the table top. She shouted, "What? No! I don't want to be the most powerful enchantress who ever lived. I don't want to wear a crown. I don't want to be a queen or a princess or fight evil or be anything but the enchantress of Hartshorn."

Misthyde lifted the first tile, the blank tile. He held it out to Aura. His white eyes blazed. Turning it in his fingers, he growled, "Then, carve this tile yourself, before someone else carves it for you."

Chapter Thirty-Two

THE RIDE BACK to Ardora Hall had been miserable. The tiles kept flashing before Aura's eyes. With them, the knowledge that the prophecy may just be true. By the time she rode into the barn, she wanted to vomit. She slowly removed Blister's saddle and bridle, hanging them up with deliberate care. It gave her something to do with her hands. Currying him required half an hour, not for any burrs but just because Aura needed to ground herself with a creature that cared nothing for prophecies or divination. Blister simply was Blister.

"I envy you," she said to the stallion. He looked at her as if to sympathize.

Now, she had to face Naurelia. Aura wasn't sure if she was more furious at Naurelia for endangering Maedyan with her prejudice and devotion to law, or more terrified of what the Eorless would do to her for breaking that law. With a sigh, she left the barn.

Naurelia stood on the veranda, as if Aura simply went for a stroll in the rose garden. She looked at Aura and smiled. "Did you learn what you set out to learn?"

Aura stepped up onto the veranda. The question surprised her. "I set out to heal a boy because you wouldn't –" Aura stopped. She narrowed her eyes. "It was a test, wasn't it?"

Naurelia's smile widened. "If you say it was. Yes, yes, why wouldn't it be?"

"Maedyan was never in any danger, was he?"

"He was dying from what I understand. But I was about to contact a fine apothecary to heal him. Then, you volunteered. I thought I'd see what happened. So, did you pass the test?"

Fury and fear faded as pure incredulity overwhelmed her. "Why don't you tell me?"

"Because I am not the examiner. You are. Do you think you passed?"

Aura tilted her head back. She adjusted her staff into the stance of a warrior at rest, but also at the ready. "Yes."

"Then that is what matters. Aura, everything that has happened to you since yesterday morning, when you accepted my offer, is all about you. It is part of your quest to discover Aura Lockhaven. Everything that happens to you from now on will be part of your quest to discover yourself, even what you eat. Yes, yes. So, what did you learn about Aura Lockhaven?"

"I learned that I am willing to break a law to save an innocent life. I also realized how much I truly believe in mercy before justice, and justice before the letter of the law. I also ..." she stopped herself before saying anything about Misthyde's divination and what the tiles revealed about her possible life. "No, I think that's all."

"What did you say? About mercy and justice?" Naurelia asked. She stepped toward Aura, her face consumed by awe. Aura stiffened. She did not want to hear one word about that prophecy.

"I said mercy before justice, and justice before the law."

"Sagacius taught you that," Naurelia said, searching Aura's eyes.

"No. It just seems like common sense to me."

Naurelia reached a hand toward Aura's face, and caressed her cheek. "I've longed to hear those words. I once believed them myself, but feel I no longer have the right." The look of awe faded into one of hope. "In our war, we divided along two lines. One side believed in absolute adherence to the law. The other believed there should be no law. There was a third party, however, yes, yes. We called them Fence Sitters, but they were nothing of the sort. They were the most courageous of us all. They believed we should have laws, but the laws should always be viewed through the lens of mercy. Law should be like lead, solid but soft and flexible. The leaders of that small group were your master, Lady Etheria, and Lord Ashthorne. If we had listened to them, we could have avoided years of misery." She lowered her hand. "I think you mean more to this Order than you realize. If anyone can remind us of who we once were, it is you." A look of astonishment clouded Naurelia's face. "The hope of the order ..."

Aura closed her eyes. Here it came. The prophecy. Instead of that, however, Naurelia said, "You look exhausted, Aura, dear. I imagine between not sleeping well and the effort of healing Maedyan, you feel quite empty. You are still recovering from your fight with Mayenne, and the injury to your leg. Miriam has something strenuous planned for you tonight. Why don't you rest before supper?"

It was a good idea. By the time Aura reached her room, she could barely move her feet. She dropped her bag and staff on the floor, then hurled herself into the bed. Before she could think about unlacing her boots, she fell asleep.

Aura sat on the veranda, leaning against one of the columns, watching dusk settle into twilight. She rubbed her stomach and begged Ystlena to kill her before she burst. Lurna cooked a pie big enough to serve ten. She filled it with roasted pheasant, dried apples, peas, and turnips. Aura despised turnips, but this pie tasted so magnificent that when Lurna offered her a third helping, she gobbled it down. Then, Lurna served tarts made from dried berries and honey. Aura ate two of those. If she remained with Naurelia for any time, she was sure she would succumb to gluttony.

She smiled the smile of one drunk on food as she reached for the goblet of wine Lurna handed her. Lurna could not be more than five feet tall. Just a little younger than her husband, she had the portly figure of a cook who tasted her food as she prepared it. She also had the broad smile that came with such a pleasant duty. The blue dress she wore did nothing to hide the powerful arms and legs earned through years of lifting sacks, meat, and kegs. Aura liked the t'Ardora's cook. Not only did Lurna have red hair, but she also had green eyes. The cook sat a flagon of wine beside Aura, then bid her a good night.

Aura waited for Miriam to return from changing clothes. She had said something about suitable attire for the night's activities. Speaking of such,

Aura looked down at her clothes. Miriam insisted that the brown dress would interfere, so she gave her a blue tangini to wear. She prided herself on defiance of social customs, but this garb bordered on the immodest. Sewn for a much more petite woman, Aura spent ten minutes adjusting the laces of the bottom to fit over her thirty-eight inch hips. If she messed with the laces of the top anymore to fit it over her bosom, she would not have enough remaining for a knot. The two parts barely covered the essentials, front or back.

Aura inherited her figure from her mother. Obviously, whoever sewed this particular one had never met a Coadic woman. Otherwise, the seamstress would have included a few more inches of linen. Even so, she liked the way it looked on her. She felt powerful, magical, and almost beautiful. The breeze enveloping her body and legs gave her a sense of freedom. When she returned to Hartshorn, she planned to ask Brythony to sew one for her. Sipping her wine, she closed her eyes and listened to nightingales sing in the growing dark. The warm breeze brought the aroma of the rose garden and evening nightshades across the veranda. Aura breathed deeply and smiled.

Hearing the sound of bare feet on the stones behind her, she stood up. Miriam had changed into a red tangini, but obviously one sewn specifically for her. Miriam sat a full goblet of wine next to Aura's.

"What I am about to show you should take your mind off hearing the prophecy," Miriam said.

"You knew I was here last night," Aura said.

Miriam smiled. "I knew the whole time. My intuition and control over it are far more powerful than even that of the t'Ardoras. I shielded your presence from Milady."

"Why? Don't you work for her?"

"I am Aitian. Loyalty is in my blood. You have brought Milady much joy just by being underneath her roof. So, my loyalty extends to you. There was no need for her to know." She narrowed her eyes. "But hear me.

Vengeance is also in my blood. Never harm Milady, or you will see that as well."

Aura nodded. "I won't cause her any harm. I promise. I wouldn't even begin to know how to fight someone that powerful. I just wish I had never heard that prophecy." She looked at Miriam. "Why do I feel I can trust you?"

"Because you can, Mistress."

"Please don't call me Mistress," Aura said with a groan. "That prophecy haunts me. It's just a bunch of words, but it's as if someone put me in a prison. I received some good advice about it today, but it still hounds me. I want to be who I am and who I will be, but because those are my desires, not the desires of someone I never met."

"If you are destined to be the most powerful enchantress who ever lived, then you would have become that whether you heard the prophecy or not. As you said, Mistress, they are but words. They really don't affect the outcome of your actions. However, I understand. Once you heard the prophecy, it was finished. What is it they say? Once heard, always remembered? Forgetfulness spells are just whimsical rumor," Miriam said.

"Actually there is such a spell. It requires a very large crystal."

"Really? How does it work?"

"You smack me in the back of the head with it and I forget everything, including my own name."

When Miriam looked at her aghast, Aura chuckled. Miriam frowned and said, "You Ayrds have the strangest sense of humor! Well, enough."

Miriam grabbed both of Aura's hands and began walking backwards, away from the veranda. She led Aura out of the circle of light cast by the torches on the columns, deep into the back yard. As they walked, Miriam transformed. Her smile widened into a girlish grin. The stars reflected in her eyes and the moon cast radiant streaks in her hair and down her bronze body. She glanced around at the trees and up to the sky, giggling like a happy child.

"Come, Mistress!" Miriam said, leading Aura further into the clearing. "Can't you feel it? The freedom! You are one with the world as you should be. The wind caresses your body. The moon and stars seduce you, inviting you for a warm kiss. All you have to do is respond and you will begin to experience the world around you with your heart. You will feel the earth, the trees, the birds."

"What are we going to do?" Aura asked.

Miriam released Aura's hands and said, "We are going to dance!"

"Dance? But there's no music."

Miriam laughed and said, "Open your ears, Mistress. The world is full of music tonight. We have the song of the trees. We have the lyrical voice of the wind. More than that, we have the music of the lute upon which we stand, the earth itself. Who needs a minstrel? He is for a party, for laughter with friends, and telling jokes while we step off reels. Tonight, this is a celebration of life."

Miriam held her arms away from her sides until her hands were even with her shoulders. She dropped her wrists so her fingers pointed toward the ground. She cocked her hip to the side, lifting her knee as she did. Then, she cocked her hip in the other direction, then back. With each step, she increased her speed, until her hips rolled from side to side in a rocking motion. Without stopping her hips, Miriam began shaking her chest, raising and dipping her breasts in the same rhythm, until they shimmied to an unheard beat.

"You're a Mran dancer!" Aura said.

"Beryt," Miriam answered, twirling while continuing to rock her hips and shimmy her chest. "Beryt is the neighboring country to Aitia, after all. This is called ran aqi, or my own form of it. How do you think I keep my figure? I must admit, Lurna is a glorious cook. I try to get Milady to dance, but she refuses. The poor woman gained ten pounds because she can't stay away from Lurna's nut bread." She stopped twirling, and swayed side to side, using her hips as a fulcrum. Her arms flowed in the air like contained water. "Dance, Mistress, dance! It doesn't matter what you do, just dance!

Jig, reel, even a tumble. This isn't about form or proper steps. This is about freedom! The more free you allow yourself to become, the more magical you will become. When you yourself are magical, your power flows."

Aura cocked her hip to the left until her knee bent and her foot lifted from the ground. She held her arms out to her side, and then let them flow up and down, gyrating in the air. As she did, she pivoted her hip back and forth, mimicking Miriam's movements. She twirled a few times, letting her back arch deeply behind her, swaying her hair in circles.

"You know ran aqi, too?" Miriam asked, coming to a stop.

Aura continued to twirl, and said, "Not by that name and not as well as you do. One of my master's best friends is from Mran. She stayed with us last year and taught me a few steps."

"I can teach you some more, if you wish."

"Please do," Aura said.

"Keep doing what you're doing, and open your heart. Try to listen with your feelings. Can you feel the music?"

Listening with her feelings was a new concept, but Aura thought she knew what Miriam meant. She often closed her eyes and listened to the songs of birds and the feel of the breeze without thinking about what she heard or felt. She just knew them and experienced them. No words, no thoughts, no analyzing. No questions such as was it a cool breeze or was that a warbler. She just knew them as they were at that second in her life. Miriam's concept sounded similar. Aura kept her eyes open so she would not collide with Miriam or dance off into the woods and smack into a tree. She shut off her thoughts.

It was difficult to not form words in her mind and yet think about the dance steps at the same time. She knew the rise and fall of her arms as she copied the woman of bronze. She knew the softness of the grass underneath her feet. She knew the nightingale in the forest. She knew her own shadow in the moonlight. She knew the chirps of crickets, the hoots of owls. The beat of the earth. The clapping of leaves. The pop of her hip. The crunch of blades of grass. It sounded like drums, pipes, and lutes.

"I ... I do feel it!" Aura shouted.

"Excellent, Mistress, excellent," Miriam said.

Aura swayed her body and thrust her hips to the side, moving in a tight circle. She expected to see a small band of musicians at the edge of the clearing. Instead, she saw only the rowans, blue in the evening shadows. The music came from within her, heard with invisible ears she never knew she had.

Miriam jumped in front of Aura, with her back to her. She said, "Follow me!"

She thrust her hip to one side, then back to the other, in a staccato motion, as if she tried to strike an unseen object with her pelvis. Letting her arms flow free in the air like snakes, she walked forward in strutting steps. Her breasts rose and fell with the same hitting motion as her hips, and she thrust her shoulders forward and backwards at the same time. Aura felt intimidated by all the motions thrown together at once, but she fell in behind her, imitating Miriam's moves. The moonlight cast shadows on the deep muscles of the handmaiden's back as they walked in a circle around the clearing. Miriam kicked to her side and touched her fingers with her toes. Aura tried it and felt a sharp pain in her hip.

"I am going to be sore tomorrow," she said.

"Dance the pain away," Miriam said, kicking to her other side. "That's what I always do."

Aura continued to hear the music, growing louder within her. She heard Garranic pipes and Cailliac fiddles and Coadic cymbals. While the moon overhead lay in its half phase, Aura felt as if she made up the fullness.

Miriam whirled to face Aura. A memory flashed through her mind, and a somewhat evil grin crossed her face. She felt mischievous, playful. It was time to return the favor to the handmaiden. Miriam stopped dancing and looked puzzled. Aura did not give her time to say anything. She grabbed Miriam's hands and flung her into a circle to her right, using her feet as the pivot point. Faster, she twirled Miriam around. The handmaiden's hair flew behind her and she yelped. Aura focused on Miriam's eyes, letting the clearing and trees pass behind her in a blur.

"What are you doing?" Miriam asked.

"It's a dance I learned as a child," Aura said.

"What do you call it?"

"A great way to get drunk fast."

When she thought Miriam reached the right speed, Aura said, "Hold on, Miriam."

"For what?"

"This," Aura said.

She let go of Miriam's hands. The handmaiden shrieked and fell backwards onto her buttocks. Aura laughed, and then realized she could not walk. A great way to get drunk fast, indeed, she thought. She hobbled two steps to her right, and collapsed onto her side on the grass. Aura rolled over onto her back and laughed. She laughed harder than she knew she could. She thought she was in love with the entire Valley, with all of Ayrdland, with the whole planet. Between her own laughter, she heard Miriam laugh.

Their laughter subsided to giggles, then to silence. The Dyrgana and the handmaiden lay five feet apart, on their backs, looking up at the half moon. As crickets sang in the trees beyond the clearing, they let the cool night air dry the sweat from their bodies. Aura felt more peaceful than she had in several evenings.

"You could have warned me," Miriam said, propping up on her elbows.

Aura rolled over onto her side to face Miriam and said, "That wouldn't have been as much fun."

Miriam smiled. Then, she asked, "So, how do you feel?"

"There is no description! I feel –"

She stopped. How did she feel? Aura knew what Miriam meant. She ran her finger from her neck, down her cleavage, to her stomach. How did she feel? She felt full.

"I feel like I could fight another balakalat," Aura said.

"Don't become too enthusiastic," Miriam said. "Your leg is barely healed. You are now one with the earth. You feel everything around you. The trees have feelings. The birds have feelings. Even ants have feelings. When you become one with them, and their feelings, there is no limit to your power other than what you can hold within yourself, and the limitations of your own body. Your vitality is fully restored now. There are other ways to build your vitality quickly or to restore it when it is depleted. This is simply my way."

Miriam and Aura walked back to the house. They sat down side by side. Miriam picked up the goblets and handed one to Aura. She held hers in her hands and looked out at the clearing in the distance. Aura sipped her wine. She liked it. She was not expecting a red wine to be sweet, much less have an aftertaste of currants.

"So many things have happened to me and they happened so fast that I haven't had time to sit down and figure them out," Aura said. "This is another. But I felt music, Miriam! I heard it! I couldn't stop my feet from dancing. Merciful heavens, Miriam, that was the most astonishing thing I've ever done! May I do it again?"

"Feel free to dance at any time, Mistress," Miriam said. "You may dance in your room, or out in the clearing. Day or night. Feel free to dance later tonight. I have altered the barrier spell to allow you to come and go at your pleasure."

"Trolls," Aura said. "I keep running into people in the Valley who believe in trolls."

Miriam nodded and said, "They are real. I've seen them myself. They're a nuisance. They infiltrate the Valley, wreck homes, destroy crops, and kill people. I haven't heard of any in the Valley in a while, but that can change any night. They have poor eyesight, but sharp hearing and a keen sense of smell. If you dance alone in the clearing, keep your guard up. Pray you don't run into one, Mistress. They are highly resistant to magic. They are why we have the Watchers."

Chapter Thirty-Three

THIS MORNING DAWNED brighter than the one the day before. Dancing with Miriam had not just restored Aura's vitality. It restored her spirits. She felt happy again, prophecy or no. As Aura brushed her hair, she hummed along with the birdsong outside. Let Lady Naurelia keep her prophecy. As long as it was not put in front of Aura's eyes, she could ignore it. She dashed down the stairs, enjoying not feeling pain in her left leg. Naurelia stood on the veranda, watching the sun drive back the shadows of the forest.

"Good morning, Lady Naurelia," Aura said.

"Good morning, Aura, dear. And it is a good morning, yes, yes. I am going to enjoy today," Naurelia said, turning to face Aura. She grinned. "I hope you do, too. Today, you learn to harness your feelings and put them to work for you. What do you know about intuition?"

"It's supposed to be a person's instinctive knowledge of something or someone. Women understand it better than men. I don't think mine works very well."

"It works better than you think it does," Naurelia said. "It practically screams in your ear. Everyone has it, and most use it, even if they don't know they are using it, which is a majority of the time, the poor dears. We enchantresses use our intuition deliberately." She smiled, and slipped her hand inside Aura's left arm. "Take a walk with me."

They stepped off the veranda. Naurelia led Aura into the center of the yard, its air already full of perfume from the rose gardens. The spring sun felt good to Aura's face.

"You feel the sunshine, don't you?" Naurelia asked. "Yet, you cannot see that warmth."

"It is the element of Light. She is excited by the great power of Sun, so she is warm during the day. At night, she relaxes into sleep by the gentleness of Moon. All of Sun and Moon's grandchildren are that way. Light is also guided by blessed Ystlena, and what element could not be warm in her embrace?"

"Ah, that's right. You follow the Gweryn. That is their philosophy. I read about the Gweryn last night so that I may better understand you. You may be surprised to know, given my daft ways, that I am a Pendurist. I believe in total balance. Yet, you and I agree on the philosophy of light. Yes, yes." She stopped, and pointed to the Sun. "In my faith, we believe the Sun sends warm light so we may see and grow. The Moon sends cool light so we may think and rest. Together, they form the element of Light."

"How is that similar to intuition?" Aura asked.

"Intuition is much like your skin feeling the warmth given from Light. Everyone has thoughts. Everyone has feelings. Those thoughts and feelings are like the sunshine, yes, yes. They radiate out from the person, even though they cannot be seen. They can, like sunshine, be felt. Have you had moments when you felt something from someone, but didn't quite understand it?"

Aura cleared her throat. She thought about her three lovers, Roderick, Jack, and Cecil. She knew in her heart that they just wanted her body to satisfy their lusts. Yet, her head told her they wanted all of her, forever. She listened to her head, and suffered embarrassment and humiliation. Her next thought made her blush. There was something about Manfred Rowanwand. She felt he wanted to be more than just friendly toward her. In his presence, her heart did not signal the clarion that it had when she was with Roderick, Jack, and Cecil. It was as if she knew his soul. Whatever she felt from him made her want to spend an entire day underneath a tree talking with him, and perhaps spend the night with him elsewhere. Aura decided to keep all that to herself. She simply said, "Yes."

"That was your intuition," Naurelia said. "I believe your intuition spoke to you when you performed your little ceremony at those graves. You did not know that an act of kindness would defeat a balakalat, but the balakalat did. Her knowledge of herself radiated into the air, like the warmth of the Sun radiates into the air. Your intuition felt it, as well as the potential for great danger. So, you responded. Your intuition also told you to destroy Mayenne's staff."

"I can understand intuiting to destroy her staff. She was consumed with fear for it. I don't know if that was intuition or reading the fear on her face. But I was a mile from Mayenne's home when I performed the ceremony at the grave. I don't mean to sound doubtful, Lady Naurelia, but how is that possible? How could I intuit something so far away?"

"Distance and time are irrelevant to those of us who are practiced in intuition." Naurelia paused and looked at the sky. With a smile, she said, "Vance the blacksmith will be here in an hour. He needs to finish installing new hinges on my carriage house. I know this, not because he does need to finish the work, but because he is thinking so at this very moment. As for you, you are unskilled at intuition. I know your master very well. Sagacius is my brother, after all. He did not teach it to you. He cannot teach what he himself never bothered to develop, the moron. I think your intuition is a latent ability. Perhaps, you are more powerful than you realize." Her smiled slowly melted into a frown. Awe crept into her brown eyes. "More powerful," she whispered.

"Pardon me?" Aura asked. Her stomach tightened.

Naurelia shook her head, and forced a smile. "Nothing. Just the old thoughts of an old woman." The Eorless stiffened. She looked in the direction of the road to Ardora. "Vance is not the only visitor I will receive. Others are coming, and they are not happy. No, no. They are most unhappy."

Leaving Aura standing in the grass, Naurelia strode toward the manor. "Juhnn! Miriam! To me!" she shouted. The valet and handmaiden appeared on the veranda at once. "Juhnn! Shutter the windows. Bar the front door. Make sure the horses are in the barn and secure it. Miriam! Get my armor and sword. Put yours on, too!"

Aura dashed up to Naurelia's side. "What's happening?"

"Lord Ashthorne and Captain Lovejoy have just arrived. This is unpleasant. Stay by my side, Aura, dear. You will be safest."

At that moment, Deofoyl and Elisabeth rounded the corner of the manor, mounted on their horses. Deofoyl wore simple chain armor, underneath a tabbard depicting a lightning bolt. Elisabeth still wore her purple garments. An iron spear with a foot long steel head dangled from her saddle, as did a folded net and a coil of rope. Naurelia glared at them and said, "Troll or ogre?"

"Neither. Would it be that simple? A wraith lion left the Weeping Moor. He was spotted in Ardora," Deofoyl said.

Naurelia's hand flew to her face. "A wraith lion. Can they even be killed?"

"The Captain will handle him."

"One lion, one Watcher," Elisabeth said, with a faint trace of a smile on her lips.

Deofoyl nodded. "I'm along just in case he bit anyone. Lady Naurelia, I can use your help. One enchanter may not be enough to extract wraith venom."

Miriam ran out into the lawn, carrying a mass of steel. She now wore bronze scale over her chest and stomach, with a matching skirt, bracers, and boots that ended just underneath the hem. Aura had seen that very armor on illustrations of Aitian warriors in books she read. The bronze armor over her bronze skin gave her the appearance of liquid metal flowing across the grass. Naurelia flung her arms out in both directions. With one motion, Miriam unfastened Naurelia's dress, letting it fall to the ground. Not even Aura blanched at the sight of a naked noble woman. She was now the protector of her shire, about to be adorned for battle.

Miriam strapped Naurelia's steel chestplate into place. The golden oak leaf emblem of the t'Ardora's blazed in the sunlight. Following that, she quickly attached the back plate and stomach protector to the dangling belts. As Miriam fastened the steel studded skirt around her, Aura looked at Elisabeth.

"Excuse me, but what is a wraith lion?" Aura asked.

"He is a lion, but not like any other," Elisabeth said. "He lives in both the world of the living and the world of the dead. His fangs are venomous, and his venom will turn the victim into a wraith. The victim will be neither alive nor dead, doomed to live in that state forever. It is rumored that some during the war dipped their weapons in the venom of wraith lions, and –"

"That is no rumor! He did it, the horsop!" Deofoyl snapped. "My apologies, Captain. I despised that man. Please continue."

"Wraith lions live in the Weeping Moor, on the western side of the Valley. This one simply got curious and went for a stroll. If you ever see a lion that looks like he was killed two weeks ago and left to rot under the sun, walk away. Do not run. That only reminds him that he is a predator. He can outrun you, and probably will."

"Why do you people have such creatures?" Aura asked.

"Are we not founded upon our feelings?" Deofoyl said. "All of them, even the dark ones. We have places in the Valley where certain feelings are strongest, such as the Forest of Desire. Those places attract creatures who feed on those feelings. The Valley serves as a refuge for them. The Weeping Moor attracts wraith lions. We leave them in peace, and try not to go into the Moor."

"Speaking of the Moor. Lord Ashthorne, rumor has reached my ears," Naurelia said. She paused for a moment, letting the air grow heavy. "The fires of Tallen Hall are rekindled." Miriam stopped with Naurelia's left boot half way up her shin. The handmaiden shivered. Elisabeth silently mouthed *Fine time to mention that, Milady.* Deofoyl closed his eyes and sighed. "We knew this would happen in time. That is your castle, Lord Ashthorne. I suggest that you do something about it."

"It is no more mine than the Castle of Damaskarose is yours," he snapped.

"We will discuss this later. Miriam, my boot." As Miriam pulled Naurelia's steel covered boot into place, the Eorless looked at the bare spots of her body. Her legs were unprotected from hip to knee. So were her arms, with only her hands protected by lobstered gauntlets. "I should invest in a full suit of armor for such outings."

"Full armor will lead to death, Milady!" Elisabeth snarled.

"Yes. I did not mean to bring up bad memories. Forgive me, Captain."

"It happened," Elisabeth said. "I know that you are First Noble, but when we leave your estate, I am in command. Are we agreed?"

"Unquestionably, yes, yes. Captain Lovejoy, as the Eorless of Ardora, I authorize you to act as you see fit in my shire, and feel free to do so in my name." She looked at Aura and said, "Aura, you will remain here."

"I can help you," Aura said.

"No!" Naurelia, Deofoyl, and Elisabeth shouted as one.

"Aura, a wraith lion is no balakalat. He bears no evil in his heart. He is merely a feral creature of the forest," Elisabeth said, the words a slurry of trilled Rs. "However, you are far too inexperienced to face one. You would only be in our way, and possibly endanger us. We cannot hunt him and watch out for you at the same time."

Aura nodded and said, "I understand. Then, go with the gods."

"Thank you, Miss Lockhaven, for your understanding, and your well wishes," Deofoyl said.

"Aura, you have the run of the manor, as long as you remain indoors," Naurelia said, as Miriam buckled a thick short sword to her waist. Then the Eorless and Miriam walked toward the barn, with Deofoyl and Elisabeth riding behind them. Aura returned to the manor. As soon as she was inside, Juhnn barred the back door.

If Aura had the run of Ardora Hall, she knew where she would spend the time. After asking Lurna for a tankard of ale, she walked to the hall's library like a girl approaching her first pony. The room had been marvelous two nights before. By day, it took on a heavenly majesty. Shafts of light creeping through the closed shutters shot through the dust lingering by the towering windows, creating brilliant godrays that danced in the air. Aura inhaled the aroma of leather, vellum, parchment, and ink. The library was a temple of knowledge and lore, magical and historical. If she did not want to be the enchantress of Hartshorn, she would have volunteered to serve as the t'Ardora librarian, just so she could remain in this room the rest of her life.

As she sat her tankard down on the desk, she spotted a book that had not been there two nights earlier. *The Story of the Gweryn*, the cover read. Lady Naurelia said she had read about them last night. This must be the book. Eager to learn more about her gods, Aura sat down at the desk and pulled the slim volume to her. The worn leather cover was frayed at one corner, revealing a piece of gray wood. Opening the book, the first page read *Copied from the original text of Princess Fayella by Angus mec Pharsan, year 679.* So, if one could believe the trail of parchment, this book contained the words of a sorceress who lived 1,000 years ago. She smiled. How many copies lay between this book and the original, she wondered.

First, there was Sun and Moon. They loved each other very much and chased each other around the heavens. They were very wise, powerful beyond comprehension, but very flirtatious. Moon loved leading her husband in a merry chase, always threatening to outrun him, but in the end, she let him catch her. In their many matings, Sun sired within Moon a son. She brought him forth and called him Sky. Later, Moon brought forth a daughter that she named Earth. Moon and Sun also brought forth Sky and Earth's sisters and brothers, great luminous beings that we call the planets, the stars, and the constellations.

Aura grinned. The words were exactly like the ones Sagacius spoke when he first told her about the faith of Coadia, of her mother's people. Perhaps the wizard learned his knowledge from this very book. She continued reading.

Sky and Earth fell in love with each other. Unlike their parents, they did not chase each other. Instead, they lay with each other constantly. Their explosive pleasures can be seen in what we call sunrise and sunset. Naturally, Earth conceived many times by Sky. She brought forth daughters Land, and Ocean, and Tree. Her sons Stone, Rain, Storm, and Ice came next. Then, Earth gave birth to six daughters known as the

Elements: Air, Fire, Metal, Water, Earth (not to be confused with her mother), and Light. When the Elements warred with each other for supremacy, Sun and Moon took matters into their own hands. They lay with each other and their great magic created the first eclipse, and brought forth a daughter of immense power that they named Spirit to guide her nieces into peace. Eventually, with her parents' blessing, Spirit rose to become the queen of the heavens.

Finally, Sky lay with Earth and she bore twin sons that they named Day and Night, powerful beings that ruled their siblings with gentle hands and guided them into creating what we know as the Seasons, based on the chase of their grandparents.

Day and Night found no wives for themselves, so with gifts from the Elements and Land, they formed the Forested Islands to be their wives, each taking two. Day and his wives, Caillia and Garrania, begat the Dyddau, four sons and four daughters of the day and forests. Night and his wives, Ayrdland and Coadia, begat the Tywelch, four sons and four daughters of the night and magic.

Aura smirked. She had caught a late addition to the text. Fayella would never have known the island as Ayrdland. It was Geilltia in her time. If she knew of Ayrds at all, she knew them as the seafaring inhabitants of the province in the north of the land of the Nebels. Fayella died centuries before Baron Reidwulf uprooted a quarter of a million people and set out on the largest single migration in known history. She returned to the book, wondering how many more exaggerations of mec Pharsan she could catch.

Stone was a wandering son, and seduced the Elements. Upon Fire, he sired the firedrakes. Upon Air, the sylphs and by Earth, the gnomes. Water bore him the undines, while Light bore him the muses. By Metal, he sired Time. Then, he slept with Spirit, who bore him the unicorns, the dragons, the elves, and the Fae. Stone desired his sister Land, who returned his affections. Their long tryst produced Avalanche, Earthquake, Mountain, and Meadow. He desired his sister Tree, but she would not have him. So, Stone besotted her with wine. In her drunkenness, he pressed himself upon her. She bore the great giants, the ogres, and the trolls. After his final thrust upon Tree, she bore Coal, the father of those we call monsters, such as vampires. Disgusted with himself, Stone retired. After that, Tree has ever sought the chance to split Stone in half when he sleeps.

"I would do the same thing, if any man ever got me with child when I was drunk," Aura mumbled.

Sky and Earth saw the great success Spirit had in unifying the Elements. They also saw the tumultuous relationship between their other children, and yearned for someone to unify them. Spirit approached Sky and Earth and suggested she with the Elements could do that, but they required a physical chalice to do so. Such a chalice would bring order to the world by giving everyone a purpose. So, Sky and Earth met with their family. They discussed a grand plan. They would create such a chalice for Spirit, Fire, Earth, Water, Air, Metal, and Light to bring all the sons and daughters of Sky and Earth together to build a world. In fact, they would create two chalices.

With the agreement of everyone, including Sun and Moon, Sky and Earth borrowed two oaks from Tree. From one oak, they carved a man named Dynnor. Then they carved a woman from the other, named Fenywa. The seven Elements gathered together and kissed Dynnor and Fenywa, and they awoke to life. These, Earth gave to the Forested Islands, the wives of Day and Night, for they, too, had been created instead of born. She charged the Islands to raise Dynnor and Fenywa and train them, and help them bring purpose to Sun and Moon's great family.

The Forested Islands suggested that Dynnor and Fenywa be given friends with whom to share life. Tree volunteered, as did Stone, who promised not to seduce Fenywa. The Elements, already inside the man and woman, were naturally friends. When Storm offered to be a friend to man and woman, Sky declined his son's offer. He said that the others should remain as they were, in case Dynnor and Fenywa needed to be reminded that they were created instead of born. To give man and woman more friends, Earth scratched her skin. From the flakes, she carved the animals, fish, and birds. From a strand of her hair, she fashioned dog, cat, and horse.

Ah, Aura thought. She had always heard the names of the first man and woman as Dyn and Fey. So, those were nicknames. Dynnor and Fenywa sounded similar to the Coadic words for man and woman. Simple, and elegant.

Sun suggested that Dynnor and Fenywa be given guides to help them throughout life. The guides would not be friends, like the animals, but benevolent kings and queens to remind them to pursue virtue. Moon looked at her many offspring, and spied the children of Day and Night. They were the most removed from the terrible power of Sun and Moon, and looked the most like man and woman.

"Let the Dyddau and Tywelch be the guides for Dynnor and Fenywa, and their children from hence forth. Let them be called gods and goddesses, our representatives to created beings," Moon said.

And so came the gods and goddesses upon the Earth. But they were mere children compared to their parents, grandparents, and great-grandparents. As children, they were jealous and petty. The Dyddau and Tywelch fought for supremacy. Each wanted to fully guide Dynnor and Fenywa and their offspring. Their quarrel turned into open warfare. In their fight, they killed many of Earth's animals, as well as Dynnor and Fenywa, who had to be recarved three times.

"Thank you for your stubbornness and your faith in us," Aura said.

When he realized that their war was causing the destruction of all that Sky and Earth had born or made, Lloer, the eldest of the Tywelch, approached his cousin Golau, the eldest of the Dyddau.

"Cousin," Lloer said. "We are but fools! We are charged with setting an example for man and woman. What example are we giving them to follow but death?"

"You are right, cousin," Golau said.

With that, the two cousins embraced.

Golau said, "There are eight of us and eight of you. Four gods and four goddesses each. None of us are married. I propose that we marry each other and combine ourselves. Let us rule and guide side by side as the Gweryn, the deities of Home."

Lloer agreed. As Lloer ruled the night, Golau did not think it proper for him to lead the combined gods, so he asked him to step aside. Lloer also agreed with this. As a consolation, he told Lloer that the Tywelch would choose their mates, and the Dyddau would consent with happiness. And so, they did, with Lloer choosing Gwernyd, the most beautiful of them all.

The book excited her more than she thought it would. Sagacius had not been so detailed. The charming language delighted her. She turned the page. Her breath caught in her throat. Before her lay a lavish painting of Golau, the supreme god, the King of the Heavens, the lord of day. The artist captured his blinding radiance, as he reached from the Sun with an extended hand. His eyes were shrouded by light. A great mane of blonde hair flowed behind him like a cloak. He wore the barest of loincloths, and was the epitome of masculine sinew and muscle, raw strength under full control of itself.

Aura placed her chin in her hand and sighed. Tracing the outline of Golau's figure, she whispered, "Forgive me, my lord, for lusting for you. I imagine I'm not the first woman to desire you. Lucky, lucky Cygfran."

Speaking of Cygfran, the next page featured her painting. The supreme goddess, the Queen of the Heavens, and wife of Golau. The lady of dark magic and mothers descended from the Moon, with open arms. Her white hair wrapped around her, covering her more than the fine silver gown she wore. Fierce love poured from her face. She looked exactly as Aura saw her when she prayed.

"Why are so many afraid of you, my lady?" Aura asked the painting.

Turning the page, she guessed correctly that this illustration depicted Lloer, the lord of night. His black hair flowed behind him, becoming the evening sky. Like his cousin, he wore only a loincloth, and had a tight body that left Aura salivating. With one hand, he commanded the stars to dance. With the other, he directed the planets in their paths.

Next came Gwernyd, the goddess of home and Lloer's wife. She certainly was beautiful, kneeling before a hearth in a lushly decorated green gown. Her blonde hair was tied back in a practical manner to keep it out of the fire. With one hand, she stoked the fire, and with the other, added a carrot to the pot simmering over it.

Aura laughed when she turned the page. Before her stood Arian, the god of abundance. He may have worn a deep red robe of velvet and fur, but it flew open around him, revealing yet again, a loincloth, although one of extravagantly embroidered silk. Unlike his brother Golau and cousin Lloer, he had a bit of a paunch. He also filled out his loincloth in almost vulgar ways. Well, why not. Abundance arrived in many forms. He sported a thick brown beard that matched his elegantly plaited hair. His beaming face was split by the grin of the generous, and he stood amid a pile of treasure. With an outstretched hand, he offered a fistful of gold to the reader.

"I'll take it, my lord," Aura said. "I need some more clothes."

Aura turned the page. Tanawynne, the goddess of the element Fire and music, burst from a sea of flames, holding a harp. Just as she thought, the goddess had red hair and green eyes. Her gown was also red. She looked like fire itself, the force of creation and inspiration.

Aura chuckled at the next page. She never thought of a god looking quite like this. Dalen, the god of the forest, lay naked on a branch, his head propped up against the trunk. He played with the leaves overhead, a boyish smile on his clean face. Dalen looked like a tree himself, with a lean body tanned golden, and brown eyes. His tangled mass of brown hair spread out like vines. He wore a wreath of ivy around his head. Various birds rested on his shoulders, while squirrels played on his legs.

Aura cocked her head. So far, the artist had depicted every god as almost naked, but completely clothed the goddesses. Then, she remembered the age of the book. Artists of old saw the curves of a woman as the best for capturing the textures of cloth, while the chiseled angles of men demanded they be bare. If this page depicted Arian, then the next should feature his wife. Surely, the artist did not cover the goddess of beauty!

He did not. Aura bowed her head in deep reverence at the painting of Ystlena, her matron. As well he should, the artist rendered the goddess of the element Light, the lady of love and bedpleasure, naked. She rested one knee upon her couch, and stretched her hand out to the reader to join her. Her seductive smile was inviting, even to a woman. Aura frowned. The goddess was blonde and had blue eyes. She so wanted her to have red hair and green eyes. That would have at least helped her feel better about her own appearance. Then, she looked at the goddess' body. The previous goddesses had all been slender and petite. Ystlena had full breasts, full hips, and a bit of a stomach. Aura looked at her own body, and thanked the goddess for giving her the same shape.

Aura lost herself praying to the goddess. She memorized everything about the painting, from the alluring curves of her body to the gleam of desire in her eyes. Then, she flipped the pages to Cynhaf, the god of harvests, and Perlyssa, the goddess of the element Metal and lady of herbs and crystals. Following them, she looked at illustrations of the god of the element Water and divination, Dyfryo, and his wife Dyoedda, the goddess of livestock. Then came Alywyn, god of the element Air and fathers, followed by the impossibly named Ysgwether, goddess of crafts. When Aura arrived at Adphyr, the god of the element Earth and healing, she kissed her fingertips, and held them to the god's cheeks. "Thank you for saving Maedyan," she said. She turned the page, knowing it represented the last of the Gweryn, Gwynn, the goddess of vineyards.

Aura caressed the edges of the book. In one sitting, she learned more about her faith than she had in ten years. Even more, she now saw all sixteen of her gods in her mind. That would make prayer easier. Aura turned the page. The title read *Children of the Gweryn*. She smiled. This ought to be interesting. She had not heard the Gweryn had any children.

A folded note rested between the pages. So, this was where Naurelia stopped reading last night, and this was her bookmark. Aura absentmindedly opened the note. Her eyes fell upon bold handwriting, penned ages ago. In fading ink, she read,

Night and Day shall war. Sun and Moon shall do battle. Only one knows which will win. She, who is coming. There is one coming who will be the most powerful enchantress who ever lived. The hope of the Order rests in her hands.

All thought of the Gweryn vanished, replaced only by the letters on the note. This was the prophecy of Damaksarose, apparently in its fullest wording. "Oh, merciful heavens! It's worse than I thought," Aura said, slowly rising. She traced the handwriting with her fingernail.

Hearing the words had been terrifying enough. Seeing them sucked all the majesty out of the library. The air felt miserably cold. Even her dress felt damp and frigid. What if this were true. The power that healed Lodd and Sire Thaddeus was still undeveloped. Her staff magnified something that shattered boulders. Naurelia said a great force lay inside Aura, like that of a god. If Naurelia was the most powerful magician Aura had ever met, and that magician thought Aura could defeat her in time, then perhaps the prophecy was true.

Marsh the Elder had written *If you know yourself better than anyone else knows you, then no one can control you.* He also wrote *If you know someone better than he knows himself, you can control him.* Aura was the Dyrgana to discover who she really was, to know herself better than anyone else. In the state of not knowing who she was, she stood vulnerable to someone who did. The prophecy told her that others knew her far better than she dreamed of knowing herself. They now maneuvered her into a cage that they built for her.

Sun and Moon shall do battle. According to Misthyde's tiles, Aura herself was the Moon. *Beware the Sun! That star is your enemy.* Aura shivered as a great chill rocked her body. What better name for the Sun than Brightstar. What better name for the Moon than Nightshade. Who else knew the entire prophecy, if this note did contain the entire thing. No wonder some people obsessed over her mother's maiden name. She felt a little more merciful toward Sagacius and his tight lips. He no doubt knew the prophecy as well as Naurelia, considering Damaskarose was his mother, too. In his silence, he prevented Aura from spending ten years cowering in the corner afraid of sunlight.

Seeing the entirety of the prophecy confused her. According to this, the most powerful enchantress who ever lived served as the judge in the conflict between Sun and Moon. If she were the Moon, and one of the combatants, how could she also serve as judge in the contest. Aura gripped the desk to ground herself to something solid.

"No," Aura said, slamming her hand against the desk top. "I'm starting to believe this. It is rubbish. It is pure horse dung. I'm acting like an idiot." She grabbed the prophecy and held it up. "I am not the Moon. I am not the most powerful enchantress who ever lived. I am Aura Lockhaven. Do you hear me? I am not a Nightshade, I am a Lockhaven! Lock Haven! You have the wrong damn woman!"

Aura tossed the note back on the book. She did not believe the words spoke of her. Someone else, however, did. That someone owned the roof over her head. That someone was only the most influential, and possibly most powerful, member of the Order she hoped to join. This required all her training as a wizardess, every last shred of her ability to think her way through a problem. While she wanted to learn everything Naurelia could teach her, she did not want to be manipulated into becoming someone else's ideal. She also did not want to say the wrong thing at the wrong time and be expelled. Becoming an outcast seemed like a silly way to defeat a prophecy that obviously referred to someone else. Getting her Lockhaven up for a phantom of herself was one thing. Doing so before an Eorless was another.

Aura looked at the note. A house to herself. A massive library that the owner knew she could not resist. A book of Aura's gods conveniently left on the desk where she would find it. The prophecy conveniently left inside the book, also where she would find it. *Everything that happens to you from now on will be part of your quest to discover yourself, even what you eat.* Even what she accidentally discovered in a book.

"Son of a bitch," Aura whispered. Perhaps Naurelia didn't know about the wraith lion. Perhaps she knew an hour before Deofoyl and Elisabeth arrived. Either way, she had set a trap for Aura and Aura walked right into it.

The rattle of metal and murmur of tired voices in the hall brought her back to the moment. Aura carefully folded the letter and returned it to its place in the book. She smoothed out her dress, and finished the ale. Closing her eyes, she inhaled and exhaled ten times to center herself and push her Lockhaven temper back into place. Then, she stepped out into the hall.

More time passed than she thought. It was already afternoon. Miriam ascended the stairs, carrying Naurelia's sword. The Eorless stood by Juhnn, giving him his orders for the rest of the day. As Juhnn departed, Naurelia looked at Aura with a weary smile.

"We were successful," Naurelia said. The air of command in her voice overpowered the rattle of the steel encasing her body. "The wraith lion bit three people, but Lord Ashthorne, Miriam, and I were able to remove the venom. That is a nasty curse, yes, yes. Captain Lovejoy was not successful."

"Elisabeth! Is she —"

Naurelia calmed her with a smile and a wave of her hand. "Oh, the Captain is unharmed. She wanted to capture the lion and return him to the Weeping Moor, but in the end, she was forced to kill him. She does not like killing animals who are simply being animals, with no trace of evil in them." Naurelia cocked her head to one side. "What is the matter, Aura, dear? I sense great fear and anger coming from your heart."

You know perfectly well what you're sensing, Aura thought. *You put it there for me to find.* Exerting her will, she held her temper back and tried to calm herself. With a weak smile, she stammered, "Nothing. I'm fine. Just a bit rattled still. The phantom. That's all."

Naurelia narrowed her eyes. "I could read your mind within the blink of an eye, but I will not. No, no. I am not the prying kind. Aura, dear, just because you are the Dyrgana does not mean you must walk this path totally alone. Rely on your friends. Perhaps that is something you need to learn about yourself, that you don't have to fight every dragon alone."

"Except for Master, I've been alone for the past twelve years," Aura mumbled.

"There are plenty who would like to change that. You have more friends than you realize. I'm one of them." Naurelia placed her hand on Aura's shoulder. With a purr in her voice, she said, "You can trust me, Aura, dear."

I just bet I can, Aura thought.

Chapter Thirty-Four

NAURELIA AND MIRIAM were both exhausted from the day, so Aura dined alone. Lurna served garlic stuffed roasted lamb and several Beryt dishes that Aura did not recognize. The tiny soft rice-like dish was kas kas and the pungent parsley and barley mixture was called taballa, Lurna said. Aura wasn't hungry, but she forced herself to eat to not draw any attention to herself.

After letting the meal settle, Aura walked to the center of the back yard, trying to dance. She danced physically, but her heart refused to join. After an hour of dancing, Aura retreated to the bathing chamber, took a bath, and tried to sleep. When she awoke from the second dream that night of herself as the most powerful enchantress who ever lived, Aura got up.

She stormed around her room, snarling to herself, "That's five times I've had that dream in two nights. Why can't I shake it? I am *not* the most powerful enchantress who ever lived! I am not some manifestation of some dead woman's prophecy. This is stupid! Get a firm grip on yourself, Aura Lockhaven! It must be this house. There's something wrong here, something making me babble to myself and dream strange nonsense and –"

Aura found herself in the back yard. She glanced around, wondering if this was another dream. After popping herself on the cheeks a few times, she decided that she had walked out of the house in an absentminded abandon, absorbed in her anxiety over the prophecy and her dream. Well, that was dangerous. While she did not believe in trolls, she did believe in other things. She had already encountered a balakalat. She knew about ogres. A rogue Guard prowled the area for her. Just this morning, four high ranking members of the Order set out to hunt a wraith lion. Not only had Aura wandered out into the yard, she she pulled on her dress without even noticing, but forgot her boots.

"Lovely," she muttered.

After reprimanding herself for her carelessness, Aura listened to the night sounds. Crickets, a few frogs, a nightingale. Ah, an owl. Hmm, it was late for bats. That was just a fox. Not sensing anything dangerous, Aura sighed, and fell to her knees. The half moon lay overhead. She knew from the shadows of the rowans that it was close to midnight. Aura clutched the grass at her knees in her hands. She felt overwhelmed and wanted help, help from someone more powerful than herself and more sane than the Eorless.

If her formal relationship with the god of Irican occurred in a temple and ended when she was ten, her formal relationship with the Gweryn occurred in a forest and began when she was twelve. On her fifth full day as his apprentice, Sagacius took Aura for a walk across the fields to the woods behind their home. Her feet hurt in new boots and her legs itched in new linen trousers. She saw it before she ever entered the woods of the Big Hedge. As she drew near the oak tree, her eyes widened and her mouth fell open. She could not see the top. Sagacius' outstretched arms only went a third of the way around the trunk. He lifted her up to the lowest branch, over his head. Aura caressed the rough bark of the tree and thought it must be the oldest living thing on earth.

As she sat on the branch, Sagacius told her that he wanted to introduce her to the Gweryn, the gods of her mother's people. She asked where they were. He said, in the tree, on the wind, across the grass, and within herself. They were gods and goddesses of Air, Fire, Water, Earth, Metal, Light, Spirit, and flesh. No temple could hold them, so they lived in the forests, mountains, rivers, and especially, with people. Several bearded sparrows landed on the branch and chirped at her as she listened to her master explain the old faith.

Aura sat higher than she ever had, looking out over the forest and letting Sagacius' words soak in. While she liked the Iricanist idea of a mystical being who lived among the stars, waiting for her in the afterlife, she loved the idea of a goddess who walked the earth, who could be touched with every slice of bread and every dip of her toe into a stream.

She begged to hear more. Sagacius launched a barrage of strange sounding names that whirled by her ears, but left her breathless to hear them again. The names intoxicated her with the smell of the rain on leaves and the smoke of campfires, the sound of laughing men and women, and the taste of roast boar and strong mead. She realized later that her master spoke in her mother's native Coadic. No wonder they called themselves Tangoi, the People of the Tongue.

By the time they left the giant tree and walked back to the house, Aura had settled on the the goddess East Linda as her favorite, mostly because she could pronounce her name. It didn't stick in her mouth like Tan Your Wind or Eggsie Weather, a name that she was just sure Sagacius made up to poke fun of her. As she grew older, Aura learned to read and speak Coadic, and grew to respect the different names and faces of the god and goddess, even the ones she butchered with her tongue that day in the woods.

As she grew, she fell in love with Ystlena, the goddess of love, bedpleasure, beauty, creativity, and laughter. Aura saw beneath the stories of the vain, lascivious flirt. Ystlena's zest for life called to the young apprentice. So did her fondness for laughing and singing. The goddess' bold pride in her nude body enthralled the young woman. Ystlena even changed her eye color at will, something Aura tried to do numerous times. Aura especially loved the way the goddess held genuine affection for her husband Dalen, the god of forests. Aura wanted to grow up to be like Ystlena.

For ten years, the goddess helped her find her way in a world where she felt like a shadow. Tonight, she needed her to calm her mind and soothe her heart. Aura lowered her right hand to her left hip. With her fingers, she drew invisible lines across her chest, forming the seven pointed Sacred Star.

"Dearest Ystlena. I came here to have more power to help people, and to find myself," Aura said. "Now, I hear about this prophecy. I shouldn't let it bother me, but it does. I keep having these dreams of turning into a power mad monster. I'm scared! If that's what I'm going to turn into, then I want to go home right now. What should I do?"

Aura fell silent, listening. She did not expect to hear an audible voice, and if she had, she would have fainted. She expected a sense of peace inside herself, something to calm her. She heard nothing but crickets and felt nothing but her gnawing fear.

Aura lifted her head to the moon and screamed, "Dear blessed Ystlena! Someone! Help me!"

As she stared at the moon, all Aura heard were more crickets and a few night birds. No voice from on high. No ethereal hand on her shoulder and a whispered, "It's all right, how can I help?" Not even a curmudgeonly, "What do you want, witch child?" Still, Aura pressed on. She believed in her deities, her gods and goddesses, both from the Tywelch half of night and the Dyddau half of day. The voice of any would have helped. She would have appreciated even the voice of Dyfryo, although on this night she especially dreaded any thought of divination. Gwynne, the goddess of vineyards, would have been some comfort, because Aura began to feel the need for a good drunk. Just someone out there with more intelligence and wisdom. All she heard were the natural sounds of the night.

"This is too big!" she said to the moon. "I just want to be an enchantress, but not the most powerful one who ever lived. No one can handle that kind of power, especially someone like me. I am an orphan. Remember? Remember me? Miss Snake Eyes? Don't give people like me ultimate power. King Albert said the world trembles when the slave becomes king. What happens when the street urchin becomes a goddess? Please! I ... I'm starting to think Lady Naurelia may be right. I ... I keep doing things I did not know I could do. Things that just seem like the right thing to do at the moment, but how could I know that. I don't know! I don't know! I'm afraid."

Aura lowered her head and mumbled, "This is nothing for you. All of you are gods. This is normal for you. I'm just a woman. I'm mortal. I cannot handle this. I wish you would just understand that I'm too frail to handle this kind of power. I'm no goddess!"

After five minutes of the deities answering with crickets and owls and nightingales, Aura muttered, "What if Lady Naurelia is right? What if I am some promised ... *thing*? Please, any of you, don't let this happen to me."

After another few minutes of just night sounds, Aura stood up and snapped, "That's the problem with you gods. You're too silent when I really need to hear you. I'm going to settle this my way!"

Aura stormed across the lawn and into the house as fast as her long stride would carry her. Furious with her god and goddesses, too preoccupied even to answer her cry for help, she knew what would answer in her time of need. She raged past the statue, through the dining hall, and into the kitchen. This night called for something stronger than prayer. She cast her glance around the kitchen, a sea of dark shadows formed by the solitary fading torch on the wall. Aura spotted her target sitting on a shelf to the right of the wine racks. Several kegs of ale with a tavern's tap in each bung. Not sure which she needed, she poured a tankard full from the first. No, this was normal ale. She didn't want to waste it, so she drained the tankard. The next keg was the one she wanted. As her mouth drew into a bow and her breath left her lungs, she knew this keg held the ale mixed with lifewater. Her father named the blend *logsplitter*, for the headache the patron had the next morning. He had called the distilled spirits of barley *ruckus juice*. A pint of ale with a cup of lifewater poured down the middle, it was good for when the day overwhelmed the soul, like today. She drained the tankard. She refilled it. Searching about the kitchen, she spotted the largest pitcher. Filling it, she thanked Gwynne for the gift of drink.

If she could not feel the spirit of a goddess tonight, then she would feel the spirit of distilled barley. She chugged the contents of the tankard as if on a dare. As the ale and lifewater warmed her throat and stomach, and snatched the breath from her nose, she refilled the mug again from the tap. With her obedient armor bearers Tankard and Pitcher at her side, she turned toward the veranda, ready to get drunk and blast anyone who even said the word prophecy.

As she passed the statue, Aura stopped and said, "I wish Master were here!"

She fumbled in her steps. Taking a long swig of ale from her tankard, she looked at the statue. It was time she learned to stand on her own two feet. She was almost twenty-two after all. She needed to face this and conquer it alone. That would make Master proud. It would make Henry Lockhaven proud. It would make Aurora Nightshade proud. It would make Aura Lockhaven proud. Now, the only one who mattered was Aura Lockhaven. As much as she loved her teacher, her father, and her mother, none of them stood in her skin.

"I don't expect you to understand a word I say," Aura said to the statue, taking a long gulp of her ale. "Oh, merciful heavens! I'm used to talking to myself, but now I'm talking to a statue! They have gaols for people like me."

Aura walked up to the statue. She held the pitcher in one hand and the tankard in the other. Between them both, she had a full gallon of fine ale to help her think. She had drank enough for her to not care who noticed, but not quite enough to drift off to sleep without dreams of destroying Ayrdland. Smiling at the statue, she said, "You know, I like you. I would love to meet you. I love your shoulders and your arms."

Aura looked around to make sure she was alone in the room before returning her gaze to the statue. She forgot her old suitors as she looked at the statue's manhood. It showed enough underneath the marble tunic to give her an idea of the stature of the sculptor's model. If he were real, he would not only fill her but also split her in painful, but ecstatic ways. Aura smirked. Something affected her mind. It could be the lifewater laden ale. It could be the damasara petal she swallowed. Manfred might be right and it was just the air of the Valley. She had never gazed so intently at a man's private area, even with her lovers. She had always let her gaze wander down, as it were.

"Oh, who cares," Aura said, taking another sip of ale. "I'm an adult. If the various gods are going to ignore me, then tonight, I'm going to enjoy myself!"

She sat the pitcher down at the statue's feet. She ran her fingers down the statue's chest, let them fingers descend to the statue's stomach, then down to the hem of his tunic. She jerked her fingers away and stepped back. Even if he was just a statue, he did not belong to her. Still, she wanted whoever this was. She groaned. She had never felt such desire before.

"I really want you to make love to me, right now, on this floor!" Aura said to the statue. "Maybe this is the ale talking, and if it is, let it give a speech!"

She chuckled at the thought of her situation. Only minutes before, she prayed and begged for help from her deities. Now, she lusted over a chunk of rock. At least, she understood lust. That came from her own desires, passions, and need to be the center of a man's universe. It did not come from a woman's deathbed profession that someone else considered carved into the walls of the king's palace. Aura glanced at the tankard in her hand. Did the drink make her feel like this, or was her loneliness greater than she imagined? She looked back at the statue. The ache she felt for the man of stone did not originate between her thighs. She realized it came from her heart.

The more she looked at the statue, the more she understood herself. It was not loneliness, she realized, but a need to join with another. On a night when everything and everyone else seemed to press on her, she felt the need to be one with a friend. This statue seemed to offer it in a way that no live man ever had. She did not desire to be lain. She desired someone with a kind ear who would simply listen to her rant.

"I wish Manfred were here," she said. "He isn't, so you'll have to do."

Aura closed her eyes and threw her head back. Then, she felt that feeling, one she knew all too well. Through her closed eyelids, she saw the world spin out of control, spiraling down into an abyss of her own creation, an utter darkness of madness. She ripped her eyes open and glared at the statue, trying to focus on something real. It was too late. She was drunk.

"What is this stuff?" Aura asked, raising the tankard to her face. "I've had ale before. I brew ale! I've had lifewater before. None of them were like this. This is good piss! May Gwynne bless the stallion this came from! That was fast. Well, let it happen. I need this!"

Aura drained the tankard, and let the empty mug fall to the floor. She did not care if the metallic clang woke the whole house. Let them be awake. If she had to suffer, everyone had to suffer! What a glorious night of suffering and fear! What a glorious night for desire! What a glorious night for telling her darkest secrets to her new confidant! She grabbed the pitcher from the floor and drank right from the rim. After several swallows, she looked at the statue.

"Well, since you can't move, maybe you can make love to me in a different way," Aura murmured through thickening lips. "You don't look like the type of man who would tell me what to do, and I really need to get something off my chest. Do you like my chest? I am rather fond of it, or them, or ... oh, this is strong ale! Really? Good. My hips? I inherited them. My legs? I rather like my legs. Oh, really? I like you! Anyway, I do hope you don't mind if I talk those marble ears off. They look like kind ears."

Aura took several swigs from the pitcher. She threw her free arm around the statue's neck and leaned against it. She chuckled a few times, using what remained of her reasoning to realize that the situation was exactly as silly as she thought it looked. A tall barefoot woman talking to a statue. Oh, she wished she had a painting of this moment. Otherwise, she would never believe it in the morning. Then, that reasoning vanished with the next mouthful of barley and yeast, succumbing to the new reality of cold marble, hard flagstones, and the unyielding darkness of a room lit by only a setting moon.

"I prayed to my goddess about this, but she didn't answer," Aura slurred. Taking another swallow of ale, she continued. "Did you know you live in the house with a madwoman? You do! She believes in this fornicating prophecy. Shh. Don't tell anyone! You do know what a prophecy is, don't you? I never liked prophecies. I think prophets like to say scary shit to manipulate people." She dropped her voice, and mimicked an angry priest. "*You shall shave your head, cover yourself with ashes, and stand on one leg. If you do not, you shall suffer great smite.* Smite of the smitiest kind of smite. Boils upon your sheep, lice upon your boils, burning snow upon your lice. That sort of balderdash and tommyrot." She sighed. "That kind of thing causes people to lock themselves in mental cages and act like fools. The worst prophecies are the ones that say *A great king is coming who will rule the whole continent.* I've read about kings who believed they were the prophesied one and after burning villages, raping women, and strangling children, they ended up as heads on pikes on battlefields. I have no desire to suffer great smite or be a head on a pike." She looked up at the chiseled face of the statue. Aura imagined the model's lips on hers and said, "Oh, you're pretty!"

Aura giggled as she turned her head from the statue. She really wanted to kiss the man of stone, but did not want to scare him too early. Better just to talk to him tonight. She tried to focus on the door leading out to the veranda. She was not quite sure which door to focus on, however. She saw three doors. Sagacius told her time and again to always look at the one in the middle. She forgot the door and looked back at the statue.

"You aren't like other men. I like you!" Aura said, her voice thick with ale. "You don't tell me what to do. You aren't telling me to spread my legs, fetch you some beef, cast this spell, get out of the way, or wipe the dirt off my face. You don't think my mother was a cat because my eyes are green or that my father was some giant because I'm tall. I like that! I never could stand being told what to do, even if Daddy told me. Even if Master told me! Ask me, and I'll do it. Tell me, and you have a small war on your hands, Mr. Statue, Sir! I don't know why I'm so independent. I just am! I just am!"

Aura took another few gulps from the pitcher and continued. "That's why I'm so damned angry. That's why I'm so frightened. A prophecy from a long time ago. Apparently, this Dumbarserose said *There's one coming who will be the most powerful enchantress who ever lived and the order of hope rests in her hands."* Aura thought for a moment. Was that right? It sounded right. She mumbled, "Look at me. I'm drunk and talking to a statue. I wonder who the madwoman is now?"

Aura's arm slid from the statue. She fell in a pile, smashing her buttocks onto the floor. She thought the thud rang throughout the house. Rocking back and forth, she drank from the pitcher, her unfocused gaze staring at the dark wall. She had been drunk many more times than she wished to remember, but none like this.

"This prophecy," Aura said. "I wouldn't care but the madwoman who owns this place ... you did know you live in the house of a madwoman, right? ... she thinks I'm the one. Me! It would be absurd, but it's wormed its way into my heart. Oh, you don't worry about worms, do you? You only worry about falling. Well, I worry about both. Worms and falling. When I was fourteen, I grew so fast that I fainted quite a bit, so I know about falling. But worms! Like that prophecy. It's getting to me, burrowing into my skin like maggots. What if she's right? Don't I have a choice? Don't I have a say in the matter? What about this order's damned self-determination? Can't I self my determination? Oh, Cyfgran's cauldron, this is good ale!"

Aura fell on her back and looked up at the statue. Her gaze lingered on the statue's groin, but she thought that his real manhood lay in the solid silence he demonstrated as she poured out her soul. He let her blabber on and on and never tried to correct her or repair her. This was heaven, she thought. Aura tried to take a deep guzzle from the pitcher, but the ale poured over her face. Instead of wasting it, she sat up and swallowed several mouthfuls.

"You don't know what it's like to have someone try to force you into being something you aren't. Oh, yes, you do. I don't suppose they asked your permission before they began hitting you with mallets and chisels. I'm sorry, Mr. Statue, Sir. I want to be asked. Daddy never told me what to do.

He asked. I obeyed because I loved him. It's that simple. Just ask me to try to be the most enchanting poweress ... the most hopeful orderess ... what was it?"

She needed more ale to loosen her tongue. She drained the pitcher. Without looking at the statue, she continued, "Don't take my power away from me. Please, don't. You don't know what it's like to be powerless. I don't mean power as in the most powerful whatever who ever lived. I mean the power to decide your own ... what's the word? There's a word for what I mean. What is it? Oh, you can't tell me. It's what the king is. Sovereignty! That's the damn word. Don't take my sovereignty away from me. They want to. I can't handle that, Mr. Statue, Sir. I just can't. They ask too much of me. This is far more than I expected. I don't know what to do or think or act or ..."

Aura stared down into the empty pitcher. Dammit. How dare it be empty! Where were her damned armor bearers? Where were those horsops Tankard and Pitcher? Where was her god Ale? Fornicating swine! She rose to her knees, then her feet, to get another pitcher. So, she thought. She lay down on her side, imagining herself walking through the dining hall. As her mind entered the kitchen, she drew her knees to her chest, cradling the empty pitcher between her breasts. Her hand reached for the tap on the keg of ale and she drifted off into blackness on the hard floor in front of the statue.

Chapter Thirty-Five

SOME LOCAL SOLDIER called the townsfyrd to arms using Aura's skull as his drum. As she lay on her back, watching the growing shafts of light cut through the dust above her bed, she knew she had a hangover, but could not remember why. The last thing she remembered was admiring the statue downstairs. That mixed with some vague snippets of a strange conversation held with no one. Now, she lay in her bed, her body cooling in the breeze drifting through the window, staring at the ceiling. She had no memory of what happened in between. From the color of the light, and the sharp angles it cut through the dust, she guessed the time to be close to midmorning.

It took Aura five minutes to climb out of bed. It took her another ten to stagger to the kitchen. Every step seemed to drive barn pegs into her brain. Lady Naurelia was nowhere to be found, but she saw Lurna cutting up a cabbage. Miriam stood by her. She looked at Aura and smiled.

"How do you feel?" Miriam asked.

"Terrible," Aura stammered.

"I found you asleep in front of the statue. I should have warned you about Milady's ale." She smiled, a look of concern and understanding on her face. She said, "You just needed to talk to someone, didn't you? I talk to the statue all the time. It was the prophecy, wasn't it?"

"I guess," Aura said. "I don't remember."

"Do not worry," Miriam said. "Milady thinks you were just fatigued from everything you've experienced so far. She's in her workshop right now, so she won't hear us talk. I carried you to your bed. As I am a woman, I can say this. You're rather heavy, Mistress."

Aura frowned. "I weigh one hundred forty-eight. That isn't terribly heavy."

"You weigh considerably more than that, Mistress!"

Aura's frown deepened. It felt as if her head rocked side to side with each throb. "We'll talk about this later. Perhaps I'll feel better after another drink."

"No, you need this," Miriam said, holding out a platter of several pork sausages, three slices of cheddar, and two fried goose eggs.

Aura looked at the food. Her stomach turned at the sight. She said, "Miriam, I'm not hungry."

"Eat, Mistress! The food will stop the headache."

Everything hurt, not just her head. She lost track of exactly how many days she had spent in the Valley, but every one of them presented some way to beat her body and soul. Ralthangarle ripped her fears out into daylight. Mayenne nearly killed her, and left her injured. Naurelia thought she was some sort of prophesied goddess. Her own inner self became all too real and tore her asunder. Misthyde showed her a possible life that was anything but serene. An criminal hunted her. A powerful lord hated her. If those weren't enough, she had discovered things that left her with far too many questions and not enough answers about her teacher and probably her mother.

As she picked at the eggs, Miriam scolded her to eat. The handmaiden may as well have whispered to the wall for all Aura heard her. Too much had happened too fast. It was as if everything that occurred since she stepped through the gates of Ralthangarle had been her fault in some way. Everything reflected some facet of herself. She just was not like most women, and that apparently caused her to be treated like the spear target for the townsfyrd. While most women feared being ravaged, Aura knew of none that cowered in moribund terror of it, like she did. All her friends hated what they saw in the mirror, but it was because their eyebrows were too bushy or their lips were too thin. She knew no one else who could arouse the insatiable lust of a soul vampire. No other woman was considered the fulfillment of prophecy, unless the poor fool walked through the doors of Ardora Hall. Even the kindest lord ignored most women. Every woman she knew would have leapt for joy at the thought of wearing a tiara in the future. Not Aura Lockhaven. She was different on the outside, and more so in the inside.

With every throb in her skull, it felt as if her head jerked to the left. Logsplitter, indeed. Henry Lockhaven had invoked understatement. She popped a fork full of eggs into her mouth. They tasted flat. She felt defeated. She wanted to go home, before today gave her something that did kill her. If nothing else, she wanted to stay near a deep, soft cushion, in a dark, cool room.

Of all her skills, her favorite was the ability to take insignificant and seemingly unrelated facts, and add them together to arrive at inescapable and profound truths. The facts of her visit to the Valley were anything but insignificant. They were also not unrelated, joined by the one common element of Aura herself. This time, however, they did not add up.

The one piece of the puzzle that held the others together was Aura herself. That was also the one piece she did not understand. There was just something about Aura that made some people want to slap her, insult her, and kill her. It also made others want to elevate her, worship her, and call her Mistress. Whatever it was led her across the threshold of drunkenness and to the brink of madness. She had almost died twice back in Hartshorn. If she didn't discover what it was about herself that unified all those other pieces, then one day and soon, she would face someone or something that did kill her. It could have happened last night. In her drunken state, she could have wandered out into the yard and into the arms of the imposter Guard.

Miriam tugged at Aura's sleeve, pointing to the untouched sausages. Aura ignored her. She returned to the reason she became a Dyrgana. Three days earlier, her reason was simply to gain the knowledge to fully help Hartshorn, and to understand the latent power within herself. Today, her reason took on a far more primal nature. She had to know herself to stay alive. A balakalat wanted to devour her soul. Misthyde's tiles spoke of a life full of more danger than just potential heart failure during an out of control healing spell. While she did not understand why she united every event she had faced, she understood one thing. Her lack of knowledge of herself no doubt drew them together, and would draw others.

Miriam nagged at her again. Aura tore into the food, not because she was hungry, but just to get Miriam to be quiet. When the platter was empty, she stood. Miriam lied. The headache had not gone away, but at least it felt more like civilized punishment. With a weak smile and a silent nod, Aura accepted a cup of tea from Lurna. Then, she followed Miriam out to the veranda. The next to last thing she wanted to see was sunlight. The very last thing she wanted to see was Naurelia t'Ardora. Both awaited her. This morning, Naurelia wore her black gown and cloak, with the belt of wands around her waist. Today would be a magic day.

Aura looked away, out into the yard. The seasons marched across the calendar day by day, each day different than that before. Some days, however, demonstrated the obvious progression of the world through the Wheel of the Year. Today was such a day. The sun shown with more intensity. The shadows of trees lay at a noticeably different angle. Birds changed their song from the announcement of birth of their chicks to the lament that their chicks needed food. The air held that languid, seductive kiss that foretold the coming of summer. Haemmont 1 drew near, the day of Parin. The day of Aura's birth.

She smiled wistfully. This would be her first birthday in ten that she would not spend with Sagacius. He would not subject her to his usual yearly pranks, nor threaten the safety of Big Hedge with his boisterous, and hazardous, celebratory spells and charms. A pang of loneliness crept through her heart. This would also be the first birthday in eleven that she spent alone. The briefest shock of her great gnawing fear passed through her, dismissed by the pleasant thought that perhaps she could find Elisabeth and they could share several tankards of ale on Parin. Perhaps she could arrange to be in Grahbale and visit Manfred.

Aura's thoughts were interrupted by a bright "Good morning, Aura."

"Good morning, Lady Naurelia," Aura said, in a hoarse voice, turning towards Naurelia.

"Aura, dear. You look awful," Naurelia said.

"Mistress Aura had a rough night, and I –" Miriam began.

"Miriam," Aura said, interrupting her. She placed her hand on Miriam's arm. "It's all right." She looked at Naurelia. "I helped myself to your ale last night. It was stronger than I thought. I have a hangover."

"Oh," Naurelia said, her voice full of knowing. "My healing spells are powerful, but they are ineffective on hangovers."

"It isn't my first. Master scolds me for my fondness for ale," she said, rubbing the slight bulge of her stomach.

Naurelia smiled, and rubbed her own chubby belly. "We like our indulgences, don't we, yes, yes." She cast a cold glance to Miriam. "Unlike *some* women." Miriam looked at the sky, a sly smirk on her lips. "Well, Aura, dear. Today, I am going to introduce you to the foundation of an enchantress' strength. How to empower your magic with your feelings. I suspect that you already use them, but don't know it, no, no."

"Believe me, Milady. I use my will, like any other wizardess," Aura said.

"Do, you really? I've spoken with Misthyde this morning. He said that Maedyan is fully recovered. You used a potion of herbs. That is a witch's remedy. Yet, I've never heard of one acting so quickly. Tell me, what did you feel when you made the potion?"

"I didn't feel anything, but I saw my father's face when my sister died. I never want to see that devastated look on anyone's face again."

A smile spread across Naurelia's lips. Her eyes narrowed into that self-satisfied look a mother casts her child when the child has been up to mischief, and the mother knows it. "If that is not empowering your magic with your feelings, then nothing is."

Aura pondered that thought. It didn't occur to her yesterday that Maedyan healed faster than normal. Healing potions were powerful, but they usually took several days to manifest. Yet, Maedyan felt well enough to eat only an hour after Aura poured the potion down his throat. Perhaps her thought of her father was enough to endow the potion with more strength. If she could do that, then she could heal the next Lodd or Sire Thaddeus without endangering herself. For the first time that morning, Aura felt good.

"Our feelings are like fire," Naurelia continued. "When fire is uncontrolled and left to its own, it can destroy, or burn itself out. When it is controlled and used deliberately, it heats our homes, cooks our food, and permits us to see at night. When you learn to harness your feelings and use your intuition deliberately, together with your knowledge as a wizardess, you will be immensely powerful. In fact ... you would be ... " Naurelia's eyes glazed over, as if she were lost in a trance. Her voice lowered to a faint whisper. Her lips barely moved as she said, "The most powerful enchantress who ever lived."

There comes a point in the filling of a bucket when it can contain no more water. One drop further, and it begins to overflow. It becomes unstable, thrown off balance by its own bloated weight, and can tip with the slightest provocation. When it tips, everything inside rushes out in an uncontrollable mass. Aura had just reached that point. Naurelia's whispered comment was the final drop of water, and her bucket tipped. The good feeling she experienced only moments before vanished. Aura winced. Her stomach roiled. Her head throbbed. "Please don't say that, Lady Naurelia," she said, stepping back. She tightened her fists, so hard that she thought the scar on her left hand would split open. The words slipped from her mouth before she could stop them. "Please don't mention the prophecy of Damaskarose."

Naurelia shot Miriam a withering look and asked, "How did she –"

"Miriam didn't tell me. I overheard *you*," Aura said. She may as well finish the thought. "You think I'm the most powerful enchantress who ever lived, the one Damaskarose told you about when she died. I also read the prophecy in the book in the library. A note you left in a book that you left on the desk for me to find in a room that you knew I could not resist entering when you were conveniently away with Lord Ashthorne."

"How ... How dare you! How dare you ... accuse me ... of ... " Naurelia sputtered. Her face tightened with anger. "I did no such thing! A t'Ardora does not engage in subterfuge. There are dozens of copies of that prophecy in my home. It was a convenient place holder. I certainly didn't mean for you to read it." Anger faded into resolve and determination. "Well, now that you know. Yes, yes. You, Aura Lockhaven, are a gift to the order. Our greatest member prophesied your coming two hundred years ago. You are the fulfillment of everything that we have hoped for and dreamed about since Damaskarose died. You, Aura, are destined to be the greatest enchantress who ever lived."

"You don't know that the prophecy was about me!" Aura said. "You believe every woman who crosses your threshold is the fulfillment of that prophecy. The true prophesied one could be a six year old girl who enters Ardora Hall three months from now."

"No. I know. This time, I know. It is you, Aura."

That was enough. She cringed at the thought of her "coming" being foreseen. No invisible hand put a hook in her nose and dragged her to the Valley. She was no mere dairy cow to moo at someone else's bidding. She had a free will. Her patience, her kindness, even her respect for authority broke like dry twigs beneath her feet.

To confound it all, she had a hangover. That was aggravated by the past two days. During that time, she saw far too much of her past, present, and future. The trance. The phantom. Misthyde's tiles. It was as if some drunken fop of a minstrel crammed a million facts into three stanzas of a song. Everything inside Aura broke. The resulting flood poured through her heart and erupted from her mouth.

Aura snapped, "You don't know the grief I've suffered for the past two days. I cannot sleep because of that prophecy! The very idea that it may just possibly be true causes me nightmares. I am bloody tired of that damnable prophecy!"

"Aura, watch your tongue!" Naurelia retorted.

"No! I will not! This whole idea infuriates me. I'm sorry about my language, but I'm angry and when I get angry, I become vulgar. I did not mean to eavesdrop the other night, but I heard you talking about me behind my back. It is my experience that when that happens that it is never for my benefit. I will not just stand by and let you, or anyone else, treat me like a puppet. No one pulls my strings and tells me to dance!"

"I am not asking you to dance, Aura," Naurelia said.

"You may as well be," Aura said. "I assure you that I have no desire to be the most powerful enchantress who ever lived!"

"Aura! It was prophesied! Just accept it and —"

"No! I will not be the most powerful enchantress who ever lived just because Damaskarose said something to you when she died. She didn't say it to me, so you really don't know that she was talking about me."

"Yes, I do! Who else could she have meant? Even now, as a novice to our ways, your power is the greatest I have ever seen. Once you are initiated, you will be phenomenal. After a few years, you will be almost a goddess."

"That's exactly what I mean!" Aura shouted. "I don't want to be a goddess!"

"You will be who you will be!" Naurelia roared.

"I will be powerful because it's my wish and I will do it through hard work and through my own efforts. I will not do it because of fate, or destiny, or whatever. As an Ayrdish woman, I value my freedom, and I am free to choose my own destiny, not fulfill someone else's. If you know my master so well, you know that he lived by self-determination and taught it to me, too."

"I don't like your tone, Aura! You haven't earned the right to speak to me like that," Naurelia said. "You do not have the right to question the prophecy of Damaskarose!"

"I never knew her!" Aura said.

"She spoke about you! You are the enchantress of promise!"

"No, I am not!" Aura said, lowering her voice and pausing between each word. "I am Aura Lockhaven, and I choose who I will be. Or will not be, for that matter. I could slit my wrists right now and that would end your precious prophecy."

Naurelia's eyes widened in unbridled fury. "What did you just say?" she asked.

"I said, I am not the prophesied enchantress," Aura snapped. "I will not surrender my hopes and dreams to mold myself into someone else's image. I reject the idea of being the most powerful enchantress who ever lived. I reject Damaskarose's prophecy!"

"If that's the way you feel, then leave! Leave my house! Leave the Valley! Leave the Order!" Naurelia shouted.

"Very well, I shall!"

Aura stormed into the house. She bounded past the statue. All traces of the hangover vanished as she flew up the stairs three treads at a time. Packing was easy. She threw the leather bag over her shoulder. Snatching her staff from the corner, she bolted from the room and tore down the stairs. Pausing in the room with the statue, she looked outside. On the veranda, she saw Miriam gesturing wildly to Naurelia. They shouted at each other in a torrent of unyielding wrath. While she wished to say goodbye to Miriam, she also did not want to face Naurelia. She wanted to punch the woman, and knew that would be a terrible idea.

Aura walked up to the statue and said, "I think you're the only one here with any common sense."

Then, she walked through the dining hall, past Lurna whistling in the kitchen, through the foyer, and out the front door with only a nod to Juhnn. Within minutes, Aura and Blister bolted from the barn, galloping down the road away from Ardora Hall. She wanted to put as much distance as possible between herself and the madwoman behind her.

When she reached the intersection of the road with the larger one running east and west, she stopped. To her left lay Ardora. At that moment, she did not want to see another enchanter or enchantress. The rogue Guard might still be in town. To her right lay eastern wall and Ralthangarle, but she wasn't sure how to reach it. She turned Blister in that direction. About one hundred yards down the road, Aura stopped. She turned aside into the shade of an oak tree to gather her thoughts.

"What have I done?" she asked, looking behind her toward the road to Ardora Hall. "I just quit." Aura hunkered over the saddle. "I'm sorry, Master. I know what I promised you. I know what I promised myself. It looks like it will not be happening. I can't go back. I just can't return and face that."

Reaching into her bag, she pulled out the map Karyl gave her. It showed no direct roads leading from Ardora to Ralthangarle. However, the road she now traversed led to Tongren's Tower, and from there another led to the eastern wall. She had to return Blister to Karyl somehow. That seemed like the best route. Either that, or follow the River Phant, and that way could be rocky and dangerous for a horse. Returning the map to her bag, she glanced toward the center of the Valley. The red tower of the Grahtur jutted above the trees.

"Goodbye, Manfred. It was nice meeting you. I wish we had more time." Then, she nudged Blister, and continued down the road to the east.

Chapter Thirty-Six

HALF AN HOUR later, the road entered a forest. Thick oaks on both
sides intertwined their branches overhead, forming a tunnel that extended
beyond the curve in the road ahead. Aura slowed her pace. This forest was
like none she had ever seen. On her left, the trees were full of birdsong,
foraging animals, and sharp shadows cast by the bright overhead sun. On
her right, she heard no birds and saw no animals. That entire side of the
road lay behind a veil of deep blue darkness, as if storm clouds blocked the
sun. Glancing up, she saw only a few puffs of springtime clouds.

She soon rounded the curve. Through the trees on her right, she saw a
tall cylinder of red stones. Half of the left side was gone, collapsed inward.
The right side jutted up, its ragged edges sticking out into the air like the
teeth of a dead animal. With one dark window toward the bottom and a
smaller one at the top, it looked like a skull. It was an old tower of some
kind.

Aura loved ruins. She often explored the ones in Hartshorn, spending
hours nosing around the old Bellician garrison on top of Piper's Knob, and
the baffling maze of nonsensical walls known as Millow's Folly. This tower
fascinated her. It looked like a good place to rest, so she turned down the
path.

She shuddered as a wave of dread passed over her. Goosebumps rose on
her skin as the cold air clung to her body. As she rode further down the
path, she noticed the trees. Although leafed out, they looked parched and
stunted, much shorter than the ones she left behind. Many were twisted
and gnarled into shapes that looked like men bent under heavy burdens.
The shadows cast on the burrs and galls on the trunks made Aura jump.
They looked like faces. Blister nickered nervously.

Piles of stones and low trenches jutted up from the leaf litter. They
looked like the hastily built fortifications down near Vine Haven. Rotted

trunks of trees lay askew across the trenches, blasted from their stumps by unknown causes. Nearing the tower, she saw low walls of stone around the cylinder, as well as more blasted trees. Grass and wind tried their best to reclaim the pockmarks of craters in the ground. A mass of sweet briars and buckthorns did little to hide the wrecked catapult underneath them.

At first, Aura thought a series of old trenches surrounded the tower. As she approached, she realized that the mass of stones had once been a wall, destroyed from the outside. Fifty yards around the tower and wall, young trees grew in an area that was clear-cut a century earlier. Foundations of long since vanished buildings lay at angles to the tower. She passed through the only spot in the wall free of stones, and guessed that it had once been the gate. This close to the tower, she realized that it had not fallen from disuse, but from force.

Unless this were an unknown relic from the Ayrdish invasion of Geilltia, she stood in the middle of a battlefield from the Order's civil war. Glancing at the thick shadows, dense mist, and lightless forest, she surmised that the gloom radiated from the tower. Whatever happened here affected the very air.

"I see some scars run deeper than others," Aura said.

Dismounting, she tethered Blister outside the gate, and stepped through. A large tablet stone sat to the left of the tower. She lay her staff against the stone and dropped her bag to the ground. Looking around the old battlefield, she wondered what drove the men and women who fought here. How could a valley of such beauty house a spot so ugly, and a people of such love turn on themselves?

Aura had sat in many cemeteries. She had also sat in several battlefields. This one felt like all of those, sacred and hallowed. She did not have to look at the ground at her feet to know she would only see dirt. Yet, that dirt held the blood of the men and women who fought and died here. From what Manfred and Naurelia said, this was the struggle between the letter of the law and no law at all.

Some said that laws were fences designed to keep intruders out, but Aura always felt many were iron bars designed to keep her in. Yet, having violated a law through anger herself, she knew all too well that some laws were necessary. People needed to know which cart proceeded first when they met at a crossroad. Predators existed who liked to kill, rape, and steal. If she still struggled with law or no law, what would happen if that struggle organized into armies.

She knew that not all wars were between right and wrong, that some were between two different forms of right. Perhaps that had been the situation. The question then became, who won this battle? In fact, no one ever said who won the war. While she also knew that the winners wrote history, she wanted to know that history. Remembering how her morning began, she sighed.

"I guess it doesn't matter now who won," she said. "I'm no longer part of this Order."

"Of course it matters who won!" a man snapped.

Tall with a dark beard and long dark hair, he leaned against what looked like the door to the tower. Leather straps from his shoulders crossed his thick chest and buckled into his belt. He wore a leather skirt studded with iron, and boots that laced to his knees. A black cape flowed down his back to his ankles. From his belt hung two long sheathed daggers.

The man snarled, "What the hell are you doing here!"

"I just paused to rest," she answered. Glancing at her staff, she inched her hand toward it.

"Don't touch that staff!" the man said. "I can toss my dagger faster than you can say an incantation."

"Who are you?" Aura asked, standing up.

The man stepped away from the door and walked toward the table stone. As he walked, he said, "I'm General Jann Ekkehart, involuntarily retired. Now, who the bloody hell are you?"

"I am Aura Lockhaven of Hartshorn. I'm a visitor, a Dyrgana if you wish. Or, I was a Dyrgana until this morning."

"I didn't think you were from around here. Terrible accent. Must be from up north."

Aura bristled at the comment. She rather liked her Lodwynnshire accent. She could say the same about Ekkehart's. He spoke like someone from around the River Pitchfork, with that southern region's nonexistent R, overemphasized T, and swallowed vowels. He also spoke as if he had gravel in his mouth.

"This is Tongren's Tower," Ekkehart continued. "Don't get too many visitors, and I like it that way. Well, you can stay for a minute. I like the love handles."

Aura still felt slim around the middle. Despite Lurna's outstanding skills, she had not eaten that much. Then, she noticed Ekkehart stared at her chest. He meant those love handles."That was rather rude," Aura said.

"Get used to it. I was cranky enough when I was alive. Less happy now that I'm dead."

"What do you mean, dead?" Aura asked.

"Dear Heittan, woman!" Ekkehart snapped. "Do I look like I'm alive? I'm a fekkin' ghost! I'm the general who lost this battle. I was killed right here by my damn cousin, Balkefor." He jerked his thumb over his shoulder toward the tower.

Her father told her many ghast tales, mostly to giggle as she huddled under the blanket. Richard once covered himself in flour and stalked the screaming girl around the house while Ester bellowed to leave their sister alone. Sagacius told her other stories. His ghasts were real. His killed. She always expected ghasts to be purple, the color of Spirit, and translucent. This one looked like any other man, solid and potentially dangerous.

Aura smiled. "Well, I won't disturb you any further, General. I do need to be on my way."

Ekkehart shrugged. His mouth twitched into a smirk. Aura picked up her staff. She turned toward the gate. Listening for any sounds behind her, such as feet or breathing, Aura walked around the table stone. Glancing over her shoulder, she saw Ekkehart standing by the tower, his arms crossed, grinning at her. As she lifted her foot to step through the gate, she smacked into something solid. Nothing stood before her. She saw only the air in the ruined gateway. Yet, something barred her exit.

"The old barrier spell keeping people out was destroyed with the gate. The one keeping people in is still in place," Ekkehart said. "I had a lot of desertions the day before the battle. I had to stop that fekkin' nonsense. You can't leave until I grant you a pass into Ardora. Don't know that I will."

Barrier spells were simple enough. She looked at the gate and deduced that it lay anchored to both sides, like a spiderweb. Clear, yet solid, this one had all the marks of any other barrier spell, the kind she had cast since her fourteenth birthday. Each one held the will and intent of its maker, but they were all erected with the same spell and dissolved with the same counterspell. Aura held her staff before her. Not sure of the will and intent contained in this particular barrier spell, she wanted all the power available.

"Pata fasa onio," Aura shouted.

The air in the old gateway shook like warm treacle as the open door spell struck the barrier. When the shaking subsided, Aura stepped forward. She smashed into the still solid barrier. Stepping back, she rubbed her sore forehead and sighed.

"Cast all the counterspells you want, lass," Ekkehart called. "I erected that barrier myself. Set it so that only I or someone who outranks me on the council can dissolve it. I don't see any council members around. Nope. None at all. Don't even think about scaling the wall, either. Not much remains, but I can throw one of my daggers faster than you can climb."

Aura returned to the table stone, but kept it between herself and Ekkehart. Wary from her fight with Mayenne, she did not trust this stranger. While she doubted he was a ghast, she did not like the way he ogled her. At least, if he charged her, she had a shield of rock in front of her before resorting to magic. If he really was a ghast, what spell would defeat him should he attack.

"What do I have to do to convince you to let me leave?" Aura asked. She thought of several possibilities, and dreaded all of them.

"Not sure yet," Ekkehart said. "I'm trying to decide if I'm going to kill you."

"Kill me?" Aura shouted. "Why? What did I do to you?"

"You're alive, godsdammit! That just boils my cabbage."

Sagacius told Aura about ghasts, just in case she ever encountered one. Some ghasts were happy and benign. They haunted people for the fun of it. Ethereal merry pranksters, he called them. They were actually a joy to be around. Others were angry and lethal. They had died through violence, or felt protective of their territory. They required special training and cunning, which he did not teach her. Such was best left in the hands of sorcerers. If Ekkehart was really a ghast, he died in a battle to defend the tower. That meant she faced a ghast who was both angry over his death and protective.

"There's no need to kill me," Aura said. "I can just leave. I'm not a member of the Order anymore."

"You're a deserter!" Ekkehart shouted. "Now I have to kill you!"

"No," Aura said. "I was forced out. Someone tried to force me to do things her way. When I refused, she told me to leave."

"Oh," Ekkehart said. He fingered his beard. "That may change things. Never could stand rules and laws myself. They only get in the way. Power bridled is power wasted. I fought on the side of freedom, against the legalists. Called ourselves Friends of Brightstar."

The name struck Aura so hard, she thought she wobbled on her feet. The whole Valley reeked of that name. And one other. At any moment, she expected to hear it. Knowing she may as well get it over with, she asked, "What did the legalists call themselves?"

"Phah, those fekkers were the Friends of Nightshade."

Aura cringed. She knew it. Of course the lawless ones were Friends of Brightstar and the all-too-lawful were Friends of Nightshade. The anarchist brother and the legalist brother. That meant that Brightstar and

Nightshade already fought. At least, those who followed the ways of the two brothers. Day and Night already had their war. Sun and Moon already battled. If that part of the prophecy had already been fulfilled, perhaps the rest of it had as well. If not for the glowering ghast before her, Aura would have laughed at the thought that Naurelia herself could be the most powerful enchantress who ever lived.

Ekkehart said, "If you don't know about those buggers, then you might leave here alive after all. That depends on who taught you."

"My master is Sagacius."

Ekkehart looked surprised, yet impressed. "The Trollslayer? Now, that's a name I didn't expect to hear."

Twice in one week, someone called Sagacius the Trollslayer. The other had apparently commanded the opposing army in the battle that felled Ekkehart. She had much to ask her teacher when she returned to Hartshorn. The general fingered his beard again and looked thoughtful.

"I almost killed him myself. Against my style to kill a fallen man, but orders are orders. I respected him. It takes a lot of guts for one of us to face down a troll! Godsdam butchers!" Ekkehart spat. "Trolls kill because they like it. At least we had a cause." The general paused. He glared at Aura. His thoughtful continence changed to disgust. "If Sagacius taught you, then you're a Fence Sitter, too. Nothing I hate more than a godsdam Fence Sitter! Now I have to kill you." He lowered his hands to the hilts of his daggers.

Aura stepped back from the table stone, and took her defensive pose, left leg forward, right leg back. Not knowing if this man was just a general, an enchanter, or both, she prepared for everything. She held her left hand up and out, ready to cast a shield if necessary. Clutching her staff in her right, she drew it to her chest to propel an attack.

She estimated her opponent. Ekkehart was taller, and a good seventy pounds heavier. His biceps, forearms, thighs and calves bulged like those of a blacksmith. He could rip her in half with one strike of his daggers. She also knew he was a general, and therefore a seasoned warrior. In a physical fight, he held all the advantages with his stronger muscles, longer reach, and earned experience. While she knew something about fighting with quarterstaves, she hadn't practiced in three years. She knew just enough to be dangerous to herself.

Ekkehart, however, said he was a ghast. Aura assumed he told the truth, and wondered if he had unlimited vitality as a spirit, or if he had none because he had no body. She decided to be safe and assume that Ekkehart was a highly skilled combat veteran with incomprehensible power, but one who chose daggers instead of magic out of honor to her as an opponent. Her best hope lay in one powerful spell, one that could knock him unconscious. Once he was out, she could scale the walls and run like a madwoman. Ekkehart gripped the hilts of his daggers and took a step toward her.

"Tenthatora!" Aura shouted, firing a throwback spell at Ekkehart's chest. The blast passed right through him and struck the door of the tower. She heard a pile of rocks fall inside the ruin.

Ekkehart grinned. "Too bad I'm dead. I get to be solid or intangible as I will, and I have a lot of will."

A movement caught Aura's attention. She looked up to see three feet of the remaining top of the tower teeter, then topple into the ruin.

"Show some respect, you bitch!" Ekkehart snapped. "This was a beautiful place once!

"Damnation!" Aura snapped.

"Oh, you curse like a soldier," Ekkehart said, grinning.

"You have no room to talk!"

"I like a woman who curses."

"If you'd like, you can just stand there and listen to me say every oath and curse I know, and I speak five languages. The Coadic oaths are actually quite poetic," Aura said.

Ekkehart snorted. His mouth twitched as he chuckled. Aura saw her chance. Just keep him talking, she told herself. Perhaps tell him some bawdy jokes. If she could convince him to like her, he may just open the barrier spell. At least, talking was better than dying.

"I know nothing about your war, General, sir," Aura said. "It happened when my father was just a baby. Obviously, I'm not from here. Please, tell me about this tower."

Ekkehart softened his stance. He smiled. Aura saw a look of wistfulness creep over his face. "You really want to know?" He spread his arms wide. "Once upon a time, when the world was younger and I was, too, there were three great strongholds in this Valley. The Castle of Damaskarose. Tallen Hall. Tongren's Tower. They were magnificent! This was the best of the lot. The others were castles, dwellings. But this place was a damn fortress! All three served as refuges from trolls, ogres, wyverns, giants, other wizards." He paused and looked at the sky. "Huh. Wonder why they even bothered with that fekkin' barrier spell. Seems everything can get through it that has a mind to. Where was I?"

"You were telling me about how magnificent Tongren's Tower was," Aura replied.

"Aye, that I was! Godsdammit, but it was beautiful. It was built to withstand a siege." Ekkehart pointed to the ragged top of the tower. "See that up there? That's the second story. Now, before the battle, it was five stories tall. You could see it for miles. Oh, it was beautiful! A fist of power and strength raised in the face of the enemies of the Order. It didn't look like this, then, nope. Around the tower lay five buildings. A great hall, a kitchen, and quarters for one hundred people. It had two walls. The inside wall was just behind you. The outside wall was further out. It was meant to be impregnable."

In her mind, Aura saw the tower rise to the sky, looming above the stunted trees. They were tall then, and as beautiful as the structure. No longer a skull of blasted rock, the red stones reached for the barrier spell. It called out a place of safety for all who saw it. A cylinder of protection, it defended the defenseless. She could see the banners waving in the breeze, marking the place of refuge, the position of the warriors who would protect those who sought safety from ogres, sorcerers, and ... trolls. From the stone foundations, five buildings emerged, low but with tall windows and slate roofs to withstand fire. The walls grew until she saw the archers, pikemen, and enchanters patrolling, ever on the watch for the enemy.

"It does sound magnificent," Aura said. "What happened to it?"

Ekkehart sagged. His great shoulders hunched. He turned to face her, crestfallen and withered. "I happened to it. Tongren's Tower stood for two hundred years. It never fell, not even to three hundred of the most vicious ogres you ever saw. Now, your master was in that fight. I saw him lay waste to dozens of ogres. They had trolls, too. Sagacius earned his moniker Trollslayer that day. I saw it with my own eyes. By Heittan, that man had guts! You must have some too, to put up with the likes of him."

Aura's chest swelled. She hoped the ghast did not notice. Sagacius always called her courageous. She liked to think she was. In the face of a physical opponent, she previously had no fear. Mayenne taught her otherwise. In the face of her memories, nightmares, and things with eight legs, she melted like wax from a candle. She did not believe in trolls. This man, however, just complimented her master, her teacher, her best friend. She felt as proud of Sagacius as he said he felt of her.

"I always dreamed of commanding here," Ekkehart continued. "When I did, what happened? I lost, and the place was demolished! I am the only man to ever allow Tongren's Tower to be infested." Ekkehart smacked his fist into the palm of his other hand. "Godsdam it, woman! You just had to make me remember that!"

That had been stupid.

"Who says you lost, sir?" she asked.

"Eh?" Ekkehart asked, looking at her.

"I know something about war, sir," Aura said. "My brother Richard commanded a company in a war against the Skols. He stood his ground on a bridge and ordered his men to retreat. He fought while they retreated. He died that day, but his company gained a great victory against the Skols the next morning. I can't say my brother lost. In fact, even though I lost him, he won his battle."

"I like him," Ekkehart said, grinning. "Now that is gallantry that I have not seen in this Valley in many a decade. Perhaps, I won't kill you after all." Ekkehart raised his hand and added, "Just for your brother, mind you!"

Praise Ystlena, Aura thought. Perhaps, she could melt his ghastly heart and she walk away. "What happened here?" Aura asked. "Why were you fighting your own cousin? Shouldn't you have been on the same side? I don't know. I'm alone in this world. I don't have any cousins."

At least, she did not think she had any cousins. She had not heard of her Uncle Cedric marrying. No woman who would marry the sourest apple in Hartshorn anyway, even if he were the richest man for miles. He was the kind who would ... no, Aura thought. Let him go. She forgave him. No reason to pick up that knife again, when one more lethal stood only ten feet away.

"Aren't you the lucky bitch!" Ekkehart said. "Believe me, family will bite your cock right off." Ekkehart looked at Aura's hips. Even with the dress obscuring his view, she wanted to cover her womanhood. "Not that you have one. Anyway, I'm an Grahbale. Balkefor is the current Earl of Grahbale, assuming the whoreson is still alive, may the gods blast his soul forever and a day. My mother was his father's little sister. As Grahbales, we were sworn to protect the Valley. Our family is the guardians of the peace here. Well, we were until that godsdam war broke out!"

"I'm afraid you're going to have to tell me about the war, sir," Aura said.

"I'm not surprised. You're a Fence Sitter. Nah, brother or no brother, I have to kill you."

Ekkehart drew his daggers. He held one underhand in his right, ready to slash upward. The other he held overhand in his left, to strike down. Aura had seen enough knife fights to know a seasoned expert. He could feint or kill with either hand.

She held held her staff in front of her with her left hand under and her right hand over and three feet from each other. Keeping her arms flexible, she shifted her weight back on her legs.

"Staves?" Ekkehart asked.

"It seems I have no choice," Aura said. "All I want to do is leave, sir."

"Goddess' nightgown, and I thought we were fools for a lost cause."

Keep him talking. "Why are you still here, sir? Why don't you go to the afterlife?"

"I can't," Ekkehart snarled. "Oh, I have to kill you for bringing that up. The unburied can't go to the afterlife. Did you know that I am the only one who wasn't buried? I died on the roof of the tower, and nobody ever bothered searching for my body. Balkefor killed me fast, the son of a bitch! But did he look for my body? No, not the Eorl!"

The flash of silver caught Aura's attention. She threw her staff up and blocked Ekkehart's downward thrust with his dagger a foot from her face. Anticipating his next move, she jerked backwards and the dagger in his right hand sailed upwards, just missing the laces of her bodice. He wasn't a general, he was a cat. The whole time he had been talking with her, he had also been walking toward her with such stealth that she did not notice. Now, her staff lay locked between Ekkehart's knives, one above and one below. With an effortless motion, Ekkehart ripped the staff from Aura's hands and tossed it aside.

"You're pretty good," he said, grinning.

As Ekkehart resumed his fighting stance, Aura looked at his daggers. They were solid. Yet, they had to be spirit knives. The real ones should be with his corpse inside the tower, unless he retrieved them. If he was solid enough to grab her staff, and solid enough to hold daggers, then he was solid enough to punch. She smashed him on the chin with a right jab. Ekkehart tottered away from her, caught his foot on the table stone, and tumbled over it onto his back.

Solid to solid, Aura thought, dashing around the stone. She ran to the door of the tower and into the ruin. Her eyes adjusted to the cold light and glowering shadows inside. She almost gagged on the lingering odors of death and decay. Glancing around, she saw rubble, piles of rocks and broken timbers. She reached for a rock, and then froze as a shadow moved over it.

"Spider!" Aura screamed, throwing herself against the wall.

Only the size of a man's thumbnail, the coin spider was still large enough to paralyze Aura where she stood. Trembling and whimpering, she looked around the destroyed chamber. Every shadow, every crevice, threatened her. How many more were in here, she wondered. She jerked away from the wall and bolted toward the door. Ekkehart's presence outside brought her to her senses. Spiders could not hurt her, but this ghast wanted to kill her.

She grabbed a timber the size of her leg and turned toward the door as Ekkehart stepped through it. As she swung the timber toward the general's head, the wood splintered in her hand. The tip sailed past Ekkehart. He grinned. Aura reached behind her and grabbed the first rock her fingers touched. She waited for Ekkehart to move closer. When he lunged for her with his right dagger, she hurled the rock into his face.

"Dammit," Ekkehart roared, falling back through the door. "I'm dead, but that bloody hurt."

"So will this," Aura snapped.

She grabbed another rock and threw it at Ekkehart. It struck the general on the side of his forehead. He spun around and fell to his knees. He sank to his face on the ground, and crawled a few feet from the tower, groaning. That should hold him long enough to find something else to keep him at bay. Glancing around, all she saw were rocks and rotten timbers. Looking up at the shattered floor of the second story, she saw the point and shaft of a spear sticking out into the air about ten feet over her head.

Hearing Ekkehart groan and curse outside the tower, Aura leapt for the spear. She missed it by four feet. She tested her weight on the pile of stones with her hands. Thinking it solid enough, she started climbing. Ignore the spiders, she told herself. Within a few moments, she climbed six feet. Reaching up, she touched the spear with the fingertips of her left hand. Just a little more. Aura put her weight on her right leg and bent her left. As she did, the stones beneath her shifted, and poured down into the floor of the tower. Aura fell forward onto the sliding pile of rocks, and slid down with them.

White light exploded in Aura's head, blinding her vision. A flame of fire shot through her abdomen somewhere below her navel. She threw her head back and roared in agony. The rocks shifted again, and she slipped further. The flame of fire drove deeper into her body. She screamed again. Her vision black now, she felt her stomach with her left hand. Something was wrong. Her fingers felt something hard, something unyielding, something cold and metal. She also felt something wet, sticky, and warm.

She tried to catch her breath and clear her vision. With black specks dancing before her eyes, she looked at her stomach. A sword, dark with disuse and rust, stuck out from the rocks. A mummified hand gripped the hilt. The other end vanished into her abdomen. Blood poured from her, around the blade, dripping in large spatters onto the stones. Aura braced herself with her hands against the stones and pushed. She slid off the sword, and screamed again. Four inches of the tip was covered in blood. Her blood.

Aura threw herself onto her back against the pile of stones. She wanted to throw up. She tried to breathe, but each gasp seemed to enlarge the wound. Watching the blood gush from the three-inch wide hole, Aura realized she was bleeding to death. She clamped her right hand over the wound, and her left hand over her right. She closed her eyes.

"Ekos entola plagia epolotha mihi!" she shouted.

She felt the flow of blood stop as the self-healing spell poured from her hands. The heat in her hands ceased before she thought it should. She had never cast a healing spell upon herself when she had a deep injury. Agony and blood loss drained her vitality faster than the spell could work. The fire continued to roar through her abdomen. Glancing down at the wound, she wiped the blood away from her skin. The closed wound still looked red and angry. A trickle of blood seeped from it. The spell was incomplete, but it would have to suffice.

Ekkehart's moaning outside the tower snapped her back to the present. If the injury didn't kill her, the ghast would. Forgetting the spear, Aura grabbed the hilt of the sword and ripped it from the grip of the corpse.

Ekkehart still lay on his face, supporting himself with his knees, as Aura staggered out of the tower. She used the sword as a crutch. With weakening, wavering steps, she walked to the table stone. Her staff lay on the ground. It looked a mile away.

"Where do you think you're going?" Ekkehart asked, standing up.

Aura tried to lift the sword in front of her. Too weak from the wound, she only lifted it two feet, holding it at a useless angle. In a raspy voice, punctuated with gasps, she said, "Just let me pick up my stuff and leave."

Ekkehart saw the sword in her hand. His expression changed. Aura thought he looked worried. He lowered his daggers. With the one in his right hand, he pointed to the sword.

"Where did you get that?" he asked. Then, he looked at her stomach and added, "It looks like you clenched it from both ends."

"It wasn't my idea," she stammered.

Ekkehart sheathed his daggers. He started walking toward Aura. She tried to lift the sword higher. The general shook his head and waved his hand.

"That sword can't hurt me," he said, approaching her. "Not any more than it already has. It's mine."

Ekkehart stood in front of Aura. Placing his hand on the sword, he pushed it toward the ground. Then, he reached up to her face and caressed her cheek. Even though his hand felt cold, his touch felt compassionate.

"Lass, that sword is cursed," he said.

Aura gulped and asked, "What's going to happen to me?"

"The worst you can imagine. It's already happening. Don't you feel it? It's called the Sword of Fate, and for good reason. The strike causes my opponent to live his fated end, whether he likes it or not. I made the curse even more blooming formidable by dipping the sword in the venom of a wraith lion. So, my enemy is neither dead nor alive, living his fate over and over and over." He looked at his right palm. "The damn curse seeped into my skin. It got me. Oh, it got me good. It was my fate to be unburied. Here I am." He nodded to Aura. "I see the blade struck true, even by accident. You're turning into a blooming wraith. Neither alive nor dead, neither solid nor spirit. For the rest of eternity, you'll be stuck here, reliving your fate, over and over. I'm sorry, lass. I really am."

Aura trembled, but not because of Ekkehart's words. The trees seemed to move back from her. The crumbling tower seemed far away. Even Ekkehart looked as if he stood on the horizon. The cooling air closed in around her, enveloping her in sorrow. Darkness penetrated her soul, chilling her. She felt alone. Aura gripped the sword tight in her right hand. She threw her left arm across her chest, under her breasts, and clutched her right arm with her left hand. She never felt so alone in her life.

"No," she whispered.

"What do you feel?" Ekkehart asked.

"Talk to me, dammit," Aura said. "This forest is like a cavern. There's no one here. I need to feel someone's soul. Please! Don't let this happen to me."

"Alone," Ekkehart whispered. "Your fate is to live and die alone."

"No!" Aura shouted. She ignored the stabbing pain in her abdomen. "I don't believe that!"

"It doesn't matter what you believe," Ekkehart said.

Aura grabbed her hair. Sagacius promised to never leave her. That was the one thought that held her together on nights when dark closed in around her. To be alone was her one great fear, greater than spiders and ravagement. She faced it in Ralthangarle, and it bested her. The phantom tormented her with it. Now, she had to live it forever. The odor of wet cobblestones and her dirty body wafted under her nose, only this time, it wasn't a mere memory or terror attack. She smelled them.

"How can I break the curse?" Aura shrieked.

Ekkehart shook his head. "You can't."

"Every curse can be broken," Aura said, gasping. "All curses have conditions that break them. That's why they're curses. You're trapped in a dark prison. You know there's an unlocked door. You can't find it. It's there. You just can't find it. You know you're cursed. So, what is it? What is the condition?"

"I don't know," the general replied. "My father and I were the only ones who could wield that sword. It was cursed when it was given to my father. Neither he nor I knew how to break it. Although, there was this apprentice. He broke it. Now, what did he do? He took the strike I meant for his master. By the gods, I've never seen such valor. I didn't know this boy's name. Wish I did. After I struck him, I was too caught off guard by his valor to finish him or his master. Such valor. I watched as he healed his master of a curse that was eating him alive." Ekkehart snapped his fingers. "That's how you do it! You break a curse on someone else."

"I already did," Aura said. "I freed Mayenne from a curse several days ago."

"Nope, nope, nope," Ekkehart said, shaking his head. "Doesn't count. You have to do the deed after you're stabbed by the sword. Considering there's just you and me here, I don't think that information will do you any good."

A flash of hope penetrated her darkening mind. Just enough to give her a ray of light, and clear the blackness spreading across her vision. There may be a way to save herself. She asked, "Only you and me?"

She took a step back, and almost fell down. Her legs felt like iron weights hung from them. She staggered toward the tower, each step sinking her further into the quagmire of loneliness. Her father's face flashed before her. Then, Richard, then Ester. No, she told herself. Not yet. There was one thing she had to do first.

"Where are you going?" Ekkehart asked.

Aura turned to him and said, "Where do you think I found that sword?"

The mummified hand stuck out from the pile of rocks at shoulder height. At least, she did not have to climb far to reach it. Her stomach revolted at the effort. She almost screamed and wanted to throw up, but she refused to surrender to her body. She had to do this. If there was a chance, she had to do it. If nothing else, she would prove to Ekkehart that his fate was only in his mind.

When she had unearthed half the corpse, she rested her head against the pile of stones to let the dark spots in her eyes fade. She found herself back in Hartshorn, walking through a warm meadow of heather and listening to the warblers sing. A shifting rock brought her back to consciousness. Realizing she fainted, she cursed and grabbed another rock. Succumbing to the stench of old flesh and decay, Aura vomited on the floor beneath her. The heaves caused pain to rip through her stomach. A trickle of blood oozed from the wound. She wiped her mouth with her hand and kept tossing rocks out the door of the tower.

After what seemed like eternity, she uncovered the entire corpse. She thought it looked intact, a skeleton held together by tight, dried skin. The age worn clothes looked like the same ones the ghast of Ekkehart wore. As she flipped the corpse over onto its back on the long cloak, she hoped that everything was there. She folded the cloak together into a bundle and grabbing it by the collar, pulled it to the tower floor.

Aura woke up a moment later with images of Manfred holding her. She had fainted again. Too weak to stand, she grabbed the cloak with her left hand, and crawled from the tower into the night air. She pulled the corpse toward the table stone. Ekkehart stood back and watched.

"What ... what is that?" he asked.

"I believe it's you," Aura stammered.

"What are you going to do?"

"I'm going to give you a proper burial," she said.

"You can't," Ekkehart said. "It's my fate to –"

"Watch me, dammit!"

Putting her hands on the table stone, Aura tried to stand up. She
looked up at the sky and wondered how she ended up on her back. Fainted
again, she thought. She tried to sit up, but her body refused to move. All
she could move were her hands. Even her arms felt paralyzed. The agony in
her stomach receded to an angry burn that consumed most of her lower
body. Even with the pain, she felt cold. So cold. So alone.

"No!" Aura snapped.

"Give up, lass," Ekkehart said. "You're only making the curse worse."

"Making things worse seems to be my specialty."

Aura managed to roll onto her stomach. Then, she rose to her hands
and knees. The corpse lay next to her. This was as good a place as any, she
thought.

"I don't suppose there's a shovel lying around here anywhere," she said.

"Nope," Ekkehart replied. "They took everything away from the battle.
Everything except that catapult and me."

"Lovely," she said.

Standing had been something Aura took for granted. As she struggled
to a crouching position, she vowed never to assume anything about her
body again. Her knees revolted. She summoned all her determination and
forced them to move until she stood upright. She walked to the sword
stuck point first in the ground on the other side of the stone. Each step
made her stomach scream. Each step reminded her that she was the last
Lockhaven left. Only Aura. Just a few minutes, and she would join her
family. No, she thought. She would not. She would be trapped in this living
abyss, never seeing her family, never seeing anyone alive either.

What was left when someone exhausted all her vitality and will, she
wondered as she grasped the sword. Her father called it guts. She chuckled
thinking about the damage to her own intestines as she pulled the sword
from the earth. Dragging it across the ground, she trudged back to the
corpse. She stuck the tip into the dirt and pushing all her weight behind it,
shoved a small clod of dirt to one side. This will take all day, she thought.
Still, it was better than sitting back and waiting to become a wraith.

"You could help me, you know," Aura said to Ekkehart as she stuck the sword into the dirt again.

"The dead are not permitted to dig their own graves," Ekkehart replied.

"Damn you and your rules!" Aura snapped. "I thought you were on the side of those who wanted no laws. Some Friend of Brightstar you are." She thrust the sword into the dirt again. As she tightened her arm to lift, a hand shot across her wrist and stopped her.

"Oh, hell. I'm already buggered! Gimme that." Ekkehart snatched the sword from Aura's hands. He thrust it into the ground and said, "Start tossing rocks this way. I want to be buried in a cairn."

Aura tried to step toward the tower, but fell onto her knees. She crawled to the tower door and grabbed the nearest stones. She tossed them toward the grave. Ekkehart dug into the dirt with his sword. With each swipe of the blade, he dug deeper. He dug with growing fury, then, growing passion. Dirt flew into a pile next to the hole. He dug deeper. More dirt flew. He started laughing. He cursed fate with words that made Aura blush. Then, he howled with joy as Aura threw more rocks into her pile.

"Godsdammit, we make a great team," Ekkehart yelled, hurling a wad of dirt out of the grave. "You'd make a good captain, lass. Hell, I'd appoint you full major, my second in command. This is it! Tell Fate to fek a broken wine jug! Who needs rules? I am the godsdam rules! Fek fate! I am fate! Ha! Look at me, working side by side with the Trollslayer's apprentice. Who'da thought it. See this, Balky? Eat my shit, you hairy bugger."

"General Ekkehart, sir," Aura said. "That's deep enough. It's a grave, not a well."

"Oh," Ekkehart said. He stood hip deep in the hole. As he climbed out, he reached for the bundle next to the grave.

Aura stopped him and said, "You died for others. Let another honor you."

Ekkehart stepped back from the grave. Aura gathered her legs under her and crawled to the corpse. Despite the agony in her stomach, she barely felt her legs. Black spots covered her eyesight. She felt for the cloak until she grasped it. Using her instinct, she pushed the bundle to where she thought the edge of the grave should be, then pushed a little further. It vanished from her grip. She heard a thud as it hit the bottom. With her hands, she pushed the dirt into the hole until the pile was no more. Then, she tossed rocks toward where she thought the grave lay. More rocks, she thought. Her mind collapsed until she ran on pure will. More rocks.

"That looks good," Ekkehart said, as Aura tossed the last stone.

"Help me up," Aura said, beckoning to Ekkehart. So this is darkness, she thought. Cold air filled her lungs with each gasping breath, yet it was never enough. So alone! So needing the touch of a human, any human. She felt Ekkehart's freezing hand on her arm, lifting her and supporting her. She could no longer see him, the tower or anything. All she knew was the pain in her stomach and the cold grip of loneliness. One more thing. One last thing to do.

"Give me the sword," she said.

She felt Ekkehart's hand move her fingers and the hilt of the sword found its way into her grasp. She asked him to lead her to the head of the grave. She knew her feet moved, but it felt like they dragged through the earth. When he stopped, she asked him to step away.

Aura raised the sword into the air. It was not much, only a few inches, but she thought it would suffice. She said, "Here lies a man who died for his beliefs. Here lies a hero!"

The thrust the sword into the ground at the head of the grave. What is magic but to give a ghast a chance at the afterlife? What was magic but to give a lost woman a chance to ... Aura took two steps to her left. She fell forward onto her face. The cold dirt comforted her. The pain in her stomach subsided into numbness. Daddy, she thought as someone rolled her over onto her back.

"I don't believe it. All this time, and some Fence Sitting visiting girl with a bad accent breaks my fekkin' curse," she heard a voice say. "You broke it, lass, right in half like a glass rod. I can leave. I can go to the gods. Who are you?"

"I am Aura Lockhaven from Hartshorn," she whispered.

"No, that is just a name. Who are you in here?" a voice asked. She felt a finger jab against her chest.

"I wanted to find out," a voice from her lips said. "Looks like ... I won't. Not today. Not ... ever."

"By the gods but you're a fekkin' warrior, that's what you are, lass. You ought to carry an axe, lass, just like women of old. You got the goddess Kregga in your blood. Stay with me. Look at me! No! Don't you dare! Your friends are here. Look at me! Look at me!"

That was impossible. Aura had no friends. She was alone in this world. There was no one but Aura, alone and unfriended, ugly and green-eyed. Only Aura. Just a green-eyed little street urchin. Green eyes. Snake Eyes. Urchin. Over now. She could give hope to the hopeless, but none to herself. What is magic?

"Aura," she heard. "Aura!"

The name, a name of someone unknown and unlovely, unfriended, but someone she thought she might like, echoed in her mind as blackness covered her eyes. Aura. What a pretty name. Was Aura pretty? Was she beautiful? Did she shine like an aura? What color was she? Was she green? No, she must be red.

So, this was nonexistence. Not so bad. She thought she smiled. She thought she saw her father's face. She thought nothing else.

Continued in

The Fires of Tallen Hall

Acknowledgements

I owe my utmost gratitude to Trish, my beloved wife of thirty years. You believed I could transform a tawdry, incomplete graphic novel into a quality written novel, and didn't stop hounding me and encouraging me until I did. It took three years, but, here it is. You were right.

Next, I thank Leanna Jackson, my Beta Reader Extraordinaire. You caught errors that slipped by Trish and me, and we had read this book a dozen times. Your suggestions also made a better story.

I also thank Ann McCutchan, former associate professor of Creative Writing at the University of North Texas. On the last night of the last class before I graduated, you said, "Go home and look at your bookcase. See what you love to read. That is what you should write." No advice has been so profound.

The funds for the publication of *A Path of Stones* was provided through a Kickstarter campaign. The following good folk kindly contributed: Karen Kelly, Jaime Bengzon, Laspe, Brian Keith McCormick, Leanna Jackson, April Milam, Eddie Ellis, Rory Block, and Stephen Lott. I heartily thank all y'all. You made the purchase of the ISBNs for the editions of this book, as well as the upgrades to my website, possible.

Finally, I thank you, the reader. No book is a solo effort. I can only tell half the story. It is up to you to finish it, as it interprets itself to you. I hope you enjoyed reading *A Path of Stones* as much as I enjoyed writing it.

Aura Lockhaven thanks you, too.

Afterward

I apologize for all the extra pages at the end, but a printed book must have a page count divisible by four. Not only that, but no page can be blank or the printer sees it as an error and kicks it back to me. Hence, the pages featuring Aura's seven pointed Sacred Star. The last two pages of a book are different. For some reason, those two pages must be totally blank, devoid of anything including page numbers.

If you were wondering, the font for *A Path of Stones* is Goudy Bookletter, 1911 at a size of 11 points. I chose it because it's one of my favorite fonts from my days as a typesetter. It is a compressed font, thus saving page count without sacrificing kerning. Some fonts, like Bookman and Times New Roman, added fifty pages to the count, even at 11 points. No need to increase your price when it can be avoided. Goudy also adds a touch of old world charm to the appearance.

Online Resources

Please visit my website at www.njbmedia.com. There, you will find Aura's Almanac. It contains maps and charts to help you make sense of Aura's world. I wrote the story as if the geography and calendar of her world were taken for granted, just as if I would write about 21st century Pennsylvania. Including the maps and charts in this book would have made it longer, and increased the price you paid. That is why they made the internet.

Also, be sure to follow me on Facebook and Twitter. My Facebook page is www.facebook.com/nathanjoshuaboutwell/. My Twitter handle is @Nathan_Boutwell. I will keep you updated about the progress of *The Fires of Tallen Hall* and the rest of the series. For in-depth discussions of writing, feel free to follow my blog; the link is at www.njbmedia.